With her roots firmly planted in the South, #1 *New York Times* bestselling author **Sherryl Woods** has written many of her more than one hundred books in that distinctive setting, whether it's her home state of Virginia, her adopted state, Florida, or her much-adored South Carolina. Now she's added North Carolina's Outer Banks to her list of favorite spots. And she remains partial to small towns, wherever they may be.

Sherryl divides her time between her childhood summer home overlooking the Potomac River in Colonial Beach, Virginia, and her oceanfront home with its lighthouse view in Key Biscayne, Florida. "Wherever I am, if there's no water in sight, I get a little antsy," she says.

Sherryl loves to hear from readers. You can visit her on her website at www.sherrylwoods.com, link to her Facebook fan page from there or contact her directly at Sherryl703@gmail.com.

Shirley Hailstock began her writing life as a lover of reading. She likes nothing better than to find a quiet corner where she can get lost in a book, explore new worlds and visit places she never expected to see. As an author, she can not only visit those places, but she can be the heroine of her own stories. The author of forty novels and novellas, Shirley has received numerous awards, including a National Readers' Choice Award, a Romance Writers of America's Emma Merritt Award and an *RT Book Reviews* Career Achievement Award. Shirley's books have appeared on several bestseller lists, including the *Glamour, Essence* and *Library Journal* lists. She is a past president of Romance Writers of America.

#1 *New York Times* Bestselling Author

SHERRYL WOODS

FINALLY A BRIDE

**HARLEQUIN
BESTSELLING
AUTHOR
COLLECTION**

HARLEQUIN®
BESTSELLING
AUTHOR
COLLECTION

Recycling programs
for this product may
not exist in your area.

ISBN-13: 978-1-335-01792-5

Finally a Bride

First published in 1995. This edition published in 2020.

Copyright © 1995 by Harlequin Books S.A.

His Love Match
First published in 2014. This edition published in 2020.
Copyright © 2014 by Shirley Hailstock

This edition published by arrangement with Harlequin Books S.A.

For questions and comments about the quality of this book, please contact us at CustomerService@Harlequin.com.

Harlequin Enterprises ULC
22 Adelaide St. West, 40th Floor
Toronto, Ontario M5H 4E3, Canada
www.Harlequin.com

Printed in U.S.A.

CONTENTS

FINALLY A BRIDE

Sherryl Woods

Prologue

"You're going to need a new roof," Ron Matthews informed Caitlyn Jones, gesturing toward the upper levels of the Clover Street Boarding House. "If you don't replace the whole thing, you'll just have me up there patching after every single thunderstorm rolls through here all summer long, and you'll still need a new roof when all's said and done."

Katie heard the news with a sinking sensation in the pit of her stomach. First the wiring, then the plumbing, now the roof. Was there any part of this beautiful old Victorian house that wasn't about to collapse around her?

The repairs were sopping up the last of her savings at a rate that made her banker very nervous. Charlie Hastings at the First National Bank of Clover, South Carolina, had already started asking pointed questions about where she was going to find the funds to make the balloon payment on her mortgage on the first of September. He was all too aware of the state of her bank balance and her pitiful cash flow.

He also knew in intimate detail what she'd already spent to make the once decrepit boarding house habitable after years of neglect. And he was just itching to remind her he'd warned her about all the pitfalls of taking an old relic and trying to remodel it on a shoestring budget. In essence, Charlie Hastings was a royal pain. Just the thought of admitting to him that he'd been right had her sighing heavily.

"Trouble?"

Katie's heart thumped unsteadily at the sound of that one single word. She recognized Luke Cassidy's voice as if she'd last heard it only yesterday. Instead it had been six years ago, on a night filled with the kind of seductive whispers that had made her heart melt. *Trouble?* Luke Cassidy's return to Clover made the problems with the boarding house pale in comparison.

She'd been dreading a face-to-face meeting with Luke ever since he'd hit town. She'd hoped it would come when she was dressed fit to kill, rather than wearing ragged cutoffs and a cast-off man's shirt that had belonged to one of her elderly boarders.

"Nothing I can't handle," she insisted, turning slowly toward the man who had broken her heart by abandoning her without a word of goodbye.

Aware that news of this meeting would spread through town like lightning, she faced him squarely. She raised her chin a notch just to show that his disappearance had meant nothing to her, that *he* meant nothing to her, despite all the years of friendship that had preceded that one stolen night of perfect bliss.

To prove just how independent she'd become and how unflustered she was by Luke's presence, she shifted her gaze to Ron. "How soon can you start working on the roof?"

"What will it cost?" Luke asked, avoiding her entirely and concentrating on the roofer who'd been one class behind Katie in school.

Ron's gaze darted from Katie to Luke and back again. Apparently he caught something in her expression that made him ignore Luke and respond directly to her.

"Week after next is the soonest, Katie," he said apologetically. "I'll put a tarp over it meantime. That should keep the worst of any rain from leaking into that front bedroom until I can get to it."

"Thanks, Ron."

"How much?" Luke repeated as if he had a perfect right to ask the question.

Ron regarded him doubtfully, then looked at Katie. She sighed. "How much?" she repeated.

"Four thousand. Could be closer to five with all those turrets. It's not like slapping up a nice straight roof on some little single-story bungalow. I'll get you a firm estimate by tomorrow."

Katie gulped. *Four or five thousand dollars!* Where was she supposed to come up with that kind of money? Right now, though, it hardly mattered. She wouldn't back down from the commitment with Luke looking on if her life depended on it.

"Fine," she said, though there was the faintest tremor in her voice she couldn't control.

"Is that a problem?" Ron asked, picking up on that tremor. "If it is, all you have to do is say the word and we can work out the payments. You know I'd do anything in the world to help you make a go of this place, Katie."

"I'll manage," Katie snapped, then winced at her misdirected anger. If anyone deserved sharp words it was Luke, not Ron, and it was way too late to be delivering them. "Just schedule the job, Ron. I had to move Mrs. Jeffers into another room until the repairs are done. I can't afford to keep a room empty for long."

"Sure thing. If I can free up someone to start sooner, I'll let you know." He glanced at Luke. "Good to see you again, Luke. I'd heard you were back. Planning to stay?"

Luke nodded. "If things work out," he said enigmatically.

As soon as the roofer had left, Kate whirled on Luke. "How dare you interfere in this? The cost of repairing my roof is none of your business."

"Never said it was," he said complacently, shoving his hands into the pockets of his worn jeans. "But you weren't asking and the question needed answering. Spelling out the details is one of the cardinal rules in business. Getting it in writing is another."

The suggestion that she had been about to make a lousy business decision and didn't know enough to get a contract aggravated Katie almost as much as Luke's interference.

"Ron and I have done a lot of business together," she said.

His knowing glance took in the old Victorian from porch to roof. "I can imagine."

His sarcasm had her gnashing her teeth. "We would have discussed the cost."

"When?"

"Later." She scowled at him, hoping her frosty reception would drive him away before she betrayed the fact that his presence had her heart hammering a hundred beats a minute. "Did you want something in particular?"

"You and Ron seem…close," he said, watching her intently. "How close?"

"Oh, I'm sure if you hadn't been here, he would have thrown me to the lawn and made mad, passionate love to me," she said sweetly.

Luke's jaw clenched. "That's not something to joke about."

"It's also none of your business."

"So you've said. Well, let's just pretend for a moment that it is my business. How close are you?"

"Oh, for pity's sake, Luke, Ron is happily married and has three kids."

"Then how come he's so eager to give you a break on the roof job?"

If Luke hadn't looked so genuinely bemused by Ron's generosity, Katie might have blown a gasket at the suggestion that the younger man might expect something in return. As it was, she figured it was about time Luke learned that not every relationship was about sex. Maybe, after all those years of well-reported wheeling and dealing in Atlanta, he needed to remember that in Clover people helped each other out without ulterior motives.

"Ron's kid sister was one of my first boarders," she said. "She was having a rough time at home. When she moved in here, I looked out for her. He credits me with keeping her out of trouble, though the truth is Janie was smarter than anyone in her family recognized. She had her whole life mapped out, and it didn't include getting smashed up with a bunch of teenage drunks out on the highway or an unplanned pregnancy. More kids today should have the kinds of goals and limits she'd set for herself."

If she hadn't had her gaze pinned to Luke's face, Katie might have missed the fleeting change in his expression when she mentioned the unplanned pregnancy. It made her wonder all over again how much the son he'd turned up with on his return had to do with his abrupt departure all those years ago. Just guessing that the timing roughly coincided with the same period in which he'd made love to her filled her with regrets. If Luke had been trapped into marriage, why couldn't she have been the one...? She let the thought trail off uncompleted. She would never have done that to him. Never.

Whatever Luke was thinking, though, he managed to banish it. He resumed that bland, inscrutable expression that tempted Katie to do something, *anything* to draw a reaction.

Regarding her evenly, he asked, "How are you going to pay for a new roof?"

The question was so far afield from the direction of her thoughts that Katie took a minute to form a response. "That's what you dropped by after six years to ask?"

Luke's mouth tightened into a grim line. "How are you going to pay for it?"

"I'll find a way," she said, injecting a misplaced note of confidence into her voice. "Well, it was great seeing you again. We'll have to catch up some other time. I've got things to do."

She tried to subtly edge toward the front door, but Luke kept pace with her. She sighed at her failed attempt to escape. He'd always had a single-track mind and an inability to take a hint.

"How? By working more hours at Peg's Diner?" he asked irritably. "You can't earn enough there in the next week to pay for the tarp Ron is going to use, much less a new roof."

She stared at him, filled with indignation at the certainty she heard in his voice. "How would you know a thing like that? And what difference does it make to you, even if it is true?"

"It's not all that difficult to get information in Clover," he said. "Nothing thrives in this town quite like gossip."

"You used to hate that," Katie reminded him.

"Yes, I did," he agreed. "I've discovered, though, that it has its uses. The rumor mill provided all the information I needed on you, including the fact that you are knee-deep in debt. Half the people I talked to are worried sick about you. They say you're wearing yourself out trying to make a go of this business. What in all that's holy ever possessed you to buy this ramshackle old place and try to turn it into a boarding house? It should have been torn down thirty years ago when the McAllisters abandoned it."

I bought it because we used to sit on that secluded porch night after night and share our innermost secrets, she thought to herself. Those were memories he'd obviously forgotten. She wouldn't have divulged them to him now for a stack of free shingles and sufficient tar paper to cover the entire roof. She decided it was best to ignore that question altogether.

"I had no idea folks in Clover were so fascinated with my well-being." She regarded him pointedly. "But they, at least, are friends. I'm not sure I'd describe you the same way. I do know that my financial status is none of your concern. I can't imagine why you would have wanted information about me, but if you did, you could have asked me directly."

"Would you have given me honest answers?"

Their gazes clashed. "I was always honest with you," she said heatedly. "You…" She let the accusation trail off. There was no point to arguing. History couldn't be changed. She had loved him once to distraction. He had left her without a word, apparently to marry a woman who was pregnant with his child. What more was there to say?

Even though Katie fell silent, Luke clearly got the message and, just as clearly, accepted the blame for whatever lack of honesty had come between them six years earlier. Guilt was written all over his handsome, chiseled face, along with something that might have been regret.

"Look, can we go inside and talk?" he asked, his tone suddenly placating.

"Why?"

He seemed amused by her reluctance. "Maybe just because it's way past time for two old friends to catch up."

Catching up—risking involvement—struck Katie as a remarkably bad idea. She didn't want to be alone with Luke. The man still had the power to wreak havoc with her senses. She'd known that the instant she'd spotted him in the back of the church at Lucy Maguire Ryder's disrupted wedding. That meant he also had the power to cause her even more anguish than he had in the past. She had wounds from the first time that, to her deep regret, felt as fresh today as they had on the day he'd walked out of her life.

"Please," he coaxed, his gaze unrelenting.

"We can sit on the porch," she said as a compromise when she saw that he wasn't about to leave until he'd gotten whatever he'd come for. She didn't for one single minute believe it had anything to do with the cost of her roof repairs. "I'll get us some lemonade."

"Afraid to be alone with me?" he inquired with a smile that never quite reached his eyes.

"Never," she denied.

"Then wouldn't it be better to have this conversation where half the town won't be witness to it?"

She couldn't imagine what he had to say that needed such privacy, but it was clear he was going to badger her until he got his way. "Oh, for heaven's sakes," she snapped impatiently. "Come on into the kitchen."

The kitchen, normally Katie's favorite room in the house because of its huge windows facing the backyard and a table large enough to seat a half-dozen friends for a good long chat, suddenly seemed the size of a closet. Luke's presence was overpowering. The effect was worsened by his pacing, which brought him brushing past her time and again as she squeezed the lemons into a big glass pitcher, added water, plenty of sugar and a tray of ice cubes. At least the process and his silence gave her time to gather her composure.

When she finally turned, handing him a glass, she was almost able to convince herself that Luke was just another old friend stopping by to catch up on the news. People—a few of them attractive, available men— gathered in her kitchen all the time, though none of them made her pulse race. Still, there was no reason to think of Luke any differently than she did all those others. She could handle his presence. She could, dammit!

Then his fingers grazed hers as he took the lemonade. Her pulse bucked. She glanced into his eyes and saw a torment that made her breath catch in her throat. Her natural compassion welled up, even as she forced herself to look away. It took every ounce of restraint she possessed to keep from wrapping her arms around him and consoling him.

Though what Luke Cassidy had to be tormented about she couldn't imagine. Everyone in town had heard by now that he'd made a fortune while living in Atlanta. He had a precious son, Robby, the merest sight of whom brought a lump to Katie's throat. And if he was divorced, well, so were a lot of people. However tragic the circumstances, people got over it. It was nothing for her to get all teary-eyed over.

"Katie?" Luke asked suddenly.

She reluctantly lifted her gaze to his. Something in his voice, a soft, cajoling note, made her pulse skip yet another beat. How many times had she heard just that note before he'd asked her to do something outrageous? She could tell by the gleam in his eyes that he intended to do just that all over again.

"What?" she asked warily.

"Marry me."

The two simple, totally unexpected words hit her with the force of a tornado. If he'd asked her to join him on a shuttle to the moon, she wouldn't have been any more stunned. Katie was suddenly very glad they weren't in plain sight. At least there was no one to see her mouth drop open, no one to witness in case she followed through on her urge to whap him upside his hard head with a frying pan. If Luke Cassidy had asked her to marry him six years ago, she would have wept with joy. Today that same request—that out-of-the-blue mockery of a real proposal—filled her with fury.

"You want to marry me?" she repeated incredulously. Her pulse, apparently unaware that the proposal merited anger, not consideration, took off as if this were a declaration of true love. "Six years without a word, and now you want to marry me? Just like that?"

"Just like that," he agreed, as calmly as if the suggestion weren't totally absurd.

"Have you lost your mind?"

He seemed to consider the question thoughtfully, then shook his head, his expression thoroughly serious. "Nope. I don't think so."

"Then I think you need a second opinion."

"Katie, I've given this a lot of thought. It makes sense."

She regarded him blankly. "Why?" she asked, when she should have been shrieking to the high heavens about the gall of any man who would walk back into a woman's life after six years and drop a marriage proposal on the table as if it were a simple hello.

"Why?" she asked again, wondering if there was a snowball's chance in hell that she would get the simple, three-word answer she'd always dreamed of hearing cross his lips.

"My son needs a mother. You need somebody to put

this place on a sound financial base again. We always got along. I think we could make it work."

Not three words, but a litany, Katie noticed in disgust as Luke ticked off the reasons matter-of-factly. He'd probably made a damn list of them. His business-like tone made her grind her teeth.

"You sound as if you're negotiating for the merger of two companies with compatible products," she accused.

The idiot didn't even have the decency to deny it.

"That's one way of looking at it, I suppose," he agreed, looking pleased that she had grasped the concept. "We both get something we need. I knew I could count on you not to get all sloppy and sentimental about this."

Katie was just itching to reach for the cast iron skillet that was sitting atop her twenty-year-old stove, when she made the mistake of looking again into Luke's eyes for a second time. Those blue eyes that had once danced with laughter were flat and empty now. Lonely. Lost.

Katie had always been a sucker for a lost soul. And from her twelfth birthday, when he'd brought her a wilted, but flamboyantly huge bouquet of wildflowers, she had been a sucker for Luke Cassidy. Regrettably, nothing in the past six years they'd been apart had changed that.

She drew in a deep, steadying breath and realized that she was going to do it. She was going to say yes and damn the consequences.

"Oh, what the hell," she murmured, furious with herself for not having the willpower to resist this man or the son he'd just turned up with. Maybe she'd just been a spinster too darn long. More likely, she'd just missed Luke too much, something she wouldn't tell him if he hog-tied her and dragged her through town in full view of every single person who'd watched the two of them grow up. Cursing herself for being a pathetic, love-starved wimp, she tried valiantly to list all the reasons to say an emphatic no. There were dozens of them, but she couldn't seem to force her lips to form the first one.

At her continued silence, a faint suggestion of a grin tugged at Luke's mouth. "Was that a yes?"

It was and they both knew it, but she wouldn't make it easy on him. Katie knew she didn't have Luke's business acumen, but she did have an instinct for self-preservation. She couldn't just cave in and accept his first offer. If he wanted a coldhearted business deal, then that's what he'd get.

"We need to discuss terms," she said, keeping her voice as matter-of-fact as his, even though her heart was thundering wildly.

She couldn't believe what she was about to do. She was standing in her own kitchen, negotiating with a man she'd loved forever, about a blasted marriage of convenience. She ought to have her head examined. She was apparently every bit as loony as he was.

Then again, as everyone who knew her well would understand, her head had never had much to do with her feelings for Luke. It was her heart he had stolen and apparently intended to claim now as his own.

Still, there was a definite call for putting some emotional distance between them, for hanging on to a shred of dignity. She would not rush into his arms, allowing herself to think for one single instant that he actually cared a whit for her. He wanted a mother for his child. She would be a baby-sitter with unusual benefits. That was it. She supposed people had gotten married for less rational reasons, but she'd never met any of them.

A few centuries back marriages like this had even been arranged by doting, practical fathers. She'd always considered such arrangements barbaric. Now she found herself in the unique position of working out such terms for herself. Well, Luke could be darned sure that she was going to adequately protect herself from any more of his foolish whims.

She went to the kitchen counter, picked up a pad of paper and a pen, then sat down at the table, pen poised. "I'm ready. Let's talk."

"Okay," he said, suddenly cautious. "What did you have in mind?"

"A contract with everything all spelled out on paper. Didn't you remind me just a few minutes ago that that's how business is done?" she asked sweetly.

"Katie," he began in a warning tone.

She ignored the warning. "This is my boarding house. I run it as I see fit." She jotted that down before he could say a word.

"Now, wait a minute," he protested. "Running it how you see fit is what got you into this mess."

She looked him straight in the eye. "I run it. I deal with the guests," she insisted. "You can handle the business end of things, if you want."

"Thank you so much," he said.

She frowned at his mocking tone. "This won't work, if you're going to be surly."

"I am never surly."

Katie rolled her eyes. "You haven't changed that much, Luke Cassidy. You were always surly, especially when you weren't getting your way."

She studied him consideringly. He wasn't exactly dressed for success today, but she wasn't fooled by the faded, skintight jeans, the rumpled yellow shirt or the battered sneakers. She knew the kind of money the man had made. She'd saved every one of the clippings from the local paper enumerating his financial achievements. Luke might not have been back in Clover for years, but his press releases had been.

"I'd say an investment in the Clover Street Boarding House would be appropriate, wouldn't you? Say ten thousand," she said and wrote it down. "That will take care of the roof and a few odds and ends I haven't been able to afford, plus some of that balloon payment that's due in September."

"You want ten thousand dollars in return for agreeing to marry me?" he repeated, his neck turning a dull red. "Selling yourself cheap, aren't you?"

She nodded as the shot hit its mark and crossed off what she'd written. "You have a point. Make that ten thousand a year for the first five years. Guaranteed," she added, "even if the marriage falls apart."

This time, he was the one who looked as if she'd tried to flatten him with a two-by-four. Katie was rather pleased with herself.

"You can't be serious," he said.

"Oh, but I am. Putting this place on a sound financial base is what this deal is all about, right? From my point of view, that is."

She beamed at him. "Now, then, as far as me being a mother to Robby, we make decisions about him together. You don't just start bullying me around or pull rank whenever I do something that doesn't suit you. A child's parents should present a united front. Squabbling will just confuse him."

"What the hell do you know about raising a child?"

"I've watched all those baby doctors on TV. Besides, you're the one who picked me to be a mother to your son. Are you changing your mind?"

Based on Luke's stunned expression, Katie had the feeling she'd finally turned this stupid game of his to her advantage. The fact that he hadn't stormed out the door was a testament to how committed he was to this plan he'd dreamed up.

"Okay," he said, his teeth clenched. "You win."

"Good." She nodded approvingly as she made a note. "Just one last thing."

"Only one more?"

Katie glared at him. "We have separate bedrooms. You can have the one that's empty right now, as soon as the roof's repaired, of course. I wouldn't expect you to sleep in it while the rain is pouring in. And we want to give Robby a few weeks to get to know me before we set the date."

"Now wait just a minute," he protested. "What the hell kind of marriage is that? Husbands and wives do not sleep in separate bedrooms."

"That's true enough for ordinary husbands and wives." She shrugged. "You're the one who established this as some sort of business arrangement. I have no idea what your code of ethics is like after all this time, but I don't sleep with business partners. I wouldn't think you'd want any messy emotional entanglements, either. Sex has a way of muddying things up."

"How would you know?" he muttered, scowling at her.

She could tell that she had taken him by surprise

with her list of demands, especially this last one. She couldn't imagine what Luke had been thinking by making this ridiculous proposition to her this morning. But if he had expected her to fall into bed with a man who could suggest this cold, calculated arrangement, then he was sadly mistaken.

She might love him to distraction, but she would never let him see her vulnerability. She knew that if Luke so much as touched her, she would go up in flames. It had always been that way. She doubted that time had dulled the effect. Time obviously hadn't done a thing to correct her inability to think straight around him. Just look at the crazy agreement she was about to enter into. She suspected it was like making a bargain with the devil. No matter how many concessions a person gained, there was no way to win in the long run. But she intended to give Luke Cassidy a run for his money.

"Those are my terms," she repeated, meeting his gaze evenly. She held out the tablet on which she'd written every last detail of their agreement. "Sign it."

He seemed a little bewildered by her stance, but he nodded finally, scrawled his name across the bottom, then held out his hand. "It looks like we have a deal."

"So it does," she said, avoiding his hand as if it were contaminated. One touch, she reminded herself. Just one and this cool attitude of hers would be ashes.

"I'll be in touch to work out the wedding plans," Luke said, sounding satisfied—or relieved?—now that the deal was concluded.

As he left, Katie clutched the signed contract and fought to contain a sigh of regret. So much for moonlight and roses and a proposal that came from the heart. That was just one more silly yearning she would have to pack away. After being a bridesmaid more times than she could recall for Hannah, Emma and all the others, she would finally have her wedding. She'd finally have the only man she'd ever loved.

But it would all be a sham.

Chapter 1

The upcoming wedding of Caitlyn Jones and Luke Cassidy was the hottest topic at the Clover Beauty Boutique on the first Monday morning in June when Lucy Maguire Ryder, just back from her own honeymoon, divulged the news. When she discovered she'd scooped the bride and groom, Lucy rushed to Peg's Diner to apologize.

Naturally Lucy's apology and the reason for it were overheard and within seconds the news had spread from one end of the diner to the other. Katie could barely squeeze through the center aisle to deliver the rush of morning orders of eggs and grits for all the well-wishers stopping her to offer congratulations and best wishes. Periodically, as she poured cups of her Aunt Peg's potent special blend coffee, she paused long enough to glare at Lucy.

"I'm sorry," Lucy said again when Katie was finally

able to take a break. "I thought for sure you would have told everyone by now. The wedding's this Saturday, for heaven's sakes."

"You sound just like Luke. He's getting impatient, too."

"Well, I can't say that I blame him. You're acting as if this is something you're ashamed of. What does Peg say about it? Is she thrilled about the wedding?"

Katie winced as guilt sliced through her. "I haven't told her yet. Thank goodness she's off this morning. If she found out like this she'd never forgive me. And I'd have you to blame for spilling the beans."

Lucy was clearly aghast. "Katie, at this rate you would have been celebrating your tenth anniversary before anyone was the wiser. People were bound to wonder why you kept the news secret. I know there are…"

Lucy hesitated, then visibly made a decision to speak her mind. "I know there are circumstances here you don't want to discuss with just anyone, but wouldn't it have been better to announce the engagement formally and get on with the wedding plans as if this were your ordinary, garden-variety, happy occasion?"

"I wasn't ready to say anything," Katie said stubbornly. She hadn't known what to say, if the truth be told. She was afraid she'd give away every blasted detail of her contract with Luke if she opened her mouth at all.

Lucy studied her worriedly. "Katie, maybe you shouldn't go through with it. Obviously you have serious reservations about marrying Luke. It's written all over your face."

"I have no reservations. I love him," Katie said grimly. "That's all that matters."

"No, it's not and you know it," Lucy countered. "You

deserve more than some weird business bargain. Katie, you're the most honest, most straightforward person I know. You won't be able to live with yourself if you have to lie to everyone. It's no way to start a marriage."

"This arrangement is between Luke and me, no one else. We'll make it work."

"How?"

Katie lost patience. She was doing her best here. She didn't need her closest friend trying to sabotage her efforts. "Dammit, Lucy, I'm beginning to be sorry I ever told you the truth."

Lucy promptly looked chagrined. "Oh, sweetie, I'm sorry. I just want you to be as happy as I am."

Katie hugged her. "I will be. You'll see. Now scoot on out of here before Peg gets in. I have to tell her before the lunch crowd shows up and starts blabbing about the news."

"Good luck. You're going to need it. I remember when we were kids Peg could always see straight through you."

"Then I'll just have to do the best acting job of my entire life."

Unfortunately, she never had the chance. Within seconds after Peg's arrival—in fact while she was still tying an apron around her waist and Katie was gathering her courage—Luke strolled in the door of the diner. Katie guessed at once from his smug expression that he had heard that the news of their engagement was finally out. He was bound to figure that Peg would have heard it as well. In fact, he was making a beeline straight for her aunt. Katie rushed to intercept him.

Before she could get in a cautionary word, he smiled

broadly at Peg, slipped an arm around Katie's waist and said, "So what did you think of our news?"

"News?" Peg had said, looking suspiciously from one to the other.

Katie jammed an elbow into Luke's side, but he kept that smile and his arm firmly in place and said, "The wedding, of course. You will be there, won't you? I know Katie's counting on you."

He dropped a perfunctory kiss in the vicinity of Katie's mouth, something he'd gotten into the habit of doing despite her protests.

"Gotta run," he said, still oblivious to the fact that he'd just dropped a bombshell. "I'll leave you two to finalize the rest of the plans."

He was gone before Katie could muster the strength to murder him, before she could recover from that slapdash kiss, for that matter. Still a little weak-kneed, she turned to Peg, who was regarding her with an expression filled with hurt and dismay.

Before Katie could open her mouth, Peg shook her head, then whirled and went into the kitchen, where she stubbornly remained for the rest of Katie's shift.

Faced with her aunt's obvious disapproval and consumed with guilt, Katie didn't have the courage to force a confrontation. She slipped away from the diner as soon as her replacement came in and drove out to the beach. It was where she'd always gone when she needed to think.

She headed straight for her favorite secluded bench, drew her knees up to her chest and huddled there trying to figure out how to handle the mess she seemed destined to make of her life.

Today, though, the soothing sound of the surf, the

scent of salt air and pine, was lost on her. She kept thinking of the hurt in Peg's eyes, the worry in Lucy's expression, and her own terrible doubts, which were mounting with every hour that passed.

It wasn't as if anything had changed during the past few weeks since the decision had been made. She and Luke still maintained a cautious distance. Their conversations about the wedding were so matter-of-fact she'd found herself grinding her teeth every time she thought about them.

How could something she'd prayed for most of her life be making her and everyone around her so thoroughly miserable? Was Lucy right? Was marrying Luke for all the wrong reasons the worst mistake she would ever make? Could she survive day after day, living a charade with Luke and hiding her true feelings from him?

So far, he'd certainly lived up to his part of their bargain. He'd deposited ten thousand dollars into her bank account the very afternoon they'd reached an agreement. He'd negotiated a price on the new roof with Ron and had somehow managed to get workers on the job within days.

Maybe it would be good to have a brisk, no-nonsense financial whiz in charge of the business aspects of running the boarding house, she told herself consolingly. She had never been wild about maintaining the books, anyway. She was better at creating a homey, welcoming, family atmosphere. It seemed, in that regard at least, that she and Luke were a match made in heaven. And Robby, well, Robby was the bonus, the icing on the cake. Kate already knew that being his mother was going to fulfill all her fantasies. He was a terrific little boy and he'd accepted her more eagerly than she could have hoped.

Suddenly, as if just thinking about him had conjured him up, she felt Luke's presence. He settled himself onto the bench beside her, as he had so often in the past, slouched down, legs sticking straight out, arms stretched across the back of the bench, fingertips just barely brushing her bare shoulder. Her entire body heated from that innocent, casual touch. Katie longed to fling herself into his arms seeking the safe haven she had once found there. Instead, sitting stiffly, she waited for him to explain why he'd come.

He regarded her worriedly. "What's up, Katie? You look as if you've just lost your best friend."

She glanced over at him. He was dressed once again in the familiar, casual attire he'd always worn. She still couldn't reconcile this Luke with the man whose picture had appeared on so many financial pages, all decked out in perfectly tailored designer suits. This look made him seem familiar, accessible. She could almost believe he was still her best friend and that nothing had ever gone awry between them.

"How'd you find me?" she asked.

"Peg said you'd taken off. You weren't at the boarding house. After that it was easy. I spent a lot of years tracking you down every time you were hurting. You always aimed straight here, even when you were too young to drive and had to walk all the way." His gaze searched her face. "So what's the deal? Are you hurting now? And why was Peg in such a snit? She practically bit my head off."

"I'm feeling guilty."

"About?"

"The way Peg found out about our plans. That also explains her mood."

He regarded her with obvious puzzlement. "I thought you had told her. Isn't that how word got out today?"

She gave him a rueful look. "No, I didn't tell her. You did."

"Me? But I didn't say a word, not until…" He studied her expression, then groaned. "Hell, Katie, hadn't you told her before I showed up this afternoon? Half the town was talking about it by then. I just assumed…"

"Believe me, I know. I suppose it's better that the news came from you, rather than some well-meaning busybody," she said wearily. "Luke, she's so hurt. She hasn't said a single word to me."

His expression turned incredulous. "You mean you didn't sit down and talk about it after I left?"

"Not a word. She went into the kitchen and stayed there."

"No wonder she looked at me the way she did. Why didn't you go after her?"

"The diner was too busy," she said defensively.

Luke regarded her with blatant skepticism. In the face of his doubtful expression, Katie hesitated, then finally admitted the truth. "I'm afraid she'll guess. I'm afraid she'll take one look at my face and know that this whole thing is some sort of sick joke."

Luke stared at her for what seemed an eternity. "Is that how you see what we're doing?" he asked, his voice flat.

"Well, isn't it? Usually two people get married because they're madly in love, not because one wants a baby-sitter and the other one needs financial backing."

Apparently the bitterness she was feeling came

through in her tone, because Luke asked quietly, "Do you want out of our deal, Katie? Is that what this is all about?"

"Yes," she said without thinking, then sighed. "No."

"Which is it?"

I want you to love me, she thought, but she didn't say the words aloud. There was no point in voicing the impossible. It would just make an already awkward situation untenable.

"We made a bargain. I intend to keep it," she said firmly, trying to blink back the tears that threatened.

For a minute Luke looked as if he might argue with her, but then his expression shut down. He reached over and gently brushed away the single tear that tracked down her cheek. "We'll make it work, Katie. I swear to you that somehow we'll make it work."

His solemn promise only served to make even more tears well up. Katie hurriedly swiped them away before they became a deluge.

When she could bear to meet his gaze, she looked up at Luke. "Thanks for coming to look for me. I needed a pep talk."

He gave her one of his patented, reassuring smiles. "In just a few more days, I'll be around whenever you need me. Don't forget that."

"I'm counting on it." She gave him a wobbly, damp smile. "By the way, why did you come if you didn't know about Peg and me?"

"Maybe I just wanted to see you," he said lightly.

Katie didn't believe that for a minute. "Is there a problem?"

"No, there is not a problem," he said with a touch of

impatience. "I just had some time. I thought maybe we could go for a drive or something."

It was the first time she could think of that Luke had so much as hinted at a desire to spend time alone with her. Katie was certain there had to be more to it. "You and me and Robby?"

"No, Katie. You and me. Period." He shook his head. "I guess it was a bad idea."

Something in his expression told her she really had spoiled what had been meant as a gesture to bring them closer together before the wedding. "We could still go."

"You need to talk to Peg. At the moment that's more important. I know how much her opinion matters to you."

"She raised me, Luke. She's all the family I have." Suddenly something occurred to her. "Speaking of family, you haven't said a word about Tommy. Will your brother be here for the wedding?"

"No," he snapped without hesitation.

The curt response startled her. "Luke?"

"Leave it alone."

Something in his expression told her to do exactly as he asked. She knew Luke had been deeply hurt when Tommy had run off years ago, but surely after all this time he had forgiven him. He had adored his younger brother. No matter how many scrapes Tommy had gotten in, Luke had always bailed him out. In some ways, she suspected, Luke had even envied Tommy his rebellious ways.

Maybe she could find Tommy and lure him to the wedding, she thought briefly before assessing Luke's forbidding expression again. Then again, maybe she'd better stay away from that troubled relationship until she understood it. Besides, she had her own family emergency to resolve.

"I guess I'd better go find Peg and face the music," she said reluctantly.

"It'll be all right. She loves you. She just wants you to be happy."

Katie didn't have the heart to tell him that *that* was the problem. Peg wouldn't believe in a million years that Luke Cassidy could make her happy, not after he'd done such a bang-up job of breaking her heart.

At four-thirty in the afternoon the diner was usually empty. The lunch crowd was long gone. The school kids had finished their soft drinks, milk shakes and ice cream cones and headed home. And the dinner crowd, always light during the week, anyway, wouldn't show up for a good hour or more.

Peg usually used the time to check the day's receipts, make lists of supplies to be ordered or simply to put her feet up for a few minutes and catch a quick, refreshing nap before the chaos started all over again.

Today, however, Katie found her aunt pacing from the front door to the kitchen and back again, clearly distracted and upset. Watching her through the window, Katie sighed as she tried to gather the courage to go in. Finally, fearing she was about to be spotted anyway, she opened the door.

When the bell over the door rang, Peg glanced through the pass-through window from the kitchen and saw her. The worry lines in her forehead deepened as she came through the swinging door. Normally an energetic whirlwind, today her aunt looked her age. Her steps had slowed. Her usually tidy, short, gray hair was virtually standing on end from the number of times she'd dragged her fingers through it.

"There you are," she said quietly. "Where'd you go? To the beach?"

Katie grinned sheepishly. No one, with the possible exception of Luke, knew her better than this woman who had taken her in and loved her for so many years. "Where else?" she said.

"Feeling lousy?"

There was an accusation behind the question that Katie couldn't mistake. She deserved to feel lousy and they both knew it. "I'm sorry I hurt you."

"Are you?"

"You know I am. I would never intentionally do anything to upset you."

"I always thought that was true," Peg said, as if she were no longer quite so certain. With her expression far more nonchalant than the situation called for, she inquired, "So, when's the wedding?"

Katie knew a loaded question when she heard one. If she could say six months from now or even a month from now, Peg might believe that the leaked news truly was fresh and that she hadn't intentionally been shut out. When she heard the truth, she was going to be hurt all over again.

"Saturday," Katie said, watching the pain gather in Peg's eyes. "Justice of the Peace Abernathy is going to perform the ceremony at eleven o'clock."

Peg simply stared at her, shock written all over her face. "A justice of the peace? This Saturday? When exactly had you planned to get around to letting me know? After the honeymoon?"

As soon as the angry words were out, Peg Jones

moved like a whirlwind. With brisk efficiency, she slapped a Closed sign on the door, poured two cups of coffee, plunked them on the counter and ordered Katie to sit.

"Okay. What's this all about?" the fifty-year-old woman demanded, her gaze pinned on Katie.

Katie winced under that penetrating look. She tried valiantly to put a positive spin on things. "Luke asked me to marry him. I said yes. It's as simple as that."

"Nothing's ever been simple between the two of you," Peg countered. "Katie, the man broke your heart. I've watched you mope around for the past six years, refusing to look at anyone else, shutting yourself off from life. Now he waltzes back into town, says let's get married and bingo, everything's just dandy again? I don't believe it. Has he even explained why he left? Has he apologized?"

"He doesn't owe me an apology."

Peg sniffed indignantly, but made no comment.

"Luke and I were...are best friends. I can't think of a better basis for marriage," Katie said defensively. "No two people could possibly know each other any better than Luke and I do. We're well suited. We know exactly what we're getting into."

She ignored the coffee her aunt had poured, stood and began cleaning the counter, which had already been polished to a shine. She didn't care. She needed to stay on her feet. She needed to be able to avoid her aunt's probing looks and pointed questions.

No matter how much her evasions hurt her aunt, Katie refused to admit out loud that Luke wasn't marrying her for love. She refused to admit that they had simply made a deal. That was no one's business, not even her beloved aunt's. Peg, who'd raised Katie to abide by an old-fashioned set of values and a romantic's notions of what marriage was supposed to be, would be appalled if she discovered the truth. Her own marriage to Katie's father's brother had been cut short by a tragic accident, but Peg's memories of that time had always brought a sparkle to her eyes.

"Hogwash," Peg said in response to Katie's claim. "Friendship has its places, but what about love, Katie? I've always dreamed of watching you walk down the aisle with a radiant look on your face. Friendship doesn't make you radiant. That takes fire and passion."

Katie thought back to the one night she'd spent in Luke's arms. There had been fire and passion enough that night. Loving him had been everything she'd ever imagined it could be. It had been...she searched for a word adequate to describe it. *Magical,* she decided finally. The stuff of storybooks and romantic movies, certainly an equal to whatever Peg had shared with Harry Jones.

Losing Luke had been worse than anything Katie had ever dreamed of, especially without knowing why he had gone. That she'd been abandoned not just by a lover, but by a best friend had tormented her for the past six years. The loss had made her question her memories of that night, made her doubt herself in ways that she could never share, not with anyone.

Then, when she had seen Luke sitting in the back of the church at Lucy Maguire's aborted wedding ceremony, holding a handsome boy with the classic Cassidy features and Luke's unmistakable blue eyes, she had guessed at once why Luke had left Clover. He had gone away to marry the mother of that darling child.

The only thing left to figure out had been where the boy's mother was now.

Naturally everyone in town had asked about Robby's mother, about the secret bride that no one—not even his very best friend—had known that Luke had taken. And Katie had heard back from most of them, in the form of idle gossip at Peg's, gossip that usually turned silent the instant anyone noticed Katie's presence. No one had learned a blasted thing. Luke had remained discreetly tight-lipped on that score, except to say that he and the boy's mother were divorced. End of story.

Katie sighed. She doubted he would say anything more to her even if she tried to force the issue. That had always been Luke's way. He'd kept his emotions bottled up inside. He'd watched his mother get old and tired very quickly after his father split. He'd been more father than big brother to that hellion of a brother of his, and Tommy had paid him back by taking off just like their father. Katie had been the only one in town who'd detected the anguish that Tommy's leaving had caused Luke. Everyone else had said good riddance, but Luke had viewed Tommy's departure as his own failure. He had blamed himself for not being a good enough surrogate father, even though only a few years had separated him in age from Tommy.

She thought about that now and realized that despite his unexplained departure from her life, in her heart she had never doubted Luke's decency. It was at the core of who he was, a decent, responsible man, determined to be more honest and honorable than the father who'd abandoned him. She didn't believe for an instant that those two traits had vanished. He might not be in love with her. He might not have made the most romantic proposal on record. But he would do his very best to make her a good husband. He would honor this commitment he was making. And he'd come to her, chosen *her* because he wanted to do what was best for his son. That wasn't the act of a man who'd suddenly turned selfish.

Somehow she had to convince her aunt of that or Peg would be worrying herself sick.

She took her aunt's hand. "Please, Peg, I know it's unexpected—"

"A pure bolt out of the blue is more like it. He's only been back in town off and on for a couple of months now."

"Since March," Katie corrected.

"Whatever. I didn't even think the two of you were speaking."

"Well, obviously we are. This is what I want. What Luke and I want." She leaned across the counter to hug her aunt. "Please, I really need your support and your love. I need you to give us your blessing. You'll be there on Saturday, won't you? I can't possibly have a wedding without you."

"If I thought that were true, I'd stay away just to prevent you from making a terrible mistake," her aunt said.

"You can't protect me forever. I'm a grown woman. If this is a mistake, it's mine to make. I love him with all my heart, Peg. You know that. I always have. I have to try. I don't want to live with even more regrets."

"Regrets aren't always the worst things to have," her aunt argued. "But…" She cut off whatever she'd been about to say and sighed. "Never mind. I love you. If you can look me in the eye and tell me you think Luke will make you happy, then of course I'll be there."

Katie thought at first that her aunt's words were the concession she'd been seeking. One look into Peg's eyes told her otherwise. Her aunt meant them as a challenge.

"Well," Peg prodded.

Katie forced herself to meet her aunt's skeptical gaze. "I wouldn't be marrying him if I didn't believe that with all my heart," she said staunchly.

The firmly spoken words clearly didn't banish all of Peg's doubts, but she nodded, her expression resigned.

"Okay, then. Let's make some plans. I'll throw the reception for you afterward. Nothing fancy," she added quickly in response to Katie's frown. "Just a few folks over for a nice brunch at the house. Maybe a champagne toast."

"But…"

Peg waved off any objections. "I don't care how small the ceremony is or how rushed, every couple should start life with a few good wishes from their family and friends."

Katie figured her wedding day was going to be difficult enough without having to pretend in front of a bunch of people that it truly was the happiest day of her life. "I'll have to ask Luke," she hedged. "We really wanted to keep this simple and private."

"Can I give you one last piece of advice before I turn you over to that man?" Peg asked. She didn't pause long enough for a reply, which Katie didn't have ready, anyway. "You don't ask him for his opinion on every little thing, Katie. You tell him what you want once in a while."

Good advice, Katie thought, as she gave a last swipe at the diner's counter before racing home to do the Monday laundry for the boarding house. But how was she supposed to tell Luke Cassidy that the only thing she really wanted from him was his love?

Chapter 2

On the night before her wedding, when most brides would be celebrating with a rehearsal dinner or a shower, Katie gathered the residents of the Clover Street Boarding House in the living room. She'd learned that afternoon that they were all terrified about what her marriage would mean to the future of the boarding house. Seventeen-year-old Ginger, who'd chewed her nails down to the quick again for the first time in months, had revealed the concerns of the half-dozen boarders.

"Katie, you haven't said. How soon will you be wanting us to leave?" Ginger had asked, her voice trembling with emotion. She'd been drying the same soup bowl for the past ten minutes, obviously trying to work up the courage to get into this with Katie.

Katie had stared at her blankly. "Leave? Who said

anything about your leaving?" Understanding dawned. "Oh my heavens, is that why I've seen Mrs. Jeffers with the classifieds every evening this week? She's been going through them for the rest of you?"

"She's been looking for rooms to let, but there aren't any," Ginger had said, suddenly tearful. "We wondered how long you'd give us before we have to go?"

"Nobody's going anywhere," Katie had replied grimly, taking both the soup bowl and dish towel from the teenager's hands. "Have all of the others in the living room tonight at seven."

Looking hopeful, Ginger had rushed from the room, yelling at the top of her lungs.

Now all of the residents were sitting quietly, watching Katie. She could see the anxiety etched on their faces.

There was Mrs. Jeffers, of course. She'd been the first to move in, a month after her husband had died. She had a starchy, prim demeanor that covered the fact that she feared no one would accept her now that she was no longer part of a couple. Once someone breached that reserve, though, the sixty-five-year-old widow had a wicked sense of humor and endless compassion and energy.

Ginger had followed. She'd been fifteen, a runaway who'd never said one single word about the past she'd left behind. For a while she had shared a room with Ron Mathews's sister, Janie. The two of them had formed a bond that had been wonderful to witness. And both of them had come to adore Mrs. Jeffers, who'd quickly become a surrogate grandmother to both teens. Janie still stayed with them whenever she came home from college.

John O'Reilly, with his round, jovial face, rimless spectacles and fringe of white hair, reminded them all of Santa Claus. A retired fireman, he'd volunteered to do the grocery shopping for Katie. She suspected he'd done it so he could stock the kitchen with his favorite snacks. Hardly a night passed that he wasn't in there at midnight with a bowl of ice cream, popcorn or, in the summertime, a peach cobbler he'd made himself and shared with the others at dinner.

When Sophie Reynolds and her daughter had moved out after Sophie's wedding, her room had been quickly let to dark-haired, energetic Teresa Parks, a young woman in her early thirties who'd just taken a secretarial job at the bank. She'd come home to Clover after a bitter divorce she never discussed. She'd told Katie only that she needed time to get back on her feet before finding a house of her own.

The remaining tenant at the moment was a salesman, in town for just a few days. Katie noticed that Dennis Brown had gone straight to his room after dinner and hadn't come back down for this meeting. It was hardly surprising since he'd be moving on first thing in the morning, right before the wedding that had thrown everyone into such a tizzy.

Just as Katie was about to start the meeting, the front door opened. Luke strolled in with Robby bounding ahead of him. An immediate silence greeted their arrival.

"Luke, what a surprise!" Katie said. She hadn't realized, in fact, that he'd brought Robby over from Atlanta where he'd been finishing up kindergarten. She'd assumed he would remain there with Luke's housekeeper until after the wedding. "What are you doing here?"

"I heard you were having a meeting with the tenants tonight. Since I'll be moving in any day now, I thought I should sit in, too. And I thought it was about time everyone got to meet my son."

"Who told you about…?" Katie began, but stopped when she saw the guilty flush in Ginger's cheeks. "Well, it doesn't matter."

She gave everyone a reassuring look as Luke found a vacant seat and pulled Robby onto his lap. "I called this meeting tonight because I wanted to reassure you that my marriage won't change anything around here."

Unfortunately her words appeared to have little effect. In fact, every blasted person at the room was staring not at her, but at Luke, whose expression suddenly seemed excessively dark and forbidding.

"Isn't that right, Luke?" she prodded pointedly, praying that he wouldn't launch into some list of changes he intended to make.

She knew he'd been making notes for the past month, hunching over her books, hovering over her as she worked, examining every nook and cranny of the place and jotting down needed repairs. So far he'd kept silent about his thoughts on the boarding house operation, but Katie knew it was only a matter of time before he would feel compelled to seize control of the place. To a man like Luke, taking charge was as natural as breathing.

"Luke, no one has a thing to worry about," she stated emphatically. "Isn't that right?"

"For now," he said.

It was hardly the enthusiastic endorsement Katie had hoped for. For some reason, though, it seemed to do what her own promise had not. Everyone nodded happily.

"It's going to be real nice to have a handsome young man in the house," Mrs. Jeffers said. Katie glanced at Luke. Before he could respond to the compliment he clearly assumed had been meant for him, the widow held out her arms to Robby, who deserted his father and bounded over to her without a hint of reservation. "I declare you are about the handsomest boy I have ever seen."

Robby grinned, his smile so exactly like Luke's that Katie's breath caught in her throat. She couldn't tell from Luke's expression if he was laughing at his own mistake or was simply pleased to see Robby being welcomed so warmly.

"Will you be my grandma?" Robby asked Mrs. Jeffers. "My real grandmas died."

"I would be honored to be your grandma," Mrs. Jeffers said, looking pleased as punch.

"You smell nice, like flowers," Robby announced.

Mrs. Jeffers, whose own grandchildren lived on the West Coast, beamed at Katie. "Dear, I do believe this is going to work out rather well."

The others nodded in agreement. Katie wished she were half so certain.

As the meeting at the Clover Street Boarding House ended with one of Mr. O'Reilly's fresh fruit cobblers being dished up and served to everyone, Luke gave Ginger a suspicious wink that had Katie crossing the room in a flash.

"Thanks for letting me know," he said as Katie joined them.

She was just in time to overhear him and guess that he was referring to tonight's meeting. If that hadn't confirmed her earlier suspicion, Ginger's blushing cheeks would have.

"It was no big deal. I just figured if you were going to be living here, you should be a part of it," Ginger said, evading Katie's gaze. "See you. I've got studying to do."

"My, my, another conquest," Katie observed, unable to curb her irritation with Luke's intrusion into her meeting. "What did you do to win her over? Offer to buy her a new car? Maybe pay her way through college?"

Luke, blast him, refused to rise to the taunt. He grinned at her indignant tone. "You're the only one around here I'm buying off, Katie. Swear to God."

Swear to God. Those were the words Luke had always used to convince her that he was being totally honest. He tended to use them loosely, which somewhat dimmed their ability to reassure.

"Buying off?" she repeated lightly. "I made a legitimate business deal. That's all."

His grin remained unrepentant. "Then you must be afraid you're losing your grip around here. Is that what's made you so cranky and suspicious all of a sudden?" he inquired in that lazy, amused tone that set Katie's teeth on edge.

Before she could reply, he gestured to Mrs. Jeffers. "Hey, darlin', would you mind keeping an eye on Robby for a bit? I'd like to take Katie for a walk. She needs to cool off."

Given the fact that it was still ninety degrees outside, Katie assumed the remark had to do with her temper, not the temperature.

Mrs. Jeffers, who'd apparently missed Luke's true meaning or assumed it was some lover's ruse to get

Katie alone, beamed. "You two young people go right ahead. Robby and I will play a game of checkers until you get back. He tells me he's world-champion caliber."

Luke brushed a kiss on the woman's weathered cheek, then whispered, "I hear you're the champ of the boarding house. Go easy on him."

Katie watched the teasing exchange with her irritation mounting by unreasonable leaps and bounds. "Trying to rub salt in the wound?" she inquired when he'd propelled her outside.

"What wound would that be?"

"That you can take over here anytime you want. You're obviously trying to win over Mrs. Jeffers. And you already have Ginger reporting every move I make to you." She paused on the front steps and frowned at him. "How did you get her to spill the beans about tonight's meeting, anyway?"

"I ran into her at the library. We got to talking. She mentioned the meeting. It was hardly a sinister, premeditated act of treason."

Katie sniffed. "That depends on your point of view, I suppose. Just in case you've forgotten, let me remind you that we made a deal. You're not supposed to interfere with my tenants."

He regarded her with amusement. "What interference? I'm just being friendly. If we're all going to be living together, we need to get along, isn't that right?"

Thoroughly exasperated, Katie couldn't think of a single way to fault that logic. "I suppose," she said grudgingly. "I just want it on the record that I don't like what you did tonight."

"Showing up?"

"Taking over."

"Katie, I did not take over," he said reasonably. "Come on. Let's walk."

She followed him without argument, still seething over what had happened earlier, even though she suspected she might be overreacting just the teensiest bit. She blamed it on nerves over the wedding that was less than twenty-four hours away.

The truth was, though, if she didn't take a firm stand now, the next thing she knew Luke would be running her boarding house and she would be doing…what? She had no idea what she would do if she lost control of the boarding house.

Starting up that business, buying the old McAllister place and making a go of it had been the only thing that had saved her sanity after Luke had left town.

"You did, you know," she accused.

He regarded her as if he'd forgotten the argument. "Did what?"

"Take over."

"Katie, I barely said two words."

"But those were the only words they listened to," she grumbled.

"Sweetheart…"

The endearment grated. "I am not your sweetheart. I'm your business partner."

"Okay, *partner*. It was only natural that they want to know where I stand. I'm marrying you. I'm moving in. I'm an unknown quantity, someone who could disrupt their lives. They wanted to hear straight from me what my role is going to be. What did you expect me to do?"

"You could have deferred to me," she said. "Maybe reminded them that it's still my boarding house, that you're only a silent partner, that you have other, more important fish to fry." Struck by an unexpected thought, she regarded him worriedly. "You do, don't you? You haven't retired or something?"

"Worried I'll be underfoot all the time tempting you to do wild, irresponsible things?"

Katie's pulse skipped a beat at the deliberate innuendo and its matching glint in Luke's eyes. "Hardly," she said.

Luke laughed, probably at her dead-giveaway, breathless tone. "Katie, stop worrying. Give them a week or two to get used to my presence and they'll be right back to relying on you for everything." He stopped under a streetlight and grinned at her.

"What?" she demanded.

"I just never noticed before how much you hate change. You're a control freak."

This from a man who'd manipulated her into marrying him, Katie thought. "I am not."

"You are. You're even more scared about tomorrow than I am, because you can't predict what will happen next."

His observation about her fears barely registered. She was too intrigued by the revelation he'd made about himself. "You're scared?" she asked doubtfully.

He didn't look frightened. He looked like a man with the confidence to take over the whole damned town of Clover if he had a mind to. For all she knew that was his devious intention. Maybe he'd just started with the boarding house, because he knew she'd be an easy mark.

Before she could work herself into a frenzy over what Luke might or might not be truly up to, he caught her off guard again by admitting to his fears straight out.

"Sure, I'm scared," he said. "It's not like I go around making deals like this all the time. It's a first for me, too."

Katie regarded him thoughtfully. "I guess I hadn't thought of it that way." She lifted her gaze to his and studied him intently, trying to assure herself that he was being totally truthful.

As if he'd guessed her intention, he smiled. "Swear to God, Katie."

Finally convinced, she grinned back at him. "Thanks."

"For what?"

"For knowing the right thing to say…again."

"I hope I always will."

He suddenly looked so sad, so filled with his own doubts that Katie very nearly stood on tiptoe to kiss him. She knew, though, that a quick, consoling brush of her lips across his would never satisfy her. It would be like playing with matches. And she had vowed that she would not risk the pain that was sure to follow.

"We'd better be getting back," she said instead, starting away from him.

"Katie?"

She turned back.

"There's something we should talk about," he began.

His tone sounded so ominous that Katie promptly decided she didn't want to hear whatever he was about to say. "Can't it wait?"

Luke looked torn. Clearly the idea of putting off whatever he'd been about to say was a relief, yet he seemed to be struggling with his conscience.

"It really shouldn't."

Now she knew for certain she didn't want to hear

it. "Please, Luke. Can't we just enjoy the night, pretend we're any other couple about to get married in the
morning, and put off all the problems until after the
ceremony? Please?"

"I suppose that's not too much to ask," he agreed,
that same mix of relief and reluctance in his voice.

He held out a hand and Katie slipped hers into it, letting his warmth and strength wash through her. They
walked back to the boarding house hand in hand and
for those few minutes, anyway, Katie forced away all
of the doubts. If she closed her eyes, she could almost
pretend that tomorrow was going to be the happiest
day of her life.

"It's not going to work, big brother!"

Luke's fingers tightened around the phone. Just the
sound of his brother's voice these days was enough to
make his blood run cold. Tommy was the last person
he'd wanted to hear from on his wedding day.

"What's not going to work?" he asked, even though
he knew he wasn't going to like the answer.

"This farce of a marriage. You're only doing it to
keep me from getting custody of Robby, aren't you?
It's just another one of your cold-blooded plots to have
everything your own way."

Despite Luke's automatic inclination to dismiss anything Tommy had to say, he couldn't deny that the accusation hurt. When had he become so cold-blooded and
calculating? Luke had a feeling it went back to the day
he had made his bargain with Robby's mother six years
ago. From that moment on, knowing that he'd have to
give up Katie to do what was right, his own soul had

been in jeopardy. He would never give Tommy the satisfaction of admitting that, though.

"Whether I'm married or not, you don't have a snowball's chance in hell of getting custody of *my* son," Luke said icily. "Why don't you save yourself the cost of this suit?"

"Because Robby's mine, dammit."

"You abandoned him," Luke reminded him. "The minute Betty Sue Wilder told you she was pregnant, you took off. You never accepted responsibility for her or your baby. I did. I married Betty Sue so that Robby would have the Cassidy name, for whatever the hell it's worth."

"Noble Saint Luke," Tommy said derisively. "Always ready to jump in and clean up my messes, isn't that right? The truth was you were glad to marry Betty Sue. She was a hell of a lot hotter than any of the girls in your life."

Luke thought of the one night he'd had with Katie, the night he'd never been able to put from his mind no matter how hard he'd tried. That night had overshadowed any experience he and Betty Sue had ever shared. Even now the memory made his blood turn hot. "Shut up, Tommy."

"You know it's true. That's why she left you, isn't it? Because you couldn't keep up with her."

Luke kept a tight rein on his temper, but it was a costly effort. He could feel his pulse throbbing dully. "Why don't you repeat some of your ugly opinions in court?" he suggested. "Let the judge see for himself exactly the kind of man you've turned out to be. The bottom line here isn't Robby. Not where you're concerned.

You don't give a hoot about your son or what's best for him. If you did, you would never have filed this suit."

"A boy should know his real daddy, don't you think so, big brother?"

"In most instances I'd agree with you. In this case I think your motives are highly suspect. You want me to pay you off to stay out of his life, don't you? That's what this is really about."

"Is that what you think, big brother? That money can make up for losing a kid?"

"Tommy, I believe that you're the kind of man who'd sell his own mother for the right price. This interest in Robby was awfully sudden. You didn't seem to give a damn until you happened to catch that news report on my net worth."

"Since we're into motives and honesty here," Tommy retorted, "how does old Katie feel about being used? Does she know she's supposed to do the mom-and-apple-pie thing when you walk into court?"

Luke winced at that. He'd told Katie nothing at all about the circumstances of Robby's birth. Nor had he told her that Tommy was trying to take the boy away from him in what promised to be an ugly court case. And because of his international reputation, that case was likely to make news around the world.

Okay, so it was a lousy secret to be keeping. He hadn't told her up front because he'd been afraid she'd turn him down if she knew exactly what she was getting into. He'd almost told her last night, but he'd been all too willing to drop the issue when she'd asked him not to get into anything too heavy on the eve of their wedding.

Afterward once she'd had time to fall in love with

Robby, once she thought of his son as her own, he prayed that she would be every bit as furious and indignant about Tommy's out-of-the-blue plans as he was.

Apparently his silence told Tommy all he needed to know. "You haven't told her, have you? Poor old Katie. You're still taking her for granted, big brother. One of these days that arrogance of yours is going to cost you big-time."

It was the only thing Tommy had said that had the ring of gospel truth. Luke did take Katie for granted. He counted on her compassion, her generosity and the deep and abiding love she'd once given him so freely. One of these days, though, he would likely pay a terrible price for taking all that she had to offer and giving her nothing but lies in return. He was likely to lose the only woman he'd ever really given a damn about.

"Goodbye, Tommy."

"See you in court, bro."

Tommy's words were still ringing in his ears as Luke dressed for the wedding an hour later. He'd chosen his most formal suit, a black pin-stripe that had served him well in the business world. Maybe it would bring him luck today as well, more luck than he had any right to expect.

He thought back over the life he'd managed to put together despite his unfortunate marriage to Betty Sue Wilder. He'd mastered finance while living in Atlanta, turning an understanding of basic accounting into an intuitive grasp of the corporate bottom line.

Between his careful personal financial management and his genius for investments, he'd parlayed a generous salary into the kind of wealth he'd never even imagined

growing up back in Clover. His tight-fisted control of
the bankbook had irritated the daylights out of his wife
and had, no doubt, contributed to her decision to take
off. Betty Sue hadn't liked being hemmed in by anything as mundane as a budget.

Luke, however, had held the opinion that having
money one day didn't guarantee he'd have it the next.
He spent it as if each dollar might be his last. He would
never, ever be left in the sorry financial mess that had
faced his mother after his father took off.

He'd been horrified upon returning to Clover to see
the kind of risks Katie had taken with her own financial stability. It was too late for him to do anything
for his mother, but Katie's situation at least was about
to change. He'd have her on a sound financial footing
in no time…if she would listen to him. She probably
wouldn't, he admitted with a sigh. For the hundredth
time he wondered why he had been so hell-bent on
making this particular bargain. He knew he could have
fought off his brother's claim to Robby on his own. He
could have hired a nanny to look after the boy.

But from the moment he'd realized that Tommy intended to fight him for Robby's custody, Luke's head
had been filled with thoughts of Caitlyn. Six years ago
he'd chosen duty over his heart. The decision to marry
Betty Sue had been forced on him by a deeply ingrained
sense of honor. Afterward, he had grimly set out to
erase all of his most precious memories of Katie.

A few months ago, with Betty Sue gone and Tommy
raising cain about the son Luke had stolen from him,
Luke had just as systematically set out to learn all he
could about Katie's life since he'd left Clover.

And then he'd formed his plan for getting her to

marry him. He'd gone about it with the kind of dogged determination and attention to detail that had made him a success in business. Major corporate mergers had been achieved with less rigorous planning.

Not once had it occurred to him to simply court her. For one thing, there wasn't enough time. For another, he'd always figured the sensible, straightforward approach was best. Most people understood dollars and cents in ways they couldn't comprehend emotions.

Caitlyn had readily confirmed his beliefs on that score. She'd seen right away that what he was suggesting would work out best all around. Hell, she'd even laid out a damned payment plan for her commitment. Ten thousand a year for five years! He'd been stunned by her audacity. He'd also admired it in a grudging sort of way.

The one thing he couldn't figure out for the life of him, though, was why her quick response had left him feeling empty and somehow disappointed.

"You never said. Is Katie going to be my new mommy? I mean is that what I should call her?" Robby asked, tugging at his tie interrupting his thoughts. His own suit was an exact replica of Luke's, but he was clearly less comfortable in it.

He was far more fascinated with the concept of having a new mother. He rarely saw Betty Sue, which was her choice, not Luke's and certainly not Robby's. For weeks after she'd gone Robby had stood silently in front of her photograph, tears rolling down his cheeks.

Now, he asked Luke, "Would Mommy be mad if I called Katie Mommy, too?"

"I think she'd want you to do whatever made you happy," Luke said.

Robby frowned. "But will Katie mind? I mean I'm not really her little boy."

"That's something you and she will have to decide."

"Will we live in her house? I like it there. Mrs. Jeffers said I could call her Grandma, and I beat her at checkers. And it won't be lonely with all those people around all the time."

Luke felt as if he'd been sucker punched by Robby's calmly delivered statement. No five-year-old should be talking about loneliness so matter-of-factly.

There was no question that Robby had spent far too much time alone in his young life. Betty Sue hadn't been much interested in mothering. She'd had a list of available baby-sitters that would just about have filled his Rolodex and she hadn't hesitated to call them morning, noon or night. As a result, Robby was amazingly adaptable and outgoing, almost desperate in his bids for approval. Some of those traits would benefit him, Luke supposed, but that knowledge didn't assuage his guilt.

"It will be like getting a big family all at once, won't it?" Luke said, wondering again at the odd sense of disappointment that had settled into the region of his heart.

What kind of privacy would a pair of newlyweds have in a crowded boarding house? And how long would it be before everyone in town knew that he and Katie were sleeping in separate bedrooms, as she'd dictated?

Of course, if every room were rented…

A slow grin crept across his face. Yes, indeed, that would solve that particular problem in a hurry. Katie couldn't very well hold him to their deal if there was a paying customer for that extra bedroom. He swore to himself that he'd have that situation resolved by the time they came back from their farce of a honeymoon in

Charleston. He'd sensed an ally in Mrs. Jeffers. Perhaps she would be willing to screen new applicants for the room. The whole matter could be handled in no time.

For some reason the thought of Caitlyn in his bed, in his arms, warmed him in a way that nothing else had in a very long time. He couldn't think of a single other business merger that had affected him quite the same way, a fact that would have surprised his ex-wife. She'd always thought the only thing that turned him on was business. He hadn't been able to deny it...until now.

Now it seemed that his best friend, the woman he was supposedly marrying solely for convenience, had the ability to make his whole damned body throb with anticipation. Something told him this marriage was going to turn out to be a whole lot more than he'd bargained for.

Chapter 3

Lucy Maguire Ryder, who was the only person who knew the whole truth about this sham of a wedding, stood back and studied Katie speculatively. The close scrutiny had Katie squirming. She was nervous enough without her best friend looking her over with the intensity of the last quality control inspector on the assembly line at General Motors.

"You look beautiful," Lucy declared finally, when she had straightened the hem of Katie's new knee-length silk dress for the tenth time in the past fifteen minutes.

"Yes, you do, darling," Peg agreed. "That pale pink brings out the roses in your cheeks, though why you wouldn't agree to a fancy gown is beyond me. This is your wedding, hopefully the only one you'll ever have. You should have all the trimmings."

"Wedding gowns are outrageously expensive," Katie

said. She didn't add that the boarding house debts had eaten up all of her savings. Such an admission might lead the conversation too close to her financial arrangement with Luke.

"I could have made one for practically nothing," Peg began.

Katie quickly cut her off. "There was no time for you to make it and there was no point in spending all that money for a ceremony that will take five minutes," she countered. "Luke and I agreed this was more sensible."

"Sensible," Peg repeated with a huff. "Weddings aren't supposed to be sensible. People in love should indulge themselves just this once."

Katie exchanged a look with her best friend and tried to avoid her aunt's penetrating gaze.

"What?" Peg exclaimed, catching the two of them. Her forced cheerfulness died, replaced at once by suspicion. "What is it that you're keeping from me? From the very beginning, I've suspected that you weren't telling me the whole truth. Now what's going on here?"

"Nothing," Katie reassured her, giving her a hug. "Thank you for everything."

Peg glanced from Katie to Lucy and back again, clearly not satisfied. Finally, apparently guessing that she wouldn't learn anything from either of them, she shrugged. "Everything? I have a cake and a few canapés at home. I always dreamed of—"

"Stop it," Katie said firmly, before Peg had them all in tears with her description of the ideal church wedding she'd envisioned for her niece. "This is what I want— just a quiet ceremony with the people I love most. Isn't that what really matters?"

To Katie's relief, the question, for which there was

only one reasonable answer, finally silenced her aunt's litany of regrets.

"I'm sorry," Peg said. "The last thing I want is to spoil this day for you." She reached into her handbag and pulled out a small package. "This is for you. It was your grandmother's."

Katie's throat clogged with emotion as she accepted it. She tugged the white ribbon free, then slid the box from its wrappings. Her fingers shook as she fumbled with the tight lid. When she finally had it open, she found a small, white leather-bound prayer book with her grandmother's name engraved in gold.

"She carried it at her wedding. It was a gift from your grandfather," Peg said.

Clasping the prayer book tightly, Katie threw her arms around her aunt and hugged her. "Thank you."

"I've been saving it all these years. Your mother and I both carried it at our weddings. Your mother wanted you to have it on your wedding day." Peg dabbed gently at the tears spilling down Katie's cheeks. "Don't cry, sweetheart. You'll ruin your makeup."

"Thank you," Katie whispered again.

"Stop that. You don't need to thank me for doing what your mother asked," Peg said brusquely, swiping at her own tears.

"I'm not thanking you for that," Katie protested. "I just want you to know how grateful I am for everything you've done for me. You took me in. You've been like a second mother, and no girl could have had a better one. I love you."

"Oh, baby." Peg's embrace tightened. "I love you, too."

With both of them about to dissolve into sentimental tears, Lucy stepped in. "Enough, you two, or Clover will be flooded by nightfall. Besides, we have a wedding to get to." She gave Katie's hand an encouraging squeeze. "All set?"

"As ready as I'll ever be."

It wasn't until she walked into Justice of the Peace Abernathy's dingy, cramped foyer a half hour later and heard the recorded sound of organ music that Katie recognized the exact consequences of the choice she'd made in her kitchen just a few short weeks earlier. Visions of all of the other lovely weddings in which she'd participated as a bridesmaid crowded into her head. This was... She couldn't find words to describe how depressing it all was, especially since she knew that she and Luke didn't even share the kind of love that might have conquered this inauspicious beginning.

Suddenly the enormity of what she was about to do struck her. For one fleeting instant she considered turning right around and running as fast and as far from Clover, South Carolina, and Luke Cassidy as she could get. She knew, though, that distance alone would never bring her peace of mind. For better or worse, this was the choice of her heart, if not her head.

"Are you okay?" Lucy asked in a hushed voice as Peg went in to take a seat.

"Peachy," Katie replied and wondered if the butterflies in her stomach could be squelched by sheer bravado. "Where's Luke?"

Lucy peered through the curtain that shielded the justice of the peace's office. "In with Mr. Abernathy. Robby's there, too. He looks so sweet. He's all dressed up just like his daddy. Peg's talking to them, but Luke keeps looking this way as if he's afraid you're about to bolt." Lucy regarded her intently. "You aren't, are you?"

Katie glanced longingly toward the front door, then sighed and shook her head as the organ music swelled and shifted into an enthusiastic rendition of the wedding march. Lucy squeezed her hand reassuringly.

"Show time, sweetie."

Katie drew in a deep breath and peeked through the archway into the room where she was about to be married. The clutter of dark antiques, the frayed upholstery and the heavy drapes were incredibly oppressive, hardly what she'd always imagined as the setting for her wedding. Before she could get too depressed, she brought herself up short. She was beginning to get as caught up as Peg on the frills, rather than focusing on what this day was really all about—a commitment to love, honor and cherish Luke Cassidy all the days of her life.

That much shouldn't be too difficult. She'd already had years of practice. If only he were coming to this ceremony with the same deep emotions, she thought wistfully. Well, there was no point in wishing for the impossible. This was the bargain she'd made and she intended to make the best of it.

Holding in a sigh of regret, she looked into that dreary office one more time. Robby was practically bouncing up and down with excitement. Luke's gaze was trained on the opening, as steady and confident as ever. Katie locked gazes with those familiar blue eyes and let them lure her into the room.

She was only dimly aware of what happened next. Mr. Abernathy read an unhurried version of the all-too-familiar ceremony. Katie hadn't been a bridesmaid more times than she could recall without learning the words by heart. She kept wishing he would get on with it. She wouldn't believe what she was doing—the emotional risk she was taking—until she and Luke had both said "I do" and the justice of the peace had pronounced them man and wife.

Man and wife! Her pulse thumped unsteadily at the thought. *All the days of our lives!* Dear heaven, was she out of her mind?

Just when she was about to panic, her gaze was inevitably drawn back to Luke's eyes. Now, with the weight of the vows spelled out, she thought she saw the same doubts and turmoil reflected in his clear blue eyes. Somehow it helped just knowing he was as nervous as she was.

Then suddenly he smiled, a slow, reassuring curve of his lips that unexpectedly calmed her. His mischievous wink had her smiling back at him.

And then, just when she was beginning to relax and enjoy it, the ceremony ended and she was wearing a simple gold band on the third finger of her left hand. Luke examined its mate on his own finger with the same amazed expression she was sure was on her own face.

For the first time Katie actually looked around and registered the pleased expression on Lucy's face, the tears shimmering in Peg's eyes and the bouquet that Luke had awkwardly shoved into her hands right before the ceremony. It was an assortment of blue, yellow and white wildflowers that was so reminiscent of the first flowers he'd ever picked for her that it brought tears to Katie's eyes. She was probably the only bride in history who was choking back sobs of regret for lost dreams within seconds after saying "I do."

"You may kiss the bride," Mr. Abernathy said jovially, startling Katie and Luke out of their private thoughts.

Luke hesitated just long enough to force a flood of embarrassed color into Katie's cheeks. Then he dutifully swept her into his arms with a dramatic flourish meant to satisfy the handful of onlookers.

Though his enthusiasm for the task seemed obviously feigned to Katie, the touch of Luke's lips on hers for the traditional post-ceremony kiss made her pulse race with predictable ease. A wildfire of emotions sparked to life deep inside her, even though there wasn't anything the least bit passionate about the obligatory gesture. She hated her own quick response to what for Luke was merely a show for their small audience.

Robby's smacking kiss and tight hug, which promptly followed, were far more natural and enthusiastic. At least one of the Cassidy men seemed happy about the marriage, Katie thought bleakly.

Too bad it wasn't her new husband.

On the ride over to Peg's after the ceremony, Luke wondered at the quick burst of anticipation that had shimmered through him as he'd held Katie in his arms for that all-too-brief farce of a kiss. He glanced over at his bride, who was sitting stiffly beside him, looking more like someone going off to their own execution than a woman who was about to attend her wedding reception. Peg had insisted that Robby ride with her to give them time alone. Luke was beginning to regret accepting the gesture.

"I didn't have a chance to tell you earlier," he said quietly. "You look beautiful."

She regarded him skeptically. "I…"

"No protest," he said interrupting. "You do. You're the epitome of the radiant bride."

She still looked as if she wanted to argue the point, but this time she managed to say a polite thanks.

"Katie, if you don't start smiling, people are going to wonder if there was a shotgun at our backs today."

That drew a startled look. "What?"

"You know," he prodded. "A shotgun. A baby."

If he'd hoped to make her laugh at the absurdity of that, the attempt failed miserably. She frowned at him.

"Well, fortunately most people in Clover are very adept at counting to nine," she said. "When next March rolls around and there's no little Cassidy, they'll figure out they were wrong."

He sighed at her curt tone. "I wouldn't mind having another little Cassidy someday, yours and mine," he said quietly. "What about you?"

"Given the fact that I have no intention of sharing a bed with you that's going to be difficult to accomplish," she retorted without even a hint of hesitation.

He grinned at her certainty that she had that situation well in hand. "Oh, there are plenty of places to do the deed other than a bed. All it requires are two people with imagination and dexterity."

Suddenly the too-serious expression on her face faltered. A grin tugged at her resisting lips. Luke wanted a full-fledged smile.

"We could pull over and I could show you," he offered generously. "The back seat of a car is a very traditional place to start."

A smile broke at last. "In your dreams, Cassidy. We have a deal."

"I would be willing to sacrifice my credibility as an honest businessman by breaking this one clause in our bargain," he said.

Finally her eyes glinted with wicked amusement. "I could never ask such a thing of you."

"You're not asking," he protested, enjoying the tint of pink the teasing was putting back into her too-pale cheeks. "I'm offering."

"Save it for someone else."

"I don't expect to have another wife."

She nodded thoughtfully. "Then that is a problem, isn't it? It's a good thing the hot water heater at the boarding house rarely works. The cold showers will do you good."

Luke vowed to replace the hot water heater the minute they got back from their honeymoon. Meantime, he pulled into Peg's driveway and cut the engine. When Katie started to open her door, he reached across her, his arm brushing against her breasts, and closed it. She turned a startled look on him.

"What?"

"Before things get too crazy inside, I just want you to know…" He hesitated, uncertain what he could say that would express the strange mix of gratitude and unexpected anticipation he was feeling. "I know that most women look forward to their wedding day their whole lives. And I imagine this isn't anything like what you dreamed about."

"It doesn't matter," she said, though a slight trembling of her lower lip said otherwise.

"It does," he contradicted. "Despite the way this whole thing came about, Katie, from here on out I intend to live up to those vows."

The tears that suddenly welled up in her eyes were almost his undoing. He reached across and pulled her into his arms. "Don't cry, darlin', please."

"I...can't...help...it," she said haltingly between sniffs. "Oh, Luke, what if this was a terrible mistake? I don't think I could stand it if you ever regretted marrying me."

"No regrets. I guarantee it. And I'm going to do my damnedest to see that you don't have any, either," he said determinedly.

Katie unexpectedly giggled at that. "You sound so grim."

A rush of tenderness washed over him as he looked into her tear-streaked face. "I was going for reassuring," he said indignantly. "Now let's get inside before they send out a search party."

"I'm sure everyone inside is perfectly satisfied that they know exactly why we've been delayed," Katie said dryly.

She started once again to open the door.

"Stop that," Luke said. "Just this once will you stay still and wait for me to open the door for you, instead of bolting like you can't wait to get away from me?"

"Maybe I'm just anxious to get to the cake before you do."

"We have to cut that together," he reminded her. "It's a tradition."

He glanced into her eyes and saw at once that she recognized as well as he did the irony of worrying about a wedding cake tradition when they'd already turned the entire concept of marrying for love on its head.

The minute they walked through the door of Peg's familiar house, Luke felt as if he'd finally come home.

As a boy he had spent more hours in this small, comfortable house with its sagging front porch and cheerful, haphazardly decorated rooms than he had at home.

And in more recent years, when the interior of his own house in Atlanta had been designed by some outrageously expensive decorator who was all the rage according to Betty Sue, he still hadn't felt as at ease as he did right here amid the hodgepodge of antiques and junk that Peg had lovingly assembled from past generations of her own family and her husband's.

Katie's own ancestors, he thought now, smiling at a memory. She had once taken him through the house and pointed out exactly which pieces had come from which relative. The furniture seemed to provide necessary and more tangible ties to her past than even the old photo album that Peg kept in a drawer of an antique, hand-carved, oak buffet.

But as familiar as everything was, today there was a distinct difference. Despite all the pleas he and Katie had made to keep things simple, the living room had been decorated with crepe paper streamers and glitter-encrusted wedding bells. A buffet table groaned under the weight of all the food Peg and the others had contributed for the occasion. In the middle sat a three-tiered wedding cake, lovingly iced and decorated with pink roses by Peg herself, he suspected. The miniature bride and groom on top were tilted slightly, as if they were as out of kilter as he felt.

The room had been filled with roses, which probably meant that every garden in Clover had been plundered for the occasion. Luke drew in a deep breath, inhaling that sweet scent, and wondered if he'd ever look at Katie and not imagine the tantalizing aroma of roses.

He glanced at her, and for the second time that day he caught the shimmer of unshed tears in her eyes. Guilt sliced through him. How could he have robbed her of the wedding—no, the marriage—that she deserved? He had to believe that given time he could make it up to her, that he could prove that she hadn't made a terrible bargain the day she'd agreed to marry him.

Don't forget the ten thousand dollars, a cynical little voice reminded him. It wasn't as if Katie was getting nothing from their deal. She had snapped up his offer of a financial bailout for the boarding house with only a token protest. Protest? Hell, she'd bargained with him for more. On balance, maybe they really did deserve each other and whatever misery today brought to each of them.

Still, he couldn't help responding to her threatened tears. He took her hand in his and squeezed it. Katie immediately turned a grateful smile on him.

"Ready?" She mouthed the single word silently.

He leaned down and whispered, "Whenever you are."

To hear the two of them bracing themselves to enter that living room and join the small celebration Peg had prepared, Luke swore anyone would have thought they were going into a battle they had no chance of winning.

Katie nodded, plastered a smile on her face that would have fooled ninety-nine percent of the population of Clover and drew him into the living room. Immediately, congratulatory cheers were called out by the gathering. Champagne toasts followed, led by Peg and echoed by all the women for whom Katie had served as bridesmaid. With each toast, Luke found himself wondering exactly what Katie had told her aunt about their relationship. Whatever she knew or suspected, Peg had clearly decided to put on a front for Katie's sake.

That front lasted until everyone was absorbed with piled-high plates of country ham, potato salad, home-made biscuits and coleslaw. Then Peg clamped a hand around Luke's elbow and steered him from the room. She had a grip that had been strengthened by years of carrying trays of food and heavy coffeepots. He doubted he could have pried her loose with a crowbar. She didn't say a word until they were alone in the backyard. She settled onto one end of an old metal glider and waved him into the spot next to her.

"I'll be good to her," he vowed before Peg could say anything. He figured this was one of those situa-tions that called for a preemptive strike. For an instant Peg indeed did look nonplussed, perhaps even a little relieved by his adamant declaration. Then her expres-sion turned serious.

"Do you love her?" she asked.

"Peg, you know how I feel about Katie," he said evasively.

The vague statement had her expression clouding over. "There was a time when that was true, a time when I thought the two of you were destined to be married," she agreed slowly. "Then you ran off."

"There were circumstances…"

"Robby," she said bluntly.

He saw no point in lying. "Robby was a big part of it. I had a responsibility to him and to his mother."

"What about your responsibility to Katie?"

Luke sighed. He had never, *never* thought of Katie as a responsibility. She had been a gift, a treasure, the one constant in his life.

But because he had believed in honor and duty, he had walked away from her and done the only thing he could do. He had married his brother's lover, had accepted their child as his own. And because he loved Robby with all his heart, had loved him from the first instant he had set eyes on him, he had always thought of the blessings of that choice and not the sacrifices.

"The past is over and done with, Peg. I can't change it," he told her. "I can only do everything in my power to see that Katie is happy now."

Peg didn't seem totally placated by that, but she nodded. "See that you do," she said forcefully. "Or I swear, Luke Cassidy, I will see that you regret the day you ever hurt my girl a second time."

Luke had no idea how to respond to that, but it didn't matter because Katie opened the back door just then. Spotting them in the shade, she crossed the yard.

Looking from one to the other of them, she asked worriedly, "Is everything okay out here?"

Peg managed an astonishing transformation. She bestowed one of her warmest, sunniest smiles on her niece. "Everything is wonderful. Luke and I were just catching up a bit," she said, standing up and slipping her arm through Katie's. "Let's go back inside where it's cooler. It wouldn't do to have the bride looking all wilted when she's about to take off on her honeymoon."

Katie didn't seem reassured by Peg's cheerful demeanor. If anything, she looked even more concerned. Her gaze shot to Luke. He managed a smile every bit as broad and every bit as phony as Peg's.

"Let's cut the cake, darlin'," he said, looping his arm around her waist. "I doubt this day will get into the record books until somebody's snapped a picture of you shoving a slice into my mouth."

"Or into your face," Katie corrected thoughtfully. She gave him a dangerous look. "I do hope you've got some fancy hankies in that designer suit of yours."

Luke figured a faceful of cake would be a small price to pay for everything he'd ever done to Katie. Once she heard all of the reasons behind his decision to marry her, she was much more likely to come after him with a shotgun. As he recalled with some dismay, she was a damned good shot.

Chapter 4

The honeymoon promised to be a disaster. Katie saw the direction it was heading the minute Luke announced that they were going to Atlanta.

"Atlanta?" she'd repeated incredulously as they drove away from her aunt's house, tin cans clanging along behind the car. No wonder he'd been so blasted secretive about his plans. He had probably guessed exactly what sort of message he would be sending and how it would be received.

It made no difference to her that she'd been the first one to declare her bed off-limits. Until the moment he'd made his announcement, Katie realized she had been holding on to a false hope. She'd dreamed that once they were alone in some romantic setting for a few days the sparks that had once flown between them might be re-kindled. She'd hoped the ensuing flames would send this coldly calculated marriage-of-convenience plan up in flames.

It hadn't been entirely wishful thinking on her part. Luke had made arrangements for Robby to stay with Aunt Peg, after all. She had taken that as a good sign. He could very well have insisted they bring his son along. Since this was hardly a traditional marriage, there didn't seem much reason to expect a traditional honeymoon, so why not include his son? And yet, he hadn't, which she had interpreted to mean something. Obviously, it did not.

Now Katie was forced to concede that even with Robby out of the picture, Luke had taken her at her stand-offish word. He apparently wasn't any more inclined than she had claimed to be to stir up any of those old sparks. He was taking her on what sounded to all intents and purposes like the perfect destination for a business trip. Worse, they were heading to the exact same city where he'd been living with his wife. In fact, for all she knew, they might be staying in the same house. The honeymoon wasn't exactly turning out to be the stuff of which dreams were made.

After a quick, disappointed scowl in Luke's direction, she fell silent. Apparently he got her message just as clearly as she'd received his. A dull red flush stole up his neck. He regarded her guiltily.

"Katie?" When she remained silent, he said, "This trip is just for show, right? We both understood that or at least, I thought we did. I figured I might as well take care of some loose ends, so I won't have to do it later."

"How efficient."

Despite her sarcasm, he smiled. "It won't be all business, I promise."

"Don't worry about me," she retorted, promptly making plans of her own to demonstrate how little it all mattered to her. "I have some friends in Atlanta I haven't seen in ages. I'm sure we can spend the next few days shopping and catching up."

His gaze narrowed suspiciously. "You hate shopping."

Katie shrugged, determined not to let him see how furious and hurt she was. "Maybe I'll like it better once I get the hang of it. Cee-Cee and Pris are grand masters. We're going to be here what? Three full days? Four? I figure we should be able to hit at least a mall a day."

"Cee-Cee and Pris? They sound like an act from some strip joint."

Despite her sour mood, Katie laughed at his assessment. "I'll have you know those names are short for Celeste Margaret Louise Pennington of the Birmingham Penningtons and Priscilla Elizabeth Warrenton of the Virginia Warrentons. Where they come from, they can call themselves anything they like and people will still be respectful, especially with all those gold credit cards in their purses."

"How on earth do you know old Cee-Cee and Pris?"

"They stayed at the boarding house summer before last and again last July. I think they were slumming it at first, but by the end of the first day, they fit right in. Cee-Cee has quite a knack in the kitchen. We ate Cordon Bleu-qualified meals for the entire week she was there both times. Mr. O'Reilly was taking notes like crazy. Mrs. Jeffers kept moaning about all the cholesterol, but she ate every bite, rich, creamy sauces and all. They could hardly wait for the girls to come back."

"Did Pris adapt to small-town life as well?"

"Pris spent her days attaining what she described as the very best tan of her entire life, then devoted her evenings to worrying about what her dermatologist would have to say about it. I think she might best be described as a conflicted personality. She could make split-second decisions about almost anything. Then she spent the rest of the time questioning herself. It was fascinating."

"I'll bet," Luke said, clearly bemused by her descriptions. "And you've stayed in touch with the two of them?"

"Absolutely. They're dying to come back later this summer." She glanced at him pointedly. "Of course, now there's no place to put them."

"That's easily solved. I'll just move in…"

Katie saw exactly where he was heading. Given the lack of seductive intent evidenced in his honeymoon arrangements, she thought he had one hell of a nerve suggesting they sleep together when they returned home.

"Don't even think about it," she warned. "And speaking of sleeping arrangements, I hope you've booked us into a suite with a very large sofa. Or will we be staying at the house you shared with your last wife?"

Luke flinched at the direct hit. "I sold that house before I left Atlanta," he said tersely. "I never liked it."

"I trust you got a good price."

He ignored the sarcasm once more. "Naturally since it's our honeymoon, I have booked us into the honeymoon suite. It has a very large bed." There was a wicked, challenging glint in his eyes as he said it.

"I'm sure I'll be very comfortable then," Katie said with satisfaction. "But you'd better check on that sofa."

"Katie…"

"I think I'll take a little nap," she said cheerfully.

"Wake me when we get to Atlanta. I want to call Cee-Cee and Pris right away. Oh, and you might want to do something about those tin cans. They're giving me a headache."

She decided it was to Luke's credit that he didn't declare that he wouldn't mind if her whole stubborn head fell off. If he was irritated with her, though, it was too damned bad. She figured it made them just about even. She was flat-out furious with him.

Atlanta had been a very bad idea, Luke decided as he glanced over at his sound-asleep bride. Her light brown hair, which had been curled more than usual for the wedding ceremony, brushed her cheeks in wayward wisps. The light dusting of makeup she had endured for the occasion hadn't covered the faint smattering of freckles across her nose. Her mouth, still pink with a shade of lipstick more delectable than any he could ever recall her wearing, invited kissing. The scent of roses, either from a perfume or from the flowers that had filled Peg's house, clung to her. She looked fresh and innocent...and furious, he admitted ruefully.

Katie was cranky as the dickens and rightfully so, he conceded. No woman, even one entering into a marriage with few illusions, wanted to hear that her honeymoon had been tacked on to a business trip. It was a tactical blunder on his part if ever there was one.

He reminded himself irritably that he was supposed to be cementing this marriage into some facsimile of the real thing. If he couldn't show a court that he and Katie were the ideal couple, who knew what some wayward judge might do about Robby's custody. Tommy was no prize, but he was the boy's natural father, albeit a single one. Luke had figured this marriage, along with Betty Sue's support, was going to give him a comfortable edge in the custody dispute. That could hardly work if he and Katie were glaring daggers at each other or, worse, not even speaking. And Tommy knew exactly how to wield that particular weapon in court. As he'd already threatened, he wouldn't hesitate to use it.

Beyond all of that, in the past few weeks, ever since Katie had declared her bed off-limits, Luke had been ridiculously obsessed with getting her into it. He couldn't even look at her without desire slamming through him. Aside from the pure frustration, it was getting to be damned uncomfortable. And wanting Katie this badly wasn't a complication he'd considered when he'd selected her for this marriage scheme of his. It suggested she held more power over him than he'd ever wanted any woman to have.

The obvious answer to that was to seduce her quickly and sate this hunger that had been building in him since the first instant he'd laid eyes on her again. He was widely regarded as being incredibly persuasive, a talented negotiator. Surely he could talk one normally sweet-tempered, affectionate woman into his arms. He knew she was attracted to him. The kind of passion they'd once shared couldn't possibly die, even from lack of nurturing. There were times even now when he caught her looking at him with a hint of blazing desire in her eyes.

So, he decided, it was all a matter of getting around her mule-headed decision to get even with him for proposing a marriage of convenience in the first place. A few dozen roses, a couple of boxes of expensive chocolates interspersed with several well-timed, bone-melting kisses, and she'd abandon this crazy stance she'd taken. If he couldn't pull it off in Atlanta—and the odds were definitely against that at the moment, he conceded with some regret—then he would just have to wait until they got home.

At his request Mrs. Jeffers was already surreptitiously interviewing prospective new tenants for the boarding house. Surely she would find someone suitable by the first of the week, when he and Katie returned home. And then, because there would be no way to avoid it without revealing to everyone that their marriage was a sham, Katie would have to welcome him into her bedroom.

It was a sneaky, underhanded thing to do, Luke admitted to himself. But every once in a while the end did justify the means. He regarded Katie worriedly and wondered if she would agree. He'd have to ask her. After they'd made love a couple of hundred times seemed like the best timing. If he asked her anytime soon, he doubted if her response would be all that encouraging.

"Katie," he called as he turned into the secluded hotel driveway. When she didn't stir, he caressed her cheek. "Hey, Sleeping Beauty, wake up. We're here."

She blinked sleepily once, twice, then stared at him as alertly as if she'd never nodded off. Her ability to come wide awake in an instant was an admirable trait for the most part. He couldn't help imagining, though, what it would be like to have her awaken in his arms, all sleepily sensual and willing.

His imagination was very vivid. His body was aroused in less time than it took her to peel off her seat belt. While he wondered if he'd even be able to move, she was already smiling brightly at the hotel doorman, who'd just swept open her door.

"Mrs. Cassidy, welcome."

Luke caught Katie's startled expression and was glad he'd at least had the good sense to call ahead and warn the hotel that he was returning with his new bride. He'd stayed there for several weeks while he and Betty Sue had been finalizing their divorce settlement. Just about everyone on the hotel's small, discreet staff knew him well.

"Good evening, Raymond," he called out to the doorman, when he was finally able to step from the car.

"It's good to see you again, sir," he said, handing Luke the suite's key. "I'll have your bags sent directly up."

"Whatever happened to check-in?" Katie inquired dryly as they were whisked to the penthouse floor in a private elevator. "And exactly why are you so well-known here?"

"I lived here for a while."

"And tipped generously, no doubt."

He nodded agreement. "It always pays to reward excellent service."

Katie murmured something he couldn't quite hear.

"What was that?"

"I said for ten thousand, you must be expecting really extraordinary service from me," she said, her chin lifting with a touch of familiar defiance. Glittering green eyes challenged him. "You probably should have tried my cooking, at least, before we got to this point. My fried chicken is good, but I'm not sure it's *that* good."

"Katie…" Luke began, then cut off his protest. What could he say to convince her that she was hardly in the

same league as the hotel staff? Or that he didn't give
two hoots about her fried chicken? He could readily
see how a case could be made that he had bought her
services just as impartially as he might those of a maid
or a concierge.

He fell into a brooding silence that lasted until he saw
her awestruck expression as the elevator door opened
into the elegant penthouse with its sweeping view of
exquisitely landscaped gardens and city lights. Apparently this much at least he'd done right.

"Oh, my," she murmured.

"Like it?"

The last of her harsh facade dropped away. "It's
amazing. I feel as if I'm in someone's very expensive, very tasteful apartment, not a hotel at all." She
glanced around slowly. "Except for the basket of fruit
and the bottle of champagne. Those are definitely hotel
touches."

Since her mood seemed to have shifted, Luke risked
taking her hand in his and drawing her over to the windows. He could see her increasingly delighted expression reflected in the glass as she stared out at their
surroundings.

Softly lit fountains cascaded amid the well-tended
displays of flowers. Romantic pathways wound through
the grounds with benches scattered in secluded nooks
for private conversations and stolen kisses. He recalled
how many times he'd observed couples on those pathways and had felt a shaft of pure envy for the closeness
they shared.

Once, long ago, he'd had that kind of uncomplicated
intimacy with someone, but he'd thrown it away. His
hand around hers tightened instinctively, and at once her

expression turned guarded. She tugged her hand free in a deliberate gesture he couldn't mistake.

"Katie…"

"It really is wonderful," she said interrupting, her voice coolly polite.

"The food is excellent. I've ordered dinner. It should be here soon."

"I'm not hungry."

"Katie, you're always hungry."

She shook her head. "Not tonight," she insisted stubbornly. She regarded him speculatively. "You stayed here for a while? How long?"

"Several weeks. I wasn't in this room, but in one very similar on the floor below. Robby stayed at home with his mother until we'd worked out the divorce and custody arrangements."

She regarded him with amazement. "Just how rich are you?"

"Rich enough, I suppose."

"You had all this and you still came back to Clover. Why?"

Luke wasn't prepared to reveal that she had drawn him back, that he'd been consumed by memories of what they'd once shared, that he'd needed something desperately—a mother for Robby—and she'd been the first person who came into his head. Duty to his son and an aching yearning that was his alone had become so intertwined he hadn't been able to separate them.

"I wanted the sort of life that's possible there for Robby," he said instead. "I want him to grow up surrounded by people who will care about him as much as I do. I don't want him to grow up afraid of going to school because of guns the other kids might have. The only sort of gang I want him involved with is a bunch of kids walking to the movies on Saturday night."

"Those are the things you wanted for your son," she said pointedly. "What about for you? What did coming home represent to you?"

He said the first thing that popped into his head. "Peace of mind. I wanted my life back the way it used to be."

Katie seemed surprised by the answer. "Luke, you always hated Clover, hated the small-town mentality. You couldn't wait to get out."

He shrugged. "Hey, darlin', I never said I was perfect. But I did learn from my mistakes, and a longing for urban life was one of them. Just read the headlines. City living these days isn't all it's cracked up to be."

The worst mistake of all, though, had been leaving Katie behind. He'd finally accepted that and come home to claim her, albeit on terms far different from those he'd once imagined. He doubted he could ever love anyone, not even Katie, as freely as he once had. He had no one to blame but himself for the shallowness of his first marriage, but the experience had soured him on the institution and on the kind of love that was supposed to be its foundation.

But surely he and Katie could build a new relationship that would be mutually satisfying without endangering the protective wall he'd erected around his emotions after Betty Sue had left them battered and bruised.

Best friends always understood, were always quick to defend. Best friends never made unreasonable demands. And they never, ever cheated. He thought perhaps that level of loyalty, always granted him by Katie without hesitation, was something he'd missed most of all in the cutthroat environment in which he'd found himself in Atlanta—at home and in business.

He caught the softening in Katie's expression, and for one brief instant he was able to convince himself that everything was going to be just fine. He circled her waist from behind and stood gazing out over her head. Already a deep sense of peace was stealing through him.

That and desire, he conceded ruefully when the evidence became unmistakable. Katie's sharply indrawn breath hinted that she was aware of it, as well, but she didn't protest, didn't pull away.

Because the moment was so fragile, so fraught with possibilities for doing the wrong thing, Luke did nothing. He just held Katie, her back tucked against his chest, her bottom brushing against his arousal, and thanked his lucky stars that they had come this far. Tomorrow would be soon enough to worry about the rest.

When the lavish dinner Luke had ordered arrived, accompanied by champagne, Katie fled. She could no longer keep up the dangerous charade without fear of getting too caught up in the seductive fantasy it promised.

She quietly but emphatically shut the door to the hotel suite's bedroom, then leaned against it and sucked in a deep breath. Talk about close calls! She had very nearly succumbed to Luke's unspoken hunger.

Surrounded by his masculine scent, enveloped by his heat, tempted by his hard body, she had felt her already flimsy resolve wavering. It would have been so easy, so natural to give in to the desire that had swept through her at his first touch. And the expensive, in-toxicating champagne would have made that capitula-tion a certainty.

How many nights had she lain awake remembering the way it felt to be held by him? How many months had she imagined the sweet torment of his touches? How many years now had she tried to forget those very same things, only to have the memories reawakened in a heartbeat?

Slowly, she stripped off the pink silk dress she'd worn for her wedding day, then the daring gossamer lace underwear. She reached for the sexy nightie that Lucy had insisted she pack, then went into the huge tiled bathroom and turned on the shower. When the room had filled with steam, she stepped into the marbled enclo-sure and let the hot water slide over her body, touching her in all the places she had dreamed that Luke would caress tonight. Before she knew it her body was sensi-tive and throbbing with need.

Groaning, she flipped off the hot water and let the cold water cascade over her until she was shivering and no longer caught up in the kind of desperate yearnings that only Luke could fulfill. The irony, of course, was that tonight he was within reach, only a few feet away, with an unlocked door between them. Legalities and proximity had made him hers, and yet, she couldn't bring herself to claim him.

Stepping out of the shower and putting on the sheer nightie that skimmed her figure, concealing virtually nothing, Katie looked at that door longingly. What was being accomplished by keeping Luke out of her bed? Was she merely trying to salvage her pride?

Or did she hope that the burning desire she'd seen in

his eyes would come to translate into love, if only she gave it enough time?

Whatever her eventual goal, the only certainty was that she was about to spend a very sleepless wedding night and for none of the usual, provocative reasons.

"Katie?"

Luke's low voice sent a shaft of pure need through her. "Yes."

"Good night," he called softly.

"Good night," she whispered, as tears brimmed over and spilled down her cheeks. Then lower still, in a voice she knew wouldn't carry through the thick hotel door, she murmured, "Good night, my love."

Chapter 5

The first thing Katie heard when she awoke after a restless night of tossing and turning was the murmur of Luke's voice coming from the living room of their suite. She rolled over and closed her eyes, thinking what a pleasure it was simply to know he was close by. This, she supposed, was one of the little-discussed benefits of marriage, a tiny intimacy that couples grew used to and took for granted. After being separated from him for what seemed an eternity, she doubted she would ever take Luke's presence for granted.

Hearing his low murmur from just behind the closed door was such a unique and wonderful experience that she very well might have stayed in bed and listened to him for hours, except she was starved. Apparently her stomach had suffered nearly as much as her libido with last night's stubborn decision to turn down the wedding supper Luke had ordered—and whatever might have come later.

Hopping out of the luxurious, albeit very lonely bed, she stretched lazily, donned her sexiest bra and panties, then tugged on tan linen slacks, a peach silk blouse, and slipped on a pair of flats. All were new and far dressier than what she usually wore in Clover. Studying herself in the mirror, she decided she could hold her own in the big city.

After a cursory brushing of teeth and hair, she skimmed a pale peach lipstick across her lips, then opened the door into the living room.

Luke was still on the phone. At the sight of her, he murmured a hurried goodbye, then hung up, a slow smile spreading across his face, transforming his too-serious expression into a look that was pure invitation.

Katie's composure suddenly slipped. Luke was wearing a pair of dress slacks, zipped up, but unbuttoned at the waist, and nothing else. His hair was curling damply. His chest was…well, his chest didn't bear too close an examination. Her heart was thumping hard enough as it was. If he'd stripped down this provocatively last night instead of offering far less intoxicating champagne, she never would have made it to that huge bed alone. Determined not to let the tantalizing effect ruin her stance this morning, she reminded herself that he, at least, was in Atlanta for the sole purpose of conducting business, not seduction.

Or so he claimed. The current dangerous gleam in his eyes suggested otherwise.

"Hard at work already, I see," she said when she thought she could get the words out without giving her susceptibility away by sounding too breathless.

"Ordering breakfast, actually," he countered with another of those smiles that could have melted an Arctic iceberg. "I hope you still love pancakes, scrambled eggs, bacon, strawberries and fresh-squeezed orange juice."

"I do, but all at once?"

"It's a special occasion."

"What are we celebrating?" she inquired innocently. "Did a big deal go through?"

That high-voltage smile dissipated. He scowled at her. "Okay, Katie, enough with the sarcasm. You made your point last night. Turning our honeymoon into a business trip was a rotten idea."

She nodded with satisfaction. "It's nice to see you grasp things so readily. No wonder you're wildly successful in business."

"However," he said, as if she hadn't spoken. "If you want a real honeymoon, then it can't be one-sided on my part. You have to cooperate."

Her gaze narrowed as she considered the suspicious glint in his eyes and the dare in his voice. "Cooperate?"

"No shopping with old Cee-Cee and Pris."

"But I was really looking forward to it," she protested just to taunt him.

"About as much as a flu shot," he muttered.

"I don't take flu shots."

"My point exactly."

Katie began to get the notion that she'd won the first round in this latest test of wills. The taste of victory was definitely sweet. She relented and grinned at him. "Okay, no business for you. No shopping for me. What'll we do?" Having three whole days stretched out ahead of them seemed to offer limitless, very intriguing possibilities.

"There are certain traditional things a bride and groom usually do on a honeymoon," he suggested hopefully.

"You wish," she countered. "How about sight-seeing?"

"Sight-seeing?" he repeated blankly as if the concept were totally foreign.

"You lived here six years. Surely you know all the most fascinating local sights. I want to see them."

"Actually, about the only thing I ever saw was the downtown skyscraper where my office was located."

His revelation was hardly surprising. Luke's single-mindedness was exactly the trait that had made him a success. Katie remained undaunted. "We'll buy a guidebook." She paused thoughtfully. "And a map."

"I can get around. We don't need a map."

"Luke, you used to get lost in Clover."

He frowned at the teasing comment. "I did not."

"What about the time we were supposed to go to Mindy Prescott's birthday party and we got there an hour late because you refused to stop and ask directions?"

"She didn't live in Clover," he said defensively. "And those country roads weren't marked. That map she drew was a joke. Whoever heard of telling someone that a house is just past the first big curve in the highway, a half mile beyond the big oak on the left and right after a dilapidated red barn?"

"Just because you couldn't tell an oak from a maple if your life depended on it, don't go blaming Mindy Prescott," Katie retorted. "We were halfway to Charleston before you finally gave in and let me call to ask where we'd gone wrong. Wandering around lost must be some macho, male thing."

He gave her a rueful grin. "Okay, we'll buy a map. Satisfied?"

About the map, definitely, Katie thought. Her body, however, was protesting vehemently. She wanted food and she wanted Luke, not necessarily in that order. Her gaze met his and something of her longing must have been in her eyes, because he suddenly went perfectly still. Electricity arced between them. The air practically crackled with it. Katie's defenses wobbled dangerously.

"Katie," he said softly, the lure in his voice almost irresistible.

"Luke," she whispered, suddenly trembling with all of the sensual anticipation she'd been fighting to keep at bay.

Their gazes locked. But before either of them could take the first, fateful step to close the space between them, the suite's doorbell chimed loudly. The sound echoed through the room, breaking the fragile moment.

As if that weren't enough disruption, the phone started ringing.

Katie viewed Luke with some regret—and admittedly a certain amount of relief. It was far too soon to allow all of those protective barriers she'd erected to be torn down, and there wasn't a doubt in her mind that they'd been about to topple. This was just further proof that she had about as much natural resistance to Luke as a badly constructed roof did to a hurricane.

"You get the phone. I'll get the door," she suggested briskly.

"Let's ignore them both," he countered, his gaze never leaving her face.

She searched his expression for evidence of sincerity. "If I agreed, would you really be able to stand not knowing who's on the phone?"

He sighed. "Unfortunately I have a very good idea who it is. My secretary. I spoke to her earlier."

"When? Before dawn on a Sunday morning?" she inquired, glancing at her watch.

"She makes herself available whenever I need her."

"I'll bet," Katie muttered.

Luke regarded her with amusement. "Jealous?"

"Hardly."

"Then you won't mind if I grab this. She's supposed to be rescheduling my business meetings for another time."

"Then by all means, talk to her," Katie said as she went to the door to admit the waiter with their breakfast order.

As she chatted with the waiter—or tried to—she heard snatches of Luke's terse phone conversation. His previously lighthearted mood had given way to an unmistakable anger that was evident not just in his tone of voice, but in his tense shoulders and sudden pacing.

"No, absolutely not," he snapped, then lowered his voice to say something that Katie couldn't hear.

The waiter, to his credit, never even looked away from the service cart, which he had pushed into a nook overlooking the gardens. He finished removing the silver tops from the serving dishes, then discreetly left them alone without any hint that he'd overheard Luke's display of temper or that he'd noticed the pile of blankets on the honeymoon suite sofa.

At first, after the waiter had gone, Katie was too caught up in sampling the strawberries and the light, fluffy pancakes to notice Luke's increasingly murderous expression or to pay much attention to his tersely-worded conversation. She assumed it had something to do with a business deal gone awry. When his sharply raised voice suddenly caught her attention, she paused with her fork halfway to her mouth.

"No, dammit! I don't want you anywhere near Clover and that's final," he said and slammed down the phone with a force that shook the delicate mahogany table on which it was sitting.

Katie regarded him worriedly. She was certain she had never seen Luke so furious. No matter how far he'd ever been pushed—by circumstances or by Tommy or by her, for that matter—he'd never exploded like this. She watched as he visibly tried to compose himself before turning and walking toward her.

"Luke, what on earth was that about?"

"It's nothing for you to worry about," he said. "How's the food?"

Katie frowned at the dismissal. "The food is fine. You're obviously not. Was that your secretary? Did some business deal fall apart?"

"Not everything in my life has to do with business," he snapped.

"Okay, then," she said, clinging to her patience by a thread. She recalled his mentioning Clover and tried to guess what that had to do with anything. "Has something happened at home? Is Robby okay?"

"I'm sure Robby's fine," he said, his voice suspiciously tight. "Everything's fine."

She didn't believe him for a minute. "If business is fine and Robby is fine, then what's wrong?" she prodded, determined to make him open up. "It's obvious you're still seething about something."

"It was nothing," he contradicted heatedly. "I'll deal with it."

Katie flinched at his determination to shut her out. That fragile thread on her patience snapped. "Well, pardon me for wanting to help. I guess I don't have this marriage business down quite yet. Our deal must not have included common courtesy."

Luke's reaction to her sarcasm was immediate and apologetic. "I'm sorry, Katie."

She regarded him doubtfully.

"I am," he insisted. "I guess I don't have it down just yet either."

Because he looked so miserable and distraught, Katie waited until her own temper had cooled before she spoke. "Luke, this is new to both of us. I don't have all the answers, but I do know one thing. It won't work if we don't learn to share what's going on in our lives. If there's some business crisis or something, I may not be able to help you solve it, but I can always listen. You know that. You used to talk to me about everything."

For an instant he seemed to be wavering. She thought for sure he was going to open up, to tell her what had ruined his mood so thoroughly, but then his jaw tightened and he shook his head. "This isn't the time to get into it."

"It? What is it?" she asked in exasperation.

He threw down his napkin and got up from the table. "Not now, Katie." He grabbed a shirt from the back of the chair and tugged it on. He was still buttoning it as he headed for the door. "I'll be back."

With a sinking sensation in the pit of her stomach, she watched him open the door. She sensed that if he walked out now, it would establish a pattern from which they might never recover. "Luke, don't go. Please."

He turned then and gave her a halfhearted ghost of a smile. "Don't worry. I won't be gone long."

He shut the door before she could protest that running out, when they should be talking, might well have worse consequences than whatever problem he had on his mind.

Damn Tommy for ruining the morning for him, Luke thought as he walked the hotel grounds in a futile attempt to calm down. Tommy's timing couldn't have been worse. Luke had sensed that he and Katie were finally getting closer just before the phone had rung. Now that he'd clearly withheld information from her, they were further apart than ever. He couldn't blame her for being furious.

At the moment, though, she was no more furious than he was, albeit for far different reasons. How typical of Tommy to wait until he was off on his honeymoon before calling and making more threats. When Tommy had said he was going to Clover to visit Robby while Luke was away, a fierce tide of anger had rolled through him. It was yet more proof that Tommy didn't give a damn about his son's feelings. He was only using the boy to taunt Luke, hoping for a big cash settlement, no doubt, in return for backing off.

Luke couldn't help wondering if his vehement protest would be enough to keep his brother away. He doubted it. Tommy had never listened to a damn thing he had to say. There was no reason to believe that that had changed. The only difference now was that the stakes were higher than they had been when they were kids.

The thought of his brother being alone with Robby sent chills through him. Tommy would never physically harm the boy. Luke was certain of that. But he would start filling Robby's head with whatever garbage suited his purposes. He wouldn't worry a bit about whatever psychological damage he might be doing in the process. It would never cross Tommy's selfish mind that revealing the truth to Robby might be devastating.

Luke suddenly knew he couldn't risk that happening. He had to call Peg at once and warn her to keep Tommy away from Robby. She would want to know why. There was no getting around that. If he expected her cooperation, he would have to tell her the truth, all of it.

At the prospect of revealing everything to Katie's aunt, he shuddered. Peg would have his hide for this, especially if she found out he had told Katie none of it.

"Damn," he muttered. It was all unraveling. He'd wanted time. Time to prepare Katie. Time for her to start thinking of Robby as her own. Time for her to become committed to being both wife and mother.

Now it seemed that his time had run out. He had to tell Katie everything. He had to let her know the fight they were in for. She had to be prepared for the bitterness and ugly accusations that were likely to come with the custody dispute.

But now? On their honeymoon? Surely it would be wrong to spoil these few days. He resolved to tell her the moment they returned to Clover. In the meantime, he knew he could count on Peg's discretion. More, he knew he could count on her to protect Robby.

The decision made, he stopped by a pay phone in the hotel lobby and called Peg's Diner. When Peg picked up, he didn't mince words. His voice tight, he just outlined the situation, then extracted her promise to keep Tommy away from his son.

"Of course, I'll see to it that he's not alone with Robby for a minute," she said readily. "I haven't seen any sign of him around town. Maybe he won't show up at all."

"He'll show up," Luke said with certainty. Knowing that, he realized what he had to do. "I think maybe Katie and I ought to get back there. We can be home by this afternoon."

Peg fell silent at that. He could practically feel her disapproval crackling over the phone line.

"Peg, it's the only way," he insisted. "I can't leave you to stand up to Tommy. This mess isn't your responsibility."

"Luke, that brother of yours doesn't scare me. He never did. It does worry me, though, that you and Katie are starting off your marriage by facing such a big problem. You need a few days by yourselves to build up the strength this fight is going to take. Stop fussing about the burden you're placing on me and think about your marriage. Let these few days alone be my wedding gift to the two of you."

Luke sighed. "Peg, I know you mean well and there's no one I'd trust more with my son, but—"

"No 'buts.' You two stay and enjoy yourselves. I'll see you on Wednesday, just the way we planned. If anything comes up I can't handle, I'll call you immediately. If I have to, I'll get Ford Maguire to set Tommy straight."

As much as he liked Ford, Luke wasn't sure he wanted the sheriff mixed up in this. "I'll think about it," he said eventually. "Is Robby there? I'd like to speak to him."

"He's sitting in one of the booths with his coloring books. I've got an order in for his breakfast now. Hang on, I'll get him for you."

Luke could hear Robby's whoop of excitement when Peg told him who was on the phone. For the first time since Tommy's call, he smiled.

"Daddy, is it really you?"

"It's me, my man. How are you doing? Are you and Peg having fun?"

"She rented a movie for me last night and she made pizza. Did you know you could make it at home?"

"So I've heard," Luke said, thinking of the times they'd ordered it in Atlanta. They'd had most of their dinners delivered the same way. No wonder Robby sounded so stunned by the concept of homemade pizza. He'd probably never guessed what the oven was for before. "How was it?"

"The best. She put pepperoni on it and everything."

"That's great, pal. What movie did you see?"

"*Flintstones*. Remember when we saw that? Mommy hated it."

Actually, Betty Sue had hated most anything with a G rating, as Luke recalled. Her whole blasted life-style would have been X-rated by the movie industry. It really was too bad Tommy hadn't stuck around. They were a perfect pair.

But then he wouldn't have had Robby, Luke reminded himself. "I miss you, pal," he said softly, an unexpected catch in his voice.

"Miss you," Robby echoed. "I gotta go. Aunt Peg just brought me pancakes. And Mrs. Jeffers said she'd take me to ride my bike as soon as I eat. And tomorrow Aunt Peg and me are going to the beach. It's her day off."

"Sounds like you have a busy time planned."

"Hey, Daddy?"

"Yes."

"I really, really like it here."

Luke closed his eyes and sucked in a deep breath. It was turning out just the way he'd envisioned. He was finally giving Robby the real home he deserved, complete with a loving extended family. "I'm glad, pal. Really, really glad."

When he'd hung up, Luke vowed silently that he would destroy Tommy if he did anything, anything at all to ruin Robby's new-found happiness.

Katie took one look at Luke's face when he finally came back to the suite, and all of her pent-up anger died at once. His face looked haggard and his shoulders were slumped, as if he carried the weight of the world on them.

Instead of verbally hurling the accusations and prying questions she'd formulated in her head, she poured him a cup of coffee and said mildly, "I saved some pancakes and fruit for you. You look like you could use them."

He accepted the cup of coffee and ignored the rest. He walked directly to the window and stood staring down at the gardens, his expression troubled.

Katie plunged on, trying to sound as if everything were perfectly normal. "Your secretary called. She said she was able to reschedule everything for the first week in July."

"That's good," he said with a distracted air.

"I'm thinking of having my hair dyed purple while we're here," she said.

"If that's what you want."

"Luke!"

His head snapped around. "What?"

Katie regarded him with dismay. "Talk about it," she ordered.

He didn't pretend not to know what *it* was. "Later."

"When?"

"Just later. Let it go, Katie."

She sighed and gave up. Years of experience should have taught her that she couldn't badger Luke into talking before he was ready. "So, what do you want to do today?"

He drew in a deep, shuddering breath before finally facing her. "I want to go home."

The last of her illusions that they could salvage this honeymoon dissolved. "You want to go home?" she repeated with dismay. "Today?"

He nodded. "I'll make it up to you. I promise."

"You've been making a lot of promises to me recently," Katie said, struggling to keep her voice even, trying even harder not to cry. "Any idea when you'll start keeping a few of them?"

Stormy blue eyes met hers. "As soon as we're home, we'll sit down and I'll explain everything."

Judging from Luke's bleak expression, Katie had an awful feeling that she wasn't going to like the explanation a bit. "Why do I have this terrible hunch that it's coming about twenty-four hours too late?"

Chapter 6

The second call to Peg Jones to let her know that he and Katie would definitely be returning to Clover had been a terrible mistake, Luke realized as they drove toward the boarding house. A collection of cars stretched for blocks in every direction. He doubted that one of the boarders had invited half the town to drop by.

More likely, the warning he had given Peg had allowed her just enough time to prepare the full-blown wedding reception she'd wanted for the two of them in the first place. He should have known that small gathering at her house the day before wouldn't satisfy her. Or maybe she was just retaliating for what he considered to be his ill-advised decision to cut the honeymoon short.

"What do you suppose…?" Katie began, then turned to Luke with a horrified expression on her face. "Oh, no, surely she didn't."

"Oh, I think it's a safe bet that we are about to be congratulated by everyone in Clover," Luke said grimly. He glanced at Katie's pale face and immediately took pity on her. "We could hide out at the hotel."

"That would be cowardly," she said, but she turned a wistful look on the two-story building that was visible a few blocks away.

"I prefer to think of it as a strategic retreat."

Katie buried her face in her hands. "What are they going to think? We've been married barely over a day and we cut short our honeymoon."

Luke honestly hadn't considered the likelihood of embarrassing Katie when he'd made the impulsive decision to come back to Clover early. He'd been focused entirely on preventing a meeting between his brother and Robby.

"I'm sorry. I wasn't thinking of how this might look." He reached for her hand, which was ice-cold. Impulsively, he brushed a kiss across her knuckles. "I'm serious, we can turn right around and stay at a motel out on the highway. We don't even have to stay at the hotel here in town."

"That's a little like closing the barn door after the horse has gone," she observed dryly. "Obviously everyone already knows we cut the honeymoon short. They've been invited here to celebrate our return."

"Maybe they'll just think Peg got it wrong."

"Yeah, right," she said in a voice laden with skepticism. "Peg has been taking orders at the diner for thirty years without making a note. She's never made a mistake. Do you honestly think anyone will believe she made a little error about something as important as our scheduled return from our honeymoon?" She shook her head. "No way. We're just going to have to brazen it out."

Filled with self-loathing for having put her in this position, Luke regarded her worriedly. "Can you do that?"

Katie's chin rose a determined notch. "I'll have to, won't I?" She turned to him, eyes suddenly blazing with fury. "But when this little charade ends, Luke Cassidy, you'd better have some damned good answers ready or this could well be the shortest marriage on record in the entire state of South Carolina. In fact, I might very well go for an annulment."

Apparently assured that Luke understood the implication of that threat, she flung open the car door and exited with the regal demeanor of a queen going to greet her subjects. Luke was left to trail along in her wake and wonder if she would make good on the threat. He decided he'd better do something damned quick to better the odds against it. Tommy would have a heyday in court with news that his brief marriage had been annulled because it had never been consummated, to say nothing of the blow it would be to Luke's ego to have the information bandied about.

Just outside the door he captured Katie's elbow and brought her to a halt. There was only one way he knew to keep Katie from blowing their charade, only one way he'd ever known to silence her—by kissing her senseless. Though he'd refrained from using the tactic thus far, he wasn't above hauling it out whenever it suited his purposes. It most definitely suited him now.

"Let's make it look good, darlin'," he said.

Before she could offer a protest, he scooped her into his arms for the traditional trip across the threshold. While he was at it, he planted a slow, lingering kiss on lips that clearly had been about to shout a vehement protest. He suspected that only the fact that a cheer had gone up at the sight of their entrance kept Katie from landing her fist squarely against his nose.

Luke discovered he rather liked holding Katie captive. It was the first moment since this entire debacle had begun that he truly felt like a newlywed. He sure as hell hadn't felt like one while he'd been trying to sleep—alone—on that cramped sofa the night before. He decided he might as well take advantage of the moment and steal another kiss that Katie would otherwise deny him. No doubt he would pay for it later, but the way his pulse was bucking told him it would be worth the cost.

As he shifted her in his arms to lower her slowly to her feet, he made very sure that Katie slid down his body until every square inch of him blazed as if it had been touched by the summer sun.

When she would have made a dash for it, he cupped her cheeks in his hands and held her face perfectly still. Katie's eyes widened as she watched him warily. Her lips parted, probably to form another vehement protest. But Luke swooped in to steal the words, sealing his mouth over hers, savoring the sweet taste.

Katie's entire body tensed for the space of a heartbeat, but if there was one thing Luke knew it was the nuances of a kiss. From that first possessive claiming, his lips turned gentle, persuasive.

The coaxing worked. He knew the precise instant when Katie stopped fighting him and became an enthusiastic participant. Her skin heated. Her pulse skittered wildly. Her tongue tentatively sought out his.

From gentle persuasion, the kiss quickly escalated

into a dark, moist, mysterious invitation that had his blood roaring through his veins. Suddenly he wanted Katie upstairs, in his bed, under him. He wanted it with a desperation that stunned him.

Staggered by this unexpected need to claim her, Luke forgot all about where they were and how the game had started. A single whoop of approval, echoed by a half dozen more, and punctuated by applause, snapped him back to an unfortunate reality. He and Katie were definitely not alone. From the dazed look in her eyes, she was no happier about that discovery than he was.

All too quickly, though, their true circumstances took the blush out of her cheeks and made her eyes blaze not with passion, but with fury. Luke knew with certainty that he would hear about this when they were alone. Worse, he suspected that would be just the beginning of what Katie had to say, none of it pleasant.

"Later," he whispered in a determinedly seductive purr he hoped would remind her of the provocative intimacy they'd just shared.

"You'd better believe it," she said tightly.

Katie might have been thinking about that bone-melting kiss, but Luke doubted it. Her tone was more in keeping with a deadly courtroom cross-examination.

Before he could try to defuse her temper, Peg swooped in to hug Katie, and Robby rushed up to hurl himself into Luke's arms. Within seconds Robby was racing off with another boy about his own age. Luke stared after them with amusement. He realized with a start how rarely he'd seen his child playing with friends. It was yet another confirmation that coming back to Clover had been the right decision.

By the time Luke glanced around, Katie was sur-

rounded by her friends, most of whom had barely a
word to spare for him, though he'd known them all his
life. He hadn't thought it possible in a town where he'd
grown up, but apparently six years away had made him
an outsider. And if the scowl on Lucy Ryder's face was
an indication, at the moment she wished he'd stayed in
Atlanta forever.

Maybe people just had long memories, he specu-
lated. Maybe they remembered with absolute clarity
that he and Katie had been best friends. Maybe they
suspected how far things had gone before he'd walked
out on her. And maybe they resented being left behind
to deal with the aftermath of his lousy treatment of a
woman they all adored.

Whatever it was, everyone welcomed Katie home
as if she'd been off on a safari for months, rather than
an abbreviated one-day honeymoon. Peg, in particular,
surveyed her niece as if looking for signs that Luke had
done anything, anything at all to make her miserable.
Katie's bright smile and glowing cheeks—the products
of determination and makeup—apparently convinced
her all was well.

Katie, whom he would have sworn didn't have a
shred of artifice in her, turned out to have superb acting
skills. Not a single person in the room—with the possible exception of Lucy—would have guessed from her
cheerful demeanor that their marriage was an uncon-
summated farce. Only he seemed to notice the tiny lines
of strain around her mouth, the faint shadows under her
eyes, the forced note of her laughter, the way she fiddled
nervously with a strand of hair.

For three hours he accepted cursory congratulations
on winning the prettiest woman in town, he endured

less-than-subtle winks about the honeymoon, and took advice from half the women in town on how to keep his new bride happy and content. Hannah, Sophie and Emma had some very intriguing ideas for the future bliss of the woman who'd been their bridesmaid.

Through it all he kept his gaze pinned on Katie, wondering exactly when she would break, worrying whether be would be able to clear out the guests before it happened. He was still worried about that when Peg cornered him.

"I'm keeping Robby at my place a few more nights," she informed him in a tone that invited no argument. Facing him defiantly, she added, "I've also arranged for the boarders to go to the hotel for the rest of the week. I can understand your feeling a need to be in Clover in case your brother decides to make good on his threat, but I will not allow you to spoil my niece's honeymoon."

Luke didn't have the heart to tell her that Katie was probably thrilled to be back among friends or that the last thing Peg's niece wanted was to be left alone with him. And, given the dire looks Katie had been directing at him for the past couple of hours, he wasn't so sure he wanted to be left alone with her.

"I'll pay for the rooms at the hotel," he volunteered since it seemed unlikely that anyone was going to go contrary to Peg's plans.

"That's what I told them," Peg said dryly.

He grinned at her. "You think of everything."

"I do try," she said cheerfully. "How did Katie take the news about the custody battle?"

Luke swallowed hard and admitted, "I haven't told her yet."

Muttering something that sounded suspiciously unladylike under her breath, Peg latched on to his elbow and dragged him into the kitchen. "Luke Cassidy, what in tarnation were you thinking of? She has a right to know. Does she have any idea at all what brought you back here in such an all-fired hurry?"

"Not exactly."

"So for all she knows, you just got tired of being alone with her," she snapped.

"Of course not," he said, but knew it was possible that that was exactly what Katie thought.

Peg clearly didn't buy the denial any more than he did. She regarded him as if he were slightly lower than pond scum. "I swear if you don't tell her everything by tomorrow morning, then I will. I can't begin to imagine what she must be thinking. Wasn't it bad enough that you walked out on her once before? Ripped the hell out of her self-esteem, you did. Now you've got her thinking you don't even want to spend three days alone with her. My glory, why'd you even bother asking her to marry you?"

Luke was very much afraid if Peg had too long to think about that question, she'd hit the answer square on the head. "As soon as everyone is out of here and we have the place to ourselves, I'll tell her everything."

"See that you do," Peg ordered, her voice tight. "Just to speed things up, I'll start clearing these folks out. Don't worry about the mess. I have someone coming in to clean up first thing in the morning."

Luke couldn't imagine Katie being patient enough to leave the dirty dishes scattered around the house. While Peg hustled everyone toward the door, he began picking up, carting trays of glasses and dessert plates into the kitchen and loading them into the industrial-size dishwasher that looked like a relic from the early days of Peg's Diner.

He'd just hauled a sack of trash to the garbage cans out back, when he looked up and spotted Katie waiting for him in the kitchen door. For one fleeting instant, he imagined that they were a typical couple, tired but elated after a night of entertaining. He could almost envision the two of them settling on the sofa side by side to nibble on leftovers, share bits of gossip, maybe even steal few sweet kisses tasting of wine. It was an image that had once filled his dreams back in the days when he'd had his entire life planned out and Katie had been at the center of it.

But as he neared the back door, one quick survey of Katie's expression told him there would be nothing sweet or simple about the next couple of hours. She clearly hadn't forgotten for one single minute her determination to get the answers that he'd been unwilling to provide earlier.

"There's a nice breeze," he observed, hoping to distract her. "Want to sit in the hammock for a while?"

She glared at him. "No, I do not want to sit in the hammock. We need to talk."

"Those two things aren't mutually exclusive. Last I heard we could talk in the hammock."

"But we won't and you know it," she said flatly.

Luke grinned. "I see you remember that old hammock Peg had in the backyard and the use we put it to."

She sighed. "I remember a lot of things, Luke Cassidy, including the fact that you've been hiding something important from me."

"That wasn't exactly what I was trying to get you to recall."

"I'm sure. Come on, Cassidy. Stop dawdling. It's time to face the music."

Luke sighed as he trudged up the back steps with Katie watching him every step of the way, probably to make sure he didn't take off. In the doorway, he could easily have walked around her, but he made sure he squeezed past, brushing tantalizingly against breasts and thighs just enough to stir his own senses, if not hers.

Sure enough, heat flared in her eyes. He seized on that. "You know, Peg went to a lot of trouble to see that we had some time alone here. It would be a shame to waste it, don't you think?"

"What I think is that you're trying to make me forget all the questions I have," she said, frowning at him.

"No doubt about it," he admitted candidly. He grinned unrepentantly.

"Why is that? What are you hiding? And what makes you think a few kisses—"

"Or more," he taunted.

She scowled. "Or anything on God's green earth will make me forget what's on my mind?"

Luke stubbornly resisted being drawn into that discussion. "If I can't distract you with images of all the wild, provocative things we could do in that hammock, let's talk about that big, old featherbed of yours."

"Luke, you could dance around the living room stark naked and I wouldn't forget what's on my mind." She waved an envelope he hadn't noticed before in his face. "Especially since this apparently arrived while we were gone. Any idea what it might be?"

From her tone, he guessed that she knew precisely what was inside that thick envelope.

"A sweepstakes entry?" he suggested.

Katie looked as if she were about to explode. "Dammit, don't you dare try to make a joke out of this," she snapped without any pretense of tolerance.

Luke heaved a sigh. It looked as if they were going to have this discussion whether the time was right or not. "Okay, you're the one who's opened the envelope. Why don't you tell me what's inside."

"Offhand, I'd say they're custody papers," she said, her voice flat. Her gaze swept over him before settling into a challenging glare. "Why the hell would your brother be fighting you for custody of Robby?"

Despite his promise to Peg, Luke really hadn't wanted to get into this tonight. They'd had a long, exhausting, stressful day as it was. He'd hoped when he laid it all out in the morning—before Peg had a chance to do it for him—Katie would be fresh, maybe even receptive. Right now she looked anything but. In fact, she seemed inclined to tar and feather him. He couldn't in all honesty say he blamed her. He reminded himself that he'd invested ten thousand dollars thus far in at least getting her to listen.

"It's a long story," he said wearily.

"As I recall our vows, there was something about till death do us part," she said. "We have time."

Luke winced at her sarcasm. It appeared the honeymoon was over.

Katie's cheeks burned with humiliation as she squared off against her new husband. It appeared she had let Luke make a fool of her not once, but twice. The papers she clutched in her hand proved that he had lied to her. As if his spoken reasons for marrying her hadn't been flimsy enough, now it appeared they were nothing compared to those he'd kept silent. She couldn't even begin to imagine what that whole story was. Why the dickens would Tommy think he had any claim at all to Robby?

"I'm waiting," she said, glaring at Luke.

"Maybe we'd better sit down. This could take a while," Luke said.

With some reluctance, Katie sat, choosing a chair rather than the sofa, to keep Luke from sitting next to her and clouding her ability to reason. The immobilizing effect he had on her brain was what had gotten her into this mess.

"I wanted to tell you," Luke swore, his gaze pleading with her to believe him.

"Why didn't you? Did the cat have your tongue?"

"You said you didn't want to get into anything serious," he reminded her.

"When did I say that?"

"Friday night."

Katie regarded him incredulously. "The night before the wedding? Wasn't that a bit late to be bringing up the little matter of a custody dispute over your son? Don't you think you should have mentioned it, oh, perhaps when you first asked me to marry you?"

"Probably."

"Why didn't you?"

"I was afraid if I got into everything, you'd turn me down."

Katie didn't deny it. She had a gut-deep feeling his fears had probably been justified. "Maybe I'd better hear what *everything* is before I tell you what my response would have been. Come on, Luke. Spit it out. From the beginning."

Luke walked over to the window and stood staring out. "It all started six years ago," he said.

His voice was so low Katie had to strain to hear him. "Six years ago," she repeated just to be certain she had heard correctly.

Luke nodded. "Betty Sue Wilder came to me and told me she was pregnant."

Katie had already guessed that much. As much as it hurt to think that Luke had slept with another woman around the same time he had made love to her, she had accepted that. "So you did the honorable thing," she said.

"It was a little more complicated than that. She wasn't carrying my baby."

She stared at him in open-mouthed astonishment. "I beg your pardon? The baby wasn't yours? Then what did it have to do with you?" she asked, even though she was already beginning to get the picture.

"Tommy is Robby's natural father."

"Tommy is Robby's father," she repeated slowly, realizing even as she said it that she wasn't nearly as surprised as she should have been.

"No," Luke said angrily, turning to face her. "Robby is my son. I'm his father in every way that counts. When Tommy wouldn't accept responsibility for Betty Sue's pregnancy, I stepped in. I was there in the delivery room when he was born. I gave him my name. I've stayed up nights with him when he was sick. I was there for his first step. I took him to his first day of school. Tommy has never even laid eyes on him."

His voice throbbed with barely contained rage. Whatever else might be true, Katie recognized that Luke considered Robby as much his as if he had made Betty Sue

pregnant. There could be no disputing the love he felt
for his son. She knew from being raised by her aunt
that the bonds formed by day-to-day parenting were
as powerful as any connection through biology alone.

And now Tommy was threatening that relationship.
She could understand Luke's outrage. What she didn't
comprehend was why Tommy would wait all this time
to stake a claim to his son. Or exactly where she fit
into this.

"Why would Tommy turn up to ask for custody after
all this time?"

Luke's mouth twisted. "Money, why else?"

"I don't understand."

"He doesn't want Robby, not really. He expects me
to pay him off to stay out of Robby's life."

Kate felt sick to her stomach. "Surely you're wrong.
Not even Tommy would turn a little boy's life upside
down just so he could get a payout from you."

"He doesn't think it will come to that, of course. I'm
sure he's convinced I'll settle with him to keep Robby
from ever finding out the truth."

"Frankly, I'm surprised you haven't," Katie said.

"If I thought that would be the end of it, I might
have," Luke admitted. "But it wouldn't. It would be
the beginning. Every time Tommy needed cash, he'd
be back making his threats again. I want it over with
here and now. I want a judge to put an end to it. Somehow I'll make sure that the truth doesn't hurt Robby."

It took every bit of strength Katie had left to voice
the fear that no amount of rational tap-dancing around
it could silence. "Could you lose custody?"

Luke finally met her gaze evenly. "With you in court
beside me, there's far less likelihood of that. What judge

would take a boy away from a happy, whole family and turn him over to a drifting single father?"

Katie swallowed hard against the bile that rose in her throat. There it was, the whole truth, spelled out plain as day. He'd wanted a wife to take into court. Any woman would have done.

Yet Luke had handpicked her to be his son's mother, not because she was so special, but because he had guessed that she was the one woman on earth who couldn't deny him anything. She was his insurance in court. The last of her illusions about their marriage shattered like so much spun glass.

Worse, she knew that even knowing the whole bitter truth, she couldn't walk away. He'd chosen well. Katie would stay by his side. She would see to it that he didn't lose his son to his ne'er-do-well brother.

And, if there was a God in heaven, Luke would never know what staying cost her.

Chapter 7

"Katie?"

Luke had to repeat himself twice before she finally looked up. The desolation in her eyes was almost his undoing. If there had been any other solution to his problem, he would have released her from her commitment to him on the spot. Something deep inside told him, however, that if he gave her up now, he would regret it the rest of his life. With circumstances as they were, he could only vow that he would make it up to her someday if only she would stick with him. He hoped that promise would be enough.

Though why she should believe anything he had to say at this point was beyond him.

"Katie," he began again now that he had her attention.

Apparently guessing that he was about to offer more

empty words, she cut him off. "Don't worry," she said tersely. "I'm not going to walk away now."

A sigh of relief shuddered through him. "Thank you. I knew I could count on you."

"Good old Katie," she muttered under her breath.

Luke heard the hint of resentment in her voice and regarded her warily. "What was that?"

She shook her head. "Nothing," she said wearily, then added more briskly, "What do we need to do to get ready to fight Tommy?"

"For starters, we have to be sure that no one guesses that this is anything less than a perfect marriage," he said slowly, watching her closely.

"Meaning?"

Her cold, impersonal, matter-of-fact tone worried him. He would almost have preferred to have her shouting at him. This docile acceptance was thoroughly out of character. He felt personally to blame for having drained all of the spirit out of her.

Or perhaps it was simply exhaustion. She had a right to be physically and emotionally tired after what she'd been through. By tomorrow she'd probably be screaming at him at the top of her lungs. Ironically, for once he had a feeling he'd welcome the change in her mood.

In the meantime, though, he recognized that this was definitely not the time to mention that Mrs. Jeffers had found a new boarder whose arrival would necessitate making new sleeping arrangements for him and Robby. He was determined that at least to all outside observers, he and Katie would appear to be typical newlyweds. If they were sharing a room, no one would know for certain what went on behind the closed door.

If they weren't in the same bedroom, who knew what people would make of it.

"Maybe we'd better talk about it in the morning," he suggested. "I've given you enough to absorb for one night."

"I think I'd rather get everything out in the open now," she countered in that same flat tone. "Come on, Luke. Lay it all out on the table so I know exactly what I'm up against."

Luke was literally saved by the bell. The front door chime was being punched with a great deal of what he recognized as childish fervor. Robby, no doubt, but what the devil was he doing back here tonight? Torn between gratitude for his timing and panic, Luke jumped up. "I'll get it."

When he opened the door, he wasn't exactly surprised to find Robby and Peg on the threshold. Still, his whole body tensed. He knew it would have taken some sort of major calamity for Peg to intrude on them.

"Well, hi," he said with forced cheer. "I wasn't expecting you two back tonight." He studied Peg's expression for some hint about why they'd returned.

"I had a call from your brother," she explained.

Her tone gave away nothing, but Luke knew at once the call must have shaken her or she would never have come back to the boarding house.

"Really?" he said, his tone just as bland. "What did he want?"

"He said he was planning to arrive in Clover tonight and hoped to see…" she glanced down at Robby, but said "…you. I thought you'd probably want Robby to be with you when he arrives."

"What on earth made him call you?" Luke muttered,

though nothing Tommy did should startle him after all
these years of seeing his brother's canniness in action.

"Obviously someone here in town is keeping him
up-to-date on Robby's whereabouts," Peg replied. "Any
idea who that might be?"

Luke shook his head. "I can't imagine who would
be in touch with him."

"What about your ex-wife?" Katie said from behind
him. "Or her parents?"

Luke had been so absorbed in digesting Peg's news
that he hadn't even been aware that Katie had joined
them in the foyer.

Robby, who was clutching his favorite fire engine
and a ragged teddy bear, seemed to pick up on the
adults' tension. "Is Mommy here?" he asked, looking
up into Luke's face.

"I don't think so, sport. When you talked to her last
week, she was still in Seattle, remember?"

"Oh," Robby said flatly, clearly disappointed, but
trying valiantly to hide it.

"Maybe you'd better be getting to bed," Luke told
his son. "Why don't I take you up and see that you're
settled in?"

"What about…" He hesitated, his sleepy, blue-eyed
gaze fixed hopefully on Katie. "I don't know what to
call you now that you and Daddy are married."

Luke's breath snagged in his throat as he waited for
her response. There was only the faintest pause and a
quick glance at Luke before she knelt to be at Robby's
level. Her mouth curved into a smile that Luke wished
desperately she'd turn in his direction.

"I hadn't really thought about it," she admitted.
"What would you like to call me?"

"Daddy calls you Katie."

"Except when he's mad," she confided. "Then he calls me Caitlyn."

Robby grinned. "He calls me Robert when he's mad at me. And his face gets all scrunched up. Sometimes I think he's gonna 'splode."

Katie chuckled, glancing up at Luke. "Yeah, it does look that way, doesn't it?"

"I had no idea I was so predictable," Luke commented. He looked at his son. "So, what's it going to be, sport? Do you know what you want to call Katie?"

Robby hesitated. "I guess I should call you Katie," he said with obvious reluctance.

Luke could see the disappointment on his son's face and realized that Robby really wanted to have someone in his life he could call Mommy, even if it wasn't his real mother. At the moment, though, loyalty to the absent Betty Sue kept him from admitting it.

"You know," Luke said lightly. "Whatever you decide tonight doesn't have to be your final choice. You can always change your mind."

"Absolutely," Katie agreed. "You call me whatever you feel comfortable with and anytime you want to change it's okay with me."

Robby nodded. "If you make me eat spinach, I'll probably call you Caitlyn."

Katie laughed, and for a minute the tension in the hallway seemed to ease. Peg was watching her niece with Robby, tears gathering in her eyes, and a smile on her lips. Truth be told, Luke was a little misty-eyed himself.

"Will you read me a story?" Robby asked Katie.

"It's a little late for a story," Luke protested. "Besides, I'll bet Peg already read you one."

"Two," Peg confirmed.

"But I'm going to bed all over again," Robby countered reasonably.

"Obviously he's picked up your negotiating skills," Katie said. "Come on. I'll read you a very short story."

"Something scary?" Robby asked hopefully as the two of them went up the stairs together. "I really like stuff about goblins and monsters and stuff."

"Hey, I'm not reading something that'll keep me awake all night," Katie retorted. "I was thinking more along the lines of, say, *Goldilocks and the Three Bears.*"

"That's baby stuff," Robby argued indignantly.

As Luke watched them climb the stairs side by side, a deep sense of satisfaction stole through him. It was going to work out just fine, he told himself. Katie was the perfect mother for his son. Whatever her own misgivings about their arrangement, she would do her best for Robby.

And, he thought with a renewed sense of conviction, she was the perfect wife for him, even if it was in name only at the moment.

"Luke?"

Peg brought him back to the present.

"Let's go into the living room," he suggested and led the way. When they were settled, he gazed into Peg's worried eyes. "I'm going to handle Tommy."

"How?"

"In court."

"But how will you deal with him if he shows up here? Maybe it's time you told Robby the truth, so he won't hear it by accident. It would be just like that brother of yours to blurt it out without thinking."

She was absolutely right. He'd known that. It was what had brought him racing back to Clover this afternoon. Luke groaned and buried his face in his hands. "God, what a mess! If only I'd known six years ago…"

Peg waved off the statement. "Would you have done anything differently?"

"No," he conceded. "I did what was right. I wouldn't have given up having Robby in my life for anything."

"Well, then, that's what you have to keep in mind. It'll give you the strength to do whatever it takes to keep your son with you."

"I've asked a lot of Katie."

"Then she knows," Peg said with a relieved expression. "Good."

For a moment his confidence in his plan wavered. "Am I asking too much?"

"Has she complained?"

He shook his head. "Not nearly as bitterly as I expected."

"Well, then, that should tell you something. You've thrown her a curve, but Katie's strong. More important, she loves you."

"I'm not sure I even understand that kind of love," Luke admitted candidly. "Maybe she's just resigned to her fate."

"Nonsense!" Peg reached over and patted his hand. "You'll just have to let Katie show you the way, won't you? Besides, anyone who's made the sacrifices you have for your son surely does know all there is to know about love and commitment." She stood. "I think I'd best be going. You two have plans to make. If you need anything, Luke, you give me a call. That's what family's for."

Luke regarded her ruefully. "Maybe some family," he noted dryly. "Others just seem bent on causing trouble."

When Peg had gone, Luke drew in a deep breath, then went upstairs to the room Katie had set aside for him and his son. He found Robby sound asleep, but Katie had remained curled up on the room's second twin bed, a pillow clutched in her arms, her gaze fixed on the boy opposite her. There was something so tender, so wistful in her expression that Luke's throat clogged and he felt the sting of tears in his eyes.

Suddenly he thought of all that he'd denied her—all that he'd denied both of them—by walking away six years earlier. Would he ever be able to make amends for all of that? Before he could start yet another apology, Katie glanced up and met his gaze.

"You're so lucky," she whispered, absentmindedly brushing at an errant tear. "He's a wonderful boy."

"I wish…" he began, but then didn't know how to finish.

Somehow, though, Katie seemed to read his mind. She reached for his hand. "So do I, but the past doesn't matter. We can't change it, anyway. We'll just have to go on from here and do the best we can."

I love you, Luke thought with a sense of wonder, though he couldn't bring himself to say the words aloud. How much would it mean to say it after all he'd done to Katie, all he'd asked of her? Besides, wasn't he the one who didn't believe in love? Perhaps what he felt was simply gratitude.

Gazing down into Katie's eyes, however, he wondered how long he could go on disbelieving in love, when he was living day in and day out with a woman who epitomized love's shining radiance and generous, accepting heart.

For all of their worrying the night before, Tommy had never shown up. Katie and Luke had stayed awake for hours listening for the doorbell and talking about inconsequential things, avoiding any of the real issues on their minds. It had been nearly dawn before they'd finally conceded that Tommy wasn't coming and had gone upstairs to their separate beds.

As Katie had lain awake in hers, she had briefly regretted the edict that had banished Luke to a room several doors away. Then she had reminded herself of precisely how he'd manipulated himself back into her life.

All things considered, Katie thought she had handled Luke's explanations about Robby rather well, in a mature, dispassionate sort of way. In the end she supposed it didn't really matter that the child wasn't Luke's. She supposed she could even admire him for taking responsibility for Tommy's irresponsible actions all those years ago, despite the way it had messed up her own dreams.

It was the fact that Luke had lied to her or, to be more precise, had left major gaps in the truth when he'd proposed, that irritated the daylights out of her. That was what kept her awake, seething with all the unspoken charges she wished she'd leveled at him when she'd first learned the whole truth. She'd been too stunned to get into it the night before. Now, though, she recognized that if she didn't get it all out of her system eventually, she'd wind up with an ulcer. Sometime after dawn she resolved to tell Luke exactly how she felt.

Now at their late breakfast, faced with the opportunity to confront him, she was suddenly less certain. Compassion welled up inside her. He looked so exhausted, so anxious about what the day would bring. He couldn't seem to tear his gaze away from his son, as if he feared what might happen if he so much as blinked.

Not until Robby was safely away from the house, on his way to the park with a very protective Mrs. Jeffers who had been briefed about Tommy, did Luke seem to let down his guard and relax. Faced with a choice between biting her tongue until the entire crisis was resolved or getting everything out into the open, Katie finally plunged in. More secrets and silences wouldn't help anyone at this stage.

"You know," she said, idly pushing her uneaten egg around on her plate. "You can't even have a decent business relationship with someone who picks and chooses which truths he's going to share."

"I never lied to you, Caitlyn," Luke said.

She suspected he had deliberately used her given name the way he always did when he wanted to make a point or, as she'd told Robby, when he was furious with her. Katie couldn't imagine what he had to be angry about. At this moment she didn't give two hoots how angry he was or why.

"No," she agreed as she stood and began clearing dishes. "You didn't lie. You just neglected to mention a few significant things. Any other little bombshells you intend to drop?"

"About my past?"

His blasé attitude had her gnashing her teeth. "About anything, dammit."

Suddenly he looked guilty as sin, a look she found extremely worrisome.

"Actually there is one thing I've been meaning to mention," he confessed. "I started to get into it last night, but you looked beat and then Robby and Peg showed up."

"What's that?" Katie asked warily. In a desperate attempt to keep busy, she searched the refrigerator until she came up with a grapefruit. Cutting out all those little sections ought to keep her hands occupied so that she wouldn't be tempted to use them to strangle Luke, whatever he had to reveal.

"I've rented out another room."

It was the last thing she'd expected him to say. She regarded him incredulously. "You've rented out a room," she repeated. "When did you have time to do this?"

"Actually, Mrs. Jeffers took care of it for me."

Katie sucked in a deep breath. No wonder they'd been engaged in such a hush-hush conversation this morning, before Mrs. Jeffers left with Robby. Katie had foolishly assumed they were talking about keeping a close eye on Luke's son. Instead, it had just been another one of Luke's conspiracies with one of her boarders.

"I suppose you paid her off, too."

"She did me a favor, that's all," Luke responded.

"How sweet of her."

Luke regarded her warily. "I thought it was. Don't you want to hear about the new tenant?"

"Oh, by all means," she snapped. "Assuming you think it's something I need to know."

"Now, Katie…"

"Oh, for heaven's sakes, get on with it, Luke."

"Okay, it's Henrietta Myers. You remember Henrietta. She leads the church choir. Mrs. Jeffers says she's getting on in years and feels she can't keep up with things at her own place." At her lack of reaction, he continued in a rush, "Anyway, she'll be moving in here at the end of the week."

Katie slammed a knife through the grapefruit in a blow that just about bounced the fruit off the counter. She did, however, manage to keep a tight rein on her temper.

"I wasn't aware anyone had moved out. Exactly which room did you give her?" she inquired testily. Surely he hadn't tossed one of the others out to accommodate Henrietta.

"Mine," Luke said and calmly took a sip of his third cup of coffee of the morning.

"Yours," Katie repeated slowly. Of course. She should have guessed as much.

He nodded and reached for another piece of toast.

"Okay. That's good. That's very good. Another paying resident is always welcome. And I've always liked Henrietta, even though she is something of a busybody." She slanted a look at Luke, who seemed very pleased with himself. "Just one question. Where do you and Robby intend to sleep?"

"I thought I'd turn the attic into a room for Robby."

"Okay," she said. "Right now it's jammed with junk and doesn't have any insulation, but I guess that could work. And you?"

"I was planning to move into our room," he said, spreading a thick layer of strawberry preserves on his toast.

Katie smiled at him. Beamed, in fact. "When pigs fly," she said cheerfully.

"Now, Katie."

"Don't you 'now, Katie' me, Luke Cassidy. We had a deal, in writing. If I need to, I'll get it so you can read it again. It was very clear on this. You and I will not sleep together. Period." She shrugged. "Seems to me you've outsmarted yourself. Maybe you'd like to try out the hammock. You seem to be partial to it."

His blue eyes blazed. "I am not sleeping in the damned hammock."

She shrugged indifferently. "Whatever."

"Katie, I think you're carrying this crazy rule of yours to extremes. How will it look to the judge if we're in separate bedrooms?"

She glowered at him. "That is not my problem. You should have thought of it before you made the bargain. Maybe if you'd told me everything that was going on, we could have come to different terms."

"Why can't we do that now?"

"Because it's too late. A deal's a deal."

"You're just being stubborn and mule-headed," Luke accused. "What difference could it possibly make whether or not I sleep in your room? We're married, for goodness' sakes. It's hardly improper."

"Propriety was the last thing on my mind when I drew up that contract," she retorted. "You wanted a business deal. You got a business deal."

Luke suddenly reached out and snagged her hand. Before she could prevent it, he'd hauled her onto his lap.

"And now I don't," he said softly. "I want a marriage, Katie, a real one."

Katie struggled to free herself before she could succumb to that coaxing note in his voice. "Well, I don't."

"Liar," he whispered, his breath fanning across her cheek.

"That's certainly the way to win my heart," she retorted. "Calling me a liar really makes my pulse race."

He grinned unrepentantly. "Something I'm doing makes it race," he pointed out as his fingers settled at the base of her throat.

"It is racing because I am furious."

"I suppose that could be one reason," he conceded, brushing an unexpected kiss lightly across her lips. He nodded in satisfaction. "Now that really seems to kick it into gear. I wonder what a real kiss would do."

"I wouldn't try it if I were you," she warned.

"Oh?" he said, sounding amused. "What will you do? Last time, you kissed me back."

"Last time I didn't know the man kissing me was a low-down, conniving jerk."

The accusation had him grinning. "Sure, you did. You just didn't want to admit to yourself that you could fall for anyone with less than perfect personality traits."

That much was true. Under the circumstances, she didn't consider her feelings for Luke to be something to be proud of. She wouldn't admit that to him if he tried to torture it out of her. At the moment with his lips barely a hairsbreadth away and his fingers caressing the sensitive bare skin at the base of her throat, it seemed a sweet, dangerous torture was definitely on his mind. Katie was not about to submit to it willingly.

Twisting unexpectedly, she broke free and stood over him, resisting the urge to wrap her arms protectively around her middle. "This can't happen again," she said emphatically.

Luke, blast him, just laughed. "Oh, but it will, Katie. I can guarantee it."

She glowered at him. "Then you're going to have a bigger problem than Tommy's return on your hands," she snapped and fled before he could say or do anything to weaken her already wavering resolve.

Chapter 8

"Well, if it isn't little Katie. Just look how you've grown up."

Alone in the backyard where she'd been weeding the vegetable garden, Katie shivered as the sleazily sensual tone and the voice registered. She knew without even looking that they belonged to Tommy Cassidy.

At one time she had tried valiantly to get along with Tommy because Luke had cared so deeply about his brother. But she'd never been blinded to his flaws as Luke had once been. The most offensive had been his tendency to regard all women as targets for his sly innuendoes and advances. Apparently he hadn't reformed.

Before responding to him now, she drew in a deep breath and considered exactly how she ought to deal with Luke's brother. Coolly polite seemed like the right approach under the circumstances. She certainly didn't want to do or say anything that would worsen the situation.

"Hello, Tommy," she said, turning slowly until she was face-to-face with the man responsible for Luke's distress and, indirectly anyway, for her marriage. She wasn't sure yet if that was something she ought to thank him for or not.

Feigning a nonchalance she was far from feeling, she deliberately continued watering the plants. She didn't want Tommy getting the idea that his arrival had startled her or that she viewed it as being of any consequence. Besides, if he really got out of line, she could always hose him down.

"It's been a long time," she said.

"Not long enough, isn't that what you'd like to say?" he challenged with a considering gleam in his eyes.

Those eyes were a faded shade of the same blue as Luke's. In fact, everything about Tommy seemed to be a second-best version of his older brother. Maybe he recognized that. Maybe falling short in any comparison was the real problem between him and Luke.

"Why wouldn't I be glad to see you?" Katie contradicted, forcing a smile. "You're family now."

Tommy's laughter was tinged with bitterness. "Yeah, right. I'm sure you'll invite me over to spend the holidays this year."

"You'll always be welcome here," Katie insisted, then gave him a warning look. "As long as you don't do anything to hurt your brother or our son."

For an instant he seemed taken aback by her directness. "Oh, so you've claimed Robby," he said after a lengthy pause. "I wonder what Betty Sue would have to say about that."

"I'm Robby's stepmother," Katie corrected. "I'd never try to take Betty Sue's place."

"Saint Katie," he said derisively. "Maybe you and old Luke are a match made in heaven after all."

Ignoring his sarcasm, Katie said, "I'm sure the court will see it exactly that way." Suddenly tired of the game, she looked Tommy straight in the eye. "Why are you doing this? What's the point? You're only going to hurt Robby."

"He's my boy," Tommy said in much the same possessive way he might stake a claim to a car or, in years past, to a bicycle or a toy.

"From what I hear you didn't care much about that fact six years ago."

"Don't believe everything you hear."

"Are you saying you didn't run off and abandon Betty Sue when you found out she was pregnant?" Katie asked.

"Oh, I left," Tommy conceded. "But I thought better of it and came back. By then, though, old Saint Luke had taken off with my woman. He didn't leave no forwarding address. Guess he was afraid if I showed up, she'd leave him for a real man."

Katie didn't believe for an instant the scenario of betrayal Tommy was painting. How dare he cast Luke as the bad guy, she thought, when he'd been left behind to deal with another of Tommy's debacles.

"Luke Cassidy is more of a man than you'll ever be," she snapped, losing her fragile grip on her patience exactly as she had sworn to herself she wouldn't.

Tommy shook his head, his expression filled with pity. "What kind of real man would take another man's leavings?"

Stunned by the crude remark, Katie simply stared, then said softly, "I wonder how the judge will react when he hears how highly you think of this son you claim to love?"

Gesturing toward the street with the hose and not one bit concerned that she had splattered Tommy in the process, she glared at him. "I think you'd better get out of here, after all."

Tommy didn't budge. "I came to see my boy and I'm not going anywhere until I do."

"He's not here," she said, thanking God that Mrs. Jeffers hadn't brought Robby home from the park yet. "If you want to see him, you'll have to call Luke and make arrangements with him."

"And exactly where would I find my saintly brother? Inside? Surely he hasn't gone off and abandoned you in the middle of the honeymoon," he said nastily.

Exhibiting astonishing restraint, Katie refused to rise to the bait. "He has an office in the new building next door to the bank. You'll find him there."

Tommy appeared ready to offer some gloating observation on that, but before he could, Luke appeared around the side of the house. Taking in the situation at a glance, he strolled directly to Katie's side. As if it were the most natural thing in the world, he slipped an arm around her waist and dropped an affectionate kiss on her cheek. "Hey, darlin', I see we have company."

All at once Tommy didn't seem quite so sure of himself. His cocky demeanor visibly faltered for an instant, showing a fleeting glimpse of vulnerability. Suddenly thoughtful, Katie wondered if Luke recognized it. A glance at his expression told her nothing.

It hardly mattered because the change in Tommy's

manner didn't last. Within seconds his jaunty, arrogant facade was back in place, leaving Katie to wonder if she'd only imagined that hint of uncertainty.

"Hey, big brother, your new bride and I were just getting reacquainted."

He managed to add a suggestive note to the comment that struck Katie as dangerous given Luke's already taxed patience with him.

"Is that right?" Luke said.

Luke studied Katie's face intently as if looking for some sign that there'd been trouble between her and his brother. She wasn't about to add to the stress of the situation by declaring that Tommy Cassidy was deliberately showing signs of behaving even more despicably than she'd thought possible.

Nor did she want to discuss the startling hint of compassion she'd felt for him minutes earlier when she'd spotted that uncertainty in his eyes. His attitude and the faint evidence of an inner turmoil struck her as being very much at odds. She wasn't certain yet which was the real Tommy. She did know that they all needed time to find out for sure.

Hoping to buy some of that time, she said mildly, "Tommy was on his way to your office to see about making arrangements to see Robby."

Katie felt Luke's entire body tense.

"Sorry, that's not possible," he said flatly, leaving no room for compromise.

Color flooded Tommy's cheeks. "Dammit, you can't keep me away from my boy."

"I can and I will, unless a judge tells me I have to do otherwise," Luke replied matter-of-factly.

Tommy's mouth twisted and his expression turned

ugly. "You'll be sorry, Luke. When the shoe's on the other foot and you come begging to see Robby, I'll remember this day, and I'll see that you regret turning me away."

Katie decided enough was enough. Tempers were bound to escalate into a nasty scene if this went on much longer. Swallowing her own anger, she said, "Maybe you both should cool down. Why don't we go inside and talk this over like reasonably mature adults?"

"There's nothing to talk over," Luke declared.

"Nothing," Tommy agreed.

"Well, isn't that just peachy," Katie retorted. "Who's going to suffer because the two of you are too pigheaded to compromise? I'll tell you who. A little boy who doesn't deserve any of this. Robby's the innocent party here, and I won't have him turned into the victim of your two giant-size egos. Now get inside, sit down and talk or I swear I'll hose you both down until you cool off." She waved the garden hose in their direction to emphasize the point.

Luke stared at her for the space of a heartbeat, then unexpectedly he grinned, a gleam of admiration in his eyes. The tension in his shoulders eased a bit and he looked at his brother. "Persuasive, isn't she?"

Even Tommy seemed amused by her threat. When he smiled, the resemblance to Luke was startling.

"A regular hellcat," Tommy agreed.

"Shall we go inside?" Luke asked.

"I don't see that we have a lot of choice. I for one don't relish getting soaked to the skin."

Katie watched with satisfaction as they walked off together. She didn't hold out a lot of hope that the negotiations would be peaceful, just that they wouldn't kill each other. Maybe, given enough time, they would remember what family was supposed to be.

Luke sat across from his brother at the kitchen table and wondered for the zillionth time how Katie had managed to get the two of them inside. Surely neither he nor Tommy had actually felt threatened by that spray of water she'd been waving around. Maybe they both knew in their guts that she was right, that it was time to start talking calmly before this entire custody mess got completely out of hand. At any rate, he had to admire her audacity in forcing them to the bargaining table. If only she had come inside to keep peace, he thought as he studied Tommy warily.

Because he couldn't decide what to say, Luke got to his feet, went to the refrigerator and grabbed a pitcher of iced tea. Holding it out, he asked, "Want some?"

Tommy shook his head. "You got any beer in there?"

Luke pulled a bottle out and handed it to him without comment. He kept his opinion of drinking before noon to himself. When Tommy saw Luke watching him swig down a huge gulp, he said defensively, "It's hot as blazes out there."

"Sure is," Luke agreed readily. Determined to stay on neutral turf, he asked, "So, tell me, are you still working over in Birmingham?"

Tommy shook his head. "The job was a dead end. I thought I might go to Alaska. I hear you can make great money up there and it's gotta be cooler than this. I'm tired of being steamed like a piece of broccoli from May through October."

"Pretty damned cold up there come February, especially for a little boy," Luke said.

The comment seemed to startle Tommy, as if he'd forgotten all about the fact that he claimed he wanted his son with him. His reaction only confirmed Luke's suspicion that what Tommy really wanted was a financial stake either to get him started in Alaska or to keep him from having to work anywhere for a while.

"But I'll bet he'd love all that snow," Tommy finally countered. "You ever seen snow, big brother? Oh, wait, what am I thinking about? You probably go skiing at least twice a winter in Aspen, don't you?"

"I've never been skiing in my life," Luke retorted. "Besides, what the hell does that have to do with anything?"

Before Tommy could snap out a reply to that, Katie strolled through the door. She glanced hopefully from one to the other, but apparently she didn't like what she saw.

"Haven't you two settled anything yet?"

Luke scowled. Tommy glared.

"Terrific," she commented wearily. "Now you're not even talking." Suddenly she brightened. "Then again, maybe that's an improvement. I'll do the talking."

"Give it a rest, Katie," Luke warned quietly. "I think Tommy has made himself clear here. His terms are unacceptable."

"What terms?" Katie said.

"Money."

Tommy shot to his feet. "I never said a damned thing about wanting your money."

"But that's the bottom line, isn't it? That's what the crack about Aspen was all about, right? You want what you think I have. You just don't want to be bothered working for it they way I did."

For an instant Tommy's outraged expression gave way to something sad and lonely. Luke was taken aback by that stark look in his brother's eyes. Was there even a remote chance that he'd gotten it wrong after all?

"That is what you want, isn't it?" he repeated, hoping for a denial he could buy.

Tommy heaved a sigh. "Would you believe me if I said no?"

Luke wished he could say an unequivocal yes. He wished with all his heart that he didn't remember each and every time Tommy had sworn something to him, only to have his promises turn out to be lies. The stakes were too high this time for him to allow himself to be taken in.

"Never mind," Tommy said. "I can see the answer on your face." He turned and headed for the door. "See you in court, big brother."

The screen door slammed behind him. Only after the sound of his footsteps had faded did Luke dare a look in Katie's direction. She seemed as shaken by the outcome of the encounter as he was.

"Luke?"

"Don't even say it," he warned. "I won't start feeling sorry for him."

"But what if all he really wants is someone to love?" she asked, voicing the thought that had been taunting him for the past few minutes. "What if this isn't just about Robby, but about you, about getting your attention and your love?"

"He's always had my love," Luke said tightly. "All those years, even when everybody said I was a damned fool, Tommy had my love. He's my brother, for God's sake."

"He had it and threw it away," she pointed out. "Maybe he doesn't realize that it's still here just for the asking."

"Dammit, Katie, don't start thinking like that. Whatever his real agenda is, he's using Robby as a pawn. I doubt I'll ever be able to forgive him for that."

Before she could turn those big green eyes of hers on him and change his mind, he set his unfinished glass of tea on the table and headed for the back door. "I'm going to the park to find my son."

Though a part of him wanted to desperately, he didn't invite Katie to go with him.

"Of all the pig-headed, stubborn, mule-brained men on the face of the earth, you are at the top of the list, Luke Cassidy!"

Unfortunately there was no one in the kitchen to hear Katie's proclamation. The back door was still rattling on its hinges from Luke's exit.

Katie stood where she was, ticking off all the logical reasons Luke had to distrust his brother. But as rational as his response was, she couldn't help thinking that maybe, just this once Tommy deserved to be heard with an open mind. If he really was just using the custody suit because it was the only way he knew to get Luke's attention again, then someone had better listen before they all wound up in court. She was hardly Tommy's biggest fan, but it appeared it was up to her to get through to Luke.

She hurried upstairs, showered and changed to a pair of khaki shorts, a striped cotton blouse that she tied at the waist and sandals. Filled with determination, ten minutes later Katie was on her way to the park.

She had no trouble at all locating Luke. He was the tallest person in the small playground area with its slides and swings and colorful climbing equipment. Mrs. Jeffers had retreated to a bench in the shade under a huge old oak tree nearby. Robby was screaming with glee as Luke pushed him higher and higher in the swing.

For a moment Katie stood still and simply watched the two of them, wondering at the twist of fate that so unexpectedly had made them part of her life. She'd been married and a stepmother for little more than forty-eight hours and yet the feelings that were growing inside her were as powerful as if Luke and Robby had been a part of her life for much longer. The need to protect them from harm flooded through her as if a dam had burst in her heart.

Right now, though, the need to shake some sense into Luke was stronger. She walked over to the swings, aware that Luke's gaze was riveted to her as she approached. He didn't seem exactly thrilled to see her.

"Hi, guys," she said casually. "Having fun?"

"Wanna swing, Katie? Daddy could push you, too."

She grinned at Robby. "I think I'll pass. I might get dizzy going up as high as you. You must be part bird."

Robby nodded enthusiastically. "An eagle," he declared. "I told Daddy I wanted to soar like an eagle. We saw one once, in Colorado."

"I'll bet that was exciting."

"Mommy got scared. I don't think she liked being up on that ridge." At a look from his father, Robby's expression faltered. "Did I say something wrong?"

"Absolutely not," Katie reassured him. "I want to hear about all the things you did before I met you. Maybe we can make a deal."

The idea seemed to intrigue Robby. "What kind of deal?"

"I'll read you a story every night, after you tell me a story about something you did. That way I can share vicariously in all of the adventures you've had."

"What's vicar...vi? You know, that word you said."

Luke grinned at him. "It means that Katie hasn't had any adventures of her own, and she wants to pretend she's shared yours."

"Should I tell her about the snake?"

Katie was beginning to regret her willingness to hear about the kinds of adventures that appealed to a small boy. "The snake?" she said warily.

Robby nodded sagely. "I know, you're a girl and girls don't like snakes. Mommy really, really hated that one, too."

"A sensible woman," Katie declared.

Luke shot a startled look in her direction, as if he couldn't believe that she would side with Betty Sue about anything. Their gazes caught and held, and for just a moment air between them crackled with aware-ness.

"Robby, why don't you go get your bike?" Luke sug-gested, his gaze never leaving Katie's face. "Maybe Mrs. Jeffers will go with you while you take another ride around the park."

"Yeah, she's probably all rested by now." He grinned impishly at Katie. "She says I wore her out before."

"I can imagine," Katie said.

As soon as Robby had scampered off, Luke gestured to the swing he'd vacated. "Have a seat. I promise you won't get dizzy."

Too late, Katie thought. Her head was spinning from

the provocative gleam she'd seen in Luke's eyes. Still, she took the seat he'd offered and allowed him to give her a slow, steady push until she was soaring almost as high as Robby. On the descent, Luke captured the swing and held it so that her back was pressed against his chest.

"Giddy yet?" he inquired softly, his breath fanning across her cheek.

Katie's pulse bucked at the seductive teasing. "Steady as a rock," she claimed.

"Then what are those goose bumps doing on your arms?" he taunted.

"It's chilly."

Luke's laughter rippled over her. "It's ninety-five degrees out here, and the humidity must be close to that."

"It was ninety-eight yesterday," she countered. "There's been a break in the weather."

"Not enough to account for those goose bumps. Must be something else."

She took a huge risk with her already wavering equilibrium and leaned back against his chest. "Such as?"

He slowly trailed a finger up her arm. "Maybe that?"

Katie shivered.

"Gotcha!" Luke murmured triumphantly.

She twisted in the swing until she could gaze up into his face. "There was never any question that you could get a response out of me," she admitted. "That was true six years ago and it's true now. The big difference is that now I'm old enough and wise enough not to act on that response."

Before he could challenge her on that, she slid out of the swing and stood facing him. "I came here to talk, not to play games."

Luke's expression sobered at once. "Forget it. I don't want to discuss Tommy."

"Then don't. Just listen. Are you willing to risk the opportunity to settle this before Robby ever finds out just because you're too stubborn to keep an open mind about your brother's motives?"

Luke scowled at her. "Weren't you the one who used to tell me repeatedly that I was too lenient, that I gave Tommy the benefit of the doubt too often?"

"That was then. This is now."

"What's the difference? Tommy hasn't changed."

"Maybe he has, maybe he hasn't. You won't know for sure until you've spent some time with him."

"I can't risk letting him around Robby."

"Then spend time with him away from the house. Take him fishing. Give him a job. Whatever it takes for you to get to know him again. Judge for yourself what his real motive is."

"I know…"

Katie shook her head. "You're reacting with all the pain and anger you felt when he ran off six years ago and left you to deal with Betty Sue."

"It's not just what happened back then. He's threatening to take my son."

"But you may be able to stop him."

"Exactly. In court."

Katie shook her head. "Maybe just by giving him his family back."

"I can't take that risk," Luke said with an edge of desperation in his voice as his gaze sought out his son who was pedaling his bike like crazy while Mrs. Jeffers struggled to keep up with him.

"You can't not take it," Katie countered.

"I married you to keep Tommy out of our lives. Now you want me to welcome him back," he said, running his fingers through his hair in a gesture of frustration. "What the hell went wrong?"

Katie ignored the pain that sliced through her at his blunt assessment of his reason for marrying her. Forcing a grin, she shrugged. "Hey, if you misjudged me, maybe you've misjudged Tommy, too."

She watched as he struggled to accept her challenge. A part of her wished he would ignore her pleas. Because if it turned out she was wrong about his brother, she knew without a doubt that she would lose Luke for the second time in her life. This time she wasn't sure she would ever recover.

Chapter 9

The next morning Katie figured that as long as she was back in Clover anyway and wide awake, she might as well go in for her regular shift at Peg's Diner. Despite Luke's promised bailout of the boarding house, she wanted to contribute as much as possible to the upkeep. She was determined that Luke not mistake for one minute that it was her business.

Peg was still checking the setups of napkins, salt, pepper and sugar on all the tables when Katie unlocked the diner's front door just past dawn. The aroma of freshly brewed coffee scented the air. Katie headed straight for the pot and poured herself a cup before Peg could even manage to snap her mouth shut.

"And just what do you think you're doing in here?" Peg inquired, facing her down, eyes blazing.

"Unless you've fired me, I work here."

"You're on your honeymoon."

Katie shrugged. "We're home. I figured I might as well get back into my regular routine."

Just then the sound of another key being turned in the front door had Katie spinning around. She turned just in time to see Ginger catch sight of her and freeze, her expression uncertain. Katie stared at her teenaged boarder.

"What are you doing here?"

Ginger regarded Katie with dismay, then turned to Peg. "You didn't tell her?"

"Tell me what?" Katie demanded.

Peg sighed heavily. "Well, the truth of it is that I hired Ginger to take your place."

"You mean while I was out of town," Katie said slowly, looking from one to the other. Both women looked guilty as sin. She began to get the idea that she was not going to like any further elaboration they offered.

"Not exactly," Peg admitted. "Actually, I figured now that you're married and have Robby and all, you'd be too busy to be carrying a full load here the way you were doing before."

"So you fired me?" Katie said incredulously. "Without even talking to me about it?"

"I didn't fire you," Peg insisted.

"Just replaced me."

"I cut back on your hours," she countered.

"How far back?" Katie challenged. "You know this place can't afford to keep two waitresses on the payroll besides you." She glanced at Ginger's crestfallen expression. "Ginger, would you mind leaving me alone with my aunt for a minute?"

"Sure, Katie. I'll help Sonny in the kitchen." She rushed through the swinging door to the back as if she couldn't get away from the tension-filled atmosphere fast enough.

"You're not telling me everything, are you?" Katie demanded. "You wouldn't do something like this all on your own. I'm practically your own flesh and blood, for goodness' sakes. You wouldn't just toss me out on my rear end without someone putting you up to it."

"I don't know what you mean," Peg replied, looking everywhere but into Katie's eyes. Her hand was shaking so badly, she'd spilled more salt all over the table, than she'd gotten into the shaker.

Katie recognized all the signs indicating the depth of her aunt's distress. Normally Peg was as steady-handed and direct as any person on the face of the earth. "Peg, you are my aunt and I love you, but you are a pitiful liar. This was Luke's idea, wasn't it?"

Finally Peg's gaze clashed directly with hers. "Well, for once, I agreed with him," she said with a touch of defiance. "You were working yourself to death before. It'll only be worse now, if you try to keep doing everything."

Indignation and outrage boiled over inside Katie. "If I want to work myself to death, it's my decision," she practically shouted. Forcing herself to lower her voice, she said, "Dammit, I like being busy. I like working with you. I like talking to the customers."

Peg's determined expression faltered. "I had no idea it would even matter to you," she said. "If I had…well, I have no idea what I would have done. Luke was very persuasive."

"Did he offer to pay Ginger's salary?" Katie inquired irritably.

Peg looked shocked by the question. "Why on earth would he do a thing like that?"

"Force of habit," Katie said. "He seems to think he can buy whatever he wants in life."

"Meaning?" Peg asked, studying her with a speculative expression.

Katie sighed heavily. That was one question she had no intention of answering. A totally honest reply would only upset her aunt. "Nothing. Don't mind me. I just resent what he did."

"He couldn't have done it without my cooperation," Peg pointed out. "I sincerely regret that I gave it to him. I really am sorry, sweetheart. I'll speak with Ginger."

Suddenly the last of the fight drained out of Katie. "You can't fire her. She needs the money."

"But you're right," Peg argued. "I shouldn't have made a decision like this without talking it over with you. Luke and I just thought it was for the best." She brightened slightly. "Maybe both of you could stay on, take fewer hours. It's summer, anyway. We're always busier this time of year. Then in the fall, when Ginger's back in school, we'll reevaluate."

Katie realized then that it was awfully silent in the kitchen. Usually by this time in the morning Sonny was slamming pots and pans around and singing at the top of his lungs. She had a hunch, though, that today he and Ginger were both hanging on every word she and Peg were speaking.

"I suppose we could try it," she agreed, loudly enough to be overheard by anyone who just happened to be listening. "As long as we're not bumping into each other in the aisles, it should be okay."

Without waiting to be beckoned, Ginger rushed

through the swinging door, a relieved smile spreading across her face. She threw her arms around Katie. "Thank you. I never meant to upset you. I guess I figured I'd be helping Peg out of a jam and earning some college money at the same time."

Katie hugged her back. "None of this was your doing. It just seems my family has a tendency to make decisions for me." She glanced pointedly at Peg. "At least my aunt knows now that this is a very bad idea."

Peg grinned at her and nodded. "You've made yourself perfectly clear to me. I'm not so sure I want to be around, though, when Luke finds out."

Her concern was well-founded. Apparently the minute Luke figured out that Katie was nowhere in the boarding house, he yanked Robby out of bed and came storming over to the diner. His clothes rumpled, his hair uncombed, Robby appeared slightly dazed by the rude awakening. Katie winked at him as he passed by, but ignored her husband.

Luke took one look at Katie serving a table of tourists and turned a furious gaze on Peg.

Peg apparently wasn't one bit daunted by his scowling demeanor. She shrugged. "Take it up with your wife."

"Oh, I intend to," he said, heading straight for a booth. He nudged Robby in ahead of him, then kept his gaze fastened on Katie with a blazing look that could have set half the town afire if the sparks had gone astray.

Katie decided this was not a discussion she cared to have in the middle of the diner with the entire town of Clover certain to hear the details before lunchtime. The decibel level was likely to reach a peak that could shatter glass. Still seething with resentment, she sent Ginger over to wait on him.

Ginger was back behind the counter in a heartbeat. "He wants you," she said in a hushed tone.

"Well, he can't have me. That's not my station."

"Actually it is," Ginger pointed out.

Katie frowned at her. "Our agreement can be canceled just like that," she said with a snap of her fingers. At Ginger's terrified expression she relented. "Oh, never mind. I'll go. Give me the coffeepot."

"I've already poured the coffee," Ginger said in a way that suggested Katie might not be trusted to pour it into a cup.

Katie plucked her order pad out of her pocket and marched over to Luke's booth. She saved her friendly grin for Robby.

"Just get up?" she asked him.

"Daddy was in a hurry. He didn't even make me brush my teeth," he said with obvious amazement over his good luck.

"I wonder why," Katie said sweetly, still not glancing at her husband. "So, what are you having?"

"A conversation with my wife," Luke said in a low, lethal tone.

"Sorry, not on the menu. The special this morning is a Western omelette."

"Fine, whatever," Luke snapped.

"I want pancakes," Robby said, oblivious to the undercurrents. "It's really neat coming here for breakfast. I can have pancakes anytime I want. Daddy burns them."

"I do not burn them," Luke said testily.

"You should see what he does to eggs," Robby added, not the least bit intimidated by his father's foul mood.

"Well, fortunately, Sonny is a whiz with pancakes and eggs," Katie said. "I like coming here for breakfast, too."

"I can't imagine when you find the time to eat it," Luke said.

"Do I look as if I'm starving?" Katie retorted.

The question was a mistake. She knew it the moment the words were out of her mouth. Luke slowly, deliberately surveyed her from head to toe with a provocative consideration that had her skin practically sizzling. Dear heaven! She barely resisted the urge to fan herself with a menu. "Nope, you do have a few curves," he observed generously. "More than I recalled, in fact."

"Thanks so much."

"Good color in your cheeks, too," he commented, grinning.

"Oh, go to—" She stopped herself in the nick of time, plastered a phony smile on her face and stalked off to place the order.

Unfortunately Sonny was one of the best short order cooks in the business. He had Luke and Robby's food ready before Katie could gather the composure necessary to fool all of the interested observers into thinking that she and Luke were not having their first marital tiff.

"I hope you're enjoying yourself," Luke said, when she thumped the plates onto the table.

She eyed him warily. "Are you trying to make a point?"

"It's your last day," he said, taking his first bite of omelette. "This is terrific, by the way."

"I'll give Sonny your compliments." Then added cheerfully, "And I wouldn't bet on this being my last day, if I were you. You'd lose."

"We'll see."

He said it so smugly, as if there were some angle she hadn't considered, that it gave Katie pause. Regarding him speculatively, she moved on to another table. If he wanted more coffee or more anything, too bad, she thought with a touch of defiance. She'd spend her energy on customers who appreciated her waitressing skills. Luke probably wouldn't even leave a tip. He probably thought he'd already tipped her well enough by depositing that check into her account.

The next time she glanced toward Luke's booth, it was well after nine o'clock. He was sitting there scribbling notes on a tablet he'd apparently filched from Peg's supply under the cash register. There was no sign of Robby.

With only one other customer in the place chatting happily with Ginger at the counter, Katie couldn't think of a single way to go on avoiding her husband. She poured herself a cup of coffee and carried it with her to his table, then slid in opposite him. He glanced up.

"All done making your point?" he inquired.

"And what point would that be?"

"That I can't run your life."

Katie regarded him intently. "I'm not sure. Have I gotten it through that thick skull of yours yet?"

"Only the first layer. Maybe you'd better try explaining to me why you want to work yourself to death this way."

Okay, Katie thought, that was a reasonable enough request. She tried to formulate an explanation that wouldn't cause him to order her to shut down the boarding house instead. Luke seemed to have turned into an either-or sort of guy. She had to make him see that both jobs were essential to her.

"I love the boarding house," she began. "I poured all of my energy into it."

"To say nothing of your money," he reminded her.

She frowned at him and he held up his hands. "Sorry," he said. "Go on."

"But Ginger and the others all have their own lives. Sometimes I just need a break from all the quiet, from doing laundry and dusting. I like coming in here and hearing what's going on around town. I like meeting the tourists. Plus I owe Peg. I get a sense of satisfaction from being able to pay her back in some small way for all she did for me. Having the boarding house and the diner gives me a sort of balance in my life."

To Luke's credit he listened to every word she said, but his expression grew bleaker by the minute. Katie didn't understand his reaction.

"You still don't understand, do you?" she asked.

"I understand," he said flatly. Blue eyes met hers. "But where in this equation do Robby and I fit in?"

Katie felt as if all the breath had whooshed right out of her. "Is that what you're worried about? That I won't have time for the two of you?"

"There are only twenty-four hours in a day," he reminded her. "You're already cramming them to the max."

Katie was stunned that he would think that he and his son would get only whatever leftover minutes she could salvage from an already overburdened schedule. Maybe what astonished her even more was the fact that it really seemed to matter to him at all.

"I suppose I hadn't thought about how it would seem

to you," she admitted honestly. She looked directly into his eyes. "But, Luke, you and Robby will always be my first priority. I meant every word I said when we took our vows."

He was regarding her doubtfully. "Every word?"

"Of course."

"What about obey?" he teased, his expression suddenly lighter.

"That word was never spoken," she retorted.

"Oh, I'm certain it was. Love, honor and obey, wasn't that it? I'm sure Justice of the Peace Abernathy read from a very traditional version of the ceremony."

"Absolutely not. I would have remembered."

He grinned and reached for her hand, lacing his fingers through hers. "You do remember the love and honor part, though?"

"Vaguely," she murmured, barely able to concentrate for all the dangerous sensations rioting through her.

"Maybe we should talk about that in more detail later, when we're alone," Luke suggested.

"Uh-huh," Katie managed when she could catch her breath. This was not good, not good at all. "I'd better go now."

Luke's grin widened. "Where?"

She shook her head to clear it, then glanced desperately around for someplace, anyplace she might be needed in a very big hurry. "The kitchen," she said hurriedly. "I have to help clean up in the kitchen."

"All done," Peg sang out.

"Now what?" Luke inquired with that lazy, smug expression firmly back in place.

"I have to go…" she racked her brain "…to the store. I have to get food for the boarders."

"They're staying at the hotel, remember?"

"That's ridiculous," Katie countered. "I'll tell them to come home. They shouldn't be spending their money on hotel rooms, when they've already paid me."

"I'm paying for their rooms," Luke said. "I'm sure Mr. O'Reilly's in heaven with room service at his command. You wouldn't want to spoil it for him, would you?"

She sighed. "I suppose not."

Luke gave a little nod of satisfaction, then stood, leaned down and kissed her in a slow, leisurely fashion that melted every single bone in her body. "I'll be waiting for you at home."

Thoroughly dazed, Katie simply stared after him as he strolled from the diner.

"Whew!" Ginger said, emerging from the kitchen waving a dish towel in front of her face. "That man is hot enough to fry bacon." Realizing what she'd said and about whom, she winced and turned an apologetic look on Katie. "Sorry."

"For what?" Peg interjected. "Appreciating a man who could turn the Arctic into steam heat?" At Katie's look of astonishment, she added, "Well, it's true. Luke does have a certain way about him."

A possessive smile crept over Katie's face. "Yes," she said finally. "He does indeed have a way about him."

She just wished she could be sure there was more to it than inbred flirtatiousness or the desperation of a man who needed to present an impression of marital bliss to a judge.

Luke sat in his new office, surrounded by all the most modern equipment, and tried to make sense of what had just happened with Katie. He'd been toying with the same question for more than an hour now. He'd bought controlling stock in entire corporations with less consideration.

The truth of it was his new wife was a puzzle to him. He couldn't begin to imagine how that had come about. After all, Katie was his oldest and dearest friend. He'd been her first lover, though he realized he had no idea if he'd been her last. At any rate, nothing about her should be taking him by surprise. That was the main reason he'd come home determined to marry her. He was sick to death of surprises.

To his astonishment, though, she wasn't the same adoring, compliant woman he'd left behind. She had a mind of her own. She'd learned to take care of herself. In fact, except for cleaning up the financial mess she'd gotten herself into with the boarding house, she didn't seem to need him at all.

Which made him wonder why she'd accepted his proposal. She could have fixed things at the bank. Despite his tough talk, bank president Charlie Hastings would walk over burning coals for Katie. Katie had probably known it, too.

Instead, she had agreed to marry Luke, become stepmother to his son and negotiated what had to be the oddest prenuptial agreement on record. Or not on record to be more precise, since they were the only people who knew about it, unless Katie had gotten it into her head to file the document at City Hall. He realized he wasn't so sure this new Katie wouldn't do exactly that.

Katie was turning out to be far less predictable than he'd anticipated. She was absolutely bursting with surprises. It was a rude discovery for a man who'd been praying for a little stability in his life. He'd come home looking for a tame old friend and found himself married to a hellion.

Yet Luke had to admit he was intrigued with this new Katie. He'd been physically attracted to the old Katie, and that much hadn't changed. But this new, fascinating woman stimulated him in ways he hadn't expected. In fact, just thinking about the way Katie had stood in the middle of Peg's Diner and blatantly defied him turned him on.

Maybe even more important, it made him smile. Ever since Tommy had declared his intent to gain custody of Robby, Luke hadn't had all that much to smile about. Now he had Katie, who made his blood race just by going toe-to-toe with him and standing up for herself. Given his penchant for taking charge and her determination to control her own destiny, he figured more battles were a certainty. In fact, he looked forward to them.

Suddenly smiling to himself, he tossed down his pen and headed for the door. It shouldn't take him more than an hour or so back at the boarding house to find something to change. With any luck he ought to be able to stir up another one of those stimulating clashes before dinnertime.

Chapter 10

It didn't take long for Luke to find exactly what he was looking for at the boarding house. He found that the way to take charge and at the same time drive Katie nuts was in plain view under the June receipts. It was already the tenth of the month and Ginger had yet to pay her rent. Mrs. Jeffers and Mr. O'Reilly paid by the week and both were behind, though only by a few days. The pattern set off alarm bells in his head.

He went back and found that Ginger hadn't paid rent on a single occasion he could find. The other two paid, but always after some delay. It seemed the only record he could find of people actually paying what they owed, when they owed it, was of the handful of people who were passing through Clover.

Luke resolved to have a chat with all three of the regulars about the need to get the boarding house cash flow back on a sound financial base. No doubt Katie would be incensed by his interference. He could hardly wait for another one of their highly charged encounters.

In fact, he decided, why put it off? All three were likely to be at the Clover Street Hotel—at his expense. Maybe it would be better to have this conversation on neutral turf and away from Katie's interference. She was at the root of the problem. Everyone knew she was a soft touch. No doubt they played on her sympathy with endless excuses.

He experienced a momentary pang of guilt for leaving Katie out of the meeting, but he ignored it. He had no doubts at all that she would hear about it soon enough. And there was no mistaking his perverse desire to be the target of more of those sparks she threw off when she was angry.

He had no difficulty at all in tracking down two of his quarry. Mrs. Jeffers was playing a cutthroat game of checkers with Robby at a table in the lobby. John O'Reilly was in the dining room with a hamburger and fries in front of him.

Luke asked each of them if they'd seen Ginger. Mr. O'Reilly claimed he hadn't seen her since the reception at the boarding house.

"I thought she was working at the diner," Mrs. Jeffers offered.

"I saw her go upstairs," Robby said. "I think she has a class this afternoon or something. She probably had to study." He turned a puzzled look on his father. "Why does she have to go to school during the summer? I thought everybody had vacation now."

"Because she really wants to get into a good college and she's taking these summer prep classes. She wants to take at least one class each summer, hoping that she'll qualify for a scholarship," Mrs. Jeffers explained. "That's the only way she'll ever be able to afford to get a degree."

Thinking about Ginger struggling to get into college against the odds made Luke stop for a minute to consider what he was about to do. Then he thought of Katie, struggling equally hard to stay afloat, and his resolve strengthened.

"I'll give Ginger a call on the hotel's house phone," he said. "I'd like to have a minute with all of you. Mr. O'Reilly will join us as soon as he's finished his lunch."

Mrs. Jeffers instantly looked worried. "Is everything okay? You haven't changed your mind about us staying on at the boarding house, have you? I'm sure you and Katie would like to have your privacy, but we all love it there."

Robby shot a look of alarm at his father. "They have to stay, Daddy."

This wasn't going nearly as smoothly as he'd intended. Withstanding Robby's accusing looks was far worse than dealing with Katie's disapproval. "Of course, everyone is staying," he reassured them. "It's just that there's something I thought we should talk about."

"Will Katie be here?" Mrs. Jeffers asked.

"No."

"But shouldn't she be in on this?" Mrs. Jeffers protested. "It is her boarding house, after all."

Luke thought how reassured Katie would be to hear one of her boarders talking this way. "I'm just trying to save her some worry," he promised. "I'll fill her in later."

"If you say so, dear," Mrs. Jeffers said, though she still sounded doubtful.

It was nearly two o'clock by the time Luke had everyone where he wanted them, in a secluded alcove in the hotel lobby where they could have some privacy.

"I was just going over the boarding house books this morning," he began. Immediately the expressions on the faces of all three boarders fell. Obviously they guessed where this was heading. "I'm sure it's just slipped your minds, but it seems that everyone is behind in paying the rent."

"But Katie knew…" Ginger began.

"Katie always…" Mrs. Jeffers chimed in.

"Now see here, young man. I don't know that this is any business of yours," John O'Reilly stated flatly. "We've all made our arrangements with Katie."

This was not going at all the way Luke had hoped. He'd been certain that once they saw how their lackadaisical attitudes toward financial matters hurt Katie, they'd all want to help her out.

"Maybe I'm not making myself clear," he said.

"Oh, I think you are," Mr. O'Reilly countered. "Pay up or get out, isn't that it?"

"No, of course not," Luke protested.

"Sounds that way to me," the retired fireman said.

"Me, too, dear," Mrs. Jeffers concurred.

Only Ginger was silent, possibly because huge tears were spilling down her pale cheeks. Luke suddenly felt like a heel. It seemed his good intentions were backfiring. He rushed on to try to set things straight before he really botched things up.

"I'm not trying to bully you," he said. "I'm just worried about Katie."

As if a switch had been flipped, they were suddenly attentive.

"What's the matter with Katie?" Ginger asked. "She's not sick, is she?"

"Well, no, but…"

"Is she upset?" Mrs. Jeffers asked.

"Not with you all," Luke replied candidly.

"Well, for heaven's sakes, spit it out, boy," Mr. O'Reilly ordered. "You know we care about Katie. She's family."

"She could lose the boarding house," he said bluntly.

His announcement was greeted with shock. The gasp he heard, however, could not be attributed to any of the three people in front of him. In fact, he had a very strong suspicion that it came from the very woman under discussion.

Apparently his guess was far more accurate than his understanding of boarding house politics, because all three people jumped to their feet and rushed to encompass Katie in hugs, while murmuring appropriate expressions of sympathy and worry. He seemed to have been forgotten—or simply dismissed as the bearer of bad tidings.

When he finally got a glimpse of Katie's face through the cluster of clucking sympathizers, his gaze clashed with green eyes that blazed with outrage. Glancing away from that look of condemnation, he suddenly realized that his son was mysteriously absent from the scene. He guessed that the little traitor had found some way to get word of the meeting to Katie.

"I'm so sorry I wasn't here when the meeting started," Katie said, urging everyone back to their places. "I was a little late in hearing about it."

"Actually, Luke said—" Mrs. Jeffers began.

Luke jumped in. "I thought I could handle it."

"If you'd handled it much better, everyone would have moved out by nightfall, according to my source," Katie replied sweetly.

Luke vowed to gag his son in the future. Maybe he ought to blindfold him and make him wear earplugs while he was at it.

"So, what's the topic?" Katie inquired. "The impending foreclosure on my bank loan?"

She said it with an edge of sarcasm that sent a dull red flush creeping up Luke's neck. He could feel his skin burning.

"So it's true," Mr. O'Reilly said, his expression grim.

"It might have been a few weeks ago," Katie conceded. She beamed at them, but saved her most saccharine smile for Luke. "But I had a windfall that saved the day and I'm fairly certain that it was just the beginning. Everything's under control."

"For the moment," Luke said ominously.

Katie glared at him. "The situation is under control," she repeated. "You all are not to worry. You know how these uptight financial types are." She directed a pointed look at Luke. "They panic at the slightest little blip in the cash-flow pattern."

"Somebody has to," Luke muttered.

"Perhaps you and I should discuss this in private," Katie suggested.

"Perhaps we should," Luke agreed, his blood already racing at the prospect of another heated exchange with his wife. If this was the only sort of passion she intended to permit the two of them, then he intended to take full advantage of it. The evening that stretched out before them seemed open to all sorts of fascinating possibilities.

Katie couldn't understand why Luke appeared so pleased by the prospect of fighting with her. He had to know that she wasn't going to let this little incident pass without comment. Calling a meeting without telling her about it had been a sneaky, underhanded thing to do. Thank heavens for Robby! Even though he hadn't understood exactly what the discussion was all about, he'd reacted to everyone else's panic. He'd had no trouble convincing the hotel desk clerk to call Katie for him.

The walk back to the boarding house was made in silence. Katie could hardly wait to get her indignation at Luke's latest high-handness off her chest, but Main Street was no place to do it. On that much at least, Luke apparently agreed. He hadn't even wanted Robby as a witness. He'd sent his son off to Peg's for the night.

Obviously, though, he was spoiling for a fight. He had to have known that calling that meeting would infuriate her and yet he'd deliberately gone ahead with it. Clearly, he hadn't learned a blasted thing from their conversation in the diner that morning. He intended to control her life, take over her boarding house and leave her with nothing to do.

As they neared the house, Katie's steps began to falter. Her temper cooled a fraction. She compared what Luke had done to what she had plotted behind his back that very afternoon. He didn't know it yet, but they were probably just about even. He might even have a slight edge when it came to justifiable outrage.

The timing was lousy for her to make her announcement, but a glance at her watch told her there was no way around it. She figured she'd better make it while they were still on the sidewalk in front of the boarding house, in plain view of the neighbors. This was one time when witnesses might save her hide.

"Luke?"

He scowled at her. "I don't want to get into this out here. We'll discuss it inside."

"In a minute. First, there's something you need to know."

"Fine. Tell me inside."

She stopped right where she was. "I'd rather tell you out here."

He met her gaze, his expression suddenly wary. "Why? What's this about?"

"I just thought you ought to know…" She swallowed hard as she met his glittering blue eyes. "I've done something."

"What?"

She plastered a bright smile on her face. "I've invited Tommy for a barbecue," she blurted out.

Luke couldn't have looked more stunned if she'd announced that she was pregnant with triplets.

"You what?" he asked slowly, as if her words hadn't been perfectly clear.

"Your brother's coming over." She glanced nervously at her watch. "In about an hour."

"Oh, no, he's not," Luke countered. "Call him and cancel."

"I can't. I don't know where he is."

"You found him to issue the invitation. You can find him to cancel it."

She shook her head. "Actually, he came into the diner for lunch."

He stared at her with an expression of complete bafflement written all over his face. "Why would you do this? How dare you meddle in something that is none of your business?"

Katie couldn't believe her ears. "Excuse me? You self-righteous son of a hound dog. Who was it who just called a meeting of my tenants without telling me? If you want to talk about meddling, let's talk about that!"

"Not out here," Luke said tightly.

"Why the hell not?"

"Because half the neighborhood is hanging on every word."

"So what? Witnesses might not be such a bad idea."

"That's enough, Katie."

Luke's voice carried a low warning that she ignored. "Enough? It's not enough by a long shot. I have plenty to say about that stunt you just pulled at the hotel."

Before she could even formulate the first thought, though, Luke tucked one arm under her knees, another under her bottom and scooped her into the air. She landed against his chest with a *whoosh*.

"You low-down, rotten..." she began, kicking futilely in an attempt to cause him to lose his balance as he strode up the walk toward the house.

She heard a distinct, low, rumbling sound coming from Luke's chest that silenced her. She gazed into his eyes and saw sparks of pure mischief suddenly dancing in the blue depths.

"You're laughing," she accused.

He swallowed hard and tried for a sober expression.

Unfortunately he couldn't seem to keep his lips from quirking into a smile.

"How dare you!" she said indignantly. "This is not a laughing matter."

Inside the boarding house he headed straight for the living room, seemingly oblivious to her protests. He settled onto the chintz-covered sofa, keeping Katie pinned firmly in place in his lap. Having his arms around her was beginning to have a neutralizing effect on her anger. It was hard to stay furious when every single part of her anatomy was tingling with awareness of the man who held her. It was absurd, really, how easily Luke was able to distract her.

Of course, she decided thoughtfully, he didn't seem as upset, either. In fact, he seemed to have forgotten all about his brother's impending arrival. He seemed much more interested in her bare midriff, where her blouse had ridden up. He was tracing a lazy pattern across the skin that had her insides trembling.

"Um, Luke," she said breathlessly. "This is a bad idea."

He ignored her and began tracing the neckline of her blouse which she'd left open about one button too far. Maybe two buttons too far. She probably should have sewn the damned thing together, given the way her pulse was kicking up.

"Luke, please," she said, trying to swat his hand away.

Without a word, he captured her hand and planted a deliberately provocative kiss against the sensitive palm. Katie's resistance melted. Another thirty seconds of this sweet torment and her blood would be sizzling. She wriggled in a half-hearted attempt to get free, but immediately realized that wriggling was a very bad idea. It had a prompt and unmistakable effect on Luke, that did not bode well for lowering the out-of-control heat rising between them with anything short of an icy shower.

"Luke," she murmured in her least effective attempt yet to get his attention.

"Ah, Katie," he said with a sigh as he kissed a spot on her neck just below her ear.

Katie shivered, which he must have taken as an invitation. He scattered kisses from the base of her throat to her chin, from her forehead to her cheeks, from the tip of her nose to her lips. Her mouth opened, formed his name, but not a sound emerged before she was caught up in the slow, sensual feel of Luke's velvet lips against her own. Her arms crept around his neck, her fingers tangled in his thick hair as she gave herself over to the kiss.

The touch of his mouth against hers, the beckoning heat that stole through her, set off a riot of memories. Sweet, wicked, dangerous memories. For what seemed an eternity, Katie indulged herself in sensation, accepting, provoking, hungering for more. She was swept away on the tide of tenderness. She lost herself to need, Luke's and her own.

A gentle, insistent caress of her breast sent her pulse scrambling. The slow slide of Luke's hand from calf to inner thigh made her heart thunder in her chest. Her entire body throbbed with a desperate yearning to know again this man who'd branded her heart as his own years ago.

She could fight it. She could pretend that she didn't want what was happening between them, but the truth of it was that she did. She wanted Luke to make love to her, wanted him to possess her as he once had. She hungered for it illogically, in a way that ignored past hurts and present problems, in a way that didn't give a damn for the emotional consequences. Every fiber of her being was straining toward fulfillment of a dream she'd thought only weeks ago would elude her forever. Logic and reason had nothing to do with it. All that mattered was a love that had never died.

Katie gave up the battle, gave herself over to the joy of the moment…just in time to hear footsteps on the front porch, a loud knock on the screen door.

"What the hell?" Luke muttered, clearly dazed and definitely unhappy about the untimely interruption.

"Tommy," she guessed, untangling herself from Luke and rising unsteadily to her feet. She straightened her clothes as she went to the door. There was nothing she could do about the flood of color in her cheeks.

Naturally Tommy couldn't let her obvious state of arousal pass without comment. His blue eyes filled with insolent amusement. "I could come back later, if I'm interrupting anything," he offered.

"Or not at all," Luke said, coming up behind Katie.

Katie saw the flash of hurt in Tommy's eyes, before he covered it with belligerence. "Or not at all," he agreed. "It's up to Katie. It's her house. I don't go where I'm not wanted."

Fully aware of Luke's disapproving scowl, she determinedly pushed open the screen door. "Of course you're wanted. I invited you, didn't I? We were late getting here. We're just running a little behind."

Tommy seemed eager to accept the explanation. Never once glancing at his brother, he asked Katie,

"What can I do to help? If the grill's out back, I can start the coal."

"Terrific. I'm lousy at it," she said, leading the way to the kitchen. "Luke, why don't you help him?"

Luke looked as if he'd rather eat dirt. Shooting her a wry look, he dutifully followed his brother out the door.

The instant he'd gone, Katie's knees seemed to give way. She sank onto a chair and released the breath she'd been holding. Sweet, heavenly days, what had she been thinking in the other room?

Of course, the point was that she hadn't been *thinking* at all. She'd been giving her hormones free rein. It appeared she owed Tommy Cassidy a debt of gratitude. His arrival had just saved her from what could have been the second most costly mistake of her life.

She listened to the low, halting murmur of voices from the backyard and gave a little nod of satisfaction. Maybe she was already repaying him by giving him time to win back Luke's love and approval.

Chapter 11

Luke couldn't decide whether to be more furious with his brother for showing up just when he had Katie on the brink of making love with him or with his wife for inviting Tommy in the first place. It was a toss-up.

But the bottom line was that Tommy was here and there didn't seem much likelihood that anything short of a shotgun would persuade him to leave. Katie, with her strong notions about family loyalty, would definitely frown on his waving a gun threateningly at his brother.

At the moment, Tommy was working intently on getting the grill started. For the first time Luke took a minute to study him with at least some semblance of objectivity. He realized with a sense of shock that Tommy was far too thin, practically gaunt, in fact. His skin was a pasty color that didn't look healthy.

"Are you okay?" he asked, drawing a surprised look.

"I'm fine."

"You look like hell. When was the last time you had a decent meal?"

"Today at lunch," Tommy said too quickly.

At the diner, Luke realized and wondered if Katie had paid for whatever Tommy had eaten. More than likely. "Before that," he said.

Tommy shrugged. "Sometime yesterday, I guess."

"Have you been drinking away your money?" Luke asked, thinking of the beer Tommy had asked for the morning before.

The question drew more emotion than Luke had anticipated. Tommy whirled away from the grill and glared at him.

"You know damn well I don't drink, not after the way Dad was," Tommy said heatedly. "An occasional beer is about it. That one I had yesterday was the first in weeks."

Something about his indignant tone rang true. It was hardly surprising that Tommy rarely touched alcohol. Neither did Luke. Watching their father's bouts with the stuff, seeing his dissolution before he'd finally taken off and abandoned them all would make anyone with sense wary.

Luke still wasn't sure what the explanation was for Tommy's appearance, but it instinctively worried him. Apparently old habits died harder than he thought. "You're sure you're not sick?"

"I am not sick," Tommy repeated emphatically, then shot him a wry look. "Though it would probably serve your purposes better if I were."

"What the hell is that supposed to mean?"

"Just that you could use it in court as further evidence of my unsuitability to be a parent to my boy."

"How can you even say such a thing? I wasn't looking for ammunition," Luke protested. "You look lousy. I wanted to know why." Suddenly an explanation came to him, one that would answer a lot of the questions he had about Tommy's motivations of late. "You said you left your job in Birmingham?"

Tommy regarded him resentfully. "Yeah, so what? I told you I'm heading to Alaska just as soon as this stuff with Robby is settled."

"How long have you been out of work?"

"Hey, man, it's none of your business. I've been getting by, okay? Now drop it."

Certain now that he was on the right track, Luke shook his head. "I don't think so. You see, it seems to me a man who's been out of work for a while might get desperate. He might do something that would never otherwise occur to him."

Tommy's shoulders stiffened. "Such as?"

"Maybe filing a custody suit he had no intention of winning, hoping to get a little cash so he could start over somewhere new." He reached for Tommy's shoulder, clasped it with a firm grip and forced him to turn around. "Is that what the suit was about?"

Suddenly Tommy looked about seventeen again, young and scared and proud. His chin lifted belligerently. "I don't want your money," he declared.

Luke sighed. "Oh, I can believe that. I worked damned hard to instill that streak of stubborn pride in you. That doesn't mean you don't need money, though."

"I'll do just fine once I get to Alaska," Tommy insisted.

Luke carefully weighed the pros and cons before he said anything more. He didn't want to make a mistake that could cost them all. But this was his brother and, as Katie had known, despite everything he loved him unconditionally. Even as angry and as threatened as he'd felt these past months, a part of him had struggled to find an explanation that would make Tommy's betrayal less painful. He still wanted to believe there was something worth salvaging.

Tommy was barely twenty-five. His whole life stretched out in front of him. Maybe all he needed was a solid push in the right direction.

Finally he said, "You could work for me." When Tommy immediately started to object, Luke added, "Just to get the stake you need, if that's the way you want it."

"Bad idea," Tommy said without giving the proposal any thought at all.

"Don't reject it just because of your stupid pride," Luke warned. "At least think about it."

"There's nothing to think about. You don't want me around my kid, and I don't want to be anyplace I'm not wanted. As soon as the judge makes his ruling, I'll take my kid and go." He glared at Luke. "I don't need handouts from you. I don't need anything from you."

Luke didn't believe him. He realized he had started to see him through Katie's eyes, and what he saw was a young man desperate for a sense of belonging. "So why are you here now?"

"You mean tonight? Because Katie invited me." He grinned faintly. "Twisted my arm was more like it."

"Yeah, I know the feeling," Luke commiserated. "But I meant why did you come back to Clover in the first place? The custody suit is being handled in Atlanta. You didn't need to come all the way to South Carolina."

"I wanted to see my son," he insisted.

"You knew I wouldn't let that happen, not under the circumstances."

Tommy shrugged. "I figured you might change your mind."

If he hadn't been so frustrated, he might have laughed at Tommy's stubborn refusal to admit what had been obvious even to Katie. Tommy had come home to be with family. Luke could see that as plainly now as if his brother had scrawled it in a note and posted it in the town square.

But until Tommy could admit he needed help, until he could accept what Luke was willing to offer, there didn't seem to be much Luke could do for him. He'd opened a door tonight, but Tommy had to walk through it.

Fortunately, before his frustration caused him to say something that would set them back, Katie emerged from the house with a platter of hamburgers. She put it down on the picnic table, then lifted her gaze to survey the two of them.

"Everything okay out here?" she asked, regarding them hopefully.

"Terrific," Tommy said with a forced note in his voice.

"Terrific," Luke echoed.

Katie looked pleased. "Well, that's…terrific. I'll be out in a minute with the rest of the food. Is the fire hot yet?"

"The coals are glowing like a lover's eyes," Tommy said.

Used to Tommy's tendency to talk explicitly when it

came to women, Luke shot him a dark look, but Katie only seemed amused by the response.

"I've never heard anyone get poetic about charcoal before," she said.

To Luke's amazement, Tommy looked faintly sheepish. "Seems like I have a turn of phrase for every occasion."

Katie seemed to forget all about the food that was still waiting inside. She observed Tommy speculatively. "Maybe you should be writing country songs," she said, clearly warming to the possibility.

Luke regarded her with astonishment. "Why the devil would you leap to a conclusion like that?"

"Because he's obviously got a flair with words," she said. "What about it, Tommy? Have you ever thought about it?"

"I've done a couple," Tommy admitted, drawing a smug I-told-you-so look from Katie. "Haven't sold 'em, though. Everybody tells me I'd be a fool to just put 'em in the mail to some singer I don't even know. Like as not, they'd just steal the song and there wouldn't be nothing I could do about it."

While Luke stared open-mouthed at his brother, Katie said, "I'm sure there must be ways to protect yourself. Maybe Luke can help." With that less-than-subtle hint, she turned around and sashayed back inside. Luke watched the sway of her hips for a minute, then turned back to his brother.

"Do you really want to write country songs?"

Tommy avoided his gaze. "Like I said, there's not much chance of selling anything. It's more like a hobby, I guess."

"But you enjoy it?" Luke persisted.

"Yeah," he admitted, shifting uncomfortably. "It helps to get stuff out of your system. Sometimes I just have to get what I'm feeling down on paper."

Luke regarded him with exasperation. "If writing music is what you want to do, why on earth are you talking about going to Alaska?"

"Because Alaska's more practical. Isn't that the sort of thing you were always preaching to me?"

"Practicality definitely has its place," Luke agreed. He turned his gaze on the screen door through which Katie had just disappeared. "Sometimes, though, you just have to follow your heart."

Tommy followed the direction of his gaze. "Is that what brought you back to Clover?" Tommy asked with a surprising perceptiveness. "Were you following your heart?"

Maybe because there were protective shadows now that dusk had fallen, maybe because he was feeling more mellow than he had in some time, maybe just because he wanted someone to whom he could admit the truth, Luke said honestly, "I'm beginning to think that is exactly why I came back."

Tommy chuckled. The low sound conveyed more than amusement. To Luke there also seemed to be a note of genuine affection behind it, a hint of understanding.

"What's so funny?" he asked his brother.

"It's just that it's about time you wised up. Everybody always thought you were the smart one, but it always seemed to me that when it came to your feelings for Katie, you were dumber than grass."

Luke laughed. "Now that's a hook for a country song, if ever I heard one."

* * *

Something had changed. Katie knew it the minute she walked back outside with the rest of their dinner and heard her husband and Tommy singing enthusiastically. Luke was wildly off-key, but Tommy had a deep, rich voice that was surprisingly sensual and definitely deserved a try at Nashville.

Of course, they were singing some improbable lyric she'd never heard before. It sounded something like, "When it comes to love, I've always been dumber than grass."

"No, no," Tommy protested. "There's no rhyme. It should be, When it comes to love, alas, I've always been dumber than grass."

"Maybe Nashville is beyond your reach, after all," Katie said to Tommy as she joined them.

"I don't know. I was thinking maybe we'd make a good duo," Luke said.

Katie lifted her eyebrows. "I'd think again, if I were you."

Luke slipped an arm around her waist. "If I stay here, will you make it worth my while?"

Luke's touch and the teasing banter shimmered through Katie, reminding her of the intimacy they'd shared just before Tommy's arrival. "What would you consider worth your while?" she inquired, daring to look into eyes that had promptly darkened with desire.

Luke glanced toward an upstairs window. It was probably Mrs. Jeffers' room, but she got the idea.

"Play your cards right and we'll see," she said, then turned to Tommy. "Are those hamburgers done yet? I'm starving."

"Me, too," Luke said, but he wasn't looking toward

the grill when he said it. His gaze was pinned directly on her.

The banter and easy camaraderie lasted through dinner. Luke seemed to have let down his guard with his brother, and Tommy's belligerence disappeared. As soon as the dishes had been cleared, all three of them by some unspoken agreement went back outside into the soft night air, where the only thing breaking the silence was the sound of crickets chirping. Lightning bugs flickered against the velvet darkness.

As if he sensed—or hoped, at least—that she wouldn't refuse, Luke took Katie's hand and led her to the hammock that was strung between two sturdy oak trees. He climbed in, then tugged her in alongside him. She went into his arms without resisting and settled her head on his shoulder.

Tommy cleared his throat and remained standing. "Maybe I should be taking off."

Katie started to protest, but Luke sent his brother a grateful look.

"Stop by the office in the morning," Luke said. "We'll talk some more."

"I told you before…" Tommy began, a belligerent note creeping back into his voice.

Katie jumped in. "There's no harm in talking, is there, Tommy?"

"Damn, but you're pushy, Katie," he accused, but there was a lightness in his voice that hadn't been there before tonight. "Seems to me you and my brother are about evenly matched."

"Does that mean you'll show up?" she asked.

"I'll show up," he said. Suddenly he grinned at the

two of them sprawled practically on top of each other in the hammock. "You two have a good evening."

"You, too," Luke said quietly.

Only after Tommy had gone did he add, "I wonder where the hell he's staying."

"He didn't tell you?"

"Not a word. I don't think he's got a dime to his name, either." He sighed heavily, and his arms around Katie tightened. "I think you may have been right. I think he's been down on his luck for a long time now and wanted to come home. Robby gave him the excuse he needed."

Though she was increasingly aware of Luke's body pressed intimately against her own, Katie tried to keep her attention focused on loftier things. If she wouldn't let Luke into her bedroom, she'd be damned if she was going to make love with him in a hammock. That would certainly violate the spirit, if not the letter of their contract.

"Are you planning to offer him work?" she asked, trying to ignore the sweep of Luke's hand from hip to thigh and back again.

"I did. And he told me to take my job and, well you know the rest."

"Can't you find some way to help him get a break in Nashville?"

"Katie, you heard us singing. Did those lyrics sound as if they stand a chance of climbing the country music charts?"

"How long did it take him to write them?"

"About ten seconds, but that's not the point."

"It is the point," she corrected. "If he can do that in ten seconds, just think what he could do if he actually worked at it. Besides, he has an incredible voice and the kind of bad-boy looks that could make him a star."

Luke stared at her. "You're serious, aren't you?"

"Dead serious. If you think I'm wrong, get him a gig closer to home and check it out. He could probably work some club in Myrtle Beach. Country music is everywhere up there."

She gazed into blue eyes that were suddenly thoughtful and added, "Besides, if Tommy finds a place for himself, if he's doing something he loves, I don't think he'll press for custody of Robby. You can end this before it ever gets to court."

Luke cupped her face in his hands. "Have I mentioned that I love you, Katie Cassidy?"

The impulsive statement sent shock waves rebounding through her. Of course, she knew he didn't mean it. Not in any way that counted. He was just grateful for the mediating she'd done that had eased tensions between him and his brother. That was all it was, she told herself sternly right before Luke's mouth settled against hers in the sweetest, gentlest kiss she'd ever experienced.

On the surface there was nothing provocative or even remotely dangerous about that kiss, but Katie's body apparently didn't know that. She responded as if it were the darkest, most sensual, most seductive invitation ever delivered. And she knew without a doubt, as her pulse scrambled and her heart thundered, that she was within seconds of losing the last fragile thread of her resolve.

It took her only one of those scant remaining seconds to bolt from the hammock, practically toppling Luke onto the ground with her.

"What the...?" Luke demanded, looking dazed.

"I'm going to bed," Katie announced with as much dignity as she could muster.

"Good. I'll—" Luke began, apparently taking her words as an invitation.

She frowned at him. "I'll see you in the morning."

He halted where he was. "I see."

He looked so taken aback, so thoroughly confused by her sudden change that Katie almost took pity on him...and herself. Only a reminder that Luke had chosen her not as a wife, but as a means to an end kept her from throwing herself back into his arms.

"I'll be at the diner by the time you get up," she said in a tone designed to put as much emotional distance back between them as possible. "Peg will probably have Robby there by then, too. If you come by..." she gazed into stormy eyes "...I'll take a break and we can all have breakfast together."

Luke looked as if he were about to protest, but finally he shook his head and turned away.

"We had a deal," Katie reminded him softly.

"I don't want to hear another word about the damned deal," he said. "Just go to bed, Katie. Go now, unless you want me to prove that you want to tear up that blasted paper even more than I do."

He was right, she thought. If she stayed, there would be no turning back, and she wasn't ready to risk it yet. She cast one last tormented look in Luke's direction, then turned and went inside. One irony did not escape her. She had smoothed over Luke's relationship with his brother, but his relationship with her was in more turmoil than ever.

Chapter 12

Luke didn't show up at the diner. Katie watched for him all morning long, delaying her break until she was practically faint with hunger. Robby had long since protested the delay and demanded pancakes with an egg on top "the way Daddy likes." Once he'd eaten, he couldn't wait to go off with Mrs. Jeffers, who was beginning to look a little frazzled, but who swore she was having more fun than she'd had in years.

At the door to the diner, Mrs. Jeffers turned and came back. "Dear, I don't want you worrying about what happened yesterday," she said, squeezing Katie's hand reassuringly. "Luke is absolutely right about the rent. We've all been taking advantage of your good nature. I'm sure we'll manage to get on the proper schedule somehow."

Katie stared at her, feeling her temper start to rise

all over again. Everyone was just assuming again that Luke was in charge. "The schedule you were on was just fine," she said tightly. "There is no need for any of you to be upset. I'll handle Luke."

Mrs. Jeffers looked alarmed by her anger. "Now, Katie, don't you dare start fighting with your new husband over this. This should be a time of joy for the two of you. Like I said, we'll manage."

"And like I said, there's no need for anyone to manage anything. You'll pay me just as you always have and that's the end of it."

"If you say so, dear," Mrs. Jeffers said doubtfully. She started toward the door, then turned back again. "One last thing, should I bring Robby back to the boarding house after our outing or take him to Peg's?"

"Bring him to the boarding house," Katie said, suddenly reaching a decision she should have made the moment she and Luke returned from Atlanta. If they were ever going to have anything resembling a normal marriage or even a decent business partnership, then they needed to get everyone back under one roof so they could all adjust together. "I think it's time everyone came home where they belonged. I'll expect to see you and Ginger and Mr. O'Reilly there tonight, as well."

The pleased expression on Mrs. Jeffers's face indicated to Katie that the woman had no idea she was part of a gauntlet being thrown down in front of Luke.

Katie was still formulating her strategy for showing Luke once and for all that he did not control the running of the boarding house, when Ginger pulled her aside.

"I heard what you said to Mrs. Jeffers," Ginger said, her voice shaking. "Do you really think you can convince Luke to back down?" Tears formed in her eyes. "I don't want to have to leave, Katie. The boarding house is home to me."

"And it will stay your home," Katie said, biting back the first sharp retort that had come to mind. "It's my boarding house. I set the rules."

"But Luke…"

"Luke may understand big business, but he doesn't know a darn thing about *my* business," Katie snapped. "I think it's time we cleared that up."

"But he told me that if I didn't pay my rent, he would evict me."

Katie saw red. "He told you that?" she said incredulously. "He actually used those words?"

Ginger nodded. "He as much as said it before you showed up yesterday. It's not like I don't see his point," she whispered, choking back a sob. "I really do, but Katie, you told me school was important. You made me see that. I can't go to school and work a full-time job to pay the rent. The hours here are about all I can manage and I'm putting that money away for college."

"Stop worrying about it. You're doing exactly what I want you to do. I'll settle this with Luke."

Ginger didn't look particularly reassured by Katie's declaration. If anything, she looked even more concerned, but whatever doubts she had she kept to herself.

Amazingly enough, so did Peg, who had come through the swinging door just in time to hear most of the conversation. Other than the inscrutable expression on her face, she might have been deaf to the obvious storm her niece intended to stir up. Katie was grateful that for once her aunt intended to let her handle her own problems.

Mr. O'Reilly, however, wasn't nearly so reticent. He

caught Katie on the front porch when she returned to the boarding house later that afternoon.

"I think it's time we had a talk," he said, indicating the rocking chair next to him.

Katie sank into it gratefully. After more than six hours on her feet, she was ready to sit down. She looked over at the retired fireman, whose expression was combative, and realized this wasn't going to be one of the friendly little chats they usually had in the afternoon. She suspected there would be no anecdotes about his heroics as a fireman in Charleston and probably not even the lecture on fire safety that she'd come to expect. The man turned positively rapturous over smoke alarms. He'd personally seen to it that the boarding house had the most technologically advanced ones on the market and he'd done it at his own expense.

"What's the problem?" she asked.

"Too many rules."

"What rules?" she inquired warily.

"These rules," he said, waving a sheet of bright canary yellow paper in front of her. "I found it under my door when I got back to my room earlier. Then your husband made it a point to let me know that he planned to enforce each and every one of them."

With a sinking sensation in the pit of her stomach, Katie reluctantly accepted the piece of paper. "Rules of the Clover Street Boarding House" headed the page. First on the list was the deadline for paying rent, with appropriate penalties for late payment. That was followed by a schedule for using the downstairs rooms that included a 10:00 p.m. curfew on weeknights, 11:00 p.m. on weekends. There were more, but when she came to rule number nine, Katie knew she'd hit on the one that Mr. O'Reilly was most upset about.

"No boarder may raid the refrigerator for between-meal snacks."

Katie groaned. What the dickens had Luke been thinking of? If he had his way, the boarding house would soon seem no friendlier than a prison. She balled the paper into a wad and said, "I'll handle this."

Mr. O'Reilly's disgruntled expression suggested he didn't have a lot of faith in her handling her husband. "If you can't," he warned, "I'll be moving out at the end of the week. Life's too short to be staying where I'm not wanted."

"Nobody will be moving out," Katie promised. Unless it was her new husband, she amended, and she might very well be chasing him out with a broom.

Katie couldn't find any sign of Luke anywhere in the house. All she found were more of those damnable colored sheets of paper, posted everywhere and shoved under every door. He'd probably placed an ad in the Clover weekly as well.

She hunted through the pile of papers on her desk until she found his new business card with the office number on it. She dialed, tapping her foot impatiently as she waited for him to pick up. When he finally did, she heard the unexpected sound of a guitar accompanying Tommy's unmistakable, sexy voice. If she hadn't been quite so furious, that might have silenced her.

Instead she said in a slow, measured voice, "Get home now, Luke Cassidy, or I won't be responsible for what you find when you get here."

Before he could say one way or the other whether he would come, she slammed the phone back into its cradle.

* * *

Luke winced as the sound of the crashing phone reverberated in his ear. Tommy must have caught his reaction, because he stopped strumming his guitar and regarded Luke worriedly.

"Everything okay?"

"Katie seems anxious to see me at home," he said in what had to be the most massive understatement he'd ever uttered. He'd never heard that particular tone of command in her voice before. He found it exhilarating...and perhaps just the slightest bit worrisome.

Tommy grinned. "Well, well, things must be heating up."

"You could say that," Luke said dryly. "Look, I'd better run. We'll talk more about this music career you want later. Give me a call tonight."

Tommy's knowing smile broadened. "Maybe I'll wait till morning, big brother. Your mood should be real mellow by then."

Luke decided to let him have his illusions. One of them might as well get some pleasure from anticipating the evening's prospects. He, unfortunately, knew better than to expect that a welcome mat was being tossed down for him.

As he walked home, he realized his timing in writing that memo to the boarding house residents might have been just a little off. Katie was putting a lot of energy into this campaign to salvage his relationship with his brother and to stave off a court battle for custody of Robby. She hadn't yet adapted to being married, though she seemed to be getting into the spirit of being a mother. She definitely wasn't quite ready to adjust to the idea that now she had someone to look out for her best interests.

Nor had she accepted that their bargain gave him some measure of control over the operation of the boarding house. Luke was willing to admit that maybe he'd been a little heavy-handed about trying to take over the financial end of things. But Katie needed to learn that she couldn't keep letting the boarding house residents pay her if and when they got around to it. He had to stop all the other ways the boarders took advantage of her as well.

Yes, indeed, he knew in his gut that he'd made the right decision in drawing up those rules. His biggest mistake had probably been talking to the tenants directly and posting the notices before mentioning them to Katie. He already knew how testy she could get about anyone trying to usurp her power around the place. She hadn't exactly welcomed his past efforts.

He found her waiting for him on the front porch, a glass of lemonade in hand that was probably only slightly more sour than her apparent mood. She did not smile when she saw him. She continued to push herself lazily back and forth in the swing as if she were trying to stir up a breeze. Her hair had been scooped up and tied with a scarf. She was wearing an old pair of cut-off jeans and a tank top. Her feet were bare. She hadn't even bothered with lipstick. She looked…entrancing.

And very, very angry, he decided with some dismay, but no surprise.

Sucking in a deep breath, Luke brazenly plunked himself into the swing next to her. She was apparently too tired to protest or to move.

"Just how mad are you?" he asked eventually.

"Mad enough."

He decided to go straight to the heart of the situation. "Do you want out of our deal?" he asked. Even as the words came out of his mouth, he realized that that thought had been behind his precipitous actions. In some weird way, he'd been testing her, hoping to discover if she would choose him over the boarding house.

His blunt question drew a startled look. "Do you?"

"No," he admitted, though he was unwilling to elaborate on just what he did want. He wasn't even sure he could put it into words or, more precisely, that he was willing to.

Katie sighed. "Neither do I." She was quiet for a long time. When she finally spoke up, she surprised him by saying, "It's not the way I imagined it would be."

"What?"

"Marriage."

"In general or to me?" It was the first time he'd even considered the possibility that she had ever cared for him enough to marry him for all the traditional reasons, rather than the trumped up business deal they'd settled for instead.

"Both, I suppose."

"That's because we're not sleeping together," he suggested, seizing the most obvious explanation he could think of—and the most convenient, given his own increasingly demanding goal. He would have seduced her right here, right now, if he weren't certain he'd get a fist in his solar plexus for his efforts.

Katie shook her head. Something in her eyes told him she pitied him.

"You really don't have a clue, do you?" she asked.

"About what?"

She sighed again. "Never mind."

Luke dared for the first time to touch the strand of hair that had escaped from her saucy ponytail. He brushed it back from her cheek, his knuckles skimming along skin that felt like satin. A thousand memories stole through him, a thousand sensations from the one night they had made love so long ago.

Was it possible that those were the memories that had drawn him back to Clover? Was it the promised joy of loving Katie that had lured him home, rather than the practical need to solve some legal dilemma that had turned his life upside down? Tommy certainly seemed to think so. He'd even begun to suspect it himself. But how would he ever know for sure? And would it even matter, if he could figure it out?

What had happened to her life? Katie wondered with a sense of desperation as she struggled to ignore the sensations Luke's casual, but persistent touch was stirring inside her. A few months ago, she had been leading a quiet, peaceful existence. She had successfully—well, almost successfully—driven Luke Cassidy from her mind. She was operating a business she loved, surrounded by people she cared about. Life hadn't been perfect, but she'd been content.

She hadn't even minded so very much that it seemed she was destined to be always a bridesmaid, but never a bride. All those couples—Hannah and Matthew, Emma and Michael, Sophie and Ford and especially Lucy and Max—were family. There would be lots of babies for her to love. Lots of people were not nearly so blessed.

Now her entire household was in an uproar because of the endless regulations Luke had instituted. And on

Friday Henrietta Myers would be moving in, which gave Katie plenty to complain about herself.

Where was she supposed to put Luke? She knew perfectly well that he intended to make himself at home in her room. She also knew that her resistance was just about taxed to the limit as it was. If the man climbed into her bed, if he so much as brushed against her during the night, she didn't have a prayer of staying out of his arms. There was so much heat between them lately, if they were caught in the rain these days they would send up steam.

It seemed to her that that risk was far more dangerous than the prospect of losing her current boarders. She could find new boarders, if she had to. Ginger, Mr. O'Reilly and the others could find adequate accommodations elsewhere, if necessary. But she absolutely could not live with the consequences of making love with Luke knowing that he wasn't in love with her, knowing that she was merely convenient, rather than the grand passion of his life as he was of hers.

If she was going to take charge of her life again, if she was going to protect herself and her boarders, then she had no choice. She had to remind Luke that this arrangement they had did not include his bullying tactics. Besides, if things worked out with Robby's custody, for all she knew he would take off. The disruptions would have been pointless, because she would never enforce them on her own.

When she could delay it no longer, she turned to face him. "I don't like what you're doing around here," she said bluntly, waving the sheet of canary yellow paper under his nose.

Luke stiffened. His hand fell away from her shoulder as if he'd been scalded. The faint teasing glint in his eyes faded as his expression immediately turned somber.

"I know I should have talked to you first," he admitted. "But I know how you are. You would have tried to talk me out of those rules."

"Damn right, I would have. The disruptions around here have gotten out of hand," she said, perversely wishing she could tease his lips back into a smile. She barely resisted the temptation to try, to run the tip of her finger along the velvet skin of his lower lip to encourage it into an upward curve. Touching him right now would be a very bad idea. Very bad.

"Our deal put me in charge of the financial end of running the boarding house," he reminded her.

"It put me in charge of dealing with the tenants," she retorted. "As it is, Ginger's terrified you're going to evict her. Where would she get an idea like that?"

"I had a talk with her," he admitted. "I thought she should understand that we're running a business. I hope you didn't undermine the message I was trying to get across."

Katie scowled at him. "I'm sure that's how you would see it. I told her we would never evict her."

"She's never paid one cent of rent," Luke pointed out in that calm, reasonable way that made Katie want to grind her teeth. "I went back over the books for all the months she's been here."

"She's seventeen years old. It's more important that she stay off the streets of some big city and finish school. Besides, she helps me out around here."

Luke shot her a look of total disbelief. "Doing what?"

Katie had to be quick on her feet to answer that one,

especially since Ginger hadn't even been around since she had gone to work at the diner. "She changes the beds, helps with the laundry, straightens up, vacuums, those kinds of things," she said, blithely ignoring the fact that Ginger probably didn't even have a clue where the cleaning supplies were kept.

"If she does all that, why do I see you changing sheets, doing tub after tub of laundry and shoving a vacuum around?"

Katie winced. "I said she helps. I didn't say she did everything. If I paid her a wage, it would more than make up for what she would have to pay for the room. I'm coming out ahead on the deal."

"Then let's make her a part-time employee," Luke countered. "That way she'll have very specific responsibilities and she'll be able to pay her own way."

"What good does it do to give her money and have her give it right back to us? That's just a bunch of paperwork."

"It'll teach her responsibility," Luke insisted.

Katie tried to make him see reason. "She doesn't need to feel responsible," she said impatiently. "She needs to feel like she's part of a family."

That silenced him.

Taking advantage of that, Katie plunged on. "Now about Mr. O'Reilly. You talked to him, too, didn't you? You didn't just hand him that piece of paper."

"We had a chat over coffee this morning, yes."

"A chat? Is that what you call it when you declare that the kitchen is off-limits between meals?"

"But…"

Katie ignored him. "How much can an occasional midnight snack cost? Besides, it—"

"Let me guess," Luke said resignedly. "It makes him feel like he's part of a family."

Katie beamed at him. Maybe he was catching on, after all. "Exactly," she said, pleased.

He studied her intently. "Do you know what would make me feel like part of a family?"

There was something in his voice that set Katie's senses on fire. Her gaze locked with his. The intensity burning between them made her tremble. "What?"

"Sharing your bed."

She couldn't seem to catch her breath. "Oh, no..." she began in a choked voice. The rest of the protest died on her lips when he pressed a silencing finger against them.

As if he sensed she was weakening, he coaxed, "I'm your husband. That's where I belong. You wouldn't want me to feel like an outsider in my own home, would you?"

"No, but..."

He lowered his head until his lips hovered over hers, so close his minty breath fanned her hot skin and his purely masculine scent surrounded her. Katie's breath snagged in her throat. When his mouth finally settled on hers, the whole world tilted on its axis. Suddenly it was impossible to recall what they were arguing about, impossible to think of anything except the indescribable way she felt when Luke touched her.

"Not fair," she murmured eventually. Her arms seemed to have twined themselves around his neck of their own free will. She couldn't find the resolve to remove them.

"I don't recall any mention of *fair* in the wedding vows," Luke said, a surprising twinkle appearing in his eyes. That spark chased away the last of the shadows. "I do seem to recall an expression that all's fair in love and war."

His expression suddenly sobered. "I want a real marriage, Katie, in every way."

Love? A real marriage? Her heart pounded ecstatically. Katie studied Luke's face to see if he realized what he'd said. Or was it one more example of words slipping out with no substance behind them? Just a convenient ploy to lure her into his bed?

Then, again, could it possibly be true that he loved her half as much as she loved him? His enigmatic expression told her nothing. Maybe this was something she was going to have to take on faith. Maybe it required a giant-size risk. She was already in this relationship up to her neck, anyway.

"You can move into our room on Friday, when Mrs. Myers gets here."

"Tonight," he argued, evidently not satisfied with the hard-won victory. He sprinkled more persuasive kisses across her brow and onto her cheeks.

"You're pushing it, Cassidy," she said without much oomph behind the protest.

"I'm desperate," he admitted in a way that gave her goose bumps. "Besides, how else will I know you're not just letting me in because my room is rented?"

His kisses deepened, leaving Katie breathless, her senses reeling.

"Tonight," she agreed eventually, because if anything, she wanted him in her bed even more desperately than he wanted to be there. Fighting it any longer seemed likely to be an exercise in futility.

"Tonight," she repeated in a whisper that only hinted at the deep, unspoken yearning in her heart. It would either be the best decision she had ever made...or the worst.

Chapter 13

There were too damned many people living in the boarding house, Luke decided about nine o'clock. He and Katie were still surrounded by boarders, to say nothing of his son who was too excited about finally living in his new home "for real" to go off to bed. If Luke hadn't recognized that it would be opening yet another major can of worms, he would have ordered every one of them back to the Clover Street Hotel so he and Katie could have some privacy.

It was another nerve-racking hour before they all finally began drifting off to their own rooms. Alone with Katie at last, Luke met her gaze and saw a riot of emotions burning in the emerald depths of her eyes. He was sure his own eyes mirrored that same sort of turbulence. He'd been aching for her ever since she'd agreed to let him move into their room that night. Longer, actually. He could trace this hunger back to the first day he'd seen her after his return to Clover.

"Ready?" he asked, holding out his hand.

Gazing at him solemnly, she stood and came slowly toward him. He couldn't miss her nervous, hard swallow, or the faint trembling as she placed her hand in his.

"Scared?" he asked, surprised.

"Of you?" she said. "Never."

He found the touch of defiance in her voice amusing. "Of us, then?"

She struggled visibly with her answer before admitting what he could already read in her eyes. "A little. It's been a long time, Luke."

"Too long," he agreed softly, his gaze locked with hers. "Far too long." He felt a smile tugging at his lips. "For the first time, I actually feel like a newlywed." Because he wanted her to understand that he was referring not just to their recent wedding, but to the past, he added, "For the first time *ever*."

Color bloomed in Katie's cheeks. "Me, too," she said with a touching shyness.

Suddenly he couldn't bear to wait a moment longer. He scooped her into his arms and headed for the stairs.

"Luke, what on earth are you doing?" she demanded, laughing.

"It's tradition," he reminded her.

"But you've already carried me across the threshold once."

"That was for show," he said. "This time it's just the two of us. Tonight's the night our marriage really begins."

With a soft little sigh, Katie settled against his chest. An emotion more powerful than anything he'd ever experienced rushed through him. Tenderness, yearning and something that even his jaded heart recognized as love filled him.

Oh, he knew there were doubts to overcome, hers and his. He knew there were obstacles in their path, not the least of which was the impending custody battle. But suddenly, with every fiber of his being, he recognized that this was where he wanted to be, where he belonged.

And the woman in his arms was the only one he would ever love. Years ago he'd fallen in love with a girl. Today Katie was all grown up, a woman of strength and beauty and generosity. Those qualities had always been there, but they'd matured.

Today Caitlyn Jones Cassidy was a spirited force to be reckoned with. And she was his, legally anyway… as long as he didn't do something stupid and blow it. Tonight was his chance to cement their relationship. Otherwise he feared that when Robby's custody was finally settled, when she had lived up to that part of their bargain, Katie could very well walk away. He knew that if she did his life would never be the same.

When Luke had nudged open the door to her room, Katie gasped in amazement. He'd filled the room with flowers—bright, splashy, fragrant flowers. The ceiling fan created a deliciously scented breeze. A bottle of champagne was on ice in an elegant silver bucket.

And somehow he had found the filmy negligee that had been meant for her wedding night. It had been shoved in the back of a dresser drawer, behind oversize T-shirts and warm flannel gowns. At the thought of Luke's hands sorting through her things, a delightful heat began to spread slowly through her. Just the sight of that pale chiffon, shimmering against the bed's dark green comforter, warmed her.

"You've been busy," she observed, looking into eyes filled with anticipation and blatant masculine desire, rather than the smug satisfaction she might have expected under the circumstances.

"I thought this called for a celebration," he said.

"Do you intend to celebrate like this whenever you get your way?" she asked, unable to resist the tart question.

"If I do, will you give in more often?"

She grinned at the teasing note in his voice. "I wouldn't count on it."

"Somehow I thought that would be your answer," he said, sounding surprisingly pleased. He held up the negligee. "Want some privacy while you change into this?"

She snatched it from his hand and headed for the adjoining bathroom.

"Don't take too long," he pleaded in a voice that had grown husky.

"You can keep busy opening the champagne," she said, wishing she had a glass to take along with her. She wasn't sure where she'd get the nerve to emerge from the bathroom in that revealing gown without it.

She recognized as soon as she'd closed the door behind her that she would collapse with a bad case of stage fright if she didn't hurry. She was all thumbs as it was as she stripped off her clothes, took a hurried shower, then pulled the filmy gown on. She stood in front of the steamy mirror and marveled at what she saw.

There was a faint hint of curl in her tousled hair. Her cheeks were bright with becoming color. Her eyes were sparkling with anticipation. She looked...like a bride, every bit as radiant as the picture-perfect bride Peg had described for her with such longing. Dear heaven, she told herself with a sense of amazement, after what seemed to be an eternity of waiting, she really was about to be a bride in more than name only. Luke's bride.

Drawing in a deep, trembling breath, she finally opened the door. She had to cling to the frame for support when she saw Luke standing at the window, wearing only his dark trousers. The well-defined muscles in his shoulders and back seemed to beckon for her touch. His skin was more bronzed now than it had been when he'd first arrived back in Clover. He looked even more breathtakingly masculine than he had six years ago.

Yet she knew exactly how he would feel if she stroked her fingers over his bare flesh. The skin would be supple, and it would burn wherever she dared to caress. She absorbed all of this in the space of a heartbeat.

At the sound of the door opening, he turned, facing her, his expression avid as his gaze swept over her. The hunger and electricity charging that gaze could have lit up the entire town of Clover, maybe the entire state of South Carolina.

Since Katie couldn't seem to move, he picked up the two flutes of champagne and came slowly toward her. She accepted the glass. Her pulse skittered wildly as their fingers brushed.

"You look…breathtaking," he said in a voice that had turned low and seductive.

"I feel…" Katie found she couldn't begin to describe the sensations rippling through her. She felt slightly breathless, slightly anxious and deliciously aroused all at once.

Luke carefully set his glass down and reached for

her. "You feel," he began, turning her words around and
filling in the space she'd left blank, "like fire and silk."

His fingers skimmed along her arms, leaving heat in
their wake. That same delicate stroking over sheer chiffon made her skin tingle with shivery awareness. Her
nipples hardened at once, responding to the repeated
return of tormenting touches. When he lowered his head
and took one sensitive, thinly covered peak into his
mouth, she shuddered, reaching for his bare shoulders
and clinging just to remain upright.

The sensation was exquisite, sweeter than she'd recalled in her wildest memories of that other time, that
other tender claiming.

Unfortunately, rather than adding to the provocative
sensations Luke was stirring in her now, the memories
suddenly cooled her ardor. Oh, her body was his, responding to his touches with predictable abandon. She
couldn't have prevented that if she'd tried. She'd waited
far too long for this moment.

But her heart withdrew into a protective shell. Even
as Luke entered her with a slow, thrilling stroke that
filled her and lured her toward an explosive release,
somewhere deep inside she remained aloof and terrified.

Terrified that once again their love was an illusion,
that once again it wouldn't last.

And when Luke saw the silent tears spilling down
her cheeks, when he asked what was wrong in a voice
that shook with concern, Katie couldn't answer. She
simply wrapped her arms around him and held on for
dear life, hoping that somehow, some way she would
never have to let go.

* * *

Ironically, after all his sneaky conniving to make it happen, Luke found that making love to Katie was bittersweet. As perfectly attuned as they had been in bed, as sweetly erotic and wickedly demanding as the night had been, something had been missing. Something had gone terribly wrong, leaving Katie in tears she couldn't—or wouldn't—explain.

A few weeks ago, absorbed with his single-minded pursuit of marriage, not love, he probably wouldn't have noticed the lack at all, but now he recognized it for what it surely had to be. Katie had made love with him, but she wasn't *in love* with him. She had held something back, some essential part of herself.

Sitting in the kitchen at dawn, drinking a cup of coffee, he couldn't help thinking about the first time they had made love. Katie had been totally inexperienced. He had been young and anxious. But love had made every touch magic, every kiss joyous. There had been no holding back for either of them.

Last night, with Katie asleep in his arms, he'd felt a fleeting sense of triumph. This morning, after hours of lying awake analyzing it, he realized that it had been a shallow victory. Katie had shared her body, but not her heart. He wondered bleakly if he would ever get that back again.

It all came back to this damned bargain they'd struck. He wondered if either of them would ever trust the other's motives as long as their deal remained on the table. Even as they had been lifted to the height of passion, even as she had murmured his name over and over, Luke couldn't help remembering everything that had led to their being together in that bed.

And perversely he couldn't help thinking that if Katie loved him, if she had ever loved him, she would have told him to take a flying leap when he'd suggested this marriage of convenience. She would have held out for the declaration of love and commitment she deserved.

No, the truth of it was that all she wanted from him was a way to save her boarding house and support this surrogate family of hers.

He had thought sex would make him part of Katie's life, part of her family. Instead, it had left him feeling lonelier than ever.

He wondered what would happen when the boarding house's bottom line was in the black and the custody suit was over. Would Katie stick with him or leave? He was more certain than ever that he knew the answer. She would go.

In those gray minutes of first light, he reached a decision. He had gotten them into this mess by thinking only of his own short-term need for a wife and a mother for his son. He would get them out again by focusing on what he really needed, Katie's love.

It shouldn't take more than what? A little ingenuity? He was acclaimed for that. A little determination? The word mule-headed had been applied to him more than once. And a lifetime of knowing Katie? There was no one on earth who knew her better.

To accomplish a miracle, though, he needed time. More time than the wheels of justice he'd oiled would give him. With that in mind, he called his attorney, oblivious to the fact that he might be waking Andrew Lawton from a sound sleep. But Andrew had disrupted his share of Luke's nights when he'd been going through his own very messy divorce.

"When are we due to go to court for the custody rul-ing?" Luke asked without even a "good morning" for the man he'd first met within weeks after he'd arrived in Atlanta. They'd been friends ever since, as well as business associates.

"Luke, what the devil..." Andrew muttered, sound-ing both sleepy and disgruntled.

Luke repeated his question.

"It's on the judge's calendar for the end of the month. It could be anytime that last week in June," Andrew told him, sounding considerably more alert once he grasped that this wasn't just idle curiosity on Luke's part. "Tommy's lawyer has been pressing to have it moved up, though. He agrees with us that for Robby's sake this needs to be concluded as quickly as possible."

It was exactly as Luke had feared. His time with Katie was running out. "Delay it," Luke said.

There was a lengthy silence before Andrew re-sponded. "I thought you wanted to get it over with," he said, sounding confused. "We're prepared. The reports are into the court. Why wait for—?"

Luke cut in. "I want you to drag this out as long as possible."

"Luke, you're not making any sense," Andrew pro-tested. "Just last week..."

"I don't give a damn what I said last week."

"Okay, what's going on?" Andrew asked quietly. "You and Katie aren't having problems, are you? Do you need time to work them out? If that's the case, the longer we delay, the more likely Tommy will find out about the problem and use it against you."

Luke sighed. "There is no problem, at least not one that I can't solve, if you'll just buy me some time. Please,

Andrew, do what you can. Take a vacation. Tell them you've got a case in Tasmania or something. Just get the case delayed."

"I'll do what I can," Andrew agreed finally. "If you need to talk, buddy, let me know."

"I don't need to talk," Luke said curtly and hung up. He turned to find Katie staring at him in open-mouthed astonishment.

"I think you do," she said quietly, her gaze cutting straight through him.

"Do what?"

"Need to talk." She poured herself a cup of coffee, seated herself very precisely across from him at the kitchen table and regarded him expectantly. "You can start anytime now. Why would you ask your lawyer to delay the custody case?"

Luke looked everywhere but at his wife. "I just told Andrew that I want to be sure we're fully prepared. This is too important to make mistakes."

"Does Andrew think everything's ready? Is he in the habit of making mistakes?"

"Andrew doesn't know everything, and everyone makes mistakes."

"What is it that your attorney doesn't know?"

The direct question stymied him. He didn't want to admit that he was buying time for the two of them, that he wanted to solidify what they had begun the night before—a real marriage. And there was also the possibility that Katie had been right about Tommy. Perhaps with just a little more time he and his brother could mend fences and Tommy would drop the suit. Time seemed the answer to everything.

"I just think it's for the best," he said finally.

Katie regarded him incredulously. "For whom? What about Robby? Don't you think he's beginning to suspect that something serious is going on? He can't help but feel the tension every time Tommy calls here. Sooner or later he's going to start asking why he hasn't met his uncle. And how much longer do you think you can keep Tommy from barging in and telling him the truth? If you're going to drag this out intentionally, then you'd better sit down with your son and tell him exactly what's happening, before he hears it from your brother."

"Katie..."

Before he could get out another word, she'd grabbed her cup of coffee and headed out the back door, letting it slam behind her. Luke stared after her.

"Well, that certainly went well," he muttered to himself. At this rate, his damned plan would land them in divorce court.

Katie had no idea what had happened to Luke between the time they went upstairs together and the moment he'd slipped out of bed and abandoned her that morning a few days earlier. No matter how she tried, she couldn't begin to figure out why Luke had placed that call to his attorney.

Over the past few days, though, she had watched in bemusement as Luke seemed to be transformed before her eyes.

She had come home one day to find him tutoring Ginger in math, leading her step by step through a tricky problem with admirable patience. Ginger's head bobbed in understanding as he explained each step. And when she reached the correct answer to the next problem completely on her own, she beamed at Luke with an expression akin to hero worship.

The next night, unable to sleep, Katie had wandered down to the kitchen at midnight and found Mr. O'Reilly and Luke there ahead of her, huge bowls of ice cream in front of them. She stayed back in the shadows and listened. Mr. O'Reilly was telling Luke all about the time he'd saved a little girl from a blaze in the rat-infested basement of a tenement. Katie had heard the story a dozen times and each time tears had come to her eyes. Luke seemed equally shaken by the near tragedy.

"Dear God," he murmured. "Maybe we'd better take a look through here tomorrow. Make sure all the alarms are in working order."

"They are," the retired fireman assured him. "I see to it myself. Nothing like that'll happen to Katie, if I'm around to prevent it. That girl is like a daughter to me." He met Luke's gaze. "And that boy of yours, he's a real pistol. Livens the place up. Mrs. Jeffers is looking downright young again, now that she has a little one to do for."

Luke's expression turned speculative. "So you've noticed what a fine figure of a woman Mrs. Jeffers is."

Red crept into Mr. O'Reilly's cheeks. "Now don't you go getting any ideas. I'm too old to be carrying on."

Luke's low laughter warmed Katie's heart.

"You're never too old," he declared.

Pleased more than she could say by the scene she had stumbled on, Katie had slipped away before either of them saw her.

Just this morning she found a stack of neat little printed notices on the table where whoever picked up the mail each day left it for the others. She picked one up and was stunned when she read that the weekly rent was being cut by ten percent. She couldn't decide whether to laugh or cry. Luke had clearly lost his mind. She'd wanted him to loosen up, but at this rate he would bankrupt her.

With one of the slips in hand, she headed straight down the street to his office. He was leaning back in his fancy new leather chair behind his fancy new mahogany desk, looking pleased as punch about something.

"Are you okay?" she asked straight out.

He grinned. "Better than ever."

She plucked the little white notice from her purse and shoved it across his desk. "Then maybe you can explain what you were thinking when you did this."

"The economy's tight," he explained without batting an eye. "We have to be competitive."

"With whom? There's no place else in town that offers people room and board. And last I heard the manager of the hotel wasn't tutoring his guests in his spare time."

Luke shrugged. "It's no big deal."

"What happened to all that talk about sound fiscal responsibility? Are you trying to bankrupt me?"

"We can afford to absorb a few losses on the boarding house. I have other investments that will more than balance things out."

Katie couldn't believe what she was hearing. "Those are your investments. The boarding house is mine. You promised to get it onto a sound financial footing."

His expression perfectly bland, he said, "Some things are more important than money."

Katie regarded him suspiciously. A statement like that sounded like heresy coming from him. "Such as?"

"Family," he replied quietly.

"Family?" she repeated as if it were a foreign concept. "Luke, what is going on here?"

He leaned forward, his gaze locking with hers. "I have finally figured out what's important in life," he said. "Now I intend to do everything in my power to see that I get it."

If there hadn't been such a note of grim determination in his voice, Katie might have laughed. She recalled the night she'd hauled everyone back to the boarding house as a way of throwing a gauntlet down in front of her husband. It seemed he'd just returned the challenge.

She still wasn't certain exactly what was going on in Luke's head, but she was beginning to grasp one thing. Finally it appeared they were both chasing the same dream.

Chapter 14

"We're going out tonight," Luke announced when he was finally able to snag Katie for a second during the morning rush at Peg's Diner.

There was a spark of mischief in his eyes she hadn't seen since they were teenagers. "Where?"

"You'll see. Just put on your party clothes and be ready by six."

"Who's baby-sitting Robby?"

"Don't worry. It's all taken care of."

"You think of everything," she said, though her tone wasn't entirely complimentary.

Ignoring the jibe, he winked at her. "Six o'clock," he reminded her and headed for the door. He stopped briefly to whisper something to Peg, who laughed and sneaked a quick look in Kate's direction.

"What the devil were the two of you conspiring about?" Katie asked her aunt.

"We were not conspiring," Peg said, regarding her indignantly. "Luke was just making a comment about the weather. It's gonna be another scorcher today." She fanned herself with a menu as if to emphasize it.

"It's air-conditioned in here," Katie reminded her before walking away in disgust. They were up to something. She knew it.

Even so, she was ready promptly at six. Luke joined her a moment later, wearing the same suit he'd worn for their wedding. Before Katie could catch her breath and comment on how handsome he looked, Ginger bounded down the stairs in a dress Katie had never seen before and slinky high heels. Mrs. Jeffers, wearing a grey silk suit and an abundance of perfume, followed on the arm of Mr. O'Reilly, who was dressed fit to kill, as well.

Obviously she and Luke were not going out for a romantic dinner, Katie decided with some disappointment just as Peg turned up wearing her best dress, the one she usually saved for holidays and weddings.

"Everybody ready?" Luke asked cheerfully.

Katie planted her feet and regarded him warily. "What's this all about? And where is Robby?"

"Robby is with Lucy and Max. Now stop asking so many questions or you'll spoil the surprise."

"I really hate surprises," she muttered.

"Since when?" Peg asked, urging her toward the door. "From the time you were a little, bitty thing, you loved surprises."

"Not anymore," she declared right before her mouth went slack with shock.

Outside, a long, sleek limousine was parked at the curb. Half the neighborhood was standing around gawking at it. Her boarders strolled down the sidewalk as regally as any royalty on earth. Even Ginger managed to act as if this were an everyday occurrence. Katie had no choice but to go along or spoil everyone else's good time, but her suspicious instincts were working overtime.

An hour later as they headed north along the coast, she began to get an inkling of where they were headed at least. There were some wonderful seafood restaurants between Clover and Myrtle Beach. Unfortunately the limo sped past most of them.

Just as she was about to demand answers to all the questions reeling in her head, the limo pulled off the road. Katie peered around at the large, unfamiliar, indistinctive parking lot, then glanced up at the marquee. A smile broke across her face as she read, Appearing Tonight Only, Country Singer Tom Cassidy.

She threw her arms around Luke's neck and kissed him. "You did it! You helped him get a job singing."

Luke shook his head. "As much as I'd like to take the credit, I can't. He did it himself. I just made a couple of calls. The club's owners wouldn't have brought him in if he hadn't performed well at the audition."

"Have you heard him sing?" She thought of the night in her backyard, "I mean really sing, not just fooling around."

"A little at the office one day," he admitted, reminding her of the time she'd called and overheard Tommy's guitar in the background. "It sounded good to me, but I'm tone deaf."

"That's true enough," Katie agreed, but she couldn't seem to stop grinning at him. The fact that he had taken a chance on Tommy, had offered him this shot, it had to mean that the two of them were finally making their peace.

The management of the small restaurant had clearly been expecting them. A special table had been set up near the stage, and they were ushered there with a maximum of fuss. Katie could see that Luke had gone out of his way to see that the others all felt as if they were as special tonight as Tommy. He was as attentive to Mrs. Jeffers as he was to Peg. He teased Ginger and joked with Mr. O'Reilly.

He treated them all like family, Katie thought with a sense of astonishment. A warm feeling of contentment stole through her at the realization.

And when Tommy finally came out to sing, there was no mistaking the pride shining in Luke's eyes. He reached for Katie's hand and clung to it. His foot tapped to the faster rhythms and his eyes shimmered with unshed tears, when Tommy's voice caressed the notes of the more emotional love-gone-wrong songs.

When the mellow tones and words of heartache ended, applause erupted with an enthusiasm that would have rivaled any Garth Brooks concert, albeit the crowd was much smaller. Luke stared around him at the rest of the audience with an unmistakable mix of amazement and delight.

"He was good, wasn't he?" he asked Katie, a grin spreading across his face.

"Fantastic," she confirmed. "Offhand, I'd say your brother has what it takes to make it."

A moment later Tommy emerged from the shadows and walked hesitantly toward them, stopping along the way to accept congratulations from others in the audience. His gaze, though, never left his big brother.

When he was only a few feet away, Luke rose and went to meet him.

Katie couldn't hear what was said, but she had no trouble at all guessing what it meant when Luke opened his arms and embraced his brother. Tears clung to her lashes and spilled down her cheeks as she watched them.

Suddenly she felt a slight tug on her arm and turned to look into Ginger's awestruck eyes. "Would you introduce me?" she pleaded. "He is totally awesome!"

Tommy? Awesome? Katie barely hid her grin. Then she took another look at her brother-in-law and realized that she'd been right when she'd told Luke that Tommy's brooding good looks would appeal to women. He'd dressed in black, from his cowboy hat down to his boots. The attire did wicked things to his blue eyes, which seemed brighter and more alive tonight than at any other time Katie could recall.

Katie slid over to the chair Luke had vacated and gestured to Tommy to sit in hers. When she introduced him to Ginger, the teenager's face turned bright red for a second before she gathered her composure. To Katie's astonishment, Tommy seemed equally dumbstruck. She thanked heaven that Ginger's eighteenth birthday was less than a week away. She got the distinct impression that Tommy would be coming to call.

Before she could start worrying about what kind of influence Tommy might be on Ginger or how Luke would feel about him hanging around the boarding house, Luke reached out and tugged her onto the tiny dance floor. His arms came around her and she nestled against his chest.

"Happy?" he asked.

"Very." She looked up at him. "You must be very proud."

"Stunned is more like it. If only I'd listened to him years ago, things might have been different."

"He told you he wanted to sing years ago?"

"Once or twice. I told him it was impractical and dismissed it." He sighed. "I think that was really behind his running off, maybe even more so than Betty Sue's pregnancy. If only I hadn't been so bull-headed, so certain I knew what was right for him, maybe you and I…"

Katie reached up and silenced him with a touch. "There's no point in looking back."

"What about forward, Katie?" he asked, searching her face. "Is there a reason to look forward?"

Katie had no ready answer for that. The future seemed so uncertain. "Let's just concentrate on the present," she said, moving even more tightly into his embrace.

"You can't just live for the moment," Luke protested. "You have to plan ahead, be responsible."

"You're backsliding," she teased him gently. "This very moment is the only one we can control and I, for one, don't want to waste it on a silly argument."

She could feel Luke's grin against her cheek.

"You have better things in mind?" he asked with a hopeful note in his voice.

"Much better," she said, looping her arms around his neck so that she could snuggle closer still.

"Ah, yes," Luke murmured with a sigh. "That is definitely much better."

One song ended and another began. They barely noticed.

"Um, Katie, do you suppose we could plan ahead just a little? Say, maybe for an hour or two from now?"

She laughed. "You can dream, Cassidy, but you can't plan."

"Okay, but just so you know, I am having one very erotic dream."

"Me, too, Cassidy. Me, too."

Unfortunately the dream got waylaid. Just about the time they'd gotten everyone settled after the drive back to Clover, there was a tap on the front door. Luke looked as if he'd like to ignore it, but Katie knew that no one would turn up at that late hour unless it was important.

"If you don't answer it, I will," she said.

"Entertaining visitors was not what I had in mind," he said, his gaze roaming over her provocatively one last time just as he opened the door. "Tommy! What are you doing here?"

"I thought we should talk."

"Tonight? Can't it wait until morning? Besides, I thought you'd be up until dawn celebrating."

"The only people I want to celebrate with are here," Tommy said, sounding wistful.

"Well, get in here, then," Katie said. She studied Tommy's somber expression and decided celebrating was actually the last thing on his mind. She stood and headed for the stairs. "Why don't I leave the two of you alone?"

Tommy shook his head. "No, stay, please. This involves you, too." He glanced toward the stairs. "Is Robby here?"

Luke shook his head. "He's spending the night with Lucy and Max."

"Good. Then there's no chance he'll overhear."

Luke tensed at once. "Overhear what? Dammit, Tommy, tonight's not the time to get into a custody discussion."

Tommy faced him squarely. "I think it is."

Katie heard the determination in his voice with a sense of amazement. Tommy had changed since his return to Clover. She could see it. It went beyond the new Western clothes, the neatly trimmed hair, his more mature face. There was a quiet resolve about him that she was forced to admire. She had a feeling that when the time came, the judge's decision wouldn't be an easy one. It would have been far more clear-cut if Tommy had remained the rebellious, irresponsible person who'd first run out on his pregnant lover.

Katie clenched her hands nervously and worried that Luke had seriously underestimated his brother's determination to become a part of Robby's life.

"I know you think I just wanted your money," Tommy began. "You've said it often enough." He met Luke's gaze evenly. "But that was never it. I suppose a part of it was that I wanted to hurt you."

"And you were willing to use Robby to do it," Luke said flatly.

"I wasn't thinking about him, not really," Tommy said. "It was a purely selfish decision. In some sort of twisted way, I think I was jealous of him."

Luke regarded him incredulously. "Jealous? Of a baby?"

Tommy shrugged. "Sounds ridiculous when I say it. But he had you in his life, and he came between you and me. I know I used to mess up, and you bailed me out over and over. Seemed like that was just the nature of our relationship. Then Betty Sue got pregnant and you chose her and the baby over me."

"I chose them *because* of you," Luke said, looking faintly bewildered by Tommy's anger and hurt. "You left me no choice. One of us had to do the right thing."

Tommy's smile was rueful. "You never gave me time to figure that out. Just wham-bang, you took care of it. You sacrificed your feelings for Katie." He shot her an apologetic look. "When I saw that, do you know the kind of guilt I felt? I had to stay away. There was no place for me here knowing how many lives I'd wrecked."

"If you felt so much guilt, then how could you fight me for custody of Robby?" Luke asked, looking shaken by everything Tommy had revealed so far.

"Because I knew in my gut it would send you running back here. I hoped Katie would take you back." He sucked in a deep breath, then admitted, "I owed you and I wanted my brother back."

Luke stood and began to pace. He raked his fingers through his hair, before he finally turned to stare down at his brother. "You were willing to go into court and ask for Robby, to try to take him from me and you thought *that* would get me back?"

"No," Tommy said quietly. "I thought it would get your attention."

"Well, it sure as hell did that!" Luke exploded. "Of all the idiotic, selfish, harebrained schemes." He stopped in front of Tommy. "So now what? Why the hell are you here tonight?"

Tommy flinched at his brother's anger, but his own voice didn't waver. "To tell you that I've withdrawn the suit. Whether you believe it or not, I don't think I could have gone through with it, no matter how things had turned out between us."

He looked from Luke to Katie, then back to his big brother. Katie waited for Luke to speak, but he remained silent.

Finally, looking dejected, Tommy sighed and stood up. "I'll be going now." At the door he paused. Without turning around, he whispered, "I love you, Luke."

And then he was gone.

"Luke?"

"Not now, Katie," he said in a tight tone of dismissal.

Katie felt as if she'd been slapped, rejected. They should have been celebrating the end of the custody battle, but there was so much more at stake. Her heart aching for her husband, Katie headed for the stairs. She paused beside him and put her hand on his cheek. It was damp with tears she doubted he was even aware he'd shed. "Are you coming up?"

"Maybe in a while," he said, his expression bleak.

"I'll be waiting," she promised.

But hours later, when sunlight began to spill through the curtains, Katie was still wide-awake and alone. And when she left the house to go to work at the diner, there was no sign of Luke at all.

It was hours before Katie finally saw Luke again. He wandered into the diner right after noon and took a booth in the back. Katie was waiting on customers at the counter. Ginger was waiting on the tables. She came back to Katie within seconds of taking Luke's order.

"He wants to see you."

"Now?" she asked incredulously. She was still too

miffed about his running out on her to risk speaking to him in a crowded diner.

"He seems really upset about something," Ginger observed worriedly. "We could switch for a while and you could take the tables. I think everybody has their order right now, anyway. You'd have a few minutes to talk."

Katie shook her head. "This isn't the place," she insisted stubbornly. She didn't want to hear that Luke intended to end their marriage in the middle of the diner. What else could he possibly be so anxious to say that would put that grim expression on his face? "But if you wouldn't mind watching the counter for a few minutes, I could use a break."

"Sure, but…"

"Thanks," she said and ducked into the ladies' room, the one place she was certain Luke wouldn't follow her.

She was still hiding out in the restroom fifteen minutes later, when the door opened and Lucy appeared. "You okay?"

Katie managed a wobbly smile for her best friend. "I've been better. Where'd you come from?"

"I stopped by to see how things were going. Luke told me you were in here. I think he was just about ready to come busting in himself." She studied Katie from head to toe. "So how are you really?"

"I'm scared, Lucy."

"Of losing Robby?"

"Of losing both of them. Tommy's withdrawn his suit. But with the custody issue resolved Luke has no reason to stay married to me."

"Hogwash! He's in love with you. He has been forever."

Katie didn't believe her, but she clung to Lucy's reassurances, anyway. It gave her the strength to emerge from the restroom and face Luke with the whole damn town looking on. There was an odd air of expectancy in the diner, as if everyone knew something was up between the two of them.

Katie would have waited until everyone left, but Luke and Ginger, with a little help from Peg, conspired to force her hand. Ginger had taken over the counter. Peg was handling the tables. They'd left her with only the one station to cover, Luke's booth. Maybe she should have just made a dash for it, but she finally resigned herself to hearing the bad news now and getting it over with.

She marched over to her husband.

"Have a seat," he invited.

"I don't think so. Are you planning to file for divorce now that you have what you want?" she demanded, hands on hips, her chin thrust forward combatively.

Luke seemed taken aback at first. Then his expression turned even more bleak. "I suppose that could be one interpretation of our deal. It wasn't in writing, though."

"Just implied," she agreed.

She drew in a deep breath and decided to go for broke. He might leave, anyway, but he wouldn't go without getting a fight. "Then there was your side of the bargain. I took a look at the books. They're a shambles. Now that everyone is getting ice cream and cookies in the evening, now that the rent has been lowered…" She shrugged. "Looks to me like you have a long way to go to get things straightened out around here."

A faint spark of hope lit his eyes. "You want me to stay?"

She refused to be the only one making an admission here. "If you want to."

"Do you want me to stay?" he repeated insistently.

Katie sighed and relented. Two stubborn people in one marriage was at least one, if not two, too many. "I've wanted you with me since I was twelve years old. Don't you know yet how much I love you?"

"You love me?"

"Oh, for heaven's sakes," she said impatiently. "Do you think you would ever have gotten across that threshold, if I didn't? It didn't have a blasted thing to do with saving this boarding house. I would have managed somehow."

Luke snagged her wrist and toppled her into his arms. Katie felt a heavy sigh shudder through him.

"When Tommy walked out last night, I should have been shouting with joy, but I couldn't. All I could think about was that it was over with us," he murmured against her cheek. "I don't know what I would have done, if you'd said you wanted a divorce."

Katie touched his shadowed cheek. "Why?"

"Because…"

"Not good enough. Why?" She kept her gaze pinned on his.

"You're my best friend."

She smiled. "Better. Keep going."

Suddenly he was laughing. "Because I love you, Caitlyn Cassidy."

"By golly, I think he's got it," she said.

Suddenly Katie heard Mr. O'Reilly's whoop of glee from the next booth, then Mrs. Jeffers' hushed admonishment about eavesdropping.

"What did they say?" Ginger demanded from clear across the diner.

"He said he loves her," Mr. O'Reilly reported.

"Then they're going to stay married?" Ginger asked.

"Sounds that way to me," he confirmed.

Katie and Luke exchanged a look. "I had no idea they even knew what was going on," she said, just as Henrietta Myers started singing a rousing rendition of "Oh Promise Me" at the top of her lungs.

"I guess she's auditioning in case we decide to try another wedding," Luke said. He caressed Katie's cheek. "What do you say? Will you marry me again? A big, splashy wedding with all the trimmings, maybe even five or six bridesmaids?"

Katie could certainly think of five she would want right by her side in front of the altar at St. John's Church—Abby, Hannah, Emma, Sophie and, of course, Lucy. Joy spread through Katie as she looked him straight in the eye.

"I will," she said, throwing her arms around him. "I will."

As it turned out, no bridesmaids were planned for the ceremony in which Caitlyn and Luke Cassidy were to repeat their wedding vows. Instead, a few days later when Abby, Hannah, Emma, Sophie and Lucy heard about Katie's plans for an all-stops-out, traditional wedding, they promptly agreed with her that it was the perfect opportunity for each of them to renew their own wedding vows. All six couples sat around in the boarding house living room making wedding plans at an impromptu gathering that Lucy had pulled together.

"And we'll throw a shower," Sophie Maguire declared. "Katie never had one."

"A lingerie shower," Emma Flint agreed, shooting a heated look at her husband.

"Only if I can come," Luke interjected.

"All right!" Max Ryder chimed in. "Me, too."

"In your dreams," Lucy said to her husband, effectively dashing his hopeful expression.

"You can forget it, too," Katie told Luke, then leaned down to whisper in his ear.

"I'll bet she's promising a private showing just for him later," Hannah guessed.

"Or maybe she's just offering to take the edge off his disappointment tonight," Ford Maguire suggested, drawing a teasing smack from Sophie, who declared that for a sheriff he had a worrisome one-track mind.

"Ever since I met you," he agreed.

Sophie grinned. "Too bad the baby's not big enough yet. She could be the flower girl." She looked at Luke. "Will Robby be ring bearer?"

"If we can keep him away from the cake long enough," Luke said. "He's become obsessed with food now that he's discovered the difference between home-made and store-bought."

"I just want to know who's going to sing?" Lucy asked. "Are we going to be stuck with Henrietta or can you get Tommy back here from Nashville?"

Katie froze as she waited for Luke's reply. He'd said very little about his brother since the night Tommy came by to tell them he'd dropped the custody suit. The next afternoon they'd heard that Tommy had left for Nashville. She started to step in to cover the awkward silence that had fallen, but Luke gave an almost imperceptible shake of his head.

"I'm not sure if Tommy will be able to make it," he said. "He's just trying to get a new career launched. That takes a lot of time."

"But it's going well," Lucy persisted. "You've talked to him?"

"Yes, we've talked," he said, surprising Katie.

The impromptu party went on for another hour, but when it was over, Katie brought up the subject of Tommy again. "You hadn't mentioned talking to him."

"There was nothing to say," Luke said tightly.

"Oh, Luke…"

"Drop it, Katie." He brushed a kiss across her lips. "We have more important things to think about."

"The wedding."

He grinned. "That's too far in the future. I was thinking about right now. Upstairs. You and me."

Katie sighed with pleasure. "Now that is definitely an intriguing notion, Luke Cassidy."

"The best one I've had all day?"

"Certainly the best one you've had since the same time last night," she agreed as she led the way up the stairs.

Epilogue

Katie's wedding gown, which seemed to be endless yards of delicate French lace, was the envy of all the other brides as they waited at the back of St. John's Church for the ceremony to begin.

"If you keep weeping on it, you're going to wilt it," Katie chided her aunt.

"It's just that you look so beautiful," Peg said with a sniff.

"I thought I looked beautiful last time," Katie retorted.

"But this time you really look like a bride." Peg squeezed her hand. "You're happy, aren't you?"

"Happier than I've ever been," Katie said as the first faint sounds of music drifted outside.

Lucy walked over. "Show time, sweetie."

Katie reached out and hugged her. "What would I do without you to feed me my cue at my weddings?"

"Hopefully this will be the very last time I ever have to do it."

"It will be," Katie said with certainty.

The six women lined up in order of their weddings—Abby, Hannah, Emma, Sophie, Lucy and finally Katie. As if she'd never gone through a wedding ceremony before, butterflies swam in Katie's stomach as she watched each of them enter the church and begin the slow walk down the aisle to join their husbands.

At last it was her turn. Robby waited until Katie was at the door before stepping into the aisle, proudly holding the pillow bearing Katie's and Luke's rings.

"Now, Mommy?" he whispered loudly enough to be heard all the way to the front of the church.

Mommy! Katie's heart flipped over. She swooped down and hugged him. "You bet. Let's do it."

Luke's gaze locked on her and never wavered as she made the slow walk down the aisle. Katie thought she would burst with sheer joy as she looked into those dear, familiar blue eyes. She was about to marry the man she loved all over again. She had a son. Her aunt's doubts about her marriage to Luke had finally been put to rest. If only Tommy could be there to share this with them, she thought, then banished the sad thought from her head as she placed her hand in Luke's and waited to repeat her vows with the other couples.

Katie was certain that her voice and Luke's could be heard above all the others, stronger and more certain. Whether it was true or not hardly mattered, because she cared only about the possessive light shining in her husband's eyes as he declared, "I will love you and honor you, cherish and keep you all the days of our lives."

Forever, Katie thought with a sense of wonder. It was

a dream come true. She gazed at the five other equally solemn couples and saw that each pair had eyes only for each other. They had been blessed, all of them.

When the vows had been said and the organ music began to swell, they turned and headed down the aisle. Not until they reached the back of the church did Katie spot Tommy in the shadows, Ginger standing at his side, a challenging glint in her eyes as if she anticipated Luke's disapproval.

Luke spotted his brother at precisely the same moment, and for the space of a heartbeat, Katie saw a muscle working in his jaw. Then a sigh shuddered through him and he closed the distance between them.

Katie watched the reunion with her heart in her throat. Then she joined them, just as Robby came racing down the aisle. He skidded to a stop at the sight of Tommy.

"You look like Daddy. Who are you?"

Tommy hunkered down in front of him and held out his hand. "I'm your daddy's brother," he said, looking up at Luke. "That makes me your uncle."

Katie released the breath she hadn't even realized she'd been holding. "Thank you," she mouthed silently to Tommy.

He winked at her. "Some things were just meant to be."

Yes, Katie thought, gazing up at her husband. Some things were just meant to be.

* * * * *

HIS LOVE MATCH

Shirley Hailstock

To my sister Marilyn
for all the joys and memories we made
and for all her acts of kindness.

Chapter 1

It can't be him.

Diana *knew* him. No computer would do this to her. Not twice in one day. Diana Greer sat at the table of the local coffee shop across from Princeton University. Her usual unshakable demeanor had just taken a hit. The place was geared up for the lunch crowd, and both students and white-shirted lawyer types poured in like Christmas shoppers just before closing on December twenty-fourth. Glancing through the wall of people, her gaze darted around bodies, hoping against hope that what she looked for wouldn't be there. Her heart sank when the human sea cleared for a second and confirmation forced a groan from her throat. He had the DVD in his hand. The one they had agreed to both carry as identification. The cover photo faced her, despite his hand cutting a wedge out of the romantic couple. There was no mistake. It could be a coincidence, but Diana doubted it. It was her suggestion that they identify themselves using this method. She'd seen it in more than one movie. Usually it was a rose or a book. She hadn't thought the suggestion would prove so close to the Hollywood version of a couple who met online actually knowing each other. She could kick herself for not insisting on a photograph before they met. But not knowing what he looked like had been intriguing, romantic even. And they were only meeting for lunch. Opinions on vanity could be judged then.

She had to get out of the shop before he saw her.

Glancing at the ceiling she cursed the universe for its wretched sense of humor. "This is not funny," she muttered. People at a nearby table looked to see who she was talking to. She smiled quickly and dropped her head, choosing to stare at the golden liquid in her cup. Maybe there was some way she could get out without him seeing her. Diana looked from side to side. She was hemmed in. The tables were very close together and crowded with patrons. She knew it would be rude to leave without talking to the man she'd spent three months corresponding with through email. But if anyone deserved being stood up it was Scott Thomas.

He looked around, stretching his neck although he already stood head and shoulders above everyone else in the place. He was obviously looking for someone—her. Diana looked down as he almost made eye contact with her. Instinctively she knew it was too late. He'd seen her. And her copy of *You've Got Mail* lay square and center on the table in front of the chair she saved for him—one she'd stopped three people from taking. She wished she had something to hide the DVD with, a

One Minute" Survey

You get up to **FOUR** books <u>and</u> Mystery Gifts...

#1 NEW YORK TIMES BESTSELLING AUTHOR

SUSAN MALLERY

California Girls

...mance

MARIE FORCE

NEW YORK TIMES BESTSELLING AUTHOR

Fatal ACCUSATION

Suspense

YOU pick your books – WE pay for everything!

See inside for details.

Dear Reader,

Your opinions are important to us. So if you'll participate in our
and free "One Minute" Survey, **YOU** can pick up to four wonde
books that **WE** pay for!

As a leading publisher of women's fiction, we'd love to hear fro
you. That's why we promise to reward you for completing our
survey.

IMPORTANT: Please complete the survey and return it. We'll s
your Free Books and Free Mystery Gifts right away. **And we pa
for shipping and handling too!** ← *We pay for EVERYTHING!*

Try **Essential Suspense** featuring spine-tingling suspense and
psychological thrillers with many written by today's best-sellin
authors.

Try **Essential Romance** featuring compelling romance stories
many written by today's best-selling authors.

Or TRY BOTH!

Thank you again for participating in our "One Minute"
Survey. It really takes just a minute (or less) to complete the
survey… and your free books and gifts will be well worth it!

Sincerely,

Pam Powers

Pam Powers
for Reader Service

www.ReaderService.

"One Minute" Survey

ET YOUR FREE BOOKS AND FREE GIFTS!

✓ Complete this Survey ✓ Return this survey

1 Do you try to find time to read every day?

☐ YES ☐ NO

2 Do you prefer stories with happy endings?

☐ YES ☐ NO

3 Do you enjoy having books delivered to your home?

☐ YES ☐ NO

4 Do you share your favorite books with friends?

☐ YES ☐ NO

YES! I have completed the above "One Minute" Survey. Please send me my Free Books and Free Mystery Gifts (worth over $20 retail). I understand that I am under no obligation to buy anything, as explained on the back of this card.

☐ I prefer
Essential Suspense
191/391 MDL GNRG

☐ I prefer
Essential Romance
194/394 MDL GNRG

☐ I prefer BOTH
191/391 & 194/394
MDL GNRS

FIRST NAME   LAST NAME

ADDRESS

APT.#   CITY

STATE/PROV.   ZIP/POSTAL CODE

▼ DETACH AND MAIL CARD TODAY!

® and ™ are trademarks owned by Harlequin Enterprises ULC. Printed in the U.S.A.

READER SERVICE—Here's how it works:

BUSINESS REPLY MAIL
FIRST-CLASS MAIL   PERMIT NO.717   BUFFALO, NY

POSTAGE WILL BE PAID BY ADDRESSEE

READER SERVICE
PO BOX 1341
BUFFALO NY 14240-8571

NO POSTAGE
NECESSARY
IF MAILED
IN THE
UNITED STATES

book or scarf—even a napkin would help. But she had none of those things handy and Scott was already weaving his way through the crowd toward her.

"Diana?" He frowned, coming to stand in front of her. "Is that you?" He deliberately slipped his DVD into his suit pocket. "What are you doing here? I thought you were meeting someone for lunch?"

Of course, he knew she was meeting someone. Hadn't she told him so this very morning? Diana raised her chin and looked him in the eye. It can't be him, she told herself again, as if the thought could transform this man who'd stood in her office only an hour ago into someone else— anyone else. *Just, please, God,* she prayed. *Not him.*

In her office that morning their encounter had been less than friendly. She wasn't in the mood for another one. Scott had come to the office to persuade her to move out and find other accommodations for the business she'd run there for the past five years. Their encounter had been unfriendly, and Diana was reminded of the sarcasm he'd subjected her to while they both attended the university that was only a few steps from where they stood now. Nothing appeared to have changed in the intervening years. He was still on the opposite side of everything she did, said or wanted.

And for no reason. At least none she could discern.

"I was just leaving," she said. As she moved to stand, he picked up the DVD. Diana flopped back down as her knees refused to hold her in position. At once Scott glanced from the DVD to her, then back again. Diana watched as he pulled his own copy from his pocket and realization dawned in his dark brown eyes.

"There has to be a mistake," she said, reaching for her copy. Scott glanced at both covers.

"I believe there is."

Diana grabbed for her DVD but encountered resistance from Scott. As she raised her eyes to him, she saw that playful disapproval that had been there when they were college students. Quickly it disappeared and he released his hold on the case.

Getting up, Diana inched around the crowded table and started for the door. It seemed as if the universe was mocking her. A line of people that hadn't been there before now stood between her and the door. She would need to wait to get out of the place, when all she wanted was to get as far away from Scott as possible. Around him she couldn't breathe. It had always been like that. Even all those years ago, when they were in college and he would harass her whenever he could, she found it difficult to breathe in his presence. Apparently time had not changed that reaction, either.

There was another door, she thought as she looked over her shoulder. She'd try to get to it. However, when Diana tried to turn around, she realized it was a mistake. Scott was directly behind her, and her body was now in contact with his. Despite the air-conditioning, her temperature flew off the scale. She was surprised she didn't double over in pain from the bends. And it didn't help that Scott's arms instinctively came up to steady her. The urge to lean into him was so great that she grabbed his hands and pushed them away with more force than she intended.

"I apologize," she said. "I'm under a little stress." That was more than the truth. Stress followed her, sat on her shoulder, worked its way into the marrow of her bones any time Scott Thomas's name came up or even entered her mind. And having him close enough that she could smell his cologne and feel the heat of his body threw her back to the one other time in her life when she was this close to him. Close enough to kiss. That time there had been a kiss. He'd kissed her. Devastated her. Left her wanting more when the passion that flared within her burned deep and hot and out of control. When it ended as abruptly as it had begun, he turned and ran away. She watched him disappear. Then she fled, too. Running across the campus in the opposite direction from the one he'd taken, competing with the wind for dominance.

And that had been the last time she'd seen him until ten months ago when, practically on the heels of his attorney's exit, he'd walked into her office and doubled the offer if she would vacate her offices. She refused.

She hadn't told her online friend about the encounter. She needed to keep Scott Thomas relegated to a corner of her brain that was as inaccessible as possible. Lately the folds in that area were vibrating with the need to access the data stored there.

"I guess leaving through the rear door is out of the question," Diana said, her voice slightly breathy.

Scott glanced over his shoulder. Looking back at her, he said, "It's just as crowded over there."

Diana turned back. She held her breath, relieved that he was no longer touching her, but still aware that he was close enough for her to feel the heat of his body. How could MatchforLove.com have paired her with Scott? They had nothing in common. Nothing except she owned a wedding planning business in a complex that he wanted.

Diana was not moving.

Finally the crowd at the door moved and she was on the street. Taking a full breath, she felt as if she could gulp the air. Not looking back, she started up Nassau Street intent on reaching her car and getting as far away from Scott Thomas as she could.

A hand curling around her arm stopped her. Diana turned, taking two steps backward to keep some distance between them.

"At least we can be civil," he said.

"If this is another of your attempts to get me to give up my offices, it's not going to work. As I told you this morning—"

"It has nothing to do with the property," Scott interrupted her.

Diana shifted her weight but said nothing. If he didn't want to make another pitch to get her offices, what did they have to discuss?

"How do you think we ended up here together?"

"Obviously by some computer glitch."

Diana knew it was a mistake to follow her partner Teddy's urging. Diana had told her that she didn't have time for a man in her life, but Teddy, in her usual persistent manner, had worn her down, and finally Diana had gone into the MatchforLove.com system and filled out the profile. And now she stood in front of Scott Thomas, a mistake if she ever saw one.

Before he could continue their conversation, his cell phone rang and Diana took the opportunity to leave. She felt she'd get to her car and be done with him. At least when she turned the corner at the end of the block she could relax. But Scott was not to be eluded. He fell into step next to her, all the while continuing his phone call.

"What?" Diana heard him say. He stopped walking, but caught up with her several steps later. "Can't you find someone else?"

He listened for a moment while she walked faster. Her shoes were the latest style, very high heels on a small platform. They elevated her five-foot-five-inch height by five additional inches.

"All right," he said as if giving in to something.

Diana got to the corner and turned. The garage was half a block away. Hoping Scott would continue up Nassau Street, her thoughts were doused as he turned with her.

"Yes, I said I'd do it." A moment later he nearly shouted into the receiver. "What did you say?"

Diana couldn't help listening while she walked.

"Who's doing it?" he asked.

Again there was a pause.

"You're kidding!" Scott said. This time he sounded as if something incredible had happened.

Diana didn't get the impression that there was any kidding going on. But she heard Scott agree to the final unheard question. "It's all right. I get it. I'll be there." He ended the call and pocketed the phone.

Diana could tell something was not as he wished it to be, but she wasn't interested in finding out what was off in his world. She had her own to deal with.

"Why are you following me, Scott? I have a high-profile wedding to get the final plans on, and I don't have time to be bothered with childish pranks. You've already said it's not about the offices, so what do you want?"

Scott hesitated a moment. "I want to know if you told the truth."

She frowned, not understanding his question.

"On your profile. Was everything you put in there true?"

Anger, hot, red and eruptive sliced through her like the knife edge of an arctic wind. "As I remember it, lying is *your* department. And since we aren't likely to see each other *again*..." She emphasized *again,* closing the door on him making further offers on her offices. "I think we should just forget this day ever happened."

Pivoting on shoes that were now hurting her toes, Diana straightened her back and shoulders and walked away from him. He didn't follow her, a good choice on his part, she thought. Practically calling her a liar to her face was enough. Another word from either of them would require police protection.

"How was he?" Theresa "Teddy" Granville jumped up from her chair the moment Diana came through the office door. "Was he as good-looking as we thought?"

Diana dropped her purse on the chair and gave Teddy the look. It should have been patented between them. It was the look they gave each other when a bride chose something that was totally wrong for her theme.

"That bad?" Teddy was nonplussed. She flopped back down in her chair. "After we had such high hopes."

"After *you* had high hopes." It was at Teddy's insistence that Diana go to MatchforLove.com. Diana had done it to silence her partner. But after she began talking to F9021@MatchforLove.com, things changed. He seemed to understand her. Even though they never identified themselves by name, he knew she owned her own business and she knew he flew airplanes. She thought he was a pilot.

"What was wrong with him?"

"He was Scott Thomas."

Teddy came forward in her chair as if she'd been pushed. "Scott Thomas? The Scott Thomas who wants us to move? *That* Scott Thomas?"

"One and the same," Diana said.

"That's impossible."

"I couldn't believe it myself. It was all I could do to get out of the coffee shop."

"Without seeing him?"

"Unfortunately, no," Diana said. She took a seat in front of Teddy's desk. The place was neat as a pin, although Teddy was juggling three weddings for the next two weeks. It was time for the brides to get crazy and the mothers of the brides to go ballistic over something minor. Luckily at this moment the phones weren't ringing with complaints. "I wished I could have become invisible when I saw him, but he spotted me and we talked."

"Talked?"

"We both agreed that the dating service had made a terrible mistake. No way are we compatible."

"That's all?"

"Pretty much."

"Pretty much, what?" As usual Teddy read between the lines and persisted.

"As we were parting he called me a liar."

"What?" Her eyes grew big.

"Not in those exact words. He asked me if everything I put in my profile was true."

"Well it was, wasn't it?" Teddy asked.

"Teddy!"

"I mean," she stammered. "We all like to embellish ourselves a little online."

"I did not *embellish*."

At that moment the phone rang. Diana got up to leave. At the door Teddy stopped her. "Well, at least he's good-looking," she said.

Diana frowned at her and went to her own office. It was a contrast to the orderliness of Teddy's. Diana worked in chaos. She knew where everything was, and she could put her hands on it without error.

Good-looking, Teddy had said. Diana supposed if she thought about him without the animosity that clouded his image, Scott was pleasant to look at. More than that. He had great eyes. They were probably his best feature, dark brown, fringed by long lashes. His cheeks had dimples that drove the women crazy in college. They hadn't diminished in effect in the ten years since they graduated. He wasn't a football player, but his lean features boded well for the diving team. Diana remembered the broad shoulders that tapered to a thin waist and strong muscular legs. Diana had to admit he *was* good-looking. If she was planning one of her bridal fashion shows, he'd be a shoo-in for a tuxedo model.

Diana glanced down at her desk. Several bridal magazines lay open in front of her. One by one she scanned the pages and studied the grooms. Not one of the men smiling up at her had an ounce of the gorgeous good looks that Scott Thomas had.

Looks weren't everything, she thought. The man was still a jerk. And even though he could turn the head of every woman in town, Diana knew the two of them should never have been matched.

* * *

Scott loosened his tie and opened his collar in the same instant he came through the garage door into the mudroom. As usual the house was cool and quiet. In the kitchen he opened the refrigerator and grabbed the container of orange juice. It was nearly empty. He lifted the container to drink, but his mother's words came back to him, and he poured a glassfull and drank it in one long gulp.

The answering machine showed eight new messages. Aside from his sister, people usually called or sent text messages to his cell phone. It was unusual for anyone to contact him on his landline. Checking his cell, he found another nine unread texts. As he scrolled through them he felt both grateful and disappointed that none were from Diana. Why he should expect to see anything from her, he didn't understand. She'd made it plain that there could never be anything between them, so why would he think she'd call? Apology, maybe. He shook his head. That was unlikely.

Pressing the button on the answering machine he listened to the calls. Most of them were either from Bill Quincy or his bride-to-be, Jennifer Embry, a couple who'd talked him into being a member of their wedding this afternoon while he was on the street with Diana. Bill thanked him for standing in for Oscar Peterson, who'd been in an accident and would be laid up for the next several weeks. He'd recover, but not in time for the nuptials. Jennifer, a numerologist, wouldn't have her numbers thrown out of whack. Scott knew she'd postpone the wedding before doing that.

The other calls were from Jennifer giving him details of where and when he needed to be. She called to change his tuxedo appointment twice.

The reason he agreed to stand in for Oscar was that Bill had told him the wedding was being planned by Diana's firm. At the time he thought it was ironic and he wanted to get him off the phone. But now he was sorry he'd agreed. Impulsiveness wasn't one of his traits. As a pilot he had to be steady and thoughtful, but Bill was a friend. To stand up for him, he'd make the sacrifice. Scott felt no disappointment at not being included in the original plans. He could do without weddings. Being involved in one was something to be avoided, like air pockets and bumper-to-bumper traffic. He was sure when Bill called him, he was last on the list and the only one available.

Scott was committed now. He had an appointment for a tuxedo fitting, and his name had been added to the programs. Jennifer expected him at the rehearsal and the rehearsal dinner. The wedding was the following weekend.

The answering machine clicked off. Scott grabbed the television remote and pressed the power button. He smiled to himself. What was Diana going to think when he showed up at the wedding rehearsal? He remembered her strutting out of sight as she walked into the garage. Her parting words told him that she never wanted to see him again. She was wrong. She'd see him. And sooner than she thought.

He'd angered her. There had been times in the past when he'd intentionally intimidated her, but today that wasn't his plan. They had rubbed each other the wrong way since their first meeting. While he'd followed her to the garage, she could have heard only one side of the conversation he was having—*if* she was listening. He was sure she was. In his experience, women always listened. But Diana had never followed the mold. He couldn't say he knew her, but he knew that beneath the facade of calm she showed to the world was a smoldering woman. He'd found that out when he kissed her on campus in broad daylight, a lifetime ago.

To think that all these years later, he could still remember that kiss. *Her* kiss. Scott had kissed his share of women. They seemed to hover around him like skydivers in formation, but none of them were memorable. None but Diana.

And next weekend he'd have another chance to piss her off.

Scott didn't know how long he'd been waiting, but he was getting irritated. He had a flight today, and he needed to get this fitting done and return to this office. Pulling out his phone, he reviewed his missed calls. His sister Piper's number and her photo appeared on the display. He couldn't help smiling. The photo was taken at her wedding four years ago. It was of the two of them, their faces near replicas of their parents. He should have returned her previous call, but with all the appointments this wedding required, it slipped his mind. He pushed the send button and waited for her to answer.

"Hi," she said. "I've been dying to talk to you. How was the meeting? What did she look like? I have a thousand questions. Did the two of you connect?"

Scott laughed from deep in his belly. His sister was a nonstop talking machine. He sobered and tried to decide how to begin and how much to tell. He should have thought of this before he dialed her number. He'd tell her about the meeting. He could describe Diana, give Piper all the answers she wanted, but he would leave out the fact that the woman in question was Brainiac.

"Well, go on. Tell me," she commanded. "Is she the woman of your dreams?"

"I'm not sure about that."

"Did she meet all those ridiculous requirements you put in?"

"I haven't found that out yet," Scott said. "We only met for lunch. I didn't have time to interrogate her." Scott's forced laugh took the sting out of his words.

He went through describing Diana. He told Piper she had dark hair, omitting that it was lustrous and fell over her shoulders and down her back like a cascading waterfall. He shared that her eyes were brown, but he didn't add that they were like looking into melting pools of coal. He said she was dressed in business clothes, but didn't say that the suit hugged her curves the way his hands wanted to or that her shoes supported legs that were as long as the Garden State Parkway.

"Did the two of you connect?" she asked.

"In a way," Scott hedged, knowing his sister would not let that go.

"What do you mean?"

"Remember the woman I told you about when I was in college? The one with the long hair."

"You mean the one who always had her head in a book?" Piper asked. "Didn't you call her something? Brain something. Yeah, Brainiac."

"Her name is Diana Greer." It was her, but Scott didn't want to tell his sister. He'd said so many things about Diana that were not flattering that he didn't want

Piper to have a more negative picture of her than had already been painted.

"Was it *her?*"

"It was her," he admitted.

Piper laughed for a moment. "It's like that movie. You probably don't know it. It's a chick flick—*You've Got Mail*. The couple don't realize they know each other. It has–"

"I know the movie," Scott interrupted.

Piper seemed to sober. "I'm sorry this didn't work out, Scott." Piper was the only person he'd told about the matchmaking service. Of course she supported him. She always did. "I remember you said she had so much hair that when she had her nose in a book, she looked like Cousin Itt."

Scott winced at that. "She's changed a lot."

"I hope so. " Piper paused. "Are you going to try again?"

"This is not over yet," Scott told her.

"You're seeing her again?" Surprise was evident in her voice.

"At a wedding next weekend." He forced a laugh for the second time. "I'm a replacement in Bill Quincy's wedding. Diana's company is the wedding consultant."

"From what you told me, I thought she'd be running General Motors by now. She's a wedding consultant?"

"Actually she owns her own business. Weddings by Diana. She's got stores in several states. While they might not be General Motors, if you put her up against the president of GM she could hold her own."

"Oh." Piper held on to the word as if it was the end of a song. She sounded impressed.

"You've heard of them?"

"Who hasn't? She's been all over the financial pages. It seems everything she touches turned to green, that's as in money. Her franchises have been expanding like they were a fast food chain. I wish I'd used her when I got married."

Scott felt his heart tug at that. When he saw Diana he was impressed that she had changed over the years, but her changes were for the better. He supposed she was always there under the hair and out of the book, but he rarely saw her or even looked at her. It wasn't until that one day in front of Nassau Hall that he saw her face. It was naked of any makeup. Her skin was flawless, and the depths of her dark eyes were enough to drive a man crazy.

And where she was concerned, he was all male.

Chapter 2

The parking lot of Darlington Wedding Gowns and Tuxedos was packed when Diana pulled into the only available space. And that was as far from the door as she could get. Darlington had been several steps away from her offices, but with Scott's new use for the property practically everyone had relocated. The store was now housed in a huge strip mall several miles from her.

Final fittings for the Embry-Quincy wedding party was scheduled for today. Diana wouldn't let anything having to do with Scott deter her. She stepped into the June heat and felt her clothes and body deflate. It shouldn't be in the nineties this early in the season. And she shouldn't be here. First she was the owner. She worked with the managers of new locations and Teddy ran the consultant staff. But Jennifer Embry came from old money, and she insisted Diana consult her wedding.

As such she was the wedding planner, not the dress approver. However, she'd learned early in this business that a wedding planner's duties were fluid. Some brides were demanding. Others only wanted her to take care of the ceremony and the reception. But she and Teddy ran a soup-to-nuts organization.

Pulling open the door of Darlington's, she silently thanked the air-conditioning gods for their invention of such a useful mechanism.

"Diana," Jennifer greeted her with a relieved smile. "I'm glad to see you."

Jennifer stood in front of a triple wall of mirrors, her white gown billowing around her.

"You look beautiful," she told her client.

"The hem is too long. The gloves aren't the same color as the gown. I can't see through the veil."

Susan Dollard, the store owner, frowned. Diana smiled back at her.

"Jennifer, remember we know that items of different materials will not be exactly the same color due to shine, weaving methods, difference in lots, and a hundred other reasons. Just focus on the day. It's going to be beautiful. I know the alterations will be completed while we wait."

The seamstress was on the floor with her needle and thread, quickly adjusting the length. Diana stepped back to get a good look at the bride. "You look gorgeous. Just wait until Bill sees you in this gown."

The praise wasn't false. Jennifer glowed in her gown. It was a perfect fit and style for the tall, majestic-looking blonde.

"The veil, Ms. Embry." Susan came forward with the altered crown.

"Let me," Diana said, reaching for the soft concoction of netting. Stepping up on the platform with Jennifer, she placed it on her head and spread out the folds of fabric. "Is it better?" she asked.

Jennifer turned back to the wall of mirrors. Tears were in her voice when she answered.

"Great," Diana said, glad to have appeased another bride. She stepped off the platform and onto the floor. "How's everything else?"

"Fine," Jennifer said. Then she turned to Susan and the seamstress and apologized. Both women smiled. They'd been through this scene a hundred or more times. "Oh, by the way," Jennifer said. "There's been a replacement for one of the groomsmen."

"I got your message." She should have said *messages*. Diana wondered if three was a significant number for Jennifer. She'd told her three times about Oscar's replacement, yet she never mentioned who the replacement was. Brides, even those as organized as Jennifer, had lapses of memory.

"He's next door getting fitted for his tux."

"Let me go introduce myself." Diana liked knowing the members of the wedding party. In case of an emergency, she knew who she was looking for. She took the digital camera she always carried from her purse. She'd take a photo and label it to be sure. Jennifer Embry had twelve bridesmaids and an equal number of groomsmen. It was impossible to keep all the names straight, even though Diana was good with names and faces. Still, she relied on file photos to help her or one of her assistants in case she had to delegate duties.

The gown and tuxedo shops were connected by a short passageway. It was designed both to keep the noise down and to provide privacy. Diana didn't use it. She preferred to enter from the outside.

The bells chimed when she entered the shop. Several people browsed the various colors and styles of men's clothing. All of the dressing room doors were closed. Judging by the parking lot, the place was full.

"Jeremy," she called.

The clerk came from the last dressing room. "Ms. Greer, how are you?" When they were alone Jeremy was very informal and called her Diana; occasionally and with several drinks under his belt, she was Di. When she came in the shop, she was Ms. Greer. To her he was always Jeremy. He and Susan were man and wife, but they kept to their separate areas unless need forced one to the other side of the causeway.

"I'm looking for the new member of the Embry-Quincy wedding. The bride told me he was here and I wanted to introduce myself."

Someone said something from behind them and one of the other clerks went to aid the customer.

"He's waiting for his fitting." Jeremy indicated one of the dressing room doors.

"I can wait a few minutes."

"It might be longer than that. I'm short-handed and swamped. Three parties are due in any moment now and I have all the dressing rooms filled." Suddenly, he put a hand to his chin. Then he looked at Diana with a strange expression. "I wouldn't like to impose, but you do know the ropes? Do you have a moment to help out?"

Diana never refused Jeremy anything. He'd helped her get started by giving her mountains of advice that saved her from some major pitfalls. Before his move to this location she had worked in his store for over a year and had learned how to take measurements.

"The Embry-Quincy wedding is in the Red Room." He smiled and offered her the tape measure hanging around his neck. "I believe the new member may need his nerves soothed."

Diana smiled. She'd often been called upon to settle a guy whose mind was on other tasks. She glanced at the dressing rooms. Jeremy named his rooms after those in the White House. It gave the place a little elegance, he said, and who wants to dress in Room 3 when they could have the Red Room? Diana still remembered the expression on his face when he gave more credence to a false name than to a nondescript number.

Taking the tape measure, she dropped her purse in his office and knocked lightly on the door of the dressing room. "I'm here to take your measurements," she said before going in. She wanted the man to know she was female in case Jeremy had told him to remove his pants. Or if he was shy.

"Come in."

Diana stepped through the door and quickly closed it. Although Jeremy's dressing rooms were huge and set up like the entrance to a home, with a foyer section and a comfortable living room, sporting a large mirror that covered one wall, Diana couldn't be sure the client wasn't standing near the door in full view of whomever was outside. When she turned back she saw only her reflection across the spacious gray-colored carpeting. The subdued floor contrasted with the bright furnishings. Walking several steps past a wall that set off the foyer area, she came face-to-face with the last person on the planet she expected to see.

Diana didn't know which one of them was more surprised.

"What are you doing here?" they asked at the same time.

Diana recovered first. "I'm here to take your measurements if you are the replacement in the Embry-Quincy wedding."

"Scott Thomas, nice to meet you." He extended a hand as if they'd never met. Diana ignored it and he folded both arms across his chest. The action brought his white shirt up a little higher over legs that were long, strong and naked. She wished her heart didn't step up its beat, but she couldn't deny it. Teddy had put the thought in her head that he was handsome. That was an understatement. He was a crowd standout. And with him half dressed, Diana wondered what he'd look like totally naked.

Clearing her throat and mentally shaking those thoughts from her mind, she asked, "Shall we get started?"

"I didn't know you worked here."

"I agreed to help Jeremy out because he has a lot going on in the shop. And I expect you have other places to be."

"As a matter of fact, I do."

"Then…" She pulled the measuring tape from her neck and took a step forward. "That is, unless you'd like a male to take your measurements. They're all busy right now, so your wait will be a little longer."

"I've waited long enough," he said. "Let's get it over with."

Diana took a deep breath and approached him. "Turn around."

He presented his back to her, and she reached up to measure its width. Then the length of his arms. She tried doing his waist from behind, but he turned in her arms. Diana caught her breath. For a moment she didn't think she'd be able to keep her feet on the floor. Gripping the tape measure, she fought to keep control of her shaking hands. Finally, she dropped to the floor to measure his inseam.

"Spread your legs, please," she said. Blood hammered in her head. She could feel the heat of his nearness. Her face flamed as blood rushed up her features, burning her ears.

"Why don't I just tell you my size?" Scott asked.

For a short moment Diana was unsure what he meant. Then sanity returned, and she realized he meant his suit size. She could feel more heat pump into her face and ears, and she wondered why they didn't melt and slide off. She dared not look up at him.

"Your suit size is not always the same. And you want to look your best at the wedding." Diana couldn't imagine him looking any other way.

"Of course. Anything less and Jennifer will have my head."

Diana raised herself up on her knees and prepared for the final measurement. She willed her hands to remain steady. Swallowing and ignoring the roar of blood and unwanted memories inside her head she touched his leg just above the knee. It was a test of her own ability to continue this procedure. She'd done this hundreds of times. She'd measured guys who were model perfect, silver-screen-idol caliber, and never had to keep her emotions in check. But Scott Thomas was throwing her usual calm into aggregated chaos.

His leg was warm, as strong and solid as a tennis player's. She moved the tape measure higher. Time seemed to slow down, and her hand moved with the slowness of passing years on its way to the juncture between his legs. The catch in his throat and the heat of his body found a place in her brain that told her to get the measurements done as quickly as possible. But that instruction didn't reach her hands. She pulled the tape measure down and extended it to his ankle, then to his sock-clad feet. Unconsciously, she brushed against him. His arousal was hard and he jerked away from her touch.

Diana's head snapped up and she met his eyes. They were dark, almost liquid. She'd seen that look directed at her only one other time. And from the same face that now stared into hers with a longing so deep it wrenched her heart.

Scott reached down and pulled her up to him. She stood as if reaching for the sky. Scott's body was long. Diana climbed the mountain of him until she was on her feet. She could feel the full length of him. For a moment she luxuriated in the warmth that covered them like a shared aura. They faced each other, their mouths only a kiss away. *Kiss.* The word registered in her brain. Lightning speed brought her up short. She pulled free of Scott's arms and hurried to the door. With her hand on the knob, she turned back.

"I apologize," she said. "I'm finished with you. You can dress and leave."

Outside, Diana stood breathing hard, clutching the tape measure as if it was an anchor keeping her pinned to the ground. She took several breaths. What had happened to her? What was she doing? She'd never done anything like that before, but this time she found it hard to control herself. She wanted to touch him, wanted to keep running her hands over his hair-roughened skin. She wanted to feel his arousal, allowing him to lengthen and grow in her palm.

Stop! she screamed at herself. She had to calm her thoughts before Jeremy emerged from one of the dressing rooms. He knew her well enough to tell if something was happening to her, and there was no doubt in her mind that something *had* happened. And more would have happened if she'd let it go on any longer. How could she feel this way? She hated Scott Thomas. She'd always hated him. How could she want to kiss her? Oh, God, how could she want to have sex with him?

She gasped at the thought. Was that what that was? Had it been so long since she had sex that she wanted to have it with a man she didn't even like? Diana stopped all thoughts of Scott. He was probably dressed by now and would open the door behind her at any moment. She didn't want to be standing there when that happened.

Rallying her thoughts, she took the card with Scott's information to Jeremy's desk and gave it to him.

"Thanks for the help," Jeremy said. "I think everything is in control now." He surveyed the shop.

Diana smiled quickly, wanting to get out of the shop before Jeremy saw how close to falling apart she was. And worse, having to face Scott so soon after she'd had her hands on him and her body melded to his. Gathering her purse, she air-kissed Jeremy and left by the connecting door, escaping into the bridal shop and out of Scott's sight. Diana didn't think she exhaled until she had finished with Jennifer's needs and returned to her car, all without seeing Scott a second time.

But there would be other times. Now that she knew he was the replacement groomsman, the two would meet at the rehearsal and the wedding. Thankfully, she did not have to attend any wedding activities with him. When the rehearsal and wedding ceremony were done, so would she be. Then she could return to her normal life. Whatever normal was. Or had been. Would it be the same ever again? Diana didn't really think so. She and Scott both lived in Princeton. The township was small even though the borough covered a larger space. They both lived in the township, and according to the card she'd recorded his information on, he lived within a good walk of her residence. Diana's business was there. She'd called it home for years not realizing she could run into Scott at any point in the day.

And for the next few days, it was inevitable.

The National Cathedral in Washington, D.C., might be larger than this one, Scott thought, but only by an inch or two. Scott should have known Jennifer would plan something this elaborate. Bill was a lot more laid-back. Or was it Diana, the wedding planner, who'd suggested this mammoth structure? Scott scanned the height of the ceiling, then brought his gaze back to the door. Where was Diana? Most of the wedding party had arrived, but Diana had yet to appear. She'd been on his mind for the last three days. Since the incident in the dressing room she'd plagued him day and night. He'd thought of her all the time. Questions arose for which he had no answers, and every question led to another. He wanted to know where it would lead, *if* it would lead anywhere. He wasn't even sure he wanted it to lead somewhere.

A few days ago he'd been a relatively happy man. Now a woman was driving him crazy. He wasn't even sure she knew it.

And there she was.

Diana opened the cathedral door and slipped inside. She walked fast down the aisle, and she looked as if she'd been running. She wore jeans and a bright pink short-sleeved sweater that accentuated her breasts. Scott remembered her pressed against him. Immediately his body began to harden. He stepped aside, forcing himself to relax.

"Sorry," she said to Jennifer when she reached her. "The flight was late and traffic delayed me."

"We're still on schedule," Jennifer said, taking a look at her watch.

"Well, let's get started." Diana put her jacket and purse on one of the pews along with a large bouquet of flowers. When she turned around, her eyes met his. Quickly she looked away, giving her attention to the rest of the party.

"Father Ryan is here," Jennifer stated. The priest came through the back of the church. He wasn't dressed in robes but wore all black, pants and shirt, no collar.

"Ladies, gentlemen, could we line up in the back of the church."

"Where's Bill?" Scott asked. "Shouldn't the groom be here?"

"He won't make the rehearsal," Jennifer explained. "His trial went to the jury yesterday. They're waiting for the verdict."

Scott thought she should be prepared for these events to interrupt other occasions in their future, but he kept his words silent.

"He'll meet us later at dinner."

Diana took over then, putting people in order by height. She explained what the church would look like in the morning after the flowers and candles were delivered and lit. She cautioned the party to be careful with the candles with their headpieces, since the netting burned easily. Couples were paired together. As the music played, they practiced their walks down the aisle.

"It's time for the bride and groom," Father Ryan said.

"The groom isn't here," Jennifer told him. "He won't make the rehearsal."

"We'll need one of the groomsmen to stand in for him." Father Ryan looked over the small assembly.

The guys looked from one to the other. "Several of us are already married," one of them said. "We've done this before. Scott, you need the practice. Why don't you stand in for Bill?"

"I'll do it," Scott agreed. He knew if he didn't it would start a back and forth banter about the state of his bachelorhood. He's been on the end of that conversation more than once and had no intention of allowing it to happen in front of a dozen women, most of whom did not know the circumstances that had led to the needling.

Scott remembered a time when they were all single and had no intention of marrying. Then one by one, they fell off the wagon. He was the last unmarried soul on that wagon, and while the guys often complained about their wives, they loved them and wouldn't trade their new lives to return to the old ones. Of course, now that they were in their thirties, their days of drinking and bar hopping all night had morphed into attending nursery school plays and walks in the playground. Occasionally they'd get together for the male bonding ritual in front of a big-screen television as their favorite teams vied for dominance on a Sunday afternoon, but at night they returned to the woman they loved.

Scott's transformation had been to the sky. Although he'd learn to fly as a child, accompanying his father on trips, Scott had made a career of flying. While piloting wasn't a sport, pilots were like athletes. They aged out early and needed a second career. He'd decided on his, but one woman stood in his way. And that woman stood at the back of the cathedral.

"Stand over here," Father Ryan said, indicating a space inside the gated nave. "The best man should stand next to you."

One of the groomsmen separated himself and followed Scott.

"Clark?" Diana called. "Remember to let Bill know the two of you will enter from that door in the back. She pointed to the door on the right side of the nave. "Father Ryan will lead you out."

Clark nodded and the two men assumed their positions.

"Now, the bride." Diana turned to the bridesmaids, who were fanned out in front of the bar separating the nave and sanctuary. "Who'll stand in for the bride? She can't do it. Bad luck, so the story goes."

As the woman looked from one to the other, they each refused to step forward.

"Ladies, there is no legend related to standing in for the bride."

"Diana, you can do it?" Jennifer said. She checked the time, and Scott understood she was keeping everyone on schedule. Not only was Jennifer a numbers fanatic, but watches could be set by her plans.

"I can't," Diana protested.

Scott stared directly at her. She wasn't looking at him, but he wondered if his agreement to stand in for Bill had anything to do with her not wanting to be Jennifer's surrogate.

"Someone do it," Jennifer ordered. "We don't want an overcooked dinner." Jennifer lifted the bouquet of flowers Diana came in with and stared at the group. Slowly they each shook their head. Eventually, she came to Diana.

"All right," she said, taking the flowers and her place at the end of the aisle.

As Diana headed down, Father Ryan gestured for the two men to come forward and take their places. Scott had a clear view of Diana as she started down the aisle. She came toward him. She was beautiful. Gone were the baggy jeans and unkempt hair that, aided by a book, hiding her face from view during their college days. She wore designer clothes, trendy shoes. If Scott hadn't seen her a few months ago when he'd come to negotiate her office lease, he'd have sworn the two women weren't one and the same.

She floated down the aisle. Scott's eyes saw the church as it would be, bathed under the yellow glow of candlelight, a white lace gown and Diana as the bride coming toward him.

Him! he shook himself. He wasn't marrying Diana and she wasn't the bride. This was make-believe, and his imagination was working on Stress Level One if his thoughts continued along their present course. He looked at her again, checking to see if her eyes were on him and if by some telepathic relay she'd heard his thoughts.

She wasn't looking at him, but she was smiling. Her staccato steps keeping time to the rhythm of the "Wedding March." Jennifer smiled at her from the front pew. The groomsmen looked at her with appraisal in their eyes. Scott stepped forward as she came to the bar. He wanted to take her arm and pull her close to his side. The groom wouldn't do that tomorrow. He stood close to her, blocking any view the other groomsmen might have.

"I won't go through the vows," Father Ryan said. "At this point tomorrow, I'll be the first to congratulate the bride and groom." He glanced at Jennifer. "Then you will kiss and turn to go up the aisle." He paused a moment, confirming the procedure with Scott before remembering to look at Jennifer. "Okay?"

Jennifer nodded.

"Not quite," Scott replied. All eyes focused on him. He took the flowers from Diana and handed them to Jennifer. Then facing Diana he put his hands on her waist and pulled her toward him. She didn't know what he planned to do until his mouth was on hers. She went rigid for a moment then she relaxed. Her mouth tasted good, chasing away his logical thought processes. She opened her mouth and his tongue swept forward. He felt her hands take his elbows. The fabric of her sweater brushed against his fingertips, a movement as erogenous as his wet mouth sweeping over hers. Her hands began a slow climb, but stopped when someone behind them cleared her throat. It was like a spark to his brain. Logic returned and Scott pushed at her arms. Quickly he ended contact. "Now, we turn and walk up the aisle." He didn't recognize his voice. Then taking her hand, he started toward the rear of the church.

Diana dropped his hand when they were out of earshot of anyone else. "Don't you ever do that again," she hissed.

Like a quick-change artist, she walked back to the congregation. All heads and all eyes were on her, but the silence in the cavernous cathedral was like a tomb.

"Father Ryan, is there any other instruction?" Diana asked, her voice strained. It gave Scott a joyous feeling to know that she had been affected by what had happened between them. His action wasn't impulsive and he enjoyed having Diana in his arms, but to provide such a public display was not his style.

"Only, good luck tomorrow," Father Ryan said.

Everyone smiled and seemed to relax. Diana could hear their sighs.

"Then I'll say good-night." Diana turned to Jennifer and gave her a wide smile. She didn't know if Jennifer was trying to put her at ease after Scott's kiss, but she was grateful for the apparent relaxation in the atmosphere. "I'll see you tomorrow morning."

Jennifer smiled and Diana moved up the aisle.

"Jennifer, Diana has to go to dinner with us," Scott said. "It'll throw the numbers off if she doesn't go."

"Oh no," Diana protested. "I've just returned from Montana. I'm tired and I need to get some rest. Tomorrow is an important day. And Bill will be at the restaurant. The numbers will work."

"Not a problem," Jennifer agreed. "See you in the morning."

Diana moved to leave. Scott stood in the middle of the aisle. "If you've just returned from a plane ride, you must be hungry. Surely you can eat before you leave."

It was no secret to anyone in the church that Scott

wanted her to go with him. He didn't care what they thought. The groomsmen smiled and gave him their silent approval. The bridesmaids only looked stunned.

"I'll get something at home," Diana told them. Her voice hadn't returned to its normal level yet.

She pushed past him and continued up the long aisle. Scott watched her go. But he wasn't finished with her. He'd wondered about her for two days. Why would the computer choose her for him?

He needed to find out. He was going to find out.

Chapter 3

Diana shut her refrigerator door with a sigh. There was nothing to eat in there that didn't require thawing and at least an hour of cooking time. She was hungry now.

She would have gone to dinner with the party if Scott hadn't thrown her off balance with that kiss. What was he thinking? And in front of people she worked for! She wasn't a member of the wedding. She was an employee—granted, a controlling and directing person, but she was still being paid for her services. He'd flustered her so that she forgot she hadn't bought food because of the trip to Montana, and she didn't think to stop and pick something up before pulling into her driveway.

She was in no mood to go out now. She'd make a peanut butter and jelly sandwich and wish she had some milk to go with it. Then a warm bath and bed would round out a long day. Tomorrow promised to be just as long and stressful, but once the reception was underway, Diana would be free to leave. And hopefully put Scott Thomas out of her mind and out of her life.

As soon as she got the peanut butter from the cabinet, the doorbell rang. Frowning, Diana wondered who would be dropping by without calling. Padding barefoot to the door, she checked the side windows and jumped back. Her heart skipped a beat or two, then hammered in her chest. Scott was out there. What was he doing there?

"I saw you," he said through the door. "Open up."

Diana hesitated a moment then taking a long sustaining breath she unlocked the door. "What do you want?" she asked, blocking his entrance.

Scott held up a pizza box and a bottle of wine. "Since you couldn't come to dinner, I brought it to you."

"How do you know I didn't already eat?"

"I assumed." He raised his eyebrows. "And it is an assumption that because you've been out of town, you didn't buy food before you left."

"I could have stopped somewhere before I got here."

"But you didn't." His voice was teasing. "Are you going to invite me in? I'll let you share my dinner."

Diana hesitated a moment. She smelled the cheese and tomato sauce. Her stomach growled. "Didn't you go to the rehearsal dinner?"

"I did."

"Then you can leave the pizza and return to the bachelor party. I'll get your money for the delivery," she said, reducing him to a mere driver. "I'm sure you'll have much more fun with your friends."

Her comment didn't seem to touch him in any way. He stared at her with the same boyish grin he had when they were students and he was chiding her for some infraction of his personal rules.

"Can't. They had shrimp in the salad. I'm allergic to seafood."

"You know everyone in the wedding party. I'm sure they'll miss you."

"Let's see." Scott tucked the wine under his arm and leaned against the doorjamb, holding the pizza box in two hands. "Sit around with a bunch of guys and drink while watching X-rated movies versus sitting around with a beautiful woman while drinking and…"

"There is no *and,*" she finished for him, even though him thinking she was beautiful made her heart do something close to a tribal dance. "The party's at the Marriott. I'm sure you can find it." Diana pushed the door to close it, but Scott proved both agile and quick. Taking the tiny space she used to step back, he slipped past her and into the room.

"Nice house," he said, looking around. He walked through the foyer and into the main living room. With just a few steps he'd taken ownership of the place. He moved as if he had a right to be here. "Is this the way to the kitchen?"

Diana closed the door and said nothing. She hadn't been in Princeton that long, but when she chose this house, it was because the kitchen was state-of-the-art. While the business kept her out of it most of the time, Diana loved to cook.

Scott walked to the great room-kitchen combination. Diana found him making himself at home as he looked through cabinets for plates. Her shoes lay in front of the sofa and the television was muted on an old black-and-white movie. Even though she was taller than the average woman, Scott dwarfed her, especially since she was without her five-inch shoes.

"Where do you keep the wineglasses?" he asked, still moving comfortably from cabinet to cabinet.

Diana went to the china cabinet and took out one glass. Coming back, she set it on the dark granite countertop.

"Aren't you having any?"

"You're assuming the glass is for you."

"You wouldn't throw a guy out on a cold winter's night without a glass of his own wine." Although his voice was completely sincere, he was still teasing, and Diana wasn't in a teasing mood.

"I wouldn't," Diana told him. "But it's June, not January. And while it is night, I need a clear head tomorrow. I've had a long day and a plane ride, wine is not a good choice for me."

"Where did you go again?"

"Montana."

"Montana," Scott echoed.

"My partner, Teddy, usually takes care of the wedding planning. I do some of it when we're busy, but mainly my focus is on additional franchise sales and operations."

"Is Teddy a man or a woman?"

It wasn't the question Diana expected. She wondered why he wanted to know. Most people wanted to know about franchising: what it cost, how was set it up. Or how she got into building her own business. "*Her* name is Theresa Granville."

Scott nodded. "So, Weddings by Diana can be found in how many places?"

"Right now we're in six states. I'm working on adding Montana." She left it at that, not going into detail about the difficulties she was having. She was sure they would iron out soon and things would return to normal.

Scott placed two slices of pizza on each plate and offered her one. "Are you putting me out or eating with me?"

Diana's stomach growled in answer.

The kitchen was too intimate. It was huge, a chef's delight with light blue walls and rich cherry cabinetry. The appliances were stainless steel, and everything was coordinated. Diana could easily see her sister and brothers gathering here for a meal, talking over old times and catching up on their lives since they were last together. But she couldn't sit here with Scott. The space would be too personal, too open to confession. And she didn't want him to learn anything more about her than she was willing to expose.

Taking her plate, she went to the great room and wedged herself in the corner of the long sofa. Stretching her legs in front of her, she rested the plate on her lap, preventing him from sitting close to her. He took a place on the love seat across from her.

Diana took a bite of the pizza triangle. "What is Jennifer going to think about you throwing her numbers off?"

"I don't know. She'll probably force the waitress to sit down just to keep the table balanced." They both laughed. Diana relaxed a moment. Scott could be charming and funny when he wanted to be. She had only seen a couple of sides of him, the angry landlord and prankster college student.

"Why did you come here tonight?" she asked. Diana didn't know if he'd tell her the truth, but she wasn't a person Scott ever sought out. He was perfectly content to let her remain a face in the crowd unless he wanted to embarrass her in some way.

"I brought you dinner."

Diana acknowledged it by glancing at the plate and the box he'd carried from the kitchen and set on the square coffee table between them.

"I see, but you were out with a lot of people who know you well enough to include you in their wedding. Yet you left them to come here." She paused. "You said it had nothing to do with my offices. So what is the draw?"

"You sell yourself short," he said.

Diana laughed. "One thing I don't do is lie to myself. We never got on all those years ago. We didn't get along when you tried to evict me."

"I never tried to evict you," he protested.

Diana went on as if he hadn't spoken. "And at the coffee shop we agreed the computer should never have matched us. So, I don't understand why you're sitting in my great room eating pizza and drinking wine, when you could be letting go at a bachelor party."

Scott set his wineglass on the table. His plate, now holding only crumbs of cheese and a slosh of tomato sauce, was set next to it. He leaned back in the chair and stared directly at Diana. She didn't think he was going to answer her. Finally he stood up. Diana thought he might go to the door and leave. Her heartbeat increased. She wanted him to both go and stay.

He did neither. He moved around the coffee table and stood in front of her. Diana bit her bottom lip to keep it from trembling.

"I came by because when we stood at the altar tonight you kissed me."

* * *

"I kissed him." Diana was dressed for the wedding, which was scheduled to begin two hours from now. She liked to be at the bride's home an hour before she was to leave for her last ride as a single woman. Often there was chaos, and dealing with that needed a level head. Unsure if that would be the case today, Diana hunted for everything she needed. The trip to Montana and her return yesterday hadn't given her time to come to the office and make sure she had everything. Consequently, she'd risen early and dropped by before going to Jennifer's.

"You did what?" Joy spread across Teddy's face like the sun rising. "Where?"

"In the church." Diana searched for her scissors. Finding them, she hooked them on the inside of her jacket. The outside was lace, but the lining held a myriad of possible necessities. Diana wanted to be prepared. Nothing could go wrong today.

"Why?"

"He volunteered to stand in for the groom, who wasn't there. And the bridesmaids were too superstitious to stand in for Jennifer. You know Jennifer's many beliefs. Apparently her friends are just as bad. So I ended up doing it."

"But you're not supposed to practice the kiss," Teddy said, her eyes following Diana as she moved from place to place collecting supplies.

"I know that. It was Scott who started it."

"And you finished it?" Teddy questioned.

"Not exactly." Diana stopped searching and turned to look at her partner. She wanted to tell someone. She wanted to explain her feelings and have someone sympathize with her. Teddy was the perfect choice, but Diana was unsure of her feelings. She hadn't had time to process the changes that she saw in Scott or the way she felt about him. And there was still the matter of her offices. Could he be using this tactic to get her to do what he wanted?

But the worst part, the reason she couldn't explain everything to Teddy was she didn't even realize kissing Scott was anything but natural. They stood at the altar. The ceremony was over. Father Ryan said, *Kiss the bride,* and Scott kissed her. She'd fallen into his arms so easily, it was as if she belonged there, that it was natural for her to be there. She'd become unaware of the other people in the church until she'd heard Jennifer clear her throat. She would have remained in his arms and gone on kissing him. Thank goodness Jennifer interrupted them.

"Did you like it?" Teddy's voice intruded on her thoughts bringing her back to the office.

"It's been a long time since anyone kissed me."

"I'll take that as a yes," Teddy said.

"Well, I only have to deal with him for one more day." Diana went back to getting everything she needed. "Once the ceremony is over and the requisite photos are taken at the reception, I'll be out the door faster than she can get the white off that dress."

Teddy laughed. It was a saying they used to mean the consummation of the vows. Diana's mother had coined the phrase and the two women adopted it.

"How did you get out of the church without explaining?"

"I asked Father Ryan if he had any further details to share. Then I left."

"Your face must have been burning."

Her entire body was burning. Even now, she felt the heat of last night. "I think that's everything," Diana said, finally feeling she was ready to leave. She looked at her desk, her bag of essentials, her notebook, assessing that everything was in order.

"What are you going to do about it?" Teddy asked.

Finally Diana looked at her partner. "About what?"

"About your attraction to our landlord. Maybe you can use that attraction to get him to back off about the offices."

"Teddy!" Diana was appalled at the suggestion. "Have you stopped to think that his attraction for me, if there is an attraction, may be for the same reason?"

Teddy's happy face turned to one of concern. "I hadn't thought of that."

"Think about it." Diana looked around one more time, then checked her watch. "I have to go. You've got everything under control here, right?"

She nodded. "My wedding isn't until five, so I'll head over to the bride's house this afternoon."

"See you tomorrow, when we can go back to business as usual." Diana threw the words over her shoulder as she headed through the door.

"Wink at him during the reception…maybe ask him to dance," Teddy shouted at Diana's back.

Diana wouldn't even make eye contact with him if she could help it. She wanted things to go back to the way they were just twenty-four hours ago. She'd been on a plane from Montana. Anything after she arrived at the church she wanted expunged from the universe.

That would include his kiss, a voice spoke in her head. Diana stumbled and twisted the toe of her shoe on the broken parking lot pavement. A large gash appeared in the front.

"Damn," she cursed. "This is Scott's fault."

Everything was his fault. Well most of it. From the moment she walked on campus ten years ago until he left her house last night, he'd been a thorn in her side. After the wedding today, she didn't want to see him again. He could deal with her lawyer regarding their offices if any more discussion was necessary—and as far as she was concerned, there wasn't.

So life could go back to normal. Diana thought it, but she didn't feel it. She knew something more would happen, something unexpected. Scott wasn't the type of man to just drop things. He had a plan in mind, and Diana wondered what it was. She needed to be on guard for whatever he might spring on her. His appearing at her home last night was unexpected and designed to throw her world out of kilter.

He'd succeeded.

Diana took a deep breath as she parked along the curved driveway of the house where Jennifer lived. The street and drive leading to the house was ringed with cars. Only Jennifer would have a procession leading to the church. For days workmen had been setting up for the reception. Thankfully, the weather was cooperating.

Getting out of the car, Diana went to the trunk and changed her broken shoe for another pair. She had learned the necessity of being prepared for every contingency. Not only did she have extra shoes, she had several changes of clothes in case they might be needed. Diana turned and took a long look at the cathedral. She'd done a few weddings here before, but this was the first one where she felt as if a huge weight was on her shoulders. Even when she first started and bluffed her way through her first solo as a wedding consultant, she hadn't been this nervous.

The limousine arrived carrying the bride. Behind her car was a succession of stretch limos carrying the twelve bridesmaids. Diana greeted the bridesmaids and ushered them into the rooms set up for them. Then she accompanied the bride. Jennifer truly looked wonderful. Her face had that bridal glow to it. Or was it that she was so in love with Bill that it was visible? For a moment Diana envied her. She wondered if she'd ever look like that when she thought of a man.

Jennifer had a perfect day for her ceremony. Diana assumed all the numbers had clicked into place, and from this point on Jennifer's life would be on the schedule she'd set up for herself.

Diana could only hope her own life had a plan. She thought it did. Or it had. Until a few weeks ago when an innocent cup of coffee had thrown her world into chaos. Maybe she should have given up the offices and been done with any dealing with Scott. But fate wasn't on her side. Fate had brought him to this wedding. Even if she had agreed to relocate, he would still be an honored guest at the head table. But they wouldn't have stood before the altar. He wouldn't have come to her apartment. And she wouldn't continue to feel the tingle of his mouth on hers.

"We're ready," Diana told the bridesmaids as she shook thoughts of Scott out of her mind. A hush settled over the women as if everyone was afraid of opening night. "Just do what we rehearsed. It'll all be fine."

She looked at one particular bridesmaid, younger than the rest. Her color was paste-white. "Breathe,"

Diana said. "And smile." She gave the girl a smile, and after a second the girl returned it. Diana leaned close to her and whispered, "Even if you fall on your face, it won't be a catastrophe. One of those hunky grooms-men will rush to your rescue." The girl tried to hide her laugh behind her hand. Diana pulled it away and watched as she relaxed.

One by one the bridesmaids floated down the aisle. Diana stood up from her crouching position as the ring bearer and flower girls took tentative steps down the long aisle. As Jennifer embraced her father's arm and headed toward wedded bliss, Diana breathed a sigh of relief. It was almost over for her. So far she'd avoided making eye contact with Scott, although she'd felt his eyes on her several times. She knew he was looking at her by the heat that surged through her body and inched up her neck. Everyone else would think it was exertion and stress from making sure every detail was going as planned. Scott would know differently.

"You may kiss the bride," Diana heard the priest say. She couldn't help remembering Scott's kiss on her mouth. The church organ started to play, and the bride and groom rushed down the aisle as man and wife. Scott looked directly at her as he went by. Diana kept her eyes on Bill and Jennifer.

As the bridal motorcade—that was the only name she could think to call it—arrived at the reception hall, Diana wanted to run and hide, but she couldn't. She was in charge. From the second car, Scott was the first person to step out. He turned to help his female companion, and Diana ushered them toward the reception line. The assembly moved like a coordinated dance. Jennifer and Bill led the procession and took their assigned places in the reception line. Obligated to go in, Scott moved away from Diana, a bridesmaid on his arm. As he passed he whispered, "You can't avoid me forever."

Diana didn't say anything. Not that she had time. He was already three couples ahead of her. She followed the last of the party. Her duties didn't take her into the reception hall, but she looked in to make sure every detail was as Jennifer had requested. Scott was shaking hands with the guests, but when she looked at him, his eyes found hers as surely as if they were destined to connect. Diana wanted to look away, knew she should, but she didn't. She withstood his stare, trying to prove that she wasn't avoiding him. The war of their eyes only lasted a few seconds before Scott had to give his attention to the next guest in line. To Diana it felt like it lasted an eon.

"You've done a wonderful job," Jennifer's mother whispered when the reception line broke up and the group headed for the dais and the sit-down meal. "Jennifer looks so happy."

"She does," Diana agreed honestly, passing a tissue to Mrs. Embry.

"The flowers, the dresses, the hall." Mrs. Embry dabbed her teary eyes and shook her head as if it was difficult to take it all in. "The church was just lovely."

Diana handed the woman a second tissue.

"Thank you," she said. "I never would have believed Jennifer could look so beautiful."

"She's a beautiful woman," Diana said.

"I know." Her mother patted her hand. "But today... today..."

"She glows," Diana finished for her. Taking Mrs. Embry's arm, she led her to the head table. Scott, who was already seated, got up and met them. "Would you help her to her seat?" Diana asked.

Mrs. Embry was not an old woman. She was overcome with emotion. Jennifer was her only daughter and today she gave her away. Their lives would never be the same.

"Mrs. Embry," Diana called. "It's not goodbye. Your lives will be different and better. In a year or so there may be grandchildren."

Mrs. Embry looked at her for a long time. Then she hugged Diana. "You're a treasure," she said. "You'll be just as beautiful a bride someday as Jennifer is today."

The compliment should have made her feel good, but the fact that Scott heard it made Diana cringe inwardly. She thanked Mrs. Embry and took a step back. Scott accompanied her to her seat. Diana turned and headed for the bride and groom, who were standing at the end of the dais and waiting for everyone to be seated so they could have the full attention of the room.

"Jennifer, Bill," she said with a smile. "It was beautiful. I hope you liked it."

"Everything about it," Jennifer said, her smile wide and happy. "Thank you so much."

"I just wanted to say congratulations again, and since my duties are over, I'm heading home for a relaxing day. Tomorrow, I start again."

"You're not leaving?" Diana didn't have to turn around to know Scott's voice. Ignoring him, she addressed the bride and groom. "Enjoy your honeymoon and have a wonderful life."

Jennifer leaned forward and hugged her. Bill kissed her on the cheek, and the couple moved away to visit their other guests.

"I wore this tuxedo just for you. Look how well it fits."

Diana was reminded of the episode in the dressing room. Her face flamed. She could feel the heat rising and her ears burned as hot as the sun.

"Good night, Scott." Pivoting, she headed for the exit and her SUV.

"You know if you leave, I'll just come by your house tonight," he said.

"I don't have to answer the door."

"I'll make a racket and wake up your neighbors."

Diana stopped walking and turned to face him. "You live in Princeton, right?"

He nodded.

"Then you know how responsive the police force is. I'll call them and tell them you're being a public nuisance."

"I'll tell them you're only acting like this because I kissed you."

Diana felt a lightning bolt jolt her. "What is it you want?" she asked. "We already know we're not compatible. The computer made a mistake. Why can't we just go our separate ways. Unless…unless this constant meeting has another purpose."

"You wound me," Scott said, placing a hand over his heart. "Seriously, the office has nothing to do with this."

"Then what does?"

"I'm intrigued," he said.

"You said that before—and believe me, I don't take it as a compliment."

"It is. I think we should talk. We could start with a dance."

Diana glanced at the empty bandstand. "The band

won't begin until after the meal. The combo will play soft music to accompany the food, but the dancing begins in another ballroom."

"So you'll have to stay. You must be hungry. I'm sure Jennifer and Bill included you in the seating arrangement."

In fact, it was traditional to allow the wedding planner a seat at a back table. As Diana had coordinated the placing of seating cards on the tables, she knew exactly where her seat was.

"You must be hungry," Scott said. "Last night you had little to eat, and I'm sure you were at Jennifer's before breakfast. Have you had more than a cup of coffee today?"

She stared at him a moment, then shook her head.

"Stay. Give me one dance, and I won't bother you again today."

"Is that a promise?"

He raised his right hand in the Boy Scout salute. "I promise."

At that moment a procession of waiters came from several doors and made a ceremony of placing food in front of the guests. The smell of an old-fashioned kitchen reminded her that she was hungry. Scott was right about her food intake. Leaving without eating was running away from him, and she didn't want him to know how much he controlled her actions.

"I will have something to eat."

"And a dance," he prompted.

"One dance," she said. "One only."

His smile broadened, satisfied that he'd won the argument. Taking her arms impulsively, he pulled her forward and dropped a kiss on her cheek. Heat poured through her. Scott started back to his seat. Diana checked to see if anyone had seen the unexpected gesture. It was not protocol for the wedding planner to act as a guest or to be kissed on the floor of the dining room. But then Scott either didn't know the rules or didn't care to follow them. Jennifer and Bill were totally engrossed in each other. No one at the head of the room noticed. However, several people at the table close to where they stood smiled at her.

She nodded to them and quickly walked to her assigned seat. What was she going to do now? She couldn't possibly eat anything and keep it down. Thoughts of Scott pressing his body against hers in a dance was too much to think about. She was sure if he took her in his arms in the broad light of a beautiful sunny afternoon, she could not say she had no feelings for this man without the world around her knowing she was lying.

Chapter 4

Relax, Diana told herself as Scott whirled her about the room. She stepped on his foot once. He didn't say a word about it, didn't tell her to relax, didn't tell her he wouldn't bite, only adjusted his arms and pulled her close to him. Diana smelled his cologne. It was mildly sweet with an undercurrent of something that seemed to come from him. She liked it.

His head touched hers, and she closed her eyes. Her body relaxed and found the perfect combination of movement. She felt everything about him, the fabric of his starched shirt, the heat of his body beneath it, his long legs, and the sureness of his hands as they held her.

Being there was like a dream, and for a moment Diana allowed herself to fantasize that she was the bride dancing her first dance with her newly minted husband. Her feet seemed to glide across the floor.

The music stopped and she opened her eyes.

"That was beautiful," Jennifer said. "I've never seen anyone dance the way you two did. You make a beautiful couple."

Diana's skin burned. She hadn't realized she was being watched. Apparently, the entire room was staring at them. What had she done? She knew. She'd fallen into the dream and let everything she felt pour through the dance. Hadn't she thought about that? She knew it was what many professional dancers wanted, strove to show on the stage. They wanted to show their feelings through the steps. Diana hadn't.

"Thank you," Scott said, saving her from having to answer anything. "I think we need a drink now."

He led her away from the prying eyes and toward the bar. The conversations resumed behind her, and she was certain that people had stopped staring at her.

"I apologize," Diana told Scott. "I never meant to embarrass you."

"You've danced before," he stated, apparently out of context. "And I'm not embarrassed."

Diana had taken lessons and learned many dances that couples used for their first dance. Often she needed to school the groom on a few steps before he took his bride onto the dance floor. At the time she viewed it as part of her full service to the wedding program. Today she regretted ever knowing a single step. Or the feel of Scott's arms holding her, almost cradling her as they traversed the floor.

"But people thought we were…" She stopped, unwilling to finish the thought.

"Thought we were what?" Scott asked.

"It doesn't matter," she said. "Whatever they thought, we're not."

"Are you sure? I can't imagine you've danced that way before."

"I may have." She took affront to his assumption, but knew she had never lost herself in a man's arms on a public dance floor.

"Then why did the color creep under your skin when Jennifer said we looked good together?"

"I'm not used to being the center of attention," she said.

"Then maybe we should get you a drink." They joined the line for the bar.

"And I'm not exactly your type."

"Type?" His brows rose. "I have a type?"

"You did once, and that usually doesn't change with age." She looked at the ceiling for a moment. Then back at him. "At college you majored in female anatomy. I don't believe I ever saw you with the same coed twice. Except for that one woman who followed you everywhere. What was her name?"

"Linda."

"Linda." Diana snapped her fingers as if the name had just come to her.

Scott listened carefully, saying nothing and only changing his expression to take a bite of his dinner or to drink from his glass.

"Your type was the leggy, long-haired, big-boobed girls. While most of us wore jeans and T-shirts to class, your women sported short skirts. The shorter, the better."

Scott nodded. "I don't believe I ever saw you with

anyone. You were always alone. Neither male nor female satisfied your friendship."

"You're wrong. I had friends."

"Really?" His brows rose.

"Who?"

"I doubt you would know any of them. They didn't run in the same circles as you and your friends. They were the nerds."

"Everybody at Princeton was a nerd. It's an admission requirement."

Diana moved a step up and Scott bumped into her. "You consider yourself a nerd?"

"On good days. What do you consider me?"

"BMOC, hands down."

Scott smiled. He'd been a campus sensation and he knew it. Even if he hadn't been on the swim team, where every woman in school could ogle his phenomenal body, he would have been known for his devastating good looks. Diana was no exception. She'd sit in the back at swim meets and watch him, too. Then she'd leave just before he got out of the pool and started talking to the many women calling his name from the gallery.

They'd reached the bar. "White wine and a glass of ice water," he ordered. The bartender filled the order, and Scott handed the water to Diana.

"I want the wine," she said.

Scott took a sip. "I'm not driving. And you are. Wine and cars don't mix."

"I hardly think one glass of wine will impair my driving, but I won't argue." Diana knew she could handle a glass of wine, but the stress she'd been under the last few days, along with an impromptu trip to Montana and missed hours of sleep, she knew she probably should stick to water. Taking a sip, she looked up and several members of the wedding party heading for them. They acknowledged her and began talking to Scott.

Diana took the opportunity to slip away. Once outside, she practically ran to her van and was out of the driveway before Scott had a chance to stop her retreat. She promised him one dance. Promised and fulfilled. She didn't need to wait for his friends to criticize her for the past or to gape at how much her appearance had changed. She could say a thing or two about the change in them. And it would be less flattering.

Scott's sister's voice broke the silence as he entered his apartment later that evening. He ran for the phone, grabbing the receiver just as she clicked off. Piper always tried his home number first. He pulled his cell out, ready for it to ring when the light on his answering machine started to glow.

Pressing the button, he listened to Piper's deep alto tones as she asked about the wedding and if he'd met anyone interesting. Scott smiled at her comment. She was almost as bad as a mother wanting a grandchild. Piper had been married twice, divorced once. While she had no children yet, she wanted them, and each time she called, Scott wondered if she would tell him she was pregnant.

He checked his cell as he listened. It remained silent, but her voice said, "You're probably still at the reception or you got lucky, so I won't interrupt you by ringing your cell. Talk to you soon."

He heard the click when she disconnected. He and Piper were close. They had always been both friends and siblings. She understood him, but he knew the real purpose of her call was to test his attitude. She knows his buddies would rib him for being the last bachelor. He'd avoided the ribbing last night by ditching most of the bachelor party. But he couldn't skip the wedding or the reception.

They cornered him at the bar and Diana had gotten away. Almost the moment she was out of earshot, the conversation started on him settling down.

Then the matchmaking began. Women didn't think men tried to set other men up, but they were wrong. Even if men weren't looking for a long-term relationship, they wanted someone to have fun with. If that fun morphed into a relationship and then into something more, all the better.

"Where's that woman you were making love to on the dance floor?" asked Dan, a linebacker-size friend who never held his tongue.

"We weren't doing that," Scott said, feeling he needed to defend the absent Diana.

The guys laughed.

"She's a beauty. You could do worse," Steven put in. "But since she's gone, the woman I accompanied down the aisle does simultaneous translations. She works at the United Nations."

"Are you trying to set me up again?"

"You're not getting any younger," Steven said.

"I'm thirty-two, not sixty-two."

"And you fly around the country, not stopping long enough to spend a night in one place."

"I spend plenty of nights here."

"Are any of them with her?"

Dan's question had them all staring at Scott, waiting for an answer. While there was noise in the rest of the room, the small circle where they stood was a bubble of silence.

"Kiss and tell," Scott finally covered. "You think I should do that?"

"Yeah," Mike answered.

"We're no longer in college, guys," Scott reminded them.

"College," Mike said. "Was she…" He stopped. "No…she's not." He looked both surprised and incredulous.

"What are you trying to say?" Dan asked.

"Brainiac?" Mike's eyebrows rose. "Diana 4.0?"

"Who's Diana 4.0?" Dan asked.

"Tell me that's not her?" Mike addressed Scott. He looked over his shoulder in the direction Diana had gone.

"That's her," Scott said.

"Oh, man." Mike spun all the way around, giving a hoot and doing a little backward dance. "Whoever would have thought you and Diana 4.0 would have anything in common?"

"I'm lost," Dan said. "Who is she?"

"She was the brain in college," Mike explained. "Wow, the difference in appearance is almost indescribable. At school she had all this hair covering her face. Some of the guys on campus called her Cousin Itt."

Dan and Steven laughed. Scott didn't.

"Her nose was always in a book and our friend Scott here taunted her to no end. She hated him," Mike went on. "And you had no love for her, if I remember right."

"I remember her now. How did you two get together?" Steven asked.

"We're not together," Scott denied.

Dan looked at the dance floor. "I think there's a permanent groove out there where you two danced."

Scott knew he wasn't going to be able to explain this or live it down. Even Jennifer had remarked on his behavior on the dance floor with Diana. The problem was he hadn't been conscious of it while it was happening. If it was just his friends ribbing him, he could endure it, but Jennifer wasn't part of the group. She was Bill's wife now, but she didn't have the same history with them.

"What about Dorothy?" Steven asked.

All eyes went to him. "Who's Dorothy?" Mike asked.

"She was my partner going down the aisle. From what I hear, she's works for an airline. That ought to be right up your alley, Scott."

"Yeah," Dan agreed. "You two could meet in different cities and—"

"Stop," Scott said. "If you guys will leave me alone, I'll find my own woman. And what if I don't? I won't be the only man in America who's unmarried and liking it."

Scott spoke with finality. He wanted this conversation to end. He and Diana had no relationship, despite the dance and the two kisses that his friends didn't know about. As he'd told her, she intrigued him. A computer had put them together, matched them on more than fifty points of interest. Never mind that they had hated each other in college or that she was the last person on the planet he'd think of as compatible. But she was the one and only name that came up after he put in his requirements.

Scott would let his friends think he and Diana came

together as a result of Bill and Jennifer's wedding. Not that he'd looked for the perfect match and got Diana 4.0.

Scott sat down, telling himself she wasn't the one. She couldn't be, yet since their meeting in the coffee shop, she was constantly on his mind. And she brought back memories he thought he'd buried ten years ago. He'd kissed her on campus. It was a prank, at least it started that way, but somewhere in the infinitesimal space between their lips meeting, she'd gotten under his skin. He'd tried to fight it off, but in the darkness, where both demons and conscious thought is true, his mind knew the truth. He was attracted to Brainiac.

For ten years he'd wondered about that day. He wanted to find out if it was just a fluke or if her kiss was as sensational as he remembered.

And then he kissed her again.

And it was.

The last American bachelor. Scott smiled at the moniker, but there was no humor in it. His buddies had given him the singles treatment. He knew some of them could be jealous and were using him to cover their true feelings, but for the most part they were happy men. And happier after they found their true loves.

Scott wondered if he would ever find his. That had been the foundation that led him to Diana. How could it possibly lead him full circle to the one woman in the universe that he'd never considered as a girlfriend, let alone a life mate? He and Brainiac had nothing in common.

So why was he aroused by her? In college he'd taunted her, trying to get a rise out of the long-haired, studious coed. He'd gone along with the guys in teasing

her because she was different. She always had her head
in a book, and some of his friends called her Diana 4.0
because she had a perfect record. She graduated with
a 4.0 average.

Scott shared only one class with her. She sat in the
back and never uttered a word unless specifically called
upon, yet she aced every test. She hid behind her mane
of straight hair and avoided looking at anyone. Her hair
remained just as long as it had in the past, but she no
longer hid behind it. She wore it in curls that framed
her face and showed off high cheekbones, dramatic
eyes and a mouth that beckoned him like a heat-seek-
ing missile. Who knew beneath that brain was a cap-
tivating beauty?

And Scott never expected her identity to pop up
when he completed the online form. He filled in a general description of the woman he was looking for, then
checked practically every criterion box: speaks several
languages; plays one or more musical instruments; owns
business; financially secure; drives a car; understands
wine, high fashion and jewels. Knows architecture; has
a sense of humor and excellent interpersonal skills. It
was more like a job interview than a relationship form.

The MatchforLove.com service notice said he would
get at least three compatible matches based on his answers. Scott clicked the submit button and waited while
the computer churned through the electricity to access
the database housed somewhere in the world. Of course,
no address was listed. The small icon on the screen circled and circled until he believed the system had frozen.
He'd chosen everything, so how could any one person
fulfill all those requirements?

After watching it for several minutes he went to get

a beer from the refrigerator. He snapped the top off and threw it in the trash, then took a long swig before returning to the computer. He heard the ping just as he sat down. "You have a match," the impersonal voice stated.

Then the screen began to scroll information. There was no picture, but almost everything he'd checked or required came back to him in astonishing color. At the end of the file was an email address and a flashing message that said, *Send an email.* Scott took an hour to decide to make contact.

And that led him to Diana Greer.

"Thanks, Edward." Diana smiled at the barista and took the two cups. As she turned to leave, Scott stood in front of her.

"What are you doing here?" she asked. She'd been coming to this shop since she moved to Princeton. Except for the day they were to meet for the first time, she'd never seen Scott in this place. Diana didn't want to give up her favorite coffee shop, but she also didn't want to take the chance of running into him on a daily basis.

"I came for coffee. He looked at the two cups she was carrying. "Unless one of those is for me."

Diana pulled back on the cups in case he reached to take one away. "One is for my partner, Teddy, and the other is mine." She glanced over her shoulder, then back at him. "The line is short. I'm sure Edward will get you whatever you want." She walked past him and out the door. Luck wasn't with her today, as it hadn't been since Scott returned to her life.

The office was too far away for her to walk. She had to get to her car. Diana had parked in one of the few spots close to the shop directly across from one of the large churches on the main street.

"Do you want something?" she asked, sitting the two cups on the roof and opening the car door. "Besides coffee?"

"You drive a Porsche?" Scott's eyes roved over the car as if it were a sex object.

Diana stared at him from the driver's side of the red sports car. She supposed he expected her to have a small compact. After all, Brainiac should drive something sensible, shouldn't she?

"I'm impressed," Scott said, laughter tinging his voice.

"Didn't think I'd do it, right? You expected me to drive a compact, something small, nondescript, something that could fade as easily into the walls as everyone expected me to do. Maybe I should have a dull green mom-mobile, or at the very least an SUV?"

"I expected a company van, logo on the side, custom-wrapped in pink with ribbons. Who would believe Diana 4.0 drove a Porsche?"

"Maybe the world will end," she told him.

Scott walked from the back to the front of the car. Several times he raised his eyebrows and nodded, giving it his approval.

"I do drive an SUV, by the way," Diana told him. He finally took his eyes off the car to look at her. "It's not pink, nor is it wrapped in ribbons. When I have a wedding or need to cart around large items, I pull it down off its cinder blocks and put the tires back on it."

"I saw it in your profile. That's why I expected... something different."

"That's the second time you've brought my profile into question."

"I just wondered if everything in it was true."

"Why?" she asked.

"It sounds extraordinary," Scott said. "You speak how many languages?"

"Four," she threw at him from the opposite side of the car. "Would you like me to reply in one of them? Or all of them?"

"And you play at least one instrument."

Diana closed her eyes and took a long intake of air. When she opened them, she set the coffee in the car and slammed the door.

Coming around the car, she stepped onto the sidewalk. The action brought her close to him and her shoes made her nearly as tall. "Follow me," she ordered. "You want to know about my profile?"

"You're so busy," Scott said. "How could you possibly do everything stated there and run a business, too?"

"I have a partner," Diana said.

"Even with a partner."

Diana went up the steps of the church in front of her car. "Open the door," she said.

Scott did as commanded. Inside Diana headed to the sanctuary, going down an aisle she was familiar with. The church piano set in the front. Sliding onto the bench, she took no time to prepare, but lit right into a Chopin nocturne. As if it were a medley, she transitioned into Bach, Mozart and Paganini. Leaving the masters behind, she flawlessly moved on to Gershwin, Bernstein, Rogers and Hammerstein, and Cole Porter, and ended with Stephen Sondheim. Standing up, she stared him in the face.

She spoke in German. "Would you like me to translate?

"'I am exactly as represented. Everything in my profile is the absolute truth. I told no lies. How many did you tell?'" he translated for her.

"I see you speak German. How about Italian, Russian and Chinese?" Diana didn't wait for an answer. She turned on her heel and marched up the sanctuary aisle.

Scott caught her at the door and turned her to face him. "There is only one lie in my profile," he said.

"Which one?" she asks.

"This one." He pulled her into his arms and delivered a kiss that curled her toes. Diana thought that phrase was the stuff of books or movies. It wasn't a real condition. People's toes didn't curl. But hers did. Her arms went around him. This wasn't like the kiss at the wedding rehearsal. There they had an audience. Here there was no one. They were together and alone. His mouth took hers in the sight of stained-glass windows, vaulted ceilings and the polished wood of the entry hall. Diana didn't think of where they were. She didn't think at all. She felt. She let his mouth tease hers and sweep her deeply into a recess of pleasure that had her groaning with delight.

His arms tightened around her waist, pulling her so close to him that not even air couldn't escape between them. When Scott finally dragged his mouth from hers, she was weak and limp in his arms. Her mind was muddled, making it impossible for her to think straight.

Diana was totally undone by his action and her complicity. This was a different experience. She'd been kissed by him before, but this kiss was the no-holds-barred kind. Yet it held a promise. This was not the time or place to continue, but in the kiss, Scott told her there would be a continuum. She might want to end their relationship because of their differences, but their time line had changed in the last few seconds.

Backing away from him, she tried to control her breathing. It took several moments before she trusted herself to speak. "That wasn't in your profile," she said.

Scott gave her a look filled with fire and desire. Then he spoke in a voice that was low and sexy and contained the same promise of more to come. "It is now."

Chapter 5

"What the hell is going on out there?" Diana said, coming into the office. She would have slammed the door if it didn't have that compressed soft-close feature.

Outside several trucks were in the parking lot. A full crew of men with jackhammers were polluting the air with the sounds of their machinery as they tore up the asphalt. This was all Diana needed. On top of dealing with Scott first thing in the morning, her coffee was now cold. And he was using a new tactic to get her to move.

"Let's see," Teddy said from the doorway of the small kitchenette where they had a microwave, a coffeemaker, a refrigerator and a small table. She leaned against the entrance, one foot crossed over the other and her arms folded. "I take it the wedding yesterday didn't go well."

"The wedding went fine," she said with a little less vehemence in her voice than the initial declaration.

"Then what did our golden boy do to upset you?"

"He's not *our* golden boy."

"But he has upset you?" Teddy dropped her arms and came farther into the kitchen. The microwave bell rang and Diana popped the door open, removing the two cups.

"He showed up at Edward's while I was getting coffee."

"Is that all?" Teddy knew there was more to Diana's anger than she had said so far. Her partner was very perceptive. Their business had taught them that there was more a bride wanted than what her words said. And while Diana wasn't a bride, she hadn't relayed the entire story.

Taking a sip of the reheated coffee, they moved to Diana's office, where she told Teddy the entire morning's activities, including the kiss just inside the church door. "And then I find this in the parking lot." She raised her arm toward the inner wall on the side of the building where the cars were parked.

"We've weathered this before," Teddy cautioned her. "This extreme reaction from you over a man is unusual."

"It's like he baits me," Diana said. "One minute he's Sir Galahad and the next he's the Grinch who stole Christmas."

"Why do you think that is?"

"I don't know. He acted like this when we were in school together. I was always the butt of his pranks. Any chance he had to embarrass me, he'd take it."

"How long have you been carrying this torch?"

Diana's head snapped up. She stared directly at her partner as if the other woman had suddenly begun speaking a foreign language.

"I am not attracted to him."

"This is me…Teddy." She placed a hand on her chest. "You can't lie to me."

That was all she needed to say. Diana dropped her shoulders and set her coffee cup on the desk.

"Damn," she said softly. Then she answered honestly, "Since my first day at college. I came out of a building and literally walked into him." She paused. "Since that day, he's only looked at me in order to belittle and ridicule."

"Don't worry," Teddy soothed her. "They say admission is the first step."

"Toward what?" Diana snickered. "A cure?"

"There is no cure for love." Teddy spoke the words as if they were a prayer.

"I'm not in love with him," Diana denied.

The two women stared at each other for a long moment. A smile raised the corners of Teddy's mouth, then grew wider. She began to laugh. Diana tried to hold it in, but Teddy's face broke into a smile that had Diana joining her. The smile grew until she was laughing. Diana tried to stop it, but only managed a hiccup and then a burst of sound. Suddenly both women were laughing as if they'd discovered the funniest thing on earth. Diana's eyes misted and she put her hand up to cover her mouth. The laughter grew until both women were dabbing at the corners of their eyes and the pent-up stress was released.

Diana could resort to only one method of getting through the days—work. She threw herself into the sale and management aspects of the business like a woman possessed.

By midmorning, she had read several reports that had piled up on her desk while she'd worked on the Embry wedding. She'd gone through her email and answered several phone calls. She updated the PowerPoint presentation she used when making an initial call.

As noon approached, her computer made a specific sound she hadn't heard in weeks, alerting her to a message from someone at MatchforLove.com. Diana's stomach clenched. She reached for her cell phone. The email address was familiar. The phone slipped from her fingers. She fought and caught it. There was a time when seeing that address caused excitement to race through her. Today it caused pain. She was not going to that site to collect a message. Her previous adventure with Scott ended in disaster. She wouldn't start it again.

Taking her leather pad emblazoned with the Weddings by Diana logo on it, she went to Teddy's office. They usually had a meeting on Monday morning. And it was still morning. At least for the next half hour.

Sitting down, she asked, "How are we set for the next month? Do we need any help?"

As usual, Teddy opened the schedule on her laptop and swung the screen around so they both could see it. There were five weddings in July.

"Can you handle them all?"

Teddy nodded. "There are several apprentices nearly ready to fly solo."

Diana didn't miss her partner's careful choice of words. Teddy was grooming the apprentices to lead, stepping in if needed, or if the bride was someone like Jennifer Embry, old money and difficult.

"Looks fine," Diana said.

"Everything's under control. What about the franchises?" Teddy asked.

Diana smiled. "I've had several calls this morning. Packets are going out. And the one in Montana is coming along. I think they'll be up and running by the end of the month."

"Any more trips out there?"

"Not at the moment, but I'll need to be there when the doors initially open."

At that moment the phone rang in the outer office. "Oops, that's me," Diana said, recognizing the ringtone.

"I'll get it." Teddy lifted the receiver and punched the button to reroute the call. "Weddings by Diana," she said. "This is Ms. Granville."

She listened to the caller. Diana read Teddy's face. It changed from surprise to a wide smile that relaxed her features. Diana wondered who it was. She thought it was someone inquiring about a franchise or a wedding. Then it sounded personal. She got up to leave, but Teddy waived her back.

Removing the receiver from her ear, Teddy offered it to Diana. "It's for you."

"Who is it?" Diana asked, taking the phone. From Teddy's expression and familiarity, it was obviously someone they knew outside of the business world.

"Scott."

Diana nearly dropped the tan-colored instrument. She put her hand over the mouthpiece. "What does he want?" she whispered.

"Only one way to find out," Teddy smiled.

Diana made a guttural noise in her throat and lifted

the phone to her ear. "This is Ms. Greer," she answered formally. "How may I help you?"

"I apologize," Scott replied.

Diana expelled a long breath. If she was honest with herself, she'd admit it wasn't all his fault. Maybe Teddy was right and he was no longer the bane of her existence as he had once been. To punctuate his point the jackhammering outside flared loudly.

"Apology accepted," she said. "Is that all?"

"Not exactly."

"Well, what else is there?"

"Have dinner with me tonight?"

"Dinner?" Diana glanced at Teddy, who leaned forward in her chair, her head bobbing up and down in agreement. "I don't think so. We only seem to rub each other the wrong way."

"That's just it. I want to prove all the hostility is behind me."

"And you think dinner will do that?" Diana didn't try to hide her skepticism.

Teddy was grinning now. *Say yes,* she mouthed silently. Diana turned away from her.

"It may not be the total answer, but it's a start." His voice sounded sincere, but she wasn't convinced.

"Are you trying to get me to go to dinner so you can bring up the offices?"

"I would not do that. This is purely a friendship dinner."

"We're not friends," she told him.

"But we could be."

"I have too much work that piled up while I worked on the Embry wedding. I don't think—"

Teddy came around the desk and took the phone.

"She'd love to go to dinner," Teddy answered. "What time?"

Diana grabbed for the phone, but Teddy eluded her. "Seven o'clock will be fine."

"I can't go," Diana said through clenched teeth.

"You can pick her up—"

"—at the office." Diana grabbed the phone, but Teddy held on tightly. She could only speak loudly into the mouthpiece. She didn't want Scott in her home. After the kiss in the church this morning, she didn't trust herself alone with him and in private.

"I'll see you at seven."

"Bye," Teddy said and replaced the receiver.

"Why did you do that? Why did you set me up with the one man I don't want to see?"

"Because he's the one man you *do* want to see." She gave Diana a pointed look. "And as my mother used to say, face the issue and get it out of your system or get it in your system."

"I don't have time for him. We've got weddings in the works. And that's where my attention should be."

"Learn to multitask," Teddy said.

The noise in the parking lot ceased around 4:00 p.m. Diana's headache kept going. Teddy usually worked late, but today she thought she'd leave early. Diana insisted that she remain until Scott arrived. Since she'd gotten Diana into this mess, she could well stay until the last possible moment. If this was a Victorian wedding, Diana could insist she act as chaperone. But they were more than a decade into a new century, and Diana and Scott already knew each other. A chaperone wouldn't be necessary. Maybe a referee was what they needed.

Both women watched from the office window as Scott got out of his car at two minutes before seven. He'd been impressed with Diana's Porsche. The car he got out of was a sleek red Lexus with vanity tags bearing the word FLYYBOY.

"He's punctual," Teddy said.

Diana's throat went dry. She watched him walk toward the glass doors. He wore khakis and a dark blue shirt, open at the neck. Even from here, the man was devastatingly attractive. He no longer sported the boyish steps of an emerging adult. He was all male, confident, sure of himself, and Diana knew how she could melt in his arms. Tonight she had to keep a lock on her emotions and make sure this morning was not repeated.

"All right, I've fulfilled my part. I'm going home." Teddy had her purse on her shoulder and was ready to leave. "Have a great night," she said. "Tell me all about it tomorrow."

"I will, and one day I hope to return the favor." Sarcasm tinged her voice.

She could hear Teddy's laugh as she headed down the hall toward the rear entrance. Her car was parked next to it, and she always said good-night to the guard who was stationed there.

Diana didn't try to stop her. From this point on, she was on her own. She could either act like a professional or she could fall over Scott like a lovesick schoolgirl. She was determined that the former happened and the latter was held in check.

Meeting him at the door, Diana unlocked it and slipped through. "I'm ready," she said. "Where are we eating?"

"I didn't know you'd be that hungry, or I'd have made the reservation for earlier."

She wasn't hungry at all. She didn't want to go to dinner. She didn't want to be in Scott's company, but she was committed.

"You look great." His eyes swept her up and down, looking admiringly at the white skirt and green off-the-shoulder sweater she wore. Unsure of their restaurant, she wore something that would work at most places in the area.

"Shall we go?" she asked.

He nodded. Diana locked the office door and they took the elevator to the ground floor. He'd parked next to her Porsche, but opened the door to his Lexus and helped her inside before walking around the hood to get in himself.

"About this morning," she said as soon as he was seated.

"Let's not talk about this morning," Scott said. "Let's enjoy the night."

Diana wasn't sure if she should press the point. She didn't know what she really wanted to say, only that something needed to be said. Some explanation needed to be rendered to set things straight. She decided against trying to find the words. The air between them was already heavy.

Scott drove through the narrow streets. At this hour a long, dark line of late-model cars was parked along the curb. Even for a Monday the population of the tiny hamlet was out in force. After circling Palmer Square, Scott pulled into a garage and shut down the engine. When he helped her out of the car, Diana immediately dropped the hand she held, but not before an electric current went up her arm.

The night was warm, and they walked the short distance to the center of town.

"I suppose if we don't talk about this morning, we have nothing to talk about," Diana said. "What happens when we get to the restaurant? We sit there looking at our food until the meal is over and we can go home?"

Scott stopped on the square leading up to Nassau Street, which was relatively empty. The small park in the center acted only as a causeway allowing cars to make a U-turn without traveling the full distance around the square.

"You want to talk about this morning?" His voice was harsh. "I'll tell you about it. The kiss was unintentional, but I enjoyed it. I thoroughly loved having you in my arms, having my mouth on yours, feeling the softness of your skin and smelling your morning soap and perfume. It was tantalizing, and despite the fact that we stood in a church, I wanted to take you right there and then."

Diana's back was to a wall. Scott was close enough for her to smell the minty toothpaste he'd used. She could move sideways in either direction, but his words pinned her to the spot.

"Is that what you wanted to hear?"

She swallowed. She didn't know what she wanted to hear, but his words had her heart singing. Did she really have that much of an effect on him? And so fast. How long had it been since they reconnected in person? A few weeks. In that time they'd shared two kisses, but they were constantly thrown in each other's path.

"Don't you have anything to say?" Scott asked. His voice wasn't as strong as it had been.

"Truthfully, I don't know what I wanted to hear. I wanted to know why you kissed me. We both know we have no future, yet twice now you've kissed me."

"Twice now, we've kissed each other," he corrected.

He moved in even closer to her. Diana tried to move back, but she had no place to go.

"Don't think I don't know you enjoyed it, too. You were right there, clinging to me, giving as good as you got."

Diana dropped her eyes for a moment, then looked back at him. "I admit it. I did like being kissed."

"By me," he challenged.

"By you," she said. "But don't take it to mean this is the beginning of anything, because it's not."

For the longest moment he stared into her eyes. She challenged him, refusing to look away no matter how much she wanted to. Scott was too close. Diana hoped he wouldn't move the half inch that would meld their mouths together. Her heart hammered in her head, and she battled her lungs to keep her breathing even. After what seemed like a century, Scott took a step back. She forced herself to exhale slowly. She didn't want him to know how long she'd been holding her breath and how hard she was trying to control her heartbeat. And, worse, how much she wanted him to kiss her again. Yet she was afraid he might.

They were only steps away from the entry gates of Princeton University and the expansive knoll of grass and walkways where Scott had first kissed her. It was a prank, a dare, and she knew it, but the result was the same as what had happened in church that morning.

She was putty in his arms. He'd nailed her on it. She had no control when it came to him.

"Why don't we go on to dinner or you can take me back to my car? It seems our evening is ruined."

"One question."

She waited, again holding her breath at whatever Scott planned to say.

"What did you feel this morning?"

Diana pursed her lips and stared straight into Scott's eyes. He looked at her steadily. She wanted to know what he was thinking, but he gave her no clue of his expectations. Searching for something to say, she came up with nothing.

"I spend a lot of time working," she finally said. "It's been a long time since anyone kissed me or held me."

Scott let out a slow breath.

"I already admitted that I liked being kissed." She paused, taking a moment before going on. "Hate me now, but you could have been anyone. It wouldn't take much for me to find comfort in a man's arms."

She raised her eyes expecting him to be angry, waiting for the color to flood or drain from his face. Knowing his eyes would darken and he'd walk away, leaving her alone on the sidewalk. Secretly, she wanted it to happen. She could already see him going.

But it didn't.

Scott's eyes darkened but with need, not anger. He stepped forward. Her back was already against the retaining wall of an office building, and she found it solid and unmovable. She was trapped, both by the environment and by the man. Scott leaned close to her, so close his lips were only a millimeter from hers. She could taste his toothpaste. Emotions, wild and passionate, rocketed through her, and it took a superhuman effort for her to remain still.

She felt his mouth move on hers as he uttered one solitary word.

"Liar."

Chapter 6

The only good thing about their meal together was entering the restaurant. Because Diana worked with many caterers, she knew most of the restaurateurs in the area. They loved to see her, and she always got the best cuts of meat and the best prepared meals.

But while the food was excellent, she tasted nothing. Both she and Scott spent the meal avoiding looking at each other. Their conversation was stilted, cloaked in an atmosphere as thick as a white sauce. Diana was relieved when it was over. All she wanted was to get back to her car and away from the strain of a situation that should never have existed.

Yet when they were on the street and walking back toward the Square, Scott stopped at the light and looked toward campus, away from the place where the night had begun.

"What are you doing?" Diana asked, her voice low and tentative.

"Let's go for a walk," he said. Taking her hand, he didn't give her time to refuse but pulled her across the street and through the entry gates of the university.

"How was your time here?" he asked.

Diana slipped her hand from his. "Why do you want to know?"

He looked at the stars in the clear sky, then back at her as they walked across the pathway told the arch. "I just wondered. We kidded you a lot. I wondered how you felt about it."

"Now?" she asked. "You want to know how I feel all these years later?"

He nodded and stopped. Diana understood where they were standing. It was almost the exact spot where he had first kissed her. Where the kiss got out of control and he ran from her. She wondered if he'd stopped there on purpose or if he didn't remember the significance of this spot.

She moved away from it. She could see the girl she'd been, the one with the long, unruly hair and her nose in a book. The one who no one dated or even thought to ask out initially. She was a fish out of water on campus, and although she had many friends, it took a while for them to like her instead of only wanting her to help them with homework. These were people like her, smart but not part of the popular segment. Scott was a BMOC, Big Man on Campus. Everyone knew him and liked him. He always had a girl on his arm, and his crowd teased and taunted her. But it was Scott's zingers that hurt the most.

"For the most part, I enjoyed my years on campus,"

she finally answered. She felt safer talking about school than about their current relationship.

"What does that mean?"

"I know I wasn't part of your group. But I made a lot of friends while I was here." She looked at the university gates.

"I'm glad to hear that."

"Why?" Diana stood in front of him and stared in the darkness. She couldn't see his full features, but the moonlight and the campus lights gave her a good enough view.

"I'm older now, and I don't like to think of the way I treated you when we were students."

"Are you apologizing?"

"I am," he said without hesitation. "It was the time and the group I was with."

"You're still with them. Wasn't Mike at the wedding?"

"He was surprised when he recognized you."

"Diana 4.0 or Brainiac? Although you were the only one who called me Brainiac."

"We were young and didn't think of how our words and deeds would affect others."

Diana resumed walking. The old hurt came back, but she refused to let him see it. "I'm a little older, too," she said. "I don't dwell on the things that were said and done then."

Scott took her arm and stopped her. When he noticed her glancing at his hand, he dropped it. "I am sorry," he said.

Diana could see it seemed important to him that she understand. His face was softer in the moonlight, and his anticipation seemed to hinge on her forgiveness.

"Thank you," she said.

It wasn't exactly an acceptance of an apology, but it was the best she could do. They gazed at each other for a while. The air around them took on a charge, and Diana knew she and Scott needed a buffer. She started walking. They continued to traverse the campus, as their hands met. She moved sideways to avoid contact. The silence between them stretched, and Diana felt that she should say something.

"We should go back," she told Scott. It was all she could come up with.

They turned and headed back toward the entrance. Diana wanted to go down a different path, avoiding the juncture where Scott had kissed Brainiac, but he steered her directly toward it. As another couple passed them, he entwined her arm with his and kept hold of her. Diana didn't wrench herself free of his touch. The feeling that came over her during their dance at the wedding was settling between them when Scott's cell phone rang.

"Damn," he cursed softly under his breath. Dropping contact with her, he pulled the phone from his pocket and looked at the display. He apologized and answered the call.

Scott listened for several seconds. "I'll be right there," he said and ended the call without saying goodbye. "I'm going to have to cut this short," he told Diana as he walked fast toward the exit. Scott said nothing about the caller or where he was running off to. "Let me get you a taxi."

"There are no taxis at this hour," Diana told him. They had reached the front gate. "I'll call Teddy to pick me up."

"Are you sure?" He stopped a moment to make sure she was all right with doing this.

"Of course," Diana said. "Go. Do what you have to. I'll be fine."

"I hate to leave you like this, but it is an emergency."

Diana took her cell phone from her purse. "Go," she said.

"I'll call you later," he said and took a couple of steps. His back was to her when the traffic light turned green. Scott didn't step off the curb. Instead, he turned back to her. In two steps she was in his arms and he kissed her. As quickly as it started it ended. He let her go and ran across the street down Palmer Square and disappeared around the corner. It was the same route he'd taken the day he'd kissed her on campus. It was night now and he was ten years older than he'd been that day, but Diana felt just as confused, uncertain and bereft as she had then.

Diana waited in the coffee shop across from the university. The place was full of jean-clad students, long-haired girls and guys with biceps the size of small trees. She looked out of place in her spaghetti-strapped dress and heels high enough to add five inches to her height. She hadn't wanted to call Teddy, but she couldn't walk in those shoes and calling anyone else would require too much explanation.

Through the glass window, Diana recognized Teddy's BMW. She gathered her small purse and giant cup of latte, which she rationalized she deserved, since Scott had left her stranded.

"You know, you two are going about this all wrong," Teddy said the moment Diana was seated. "You're supposed to be on a date. That's where the man sees you home and makes sure you're safely inside your house before leaving." She glanced sideways. "Or if you're lucky, he kisses you goodbye after breakfast. *Really* lucky would be breakfast, lunch and dinner."

"Obviously, my luck has run out," she said flatly.

Teddy was quiet for a moment. "What happened?" she asked as she navigated the streets.

"I don't know. We were walking on campus and he got a phone call. He explained it was an emergency and he had to go."

"He left you stranded here?" Her voice rose several notes.

Diana shook her head. "He didn't." She explained that she told him to go. That she would find her own way home.

"What was the emergency?" Teddy asked.

"I don't know."

"He didn't tell you?"

Again she shook her head.

"Was it female?"

"I don't know." Diana didn't want to answer any more questions. She didn't know anything, didn't understand what had happened.

"Do you think it was staged?"

"Staged?"

"Yeah, you know. When you aren't sure that you want to spend time with a person, you arrange for someone to call you at a specific time. Depending on your answer to the call, you either continue the date or you have a method of cutting the night short."

Diana came to that thought at the same time Teddy voiced it. She didn't want to believe it. Not after the way Scott had told her that he enjoyed their kiss this morning. And not after their walk through the university grounds. Or the final kiss.

"I don't think that was it," she said, but she wasn't sure. "Scott already knew who I was. If he didn't want to spend time with me, there was no reason for him to even ask me out."

"True," Teddy agreed, but her voice indicated she still had reservations.

"My car is still at the office. Take me there," Diana said, as Teddy turned down the street that would lead toward Diana's house.

"I don't think I should take you home. We should go to Winston's for a glass of wine. You can drown your emotions or at least dull them, and I could be the designated driver."

"There's nothing wrong with my emotions. I'd rather go home."

"This is Teddy, remember?"

"You said that this morning, before I got mixed up in all this."

"All right, it *is* partly my fault. I'm sorry I insisted you go to dinner with him. I never thought it would end like this."

Teddy pulled the car into a parking lot, but not at their office. She'd driven to Winston's, a local bar and restaurant not far from their office or the new hospital.

"What are we doing here?" Diana asked. Instead of answering, Teddy got out of the car, purse in hand, and closed the door. Diana could only follow. Even if she hadn't wanted to, Teddy took her arm and pulled her along.

"We're going to drown."

* * *

Scott set the plane down with barely a bump. He braked, bringing the huge bird to a slow speed before taxiing to the hangar. A medical team waited for him. The moment the fuselage doors opened they rushed into action. Within minutes an ambulance sped away, its lights flashing and sirens cutting the night air. Scott witnessed this scene many times and it never got old. He was helping to save someone's life, delivering transplant organs. He no longer asked for information about the patients, because he'd found that knowing compelled him to think about them rather than place his full concentration on flying. And in the air, mistakes were unforgivable.

As the lights of the ambulance faded he thought of Diana. Pulling his phone out, he headed for the hangar to call her. He got no answer on either her cell or her home number. He frowned, wondering where she was.

He'd left her abruptly. Without explanation. He didn't have time to tell her about the call. He knew that minutes could make a difference between life and death for someone. He had to go. His friends understood. Often he'd take a call and be gone without a word. But he wasn't sure she knew or understood.

Trying her number again, he was met with the same answering machine. Calling the office, a business voice that was unmistakably Diana's came over the line asking him to leave a message. Scott could hear the sexy undertone in it. Where was she? His flight had taken two hours after he got to the airport. It was nearly midnight in Princeton, and he knew she wasn't at a wedding tonight. So where was she? Had she reached Teddy'

Had anything happened to her? Scott worried. Leaving a woman on the street wasn't like him.

Normally at this hour Scott would stay the night, but he was back in the air the minute the plane was refueled and serviced. It was three o'clock in the morning when he arrived in Princeton. Diana's car was still in the office parking lot, but there was no sign of her. Worry surfaced. Scott wished he knew Teddy's number. Or where she lived. Maybe she knew where Diana was.

At five o'clock in the morning Diana answered her landline. "This better be good," she said, her voice slurred.

"Diana?" He was surprised at the way she sounded, but relieved that she was home.

"Go away," she said.

"It's Scott."

"Scott, go away."

He was unsure if she was half asleep or ill. She sounded strange. "Diana, are you ok?"

"Go away," she said again. He heard the phone click in his ear. She'd hung up on him.

Something was wrong, Scott thought. He didn't like the sound of her voice. He redialed the number and started the car at the same time. She didn't answer. He didn't know how long it took him to get to her house, but it was less than it should have taken if he'd obeyed all the traffic laws.

Jumping out of the car, he was on her porch in a matter of seconds, his finger pushing and holding the doorbell. His mind imagined she was hurt, attacked, unconscious, unable to get to the door. He started knocking loudly and calling her name. Half a minute later, she opened the door a crack.

She pushed his hand off the bell. "Could you stop that noise?"

"You're drunk," Scott said. Still he was relieved.

"I am not drunk," Diana countered. "I was drunk, but I'm past drunk now. So go away."

Instead of leaving, he pushed the door open and walked inside. Diana lost her balance, her arms flailed as she tried to keep from falling. Scott caught her hand and pulled her upright.

"Maybe you better sit down."

"Maybe you better leave." Her hands moved in the air like she wanted to point at him, but couldn't find his image in the many she was seeing. If Scott hadn't been so relieved that she was only drunk and not hurt, he'd laugh. He moved her to the sofa and sat her down. "You left me at the altar."

"Where?"

"Where did the moon go?" She laughed. "I know... I know," she repeated. Then she fell sideways and passed out.

The groan Diana heard woke her. She felt terrible.

"Ugh." Her mouth tasted like copper. Raising a hand to her head, she pushed her hair aside. The effort hurt and she groaned again. What had she done? She tried opening her eyes, but the effort was too much. She squeezed them shut and found even that hurt. With a harsh moan she flopped back against the sheets. Something was behind her. This wasn't her bed. Where was she? Again she tried to open her eyes. Squinting, she peered through slits. What was she doing in the living room? And why was... *No,* she thought. Her brain was still soaked in wine. She thought she saw... But she couldn't have.

Diana tried to turn over, away from the light filtering through her eyelids. She fell. Her eyes opened wide. She was on the floor. She heard something. Then hands touched her. She jumped and began to fight.

"Stop it!" Scott shouted. "It's me."

Diana looked up, startled to see Scott staring down at her. She immediately stopped struggling. And closed her eyes. She had to be dreaming. But if she was, it was the first time she felt, really felt, hands. She opened her eyes again, then squinted. Pain shot through them, but not before she recognized Scott.

"What are you doing here?" Every word she spoke hurt her head. She put her hand up to it. Scott's hands were still at her waist and she was still lying on the floor.

"You don't remember letting me in last night?"

"I let you in?" Diana asked, raising her voice at the end making it a question.

"It's a good thing I'm an honorable man."

Diana levered herself up and sat with her back against the sofa. The effort took most of her energy. She needed to close her eyes, but forced them to remain open. "If you were honorable, you'd have gone home and let me wake up without anyone knowing how bad I feel."

Scott laughed. "Is this your first hangover?"

"Is that what this is? Why do people drink like this? My head feels like it will either fall off or explode."

"Why did you go drinking?"

"It was Teddy's idea. At least I think it was."

"Did she have something to drown?"

"Me," she said.

"Why you?"

Her head was clear enough that she knew better than to answer. "I'm all right now. You don't have to baby-sit me."

"You owe me a walk," he said.

"I owe you nothing. I completed the walk—*alone*." Her voice wasn't strong enough to prevent the pain the word evoked, but she endured it.

He stood up and pulled her to her feet. For a moment she was unsteady and clung to him. She still wore the dress she'd had on last night, but she had no memory of getting home or falling asleep on the sofa. Where was Teddy, and why wasn't she the one who stayed the night?

"Did you see Teddy?" Diana asked.

"Not today."

Diana, feeling strong enough to stand on her own, pushed herself out of Scott's arms. Then realizing her mistake, she sat down on the sofa and fell sideways, gathering a pillow she hugged it to cushion her head.

"I need something to drink. Would you get me a bottle of water?"

"That's the last thing you need," Scott told her.

"Why?"

"It'll make you drunk all over. Got any tomato juice? I'll make you a hangover cocktail."

"Too much salt," she said with a frown.

Scott disappeared. Diana tried to go back to sleep. At lease there she wasn't in pain.

"Diana?"

She heard her name called, but didn't want to answer. Answering caused pain.

"Diana?"

"Go away," she muttered, turning her head away from the sound.

"Turn over and drink this. It'll make you feel better."

She wasn't sure she believed him, but her head hurt so bad, only death would make her feel better. She heard Scott sit a glass on the coffee table. The sound of the glass rang like a loud bell. The seat next to her depressed as Scott sat down on the sofa. His body was hot next to hers. Hands took her shoulders and turned her gently. She faced him.

Picking up the glass, he offered it to her.

"What is it?" she asked.

"Orange juice and a few ingredients from your refrigerator and cabinets. Don't ask, just drink."

Lifting her head off the sofa, Scott supported her and held onto the glass while she drank.

"Yuk," she said. "It tastes like Drano."

"Drink it all," he ordered, pressing the glass to her lips.

Diana did as she was told, then let her head fall back against the sofa pillow.

"Fresh air is the next best thing," Scott said. "Come on. We'll go for a walk."

"Walk! I don't think I can stand, let alone walk."

Scott levered her to her feet. "You can lean on me."

She stepped sideways, testing her ability to stand alone. "I need to change clothes."

"Can you do it alone?"

"Of course, I can." She wasn't sure if that was true. She could get out of her dress and into pants and a shirt. It was getting to the second floor that posed a challenge. She took a tentative step, grabbing the newel post and closing her eyes. Nausea threatened, and she waited until it passed. She got to the fourth step and stopped. A moment later she made it the rest of the way. At the top, she headed to the bathroom to brush away the taste of last night's alcohol as well as whatever Scott had given her.

Diana felt no better returning to the living room, but she was dressed in more appropriate clothing for walking. She couldn't explain why she went with Scott. After he left her standing on the street corner last night, she shouldn't even be talking to him.

Scott led her to the door and turned to her. "You might want to get some sunglasses," he suggested.

Even with the glasses, the sun was strong. Scott offered Diana his arm, and she had to take it. She was unsteady on her feet and constantly closing her eyes against the glaring pain. Scott took the lead, deciding where they walked and how they got there. After a while she realized they were in the center of town near the campus buildings that had dominated Princeton for more than two centuries.

"What are we doing here?" Diana asked. "I didn't realize we'd walked so far."

"That's a good thing. You must be feeling better," Scott said.

Or going blind, Diana thought, but didn't voice it. Her head pounded, but the ringing in her ears was gone, and the traffic along Nassau Street no longer sounded like a cacophony of poor-quality steel drums.

They wandered toward Blair Arch. It was a meeting place, home of several choruses, and a natural division between upper and lower areas of campus. When they reached it, Diana stopped. She took a seat on the steps facing the lower campus and let the shade soothe the pain in her head.

"You asked me if I enjoyed my time here," she said.

"And you said you did." Scott looked over the area, sitting next to her.

"What about you?" she asked. "Did you enjoy being a student here?"

"I did," he finally said, but his voice conveyed something else.

"What's wrong? You sound like you didn't really like it."

He looked over the campus in front of them. Green lawn spread out like a carpet. Diana wondered if he was seeing the young man he once was.

"It was a long time ago," she told him, soothing whatever it was that appeared to haunt him.

"I wish I could go back and change some things."

"What would you want to change? You had everything. You were a BMOC. Everyone knew you. Everyone liked you. There was always a girl trying to get your attention."

"All except one." He looked directly at her when he said that. His voice was quiet as if they were in a library or one of the campus chapels.

"Me? You didn't want my attention."

"I would have changed how I treated you," he said.

"I don't think about it. It was a lifetime ago. I'm no longer the girl who went to school here. I'm older, hopefully wiser." She smiled, trying to lighten the mood.

"Don't you feel something every time you pass by?"

"Feel what? Envy. Pride. Hostility? My memories are good ones. You might not know it, but you and your group weren't the only people I met as a student. It isn't the campus that causes memories." She left the unspoken sentence hanging in the shaded air. "The ground and buildings are just that. The people are gone."

For long moments they were quiet, each lost in their own thoughts. In college Diana had watched Scott and his friends from afar. While they played with a Frisbee on the campus lawn or gathered in a hall, she'd had to study extra hard to keep her scholarship and work for extra money. She'd gone on a few dates, had friends, but there had been no one special in her entire college career.

"We'd better start back. It's a long way, and I feel better," Diana said.

They got up. Scott took her arm when she appeared unsteady. He dropped it as soon as she was able to stand. They headed back toward the front gate.

"How's your head feel?" Scott asked as they began to walk.

"Better," Diana said. "Thanks for the walk and the medical advice."

"I've been where you are, many times." He smiled, apparently remembering past mornings-after.

Classes ended and the grounds were suddenly dotted with young men and women moving back and forth across the campus. Despite it being summer, classes were in session.

"You know, when I went to class here, I never walked through those gates." She indicated the main gate a few yards away. It wasn't a real gate, not one you could close to keep people either in or out. It was a passageway, two high brick pillars with stone lions atop them.

"Why not? You weren't superstitious, were you?" Scott stepped off the path allowing a couple walking hand in hand to pass them. The girl smiled at him. Many students felt that walking through the gates meant they would never graduate, so they avoided the use of them.

"I wasn't superstitious. It's just that there was always a lot of activity going on here," Diana said. "I was forced to go another way."

"You mean we were out here playing. And you were avoiding us," he accused.

"Not all the time," she said. "I didn't intentionally avoid you and the others. But now, I always come in this way."

"You stage weddings here?"

Diana laughed. "I'm on the alumni board and usually park on a side street. Going in that way is more convenient."

Silence settled over them as they approached the spot in the walkway that Diana thought of as the kissing place. She didn't stop there, but passed it.

"Do you mind if I ask a question?" she asked.

He turned and looked at her inquiringly.

Teddy's comment that he might have arranged the call to cut their time together short was on her mind. But if he had, it made no sense. Why would he stay the night with her if there was another woman he wanted to see?

"Where did you go last night in such a hurry?" Diana asked.

"I had an emergency flight to take."

"I thought you were a corporate pilot," Diana said.

"Even corporate pilots have emergencies. But I'm not strictly a corporate pilot."

Diana waited for further explanation.

"I fly corporate executives from Centex Biologics. In

addition, I sometimes deliver human organs for transplant."

"Transplants." Diana was relieved. "This is what you did last night. You flew an organ to save someone's life?"

"I tried. I deliver the organ. I can't tell if the operation is successful or even if the recipient is male or female."

Diana lifted herself up on her toes and kissed him on the cheek.

"What was that for?"

"For being one of the good guys."

She didn't think anyone would make up that kind of explanation. Diana didn't know what she would have thought if Scott had decided to leave her alone after he'd invited her to have dinner with him. Diana wanted to go, but she wouldn't let Teddy or Scott know that was the case. She'd have refused Scott's invitation if Teddy had not taken the phone.

But all the tumblers had fallen in place and they were together. Dinner hadn't been all she wanted it to be, but the walk on campus had begun well enough. Then Scott left her, but he was saving someone's life. Of all the things she could fault him for, that wasn't one of them.

They resumed walking, this time Scott took her hand. Just as they were passing Nassau Hall, the main building seen from the front gates, a group of people exited the building. Most of them were students, but a few were faculty.

"Hi, Diana," Dr. Rhys-Weisz said.

"Hello, Diana," said her colleague, Dr. Lange. "There's no committee meeting tonight, is there?"

Diana shook her head. "I'm just showing a friend

around." She glanced between Scott and Dr. Lange. "This is Scott Thomas," she said.

They shook hands, and the two teachers excused themselves to hurry along to class. Dr. Lange and Dr. Rhys-Weisz were on a committee with Diana.

"They didn't recognize you," Diana said, surprise evident in her voice.

"Why should they?"

"You don't know who they are?"

Scott watched the two people walking away from them. He cocked his head as if trying to pull a memory into focus.

"Wait a minute," he said. "That was Professor Lange."

"He got his doctorate a few years ago," Diana told him.

"And Dr. Rhys?"

"She got married," Diana supplied. She's Dr. Rhys-Weisz now."

"You know them?"

She nodded.

"How?" he asked.

Before she could answer, Dr. Rhys-Weisz called her name. "You are coming next Saturday, right?"

Diana nodded. "I wouldn't miss it."

"I'm amazed she's still here," Scott said as the teacher left. "We used to walk all over her."

"She's still here," Diana said. "And I guess she learned from you, because she's a force to be reckoned with now."

They continued to walk, and a few other people smiled and spoke to Diana by name as she and Scott approached the main gate.

"You seem to have a presence here."

She nodded, not explaining.

"Can I surmise that your memories of being here continue to form?"

"You can," she said with a bright smile.

"What's happening next week?" he asked. "If I'm not overstepping my bounds."

"A few people are coming in for dinner."

"You mean the alumni?"

"Of course, they're all alumni." Diana made light of the situation as if the event was no big deal.

"It's the annual scholarship dinner," Scott said. "I have an invitation at home."

"They were sent to all alumni," Diana said. "Most people don't appear in person. If they did we couldn't accommodate them. Many send donations. About three or four hundred people attend the actual event."

Scott had never been there as far as Diana knew. He made regular donations. She got the list of attendees and patrons every year. Her first job on the dinner-dance committee was to send acknowledgments to the alumni who donated to the fund. She hadn't looked for his name, but it had jumped out at her like an unexpected snake.

"You're going?" he asked.

"I'm on the committee."

"How about we go together?" Scott asked. "You let me make up for running out on you yesterday, and I'll make sure I'm not on call next Saturday. This is not a major reunion. It's not likely they'll be many people there either of us know."

"Then why do you want to go?" she asked. "Isn't

the point of a reunion to see people you haven't seen in a long while?"

"I'm sure there'll be at least a few people I remember. And since we're both right in Princeton, maybe we should go together."

"Scott, the BMOC and Diana 4.0. *together.*"

Chapter 7

Scott's car blocked the driveway when the campus taxi dropped them off several minutes later. They had walked to the center of town to clear their heads. Traversing the distance back over small hills that looked like mountains was more exercise than she wanted.

"I'm hungry," Diana told him when they were inside. She headed for the kitchen. "Want some breakfast, or is it lunchtime?" She checked her wrist. It was bare. Her watch was upstairs on the bedside table. At least that was where she hoped it was. The events of last night were still a little fuzzy.

"I'd love some. Anything I can do to help?"

"Set the table and make coffee." She indicated where the coffee was and pointed to the coffeemaker.

Diana moved around the space with steps as precise as a dancer's. In just a few minutes they were sitting down to a full breakfast of British bangers, scrambled eggs, Nutella crepes and buckets of coffee.

They ate in companionable silence, enjoying the food, but when Diana finished and poured a second cup of coffee for herself, she leaned back in the chair and gazed at Scott. He was an enigma. She wondered how the two personalities could occupy the same gorgeous body. One of his personalities left her in the dark. The other spent the night making sure she was all right and then helping her through the worst day of her life.

"What are you doing?" Scott asked. He had another cup of coffee and she hadn't seen him get up to get it or even remove both their plates.

"I was thinking of something."

"Was it about me?" he said with a smile.

"As self-centered as ever, aren't you?"

He sipped the hot liquid and shook his head. "I just hoped I was the object of your thoughts."

"Good or bad?"

"Your expression said good, so I went with that."

Diana waited a long moment before she answered his question. "I don't know if it was good or bad."

"What?"

"Why did you kiss me that day?" Diana asked.

Scott's face didn't change, but she knew he understood she was referring to the kiss he'd given her in front of Nassau Hall and not the one last night before he'd left her. Whatever his reason was, it had bothered her for years. She wanted to put it out of her mind. She'd tried, but suddenly without notice, she would remember it.

Some days she would hear a voice that sounded like his, only to turn and find it belonged to a stranger.

There were television actors who showed traits she remembered him having; the way they ran or drew a hand through their hair. When a movie got to a love scene, Diana would fantasize that the man was Scott and she was the leading lady. For a time she only watched plotless actions movies.

"When we were students," he stated, knowing exactly what day and what kiss she meant.

She nodded. "It was one of the only times you talked to me without harsh words, without an audience. I thought you were changing. Then you kissed me. And you ran away."

"We had an audience." He lowered his head and looked at his hands. "It was a joke, another prank against Diana 4.0."

She listened without a word.

"They were in the window of the building behind us. We saw you coming across campus and someone said something about how you probably had never been kissed. Of course, the conversation quickly got out of control. And then they thought one of us should go out and kiss you."

"And you lost."

"That wasn't how it was."

He was silence for a while. She was about to prompt him when he began speaking again. "I liked my friends back then. I still like them. They're married now and settled, but at the time I was unsure what they might do if someone else tried to complete the bet."

"So your act was to save me?"

"It doesn't sound noble, and at the time I didn't think of it that way. I was just unsure what would happen if one of them tried something and you didn't like it."

"You thought I might hurt one of them?"

"I doubt you could have. You were so much smaller than any of them. And they were either basketball or football players."

"You were on the diving team, but just as strong as any of them."

"But I wasn't about to hurt you," he said. "At least not physically." The last he added in a lower voice.

"I remember you started talking about a class. It had something to do with political science. You mentioned joining a campaign and wanted to know what I thought of the current presidential candidates." Diana didn't relay all he had said. She could repeat that conversation word for word if needed.

"You were skeptical of my motives," Scott reminded her. "I remember the expression on your face and you asking me why I wanted to know anything."

"You said you were interested in running for office, and you wanted to know how to change someone's mind that you had offended. I was the perfect patsy for that."

Scott winced, remembering that long-ago conversation. He reached across the table and took her hand. "I'm sorry for that day."

"What do you think your kiss did?" Diana asked.

"I've wondered about that for years. I thought you'd forgotten it. That it meant nothing."

"Is that's why you ran away?"

He shook his head. "I was surprised," he admitted.

"That the kiss was not my first time?"

"That I liked it and every time I saw you I wanted to kiss you again. After that I never teased you again."

"I know," she told him. "And you must have convinced your friends, because most of them stopped, too. I thought they'd found another target, but I knew it was you."

"We didn't find another target. I think we grew up at that moment and realized what we were doing was something we wouldn't want done to us. All except Linda."

"She thoroughly doesn't like me. Her harsh criticism continued." It had actually stepped up a few notches after the kiss.

"I never understood that. What did you ever do to her?" Scott asked.

"Nothing," Diana said. "I existed, and she knew about the kiss and your abrupt exit." It was a woman thing, and Diana wouldn't reveal it to Scott. It would tell him too much about her. Linda instinctively knew that Diana was a threat to her—competition for Scott's affections. Once she found out Scott had kissed her and no longer wanted to tease her, Linda would know that deep down Scott felt something for Brainiac.

"Yeah," Scott said, as if Diana had asked a question. "So?"

"While your male friends didn't get it, Linda did."

Scott frowned. He still didn't know what she meant.

"I was a threat to her. She wanted to make sure that she had your full attention, that she was the woman on your arm and no one else would replace her."

"She thought you would replace her?"

Diana gave him a long look. "It wasn't a peck on the cheek. When you kissed me, we were both surprised at the intensity that overtook us. Your friends were watching, and they embellished what they saw. So she continued her waspish comments and her belittling of anything I did."

"Good thing she married and left the area," Scott said.

That came as a surprise to Diana. The way Linda clung to him, she was sure they would have gone down the aisle together. She wanted to ask what had happened with the two of them, but didn't.

"She's probably a lot different now," Diana told him, and left the sentence obviously unfinished.

"Yeah, we're all different."

Scott got up and reached over to Diana. He pulled her to her feet and circled her waist. "I'm going to kiss you," he said. "And this time I'm not running away."

Teddy had come through for her. Diana knew she would. After Scott offered to take her to the dinner-dance, she wanted to look good, but after they made love, she wanted to outshine any woman he'd ever been with. She wanted to obliterate Diana 4.0 and Cousin Itt from his memory and let him see that she was a sexy, flesh-and-blood woman. And her blood ran hot for him.

Diana needed a gown. "Not just any gown," she told Teddy. "I need a gown that says WOW! Something that will knock Scott's eyes out when he sees me."

"Gee, this sounds serious, and over someone you said you weren't compatible with," Teddy teased.

Diana's face crimsoned under her makeup, but she only smiled at Teddy. Diana knew the inner glow she felt was evident. *Not compatible.* All that had changed. It was never really true. Diana had given herself that excuse to keep from confronting the fact that she really liked Scott. She thought about him the moment she woke up and every minute throughout the day.

"I'll see what I can do," Teddy said.

And now they were together. The BMOC and Diana

4.0. And they liked each other. She smiled to herself as she looked in the mirror. The dress was superb, a strapless royal-blue concoction that looked like blooming roses along the bustline. It pinched tightly in at the waist before flaring out as it fell to the floor. Teddy called in a favor and in a week got a dress fit for a queen. She knew exactly what Diana wanted, and the drawing Teddy sketched lived up to Diana's expectations.

She was rewarded when Scott arrived to pick her up. When she opened the door, he stared at her open-mouthed and speechless.

"Wow," he finally said, and she smiled.

Her hair was off her face, removing all traces of the Cousin Itt persona. This Diana bore no resemblance to the old Diana who moved about the Princeton campus. From looking at her, no one would know that Diana 4.0 resided under the ringlets of curls or inside a person who was dressed to kill.

The dinner was going well when they arrived. Before people sat down, there was a reception for mingling and renewing friendships. Diana was apprehensive. She knew some time during the night, someone was going to comment on the BMOC being with the 4.0. Scott supported her, even understood her feelings. No one seemed to notice anything unusual. She got a few appraising glances. Finally she relaxed, sipping her drink and smiling at some of the people she had once known who hadn't been at a dinner before. Many of them didn't recognize her and looked at her admiringly.

But her relaxation was short-lived. Her heart stopped when she saw the woman and realized the night was just beginning.

Diana recognized her as soon as she walked through

the door. She was as gorgeous as she'd been when they were students. Marriage and divorce hadn't changed her God-given beauty. But the inner working that made a person beautiful from the inside was missing from Linda Engles, Scott's old girlfriend.

She stood in the doorway, searching for someone. Diana knew without asking who she was looking for. Gripping her drink tighter, she touched Scott's back.

"Scott," Linda called the moment he turned. Her steps were determined as she rushed across the room, making a line for him as if she'd only been to the ladies' room and was returning to their date.

Scott turned as did everyone else in the room. This was the way Linda liked it. She loved being the center of attention and would do anything to make sure all eyes were on her.

Linda went straight into Scott's arms and kissed him on the mouth. "Scott, darling, it's so good to see you again."

Scott pushed her back. "Linda," he said, surprised. "It's great to see you, too." His voice seemed a little embarrassed to Diana. Taking his handkerchief from an outer pocket, he removed her lipstick.

Scott put his arm around Diana's waist and pulled her close.

"This is Diana Greer," he introduced. "You remember her?"

"Oh...my...God," Linda shouted loud enough for the entire room to hear. "I don't believe it. What a *transformation*." The tone she used said it was impossible. "What is she doing here?" Her question was directed at Scott.

"Diana is on the committee for this dance." Again his

hand went to her back, settling just at the place where the zipper separated her bare skin from the fabric. "She runs a business now called Weddings by Diana."

Linda looked around at the crowd. Diana knew it was coming. If no one in the room realized who she was, Linda would make sure they all knew. And in the worst light. Scott tightened his arm around her and turned her away.

"We were about to get a drink. Excuse us." They took a couple of steps and Diana realized he was trying to work them to another part of the room. But obviously Linda was having none of that.

"Wait," she said. "This is Brainiac." She stepped forward and grabbed Diana's arm. "You guys remember her? Diana 4.0." Linda stepped back, placing both hands on her hips and inspecting Diana. "You're a Cinderella if I've ever seen one."

Diana heard the expelling of air as people remembered who she used to be. She leaned toward Linda and whispered only for her ears, "That means I get to go home with the prince."

Linda's face reddened then drained. Diana turned to the crowd and lifted her head with a large smile on her face. "You all probably remember me as the studious girl who always had her head in a book." A low giggle went through the room. "Well, I was a scholarship student, and I had to keep my grades up if I wanted to stay in school. So I'm glad you're all supporting the fund tonight. After all, there may be someone out there just like me. And look how I turned out."

Diana lifted her arms and twirled around. Thanks to Teddy and her contacts in the world of high couture, Diana was dressed to the nines. Her hair was swept up completely off her face in a ponytail of cascading curls that fell to the middle of her back. Her only jewelry was a huge sapphire teardrop necklace that was circled with tiny diamonds and matching earrings.

She heard the approval from the audience, especially the males in attendance. At one time, most of these now ex-classmates wouldn't speak to her except to ridicule her. Now they looked upon her as eye candy.

Scott came up beside her and took her arm. "Thank you all for coming," he said. "And don't forget. Be generous."

They headed for the bar. Linda Engles was left standing alone, clearly bewildered that her little attempt to embarrass Diana had backfired. Diana gave the other woman a pointed look and followed Scott.

"That was interesting," Diana said when they were seated at their table with fresh glasses of wine.

"When did she get back in town?" he asked another guest sitting with them.

"I don't know, but I hear she's divorced."

Diana glanced at Linda. Her back was to them. She was speaking to another couple with animated, if not exaggerated laughter. But she already had her sights on Scott. Diana didn't tell him how apparent it was that Linda wanted to continue the relationship they'd once had. She couldn't say it was where they had left things, because she didn't know the circumstances of their parting. But from the way Linda wanted to tear Diana's eyes out, she was gunning for Scott and didn't think Brainiac was an obstacle. Little did Linda know that Brainiac had learned a thing or two and she wasn't ready to crawl into her dorm room and hide from any insults that might be inflicted upon her.

"I hope she's only here for the dinner," Scott said.

"Sorry, but the word in the ladies' room is she bought a house in Rocky Hill," a woman sitting across from Scott said. Rocky Hill was small town fifteen minutes north of Princeton.

"Let's hope she's learned something in the ensuing years and she won't let things get out of hand," Scott said.

"From the way she looked at you, I believe she wants to pick up where you two left off," Diana whispered.

"That's not going to happen," Scott said in a tone that had Diana staring at him. "It wasn't the best of times," he told her. "And what makes you think she's after me?"

"I'm not blind. It was obvious from the way she looked at you, gave you all her attention to the exclusion of the rest of the room."

She'd only glanced at Diana before she recognized her and then tried to resume her past association with Scott, using Diana as a punching bag. She probably expected Scott to do the same.

Thank heaven he'd been the attentive date. But Diana still wondered. Scott and Linda had been a couple for three years. They hadn't parted until after graduation. Diana moved to take a job and lost track of the two. She heard that Linda had married a few years later, and was relieved to discover she had not married Scott. She didn't know where Scott was, and her business was getting started. All her energy went into it, and she didn't think about him until the day he walked into her office an hour after his lawyer left.

Now she was glad to be on Scott's arm. But whatever Linda wanted…Linda got.

And Linda wanted Scott. But so did Diana.

* * *

As soon as the dinner and the speeches ended, the dancing began. Scott led Diana to the floor and straight into his arms. The two circled the floor for several dances, keeping step to the music as they held each other for all to see. As soon as the band gave them a breather from all the fast-tempo songs and played something slower, Linda Engles made her move.

"You can't monopolize him all night," she said. "Scott, let's dance for old time's sake." Linda grabbed his arm and pulled him away, then pushed herself into his arms. Scott looked back at Diana, But Linda turned his head so he faced her.

Diana moved back, intent on going to her table, when Mike grabbed her arm. "Dance with me," he said, leading her to the floor. Without a thought the two began to dance.

"I see those two are back where they started."

Diana looked at Scott and Linda to make sure they were the couple he was referring to."

"She's only just back in town."

"Yeah," he said. "But she's got an agenda, and it's on the floor right now."

Diana checked the dancers. Sex on the floor was all she could think of when she saw the way Linda danced with Scott. Her gown was skintight. Every voluptuous curve she had was outlined in the shimmering gold fabric. Her body was so close to Scott's, Diana was sure no air was between them. It was a reenactment of their college days. If you saw Scott, you saw Linda. The two were so closely associated that people spoke of them almost as one name.

Diana scanned the faces of Scott's friends. Approving smiles showed white teeth and envy. She felt like the outcast. The best couple was on the floor, and few people remember the others. And Diana's name was never on anyone's list for any of the "most likely" awards. Linda and Scott, most likely to marry and have beautiful children. Diana, most likely to be forgotten.

But she hadn't let that stop her. She might be forgotten by Scott and Linda's crowd, but she was known well in her own circle. Her group of people were not superficial and interested only in themselves. They went on to become the quietly rich and famous in the background, not looking for the limelight. In many ways Diana could see in them the same qualities she found in the high-profile weddings she planned. They wanted quantity, not realizing that something of quality would add more elegance. While Linda might be dressed in the finest Versace had to offer, she still looked like a peasant. And Diana wasn't just being catty.

The dance finally ended, and the two went to get a drink from the bar. As soon as Scott handed a glass to Linda, he excused himself. Diana smiled. Her heart bloomed in her chest that he was forsaking Linda for her. Unfortunately, he was waylaid by his friends. Diana knew what they were doing. They were congratulating him on the dance. Linda joined the group. Diana got up, lifting their drinks and headed toward them. Wedging herself between Scott and Linda, she handed him one.

"This is for me, right?" Scott asked. He put his arm around her waist, and she doubted a soul in the group thought he meant the glass of wine.

Chapter 8

Decorated as a throwback to the art deco period, the hotel's ladies' lounge included private cornices where women could adjust their makeup under flattering lit mirrors. Diana sat in one of these at the end of the room. She'd checked her gown, which still sported perfect roses despite the heat her encounter had provoked.

Unknown to her, Linda Engles sat in one a few feet away.

"You won't believe what she looked like," Linda said to a woman Diana couldn't see.

"Has she gained a lot of weight?" the woman asked.

"It's not that. She's thin, but that rag of a dress she's wearing looks like she made it herself."

"Hmm," the other woman said. "I thought it was rather nice."

"Nice?" Linda questioned. "Could you imagine wearing that?"

"Are you kidding?" the woman said, her voice rising as if in surprised. "That dress is a Naeem Khan design, the same woman who designed a dress for Michelle Obama. Of course, I could imagine wearing it. I should be so lucky, but if Michael knew what that cost he'd divorce me."

"Well, she's no Michelle Obama."

"None of us are," the other woman said. "I better get back."

"I'll see you in a minute," Linda said as the door closed. "Designer, humph!" Linda said the word as if it tasted bad. Then she laughed, a high-pitched sound. It was the final straw. Diana had been trained in customer service. She knew how to defuse a situation, how to allow the customer to rant and rave until they were out of breath or had expended all the anger inside them. She'd spent years soothing nerves and offering alternatives, compromising angry patrons. She took all that knowledge, balled it in to a tight little wad and pitched it in the trash.

Approaching Linda, she walked right into her personal space. She knew what the reaction would be and Linda did not disappoint her. Sudden fear appeared on Scott's former girlfriend's face. She leaned away from Diana. Maybe she could feel the anger in the woman she'd teased for years, the one who was through with being the scapegoat or butt of jokes. Maybe Linda was or maybe she wasn't, but she was about to hear and see something she'd never seen before.

Diana kept her voice menacingly low even though the two of them had the room to themselves. Through clenched teeth she spoke, her lips barely moving. "I am not your whipping girl," she began. "I will no longer

ake your barbs or be the person on which you inflict
arts. I am here with Scott Thomas at his invitation. If
ou don't like that, then I suggest you find your mink
r sable or rat and get out of here. If you try this with
ne one more time, the secret you've been harboring for
he last ten years will be spread all over Facebook and
'ouTube, as well as throughout Princeton and Rocky
Iill. Then you'll know what it's like to be the butt of
okes. The lapdogs who crowd around you awaiting the
avors you offer them will learn the truth about Linda
:ngles. See how quickly they abandon you and that
hony smile you give them."

"What...what could you know?" She tried to act
rave. "There is nothing to know."

Diana smiled at her, although the smile held more
ostility than mirth. "I know it all. From the moment
ou entered that house on Michigan Avenue until you
eturned to your dorm. I know how many times you
vent there and what you did inside. And with whom?"

"How?" she asked.

"Does that matter? The point is I know."

Linda gasped. "Why...why wouldn't you have used
his information before, *if* you have it?"

"Because, unlike you, I don't tell other people's se-
rets."

"But you're willing to divulge mine." Her voice was
tronger.

"I've been pushed to the limit by you. I'm at the
vall and there is no place else for me to go. If you
hink I'm going to let you grind me into the floor every
ime I see you, I want you to know that is not going to
appen. You're done making fun of me and everyone
lse within my hearing. When you return to that room,

you'll be the model of feminine hospitality. If you fo
one minute don't believe I'll make good on my prom
ise, just try me."

Diana glared at her punctuating the point that thi
was no threat. It was a promise.

"I went there to volunteer," Linda stammered.

"Sure you did. You volunteered community servic
as part of your parole."

Linda's hand went to her breasts. Diana knew he
heart was about to jump out of the strapless gown sh
wore.

Diana moved back, standing up straight. She ke
her gaze on Linda who'd gone as white as paste an
looked as if a single breath could push her through th
back wall.

"There has to be another reason," Linda said. "Yo
wouldn't keep that information to yourself all thes
years to protect me. Not after the way I treated you.
She stared at Diana for almost a minute. Then she sa
up straight. The truth dawned on her. "You're in lov
with him," Linda stated.

Diana remained quiet, silenced as surely as if sh
had tape over her mouth.

"That's why you're doing this. Does he know?"

"I doubt it. And I doubt you're going to rush out o
here and share the good news."

"What does my record have to do with Scott?"

"Don't you know? Can't you remember what he wa
back in school?"

Linda looked confused. "He was popular, outgoin
invited to all the parties. A big man on campus."

"All those things," Diana said. "He was a PolyS
major. Political Science. Think about that."

"Yeah, so?" She opened her hands, questioning what one had to do with the other.

"He talked about law school, going into public office."

"That was all talk. None of us knew what we really wanted to do."

"Going to law school was a first step," Diana reminded her. "He even had application papers for the LSAT. I saw them."

"Scott has an uncle who's a lawyer. He worked in his office one summer and talked about going into that profession."

"And if he had, he'd be linked with you, a felon, a woman who had once served time for theft. What do you think his chances of getting elected would be then?"

"That's silly, no one would look at me. I wasn't married to him."

"But you wanted to be. You did everything in your power to get his ring on your finger. You'll have to tell me why that didn't work out someday."

Linda's face turned as red as it could under her over made up face and Diana's menacing countenance.

"My record is clean. No one could find a thing."

"*I* found it," Diana said. She straightened, stepped back and let the point sink in. "Have a wonderful evening." Diana walked to the door and left the room. Outside she stopped and inhaled a long breath. She'd never expected to let Linda know that she found out that she was seeing a parole officer during college. She came to Princeton a couple of years older than most freshmen. She told the story that she'd worked and decided to return to school because she understood that she wanted

a career and not just a job. It sounded good comin~
from her, but what she'd really wanted was a husban~

  She'd been caught shoplifting several times. She wa~
convicted of theft and given parole and community se~
vice. She kept it quiet and far away from the old-mone~
structures of Princeton proper. But Diana discovere~
her secret by accident. She'd been heading to New Yor~
to meet her sister when she saw Linda getting on th~
train. Why she followed her, Diana didn't know, bu~
Diana got off the train and went to the house on Mich~
gan. After that, Diana used her many skills as the gee~
Linda accused her of being and found out the rest.

  Following her and finding out what was in that buil~
ing was easy. Posing as a student doing research on th~
percentage of young felons who turn their lives aroun~
she interviewed Linda's parole officer right after sh~
left. With Linda's discussion still fresh in his min~
the parole officer gave Diana examples of young fe~
ons. While he didn't break any laws or infringe on an~
protocols, he cited the details. Diana filed the informa~
tion away. Because Linda had been a minor, her recor~
was expunged.

  In a way Diana felt sorry for Linda. But tonight wa~
the last time that Linda would walk on her. Diana wa~
ready to battle anyone determined to wreck her rela~
tionship with Scott.

  Scott smiled as Diana approached their table. H~
stood as if greeting her for the first time. Diana lifte~
her drink when she reached the table and drank befor~
being reseated.

  "Everything okay?" Scott asked.

"Everything is fine," she said, flashing him a brilliant smile. "Dance with me."

Together they went to the floor and she slipped into his arms as easily as anyone who knew her lover's every move. Diana felt great. She'd unleashed ten years of pent-up frustration, and the release was almost sexual.

"What happened in there?" Scott asked.

"In where?"

"Don't act you don't know what I'm taking about. I saw who went in first and who came out last. Did she—"

Diana shook her head. "Nothing happened. We talked. Everything is fine." And it was. Diana had only had a couple of glasses of wine, neither of which she finished. Yet she felt as if she were flying.

Scott leaned back and looked skeptically at her. "Are you sure?"

Diana's smile dazzled. She put her head next to his and danced. She wanted to close her eyes and fall into the music with him, but she remembered what happened at the Embry wedding and kept herself in check.

At the end of the night, the usual "let's keep in touch" messages and the exchanges of cell phone numbers and email addresses was done as the party broke up.

When they entered Diana's house minutes later, she was humming.

"You sound like you enjoyed the evening," Scott said.

"I did. It went much better than I thought it would."

"So you had reservations?" Scott asked.

"Didn't you?"

"Some," he admitted.

Diana sat down on the sofa and slipped her shoes off.

"It was amazing to see the look on everyone's faces when we walked in." Scott laughed.

Diana enjoyed hearing him laugh.

"And you were great when you defused that situation Linda started."

If only you knew. "It's my customer service training."

Scott moved to sit next to her. "Whatever it was," he said, "I was ready to change the dynamics of what was going on if need be. I didn't want this to turn into a night that humiliated you."

"I thank you for that," Diana told him. She propped her feet on the coffee table and stretched her legs out in front of her. Scott put his arm around her and she leaned against his shoulder. "You know," she began. "I *can* fight my own battles."

Silence followed her last statement. It stretched between them changing the friendly nature of the room to awkwardness. Scott stared at her. They were suddenly strangers, not knowing what to say or do next.

"Would you like something to drink?" Diana asked.

He shook his head, answering her silently. Then after another long moment, he stood up. "I think I'd better leave."

Diana was at a loss as to what to say. She didn't want him to go. Linda had read her right when she said Diana was in love with Scott. She was. They had made a deal to go to the dinner-dance together. It was a joke to begin with, but the last week had changed her. She thought it had changed him, too. Somewhere along the way, she'd begun to think their relationship was real, especially when he came to her aid in front of his friends and everyone else. The old Scott wouldn't have done that. The old Scott would be hand and fist in the corner with the Lindas of the world.

But this Scott wanted to kiss her. She knew it. The air between them sizzled with unfulfilled sex. Even when they danced, when he held her, she felt it, knew they wanted each other. But he was leaving. Diana felt as if the room got longer as he approached the door. But finally he had his hand on the knob. He was really going to leave. And she was going to let him. She didn't want to, but if she asked him to stay, everything would change. Diana wasn't ready for changes. She had her business to run and it was flourishing. She was involved in the community, sitting on several committees. She had friends, people who liked her for who she was. They didn't come with the baggage of her college years. They didn't know Brainiac or Diana 4.0. They accepted her for who she was now.

Scott opened the door and went through it. He pulled it shut. Diana heard the click of the lock. She went to the door to throw the deadbolt. The house was quiet, but she heard a rushing in her ears to rival the home team winning the Super Bowl.

Diana didn't understand how the door came to be open, but she was standing in it calling Scott's name. Her feet were bare, cold on the wooden porch. He stood next to his car, key in hand.

"Please stay," she said. Diana heard the words, recognized her voice, understood the implication of her request. And threw any caution her mind had left to the east wind.

Scott remained where he was. His body went still as he stared at her. Time seemed to stop its forward march as the two of them gazed at each other. Slowly he closed the car door and walked back to where she stood. Diana's mouth went dry. He was the sexiest man she'd ever seen. No longer was there any boyishness about him. Neither of them said a word when they were face to face. He cupped her face and stared in her eyes. Then let his eyes rove over her features until they settled on her mouth. Diana couldn't breathe. The noise in her head grew louder. He kissed her, tenderly, brushing his mouth over hers, teasing, tantalizing, promising more to come. Her arms wrapped around him and she pulled him close.

Scott pushed her backward and kicked the door closed. Reaching behind him, he secured the deadbolt without once lifting his mouth from hers. Diana felt his length pressing against her. His arousal was unmistakable. She moved against it, and he groaned in her mouth, a sound so guttural and pleasurable it sent prickles up her arms. Scott's hands caressed her back, making long, slow sweeps over the fabric of her dress. She could have been wearing a sheer nightgown. She could feel the heat of his hands all the way to her skin.

When his hands smoothed over her bottom, a wave of pleasure slammed into her, pushing her further into him. She heard the rasp of the dress zipper as he pulled it down. Cool air replaced the heat building inside her. When he reached the base of the dress, his hand slipped inside. Diana's head fell back. Her body was suffused with a red-hot fire that had her crying out. Scott pushed it away from her. A royal-blue puddle formed at her feet.

Wearing only a bra and panties, Diana bit her lip to hold in all waves of rapture vying for an outlet. This was the climax of her life to this point. She'd always wanted Scott. From that first encounter on campus to this moment, she wanted him to make love to her. She wanted to be in his arms, wanted to hold him and have him hold her. She wanted his mouth of her body and wanted his skin on her skin.

Scott must have pulled his tie loose after he left her front door. Diana caught one of the ends and slipped it free of his neck. She held it out the length of her arm and dropped it to the floor. Then her fingers worked the buttons of his dress shirt. As she released one button, her head bent and she pressed her mouth to him. His skin was moist as her sure fingers spread over him. Together they undressed each other, leaving a trail of clothes as they circled each other on the way to her bedroom.

The room was lit only by the moonlight. Scott released her bra and it fell to the floor. His thumbs brushed over her nipples, which grew to hard peaks under his tutelage. Diana clung to him. Her knees were weak, and with what he was doing to her, she wasn't going to be able to support herself much longer. They divested themselves of their final garments, and her heated skin met a torrent of fire. Scott turned Diana around and pulled her back into his front. His hands traveled all over her then settled over her breasts, and he brought her body to life as he gently massaged them.

The gentle pleasure Scott evoked in her as his hands moved over her, stopping and starting in places she never knew could add to her pleasure, built until she was panting and turning in his arms. Her body was hot and ready. She could feel herself flowing, wanting to be satisfied. Her inner muscles tightened to the point that she had to have him.

Together they fell on the bed. Scott quickly grabbed a condom, then he protected them and in one swift movement they joined. His mouth found her and he began the timeless rhythm of love. She opened her legs, allowing him greater access and wallowing in the pleasure that went through her with each pull and push of their bodies. His hands reached around to clasp her bottom. He lifted her to him, stroking harder and harder, increasing the pleasure quotient. Diana heard the sounds around them. She was unsure if they were from her or from him, but with each joining of their bodies the rhythm grew. They worked harder and faster. Her heart beat out of control. Her hands and arms held him, moved over him, pulled him into her, filling her with the love she always knew would be there.

Together they headed for oblivion, for the climax that came like a crashing wave. The roar started low then stepped up one stair at a time until it reached the zenith of intensity, until it was impossible to do anything other than explode.

And explode they did.

The coffee cup on Scott's desk had the Edward's Coffee Shop logo on it. He lifted it and looked at the black writing on white paper. It reminded him of Diana. During the past couple of weeks it seemed everything reminded him of her. And it was all good. He laughed to himself. Some of it was fun. Not like the fun he had when he was a sophomoric prankster. He didn't want to make fun of her. He wanted to have fun *with* her. Last night had created a memory he could hold and bring out when he needed to think of something good. It was their dance together. Despite his buddies' comments, he enjoyed holding her close, and he wasn't even sorry that they had seen him dancing with her as if she was the only woman for him.

He wasn't sorry when they made love, either. He wanted to stay with her to repeat the all-consuming act again and again. But eventually they had to eat, and both had to work. This was what Scott should have been doing now, instead of reliving their wild night on the sheets.

The door opened, and in walked three burly men. Scott sat up straight in his chair. He recognized them, had been expecting them in some form: a phone call, email, text. But they were here in person.

They were his friends, had been since college. And each one knew him and how they all treated Diana. When he was not flying a corporate executive to a meeting or going up to Maine, they got together for a guys' night out. They'd drink and talk about their wives, sometimes about the women who got away, and invariably come around to Scott's state of singleness. Someone would always ask if he'd met anyone special, when was he going to settle down or mention someone they'd known in their collective pasts who was now divorced. Women would be surprised to know that men tried just as hard to introduce their single male friends to women as they did.

Dan's and Mike's wives were willing to introduce him to one of their friends. Scott declined every time. From what he heard them saying, marriage was great, but there were times when it was trying. So far he hadn't met anyone he wanted to spend his life with.

Scott set the paper cup down and leaned back in his chair, linking his fingers together and placing his hands on his abdomen. The guys approached him seemingly

in slow motion, like the astronauts in *The Right Stuff.*
And undoubtedly, he was about to be told the right stuff.

"You're late," Scott said, getting in the first strike.
"I expected you to show up for breakfast."

When they met, they always had beer. Today, Hunt
set a bag of sandwiches on the desk along with mega-
size cups containing soft drinks. Without a word they
dove in and pulled out food. Scott didn't reach for the
bag, but Hunt slid a wrapped sandwich and a cup toward him.

"What's going on?" Mike asked. He spun a chair
around and straddled it. Dan lowered his bulk into the
worn leather chair of questionable origin. And Hunt-
ley Christenson, called Hunt by everyone who knew
him, pulled a rolling office chair from a nearby desk.
They looked like the dissertation committee except for
the food.

"I'm sorry I missed the party," Hunt said. "Sounds
like you and Diana 4.0 were the highlight of the evening."

"Don't call her that," Scott snapped. He came forward in the chair. Three pairs of eyes stared at him.

"Scott are you serious about her?" Dan asked.

"No," he said quickly. The truth was he didn't know
how he felt about Diana. He did have feelings for her,
more than even he was willing to admit.

"What was the dance about then?" Dan asked. "You
showing up with her was bound to spark rumors."

Scott smiled. He thought of them sitting in the arch
and planning this. "At first it was a joke," he said. He
explained about them seeing the irony of a date together,
especially one that would take them in direct view of
the same people they went to school with.

"So you two came as a joke?"

"It started out that way."

"Okay," Hunt said. "Why don't you start at the beginning and tell us what's going on?"

"And I would do this why?" Scott asked. "You're my friends, not my parents."

"It's damn interesting," Dan said. "And Diana 4.0 is the last person we'd ever pair with you."

"Don't call her that," he said again. "That was a college thing and a poor one at that. We should all have had 4.0 averages. She's a professional now with her own business."

Silence spread over the small group.

"This is your fault," Scott said, looking at them.

"How's that?" Mike asked.

"It started at your wedding."

"Mine? I've only been married a few months. Don't you mean Bill's wedding?"

"You weren't there," Scott told Mike. "You were off on your honeymoon. After the reception, we were all sitting around. The usual began and as usual conversation rolled around to my love life."

"Or lack thereof," Hunt interjected.

"We always do that," Dan defended. "It's all in fun. We don't mean anything by it."

"Just because we always do it doesn't mean we should," Scott told them. "Like we shouldn't continue to think of Diana in the negative because of her brain."

"This coming from the leader of the pack."

Scott nodded. "I admit it. I did taunt her when we were in school, but we're in our thirties now. We have jobs, responsibilities, you have wives. Would you want someone from their pasts referring to your wives with negative comments?"

They sobered and looked at each other.

"You're really stuck on her," Hunt said. "When did this happen?"

Scott took a moment to collect his thoughts. "After Mike's wedding, you guys really laid it on heavy."

They hung their heads a moment then nodded.

"It stayed on my mind, and one night while I was online one of those ads for singles popped up. I don't even remember clicking on it, but when the window opened I had no intention of doing anything but reading. Then I saw the questions and I started answering them, entering information."

"And you got Diana—" Mike stopped himself from adding the *4.0* to the end of Diana's name.

Scott nodded, keeping the rest of what he'd entered to himself. "I didn't know it was her for months. We didn't include photos and we never used real names. It wasn't until we met in person that we discovered we knew each other."

"And you started dating."

Scott shook his head. "We had one dinner, but I was called away. The scholarship dinner-dance was the first time we went anywhere together."

"Are you going out again?" Dan asked.

"We have no plans, but I'm thinking of it," he answered honestly. "She's different from how we perceived her in school."

"What about Linda?" Hunt asked. "I hear she's back and gunning for you."

"Not interested," Scott said. "She's not much different from when we were in school. I suppose we all don't change."

"Maybe she *is* changing, too," Mike said.

Scott looked at him for an additional explanation.

"At first she was as mean to Diana as she always was. But later in the evening I heard her give Diana a compliment."

"What did she say?" Scott asked. He'd witnessed Linda's treatment of Diana. But after Diana returned from the ladies' lounge something was different.

"She liked her dress and her hair," Mike said.

Scott remembered the royal-blue dress Diana wore and the way her hair was. She'd done it in a huge, thick collection of curls that dangled down her back. He also remembered removing the dress and undoing her hair. After that he was the one who was undone.

"Are you sure that was a compliment?" Scott asked.

"She didn't sound as if it was tipped with her usual venom. In fact, I was surprised to hear her speak without the sarcasm that usually poured from her lips."

Scott remembered the comment from across the years. Diana wasn't the only person they ridiculed. Linda got her share of colorful remarks from the group, some in private, some to her face.

"If Linda complimented Diana," Scott said, "she wants something."

"Or she's planning something," Hunt added. His tone had them looking at him.

"Do you know something about Linda?"

"Not about her and Diana, but I know what she wants."

"How?" Dan asked. "You weren't at the dance."

Hunt said nothing, only stared back at Scott.

"Well, don't keep us in suspense," Dan finally said.

"What's she's always wanted—you," he said quietly.

All eyes turned to Scott.

Chapter 9

Scott set the plane down and rushed to complete the postflight paperwork. He was meeting Diana and that was uppermost in his mind. He knew he couldn't skimp on what was necessary with the plane, but he was glad to be able to turn it over to the mechanics and take a quick shower before heading into town.

They had no formal plans, just dinner and relaxing at his place.

Teddy was leaving as he arrived. "Hello, Scott. Good night, Scott," she called with a wave as she headed toward her car. The parking lot was crowded with construction material. The men had ended their work for the day. Scott had to step around cement bags and discarded wood and broken pieces of drywall to reach the door.

He brushed away a sheen of dust before climbing the

stairs to Diana's office. She met him at the door, and all thoughts went to her. Kissing her on the mouth, he stepped back and surveyed her.

"You look like you had a successful day."

"I did. I only have a few details to complete and another Weddings by Diana will be up and running.

"Congratulations. We'll have to celebrate. But let's not do it here. There is so much debris outside."

"Where did you go today?" Diana asked when they were in his Lexus and heading away from the parking lot.

"Tennessee."

She laughed. "That sounds so interesting. Most people would answer 'nowhere' or 'out to lunch.' You get to visit entire states."

"Today I didn't get to see much of it. I only thought of getting back to you."

"Ooooh, pretty words. I love hearing them."

The drive was short. Scott led her to one of the older neighborhoods outside Princeton proper. While both the borough and the main section of town referred to as Princeton proper had merged, it would take a while before the sense of separation ended. Scott lived on one of the side streets close to the gothic-looking high school.

They got out of the car and he carried in several bags.

"What are we eating?" Diana asked.

"Wine and cheese."

"Is that all? I think I'm starving tonight."

"There might be a steak in one of these."

"Red meat. Suppose I don't eat red meat?"

"I've already seen you eat it."

He put the bags on the kitchen counter and started to remove the items. Diana looked around the room. His kitchen wasn't state-of-the-art like hers, but it was functional and easy to get around in. She moved through and looked into the living room.

"The light switch is on the right," Scott said. Diana found it and turned it on. The room had the basic furniture and artifacts he'd brought back from his travels.

"This is beautiful," she said and stepped into the room. Scott went to the doorway and watched her. She stared at a painting over the fireplace.

"It's the Maine house," he explained. "We used to go there often. I learned to fly there. Ever been?"

Diana shook her head. Scott handed her a glass of sparkling wine and told her it was her turn to make the salad. She rejoined him in the kitchen and opened several drawers looking for the silverware. The kitchen quickly filled with savory smells. Once dinner was ready, they sat down in his kitchen and ate.

"I had a very interesting meeting last week," he said. He didn't know why he wanted to tell her about it, but he wanted her to know.

"Really?" she said, smiling as she sipped wine. "Was it about me?"

"As self-centered as ever," he teased, using the same phrase she had when he'd asked the same question. She laughed, and he loved hearing the tinkle in her voice.

"The meeting was no laughing matter. It was almost an intervention."

"Intervention?"

They got up and moved from the kitchen to the living room. "And your name did come up."

"This doesn't sound good."

Scott related what had happened, casting a good light on it.

"So they've changed and no longer think of me as Diana 4.0?"

"That might take some time," he admitted. "But being a 4.0 student is a compliment."

"Not the way they said it. But I suppose since you've changed your thinking, I can at least give them the benefit of the doubt until proven otherwise."

"You say that as if you expect them to prove otherwise."

"Well, there is Princeton borough and Princeton proper. And never the twain shall meet."

"They'll come around when they get to know you."

Scott realized he wanted them to get to know her. He wanted them to realize how they had misjudged her when they were in school, but now that they were older, more mature, they could see her for the warm, loving person she was.

"What are we going to do tonight?" she asked, apparently relegating his friends to another subject area. "We could go for a walk."

Scott stood up. "I have a better idea, but it does involve a walk."

Diana looked at Scott and a slow smile teased his mouth. He came to her. Diana didn't turn away. She was no longer Diana 4.0 or Brainiac. She was a woman, and Scott was the man attracted to her. His hands were on her waist, the same as they had been at the Embry wedding rehearsal.

"Shouldn't we clean the dishes?" she suggested, her voice a low whisper.

"What dishes?" he asked.

She looked in his eyes, seeing the need there. His

mouth slid down to hers. The moment their lips touched, Diana was transported back to school on *that* day, back to the kissing spot. Scott's arms went around her, pulling her close to him. He tilted his head, took her full mouth. His tongue swept inside and she joined him, weaving her arms around his neck and feeling the warm softness of smooth skin.

Without her high heels, Diana felt short next to Scott. Pushing herself up on her toes, she leaned into him, wrapping one leg around Scott's. The action brought her body closer to his. She could feel his erection grow hard against her belly. A low, pleasurable sound came from him. The feeling was too good for her to stop. She didn't want to think about anything but him. Scott's hand caressed her back, traveling up and down over her contours.

His hands warmed her where they touched. And he touched her everywhere. Each part of her shirt and the tops of her pants turned to fire as Scott skimmed over them. Diana was sure her skin would burn and slide off. Her second leg raised as she could think only of getting closer to him. Scott grasped her bottom and held her, pushing into her. The two became one.

"Where's the bedroom?" she asked in a croaky voice.

"Top of the stairs."

Diana didn't know how they made it. It seemed to take hours to get there. Scott stopped along the steps, pushing her back into the rungs and deepening the kiss with each lift of his head. His fingers slid between hers and they stretched along the stairs. She could only marvel that they kept themselves from sliding down the stairs. By the time they got to the bed, both were frenzied. They tore at their clothes and undressed each other, separating and coming together as if each needed the other to survive.

Scott pulled Diana back to him and kissed her. Each stood naked in the other's arms. Diana inhaled Scott's scent. She smelled his flight jacket combined with the outdoors. His body was hard and smooth. Her hands ran over him as if he were clay and she was the artist forming him into a man. His butt was strong, and she reveled over the curves leading to his long legs. Her fingers forced him to arch into her.

The whole room smelled of sexual electricity, combined with the guttural stock of human pleasure. Scott laid her on the bed and joined her there. His eyes gazed over her, taking in the smooth skin of her breasts and legs. He kissed her neck, then her cheeks, neck and shoulders. As he neared her breasts, Diana could feel them grow heavy and point upward in anticipation. She was having trouble controlling her breathing.

Scott paused at her navel, giving it wet attention. Diana writhed beneath him. She wanted him now, but he wasn't finished with his torture. His hands stretched down the outside of her legs and came up the inside. When he reached the juncture of her legs, he used his thumb to give attention to the sweet spot of her sex.

"Awww," she cried out. Her hands took his shoulders and assisted him up to her. She opened her legs in invitation, and Scott protected himself before entering her. Diana's eyes fluttered shut as she moved ever so slightly. Yet the pleasure he evoked shot through her like a narcotic, instantly taking her on a high greater than she'd ever felt before. Three, four, five times the rapture embraced them. Waves burned inside her. Her fingers grabbed his back and held him, guided him, showing him where her pleasure points were and having him tap into each of them.

With each thrust of his legs, Diana was sure she would die. Yet each was greater, harder, more intense, more sensitive and found a higher level of pleasure than the one before. Unsure if she could endure this plane of erotic saturation, she still didn't want him to stop. She anticipated each thrust, waited for it, wanted it, wanted more and more, wanted it all.

She heard Scott's sounds as he pushed into her. Her head banged against the bed's headboard. Diana pushed against it, stretching her body and allowing him greater access to the core of her being. It could have gone on for years or been over in a few seconds, she didn't know. Time had no place in their lovemaking. Only feelings counted. Only the area of space where they ascended— where the universe was composed of sensation, where the giving and receiving of pleasure was the purpose of life—existed. And only the two of them inhabited it.

The break happened, the big bang, the eruption of a shattering star penetrated her mind. Diana felt the wind of creation rush over her. She heard the scream, yet didn't know it came from her. When they could get no higher, feel no greater pleasure in each other, they came, climaxed, in the bright light of their new world.

Seven nights, Diana thought. Seven glorious love-filled nights. She glanced from the mirror to the hotel bed. She would miss him tonight. Scott had been with her every night, and they'd burned up the sheets with their lovemaking. Diana whirled before the mirror. She wore a business suit, but she felt beautiful.

The opening of the latest franchise was days away,

and she'd flown to Montana for some last-minute details. Several calls to Scott proved fruitless. She missed
him every time. She assumed he had an emergency and
had to fly out quickly. But he was never far from her
thoughts or from the infusion of heat that accompanied
those thoughts.

Going to the new office, Diana worked with Carrie
Osgood, its manager. They spent hours together and by
the end of the day the room was cluttered with material: glossy magazines, wedding veils, blueprints and
flowers. Coffee cups and the debris of a working lunch
lay on the credenza in the corner.

"Many of the details have been worked out. I've been
arranging for furniture and inventory. The suppliers
you use have been wonderful to work with, and several orders are in the works. I made a contact with a
local office supply company, and our furniture arrives
tomorrow."

Diana listened as Carrie updated her on the franchise's progress since Diana's last visit.

"Are we still on for the grand opening?" Diana asked.

"We'll be ready," she said without hesitation. "The
shelves are all in place. Our inventory will be here in
a few days." Carrie spread her arms and Diana looked
at the empty shelves, glass cases, mirrors and dressing
rooms. Carrie's idea was that the franchise should have
a working bridal shop in case brides wanted a one-stop
for all wedding consultants. Diana loved the idea. And
it was another place to showcase Teddy's designs.

"I've worked with the advertising firm I used in the
past," Diana told her. "They've begun the program. A
reception and fashion show to introduce the business
usually works well to bring in potential clients." Diana

held her hands out with her fingers crossed. "It will work again."

"I already have a client," Carrie said.

"Is it a friend?" Diana asked. That was the usual way planners began.

"Not a friend. It was a recommendation. She's not the richest person. She took the basic package."

"No matter the package, treat her like royalty. This is her day. If she likes what she gets, she'll tell her friends, and our business lives or dies on word of mouth."

Diana gathered her papers and briefcase. Sliding her purse on her shoulder, she smiled at Carrie. "You'll do fine," Diana told her confidently. "And you won't be alone. We'll have one of our best consultants come out and help you until you can hire someone of your own."

Carrie took a breath. Diana smiled and squeezed her shoulder. "I'm off to the airport. Just follow the details we set out in the package and everything will work out fine."

Carrie nodded, but Diana understood she wasn't taking to being alone for the first time. She'd be fine. Mistakes could happen, but usually they were fixable. And Diana had a full team of people who came as backup.

She only wished she had the same kind of team for her life. Things were going well—too well—and that scared her.

Diana was both tired and exhilarated when she returned to the hotel that night. Her plans were to order room service, take a hot shower and turn in early. She'd fly home in the morning and straight into Scott's arms if he was back.

She called him as soon as she got to the room. He

answered, and her heartbeat accelerated just hearing his voice.

"Where are you?" she asked, expecting to hear he was in New York or Timbuktu.

"Montana," he said.

Diana was sure she hadn't heard him correctly. She moved her hair and pushed the phone closer to her ear. "Where?"

"Outside your door," he said.

Diana was robbed of the ability to speak. She tried saying something, but nothing came out. She turned and stared at the closed door. She was sure she hadn't heard correctly. It had to be the phone. She was due for a new one. This was the time to get it.

"Open the door," he said.

Obediently, she went to the hotel door and peered through the fisheye lens. Scott stood there in his flight suit. Yanking the door inward, she found it was true.

"What are you doing here?"

He didn't answer. He swept into the room and took her into his arms. They kissed for a long time.

"I couldn't wait one more day for you to come back," he said, kissing her again.

Diana couldn't get a word in, and after a moment she didn't want to. Feelings took over her body, and she only wanted to know Scott's hands on her, feel him filling her with more pleasure than should be legal.

Diana opened her eyes and groaned at the sound of Scott's ringing phone. Reaching across her, he grabbed it from the bedside table.

"Hello," he said. Then, like a soldier coming to attention, he was instantly alert. He got out of bed, listening intently.

"Linda," he said. "What?"

He waited for her to answer.

"Where?" After another pause, he said, "I'm on my way."

Scott ended the call and grabbed his clothes. Looking around for his socks, he suddenly remembered Diana. She lay in bed, her body raised on her elbows, the sheet covering her naked breasts.

"I have to go," he said. Going into the bathroom, he showered and dressed in ten minutes. Taking a second, he kissed her quickly and left the hotel room. It was unusual for him to get a job outside his usual flying area, but he'd been called to pick up a sick child in need of emergency microsurgery. Scott understood the crucial nature of his job. He was at the airport and onto his plane in record time. Soaring through the air, it suddenly hit him. What he'd said. What Diana had heard. And the worst of it was the dispatcher's name was Linda. She probably thought he was rushing off to meet his former girlfriend Linda.

Nothing could be further from the truth. Scott need to call Diana. Explain. Let her know where he was and who had called to give him the message. Anything he'd say in the cockpit would be recorded on the black box that had been placed there for security purposes in case of an accident. There was an air phone in the cockpit, another FAA safety feature in case communication was interrupted by other sources.

He grabbed it and dialed. No answer.

Slamming the phone back into its cradle, he mentally kicked himself. He remembered her lying under the sheets. Her hair was all around her, but the expression on her face had been questioning. He had seen it, but didn't think too much of it. His mind was on the life he had to save. But Diana didn't know that was his destination. He was sure she only heard the word *Linda*. It was Linda Tisdale, the dispatcher for the medical air facility. Not Linda Engles, his former girlfriend. But Diana didn't know there were two different Lindas.

Even after last night, after the passionate and uncontrollable fervor of their lovemaking, the pure consummation of the universe, she would think it was all a lie, that he'd left her bed only to jump into one with his former girlfriend. He needed to talk to Diana, but there was no way. He had an injured child on board and every minute counted in getting that child medical care.

Scott would have to explain later. He'd come to Montana to explain that he loved her. Yet he'd never said the words. He'd shown her in every way possible, but the three little words remained in his mind and his heart. On the outside, the side she could see and hear, his actions said he was leaving her.

He checked the controls. Everything was in order. His life was a mess, but the plane was flying as he had programmed it to. Every second it took him farther and farther away from the woman he loved. She was probably on her way traveling east. He was flying to Los Angeles. The child behind the closed door of the aircraft was a six-year-old brain-tumor patient on her way for microsurgery at the world-renowned Oceanic Clinic. When Scott had got to the airport, the ambulance was already there and she, along with a truckload of medical equipment, was on board.

The tower cleared him immediately and then they

were airborne. He was winging his way four thousand miles from where Diana was headed. He could only hope when he got to the ground she would answer the phone and allow him to explain.

But that wasn't going to happen. Scott wasn't allowed to take off immediately and return to his home base. He'd been in the air too long within the last twenty-four hours. He had to stay where he was for at least another night. Diana not answering his calls told him she believed he was with Linda Engles. No matter how many messages he left, she returned none of them.

Packing wasn't one of the things Diana did well. Even though she traveled a lot, she'd never learned to pack her clothes efficiently. After Scott left, she cared nothing about packing. She virtually threw her clothes into her suitcase and smashed it shut. If the people at the airline wanted to open and inspect it, so be it. She didn't care if they found her dirty nightgown and underwear.

How could Scott just jump up and leave without a single word? And how could he go to Linda? He'd told her Linda was old news. That she was not coming back into his life, yet one call from her when he was two thousand miles away and he'd grabbed his clothes and left Diana's bed.

She'd never felt so abandoned. Diana hated to admit it, but Scott still had feelings for Linda. Diana couldn't compete with that. She'd already known they'd had no future together, but he'd treated her well, made her feel special. But she only had a few months with him, and he and Linda had years of time that linked them together.

"Checking out," she told the woman at the hotel desk and then settled her bill.

"I hope you enjoyed your stay and you'll come back again."

Diana returned the young woman's smile, although she felt more like crying than smiling. She never wanted to see this place again. The best and worst day of her life had been spent here. Scott had made love to her so sweetly and so tenderly that she felt as if nothing on earth could top it. She'd thought of happily-ever-after, of being the bride in her own wedding. And then the worst had happened.

He'd left her.

Alone.

And without a word.

Princeton, New Jersey, was as much a tourist attraction as the Statue of Liberty. Droves of people flocked to see the university. Scott was among the many locals walking along the short stretch of land that comprised the center of town. He hoped to see Diana going into the coffee shop. He'd been back a day and she hadn't answered her phone or returned any of his messages.

She loved Edward's coffee. Scott figured he'd run into her here sooner or later. Going through the door, he looked around, but she wasn't among the patrons. He ordered a coffee and sat on one of the high chairs near the window that faced the university. If she came in he could talk to her. If she passed by he could go out and meet her.

"Is this seat taken?" someone asked.

"No." Scott turned and spoke at the same time. Slipping into the empty chair next to him was Linda, the last person he wanted to see. And the one person he didn't want Diana to find him with.

"I was hoping to run into you." Her voice was as soft as purring kitten.

"Why is that?" Scott wanted to leave. His strategy for the day had been thwarted. He couldn't leave now that she'd begun a conversation.

"Well, I'm back in town, and since I haven't been here for a while, I thought we might get together for old time's sake. You could tell me what's happening with the old crowd and we can catch up on each other's lives."

"You know this is a small town, but I was never the one who had that information. You should contact one of the women you used to hang out with. A couple of them are still around. At least they were at the dinner. I'm out of town a lot."

"I know, but they don't…" She moved closer to him.

Scott recognized the move. He and Linda had once been a couple. He didn't know what he'd seen in her.

"Linda," Scott began before she could go on. "We spent a lot of time together in the past."

"Yes," she smiled.

"Both of us have changed since then. You've been married and divorced. You're putting down roots in Rocky Hill."

"And you've flown all over the world. We could—"

"No," Scott stopped her. "We had—"

"I was only going to say that we had a great time at the dance, but don't read anything into it."

Scott understood she knew where he was going and had interrupted him to save face.

"Like you say, I've just moved back to the area. And

I need to give myself some time since the divorce before I rush into anything." She laughed. He knew she was attempting to lighten the mood, but it failed. "I wouldn't want to make another mistake like the last one."

"Taking time to think things through is always a good decision."

She gave him a brilliant smile. "There is one thing I want to say."

"What's that?"

"Thank you."

Scott frowned. "For what?"

"For being my friend. I don't have many. I hope in the future I can continue to count you among them.'

"You can."

She leaned forward and kissed him on the cheek. At that exact moment, Diana's car stopped across the street to wait for the light. She looked directly at him, holding her gaze for a long moment.

"Damn," he cursed. Could things get any worse?

"Anything wrong?" Linda asked. Her gaze went to the Porsche.

The light turned green and Diana drove away.

Scott had no doubt that she'd recognized Linda.

"Is she the one?" Linda asked.

Scott barely heard the question. He continued to stare through the glass, looking at the space where Diana had witnessed an innocent kiss, a friendship kiss, between him and a former girlfriend. He knew Linda could be a conniving individual, but he didn't think she was insincere.

"I have to go," he said.

He left the cup on the counter and moved toward the door.

"Scott," Linda called.

He looked back at her.

"Tell her," she said.

Chapter 10

Diana knew she was acting like an idiot, but she didn't care. It was childish not to answer a phone or respond to a text message. She could tell Scott she didn't want to talk to him or she could listen to his explanation. Instead she'd taken the coward's way out and just refused to confront the fear that he might want to be with Linda Engles and not with her.

Diana had never called him and asked him to drop everything and come to her. She wondered it he would. Even if he was halfway across the country, would he fly to her the way he'd flown to Linda? She wasn't sure. She'd never tested anything and had no will to do so now. She didn't have the same history with him that Linda had. He and Linda had been lovers for three years. Diana barely had three months. But she thought the degree of intensity of their lovemaking made up for the shortness of time. It had for her.

When she thought about it, she and Scott didn't know each other that well. They knew the basics, like what it was like to make love, where they could touch each other to send their bodies into overdrive, but the mundane things—like what it was like growing up, when was his birthday, what was his favorite color—were things they hadn't been together long enough to learn. And now it was likely they never would.

Diana got out of the car feeling like stamping her feet. Instead, she slammed the car door, deciding it was time to chart her own life—without Scott. He preferred women like Linda. Diana would never be like her. And she'd make sure Scott didn't figure into her plans. She knew the Lindas of the world, and if he wanted to spend his time or his life with someone of her character, he had her permission.

And good riddance.

Diana entered the church. Seeing Scott and Linda in the window kissing had sent her nerves into burning jealousy. She hated to admit it to herself, but she wanted Scott and didn't like knowing he preferred Linda.

The quiet solitude of the sanctuary calmed her. She was backing Teddy up, but her partner was in control. Diana breathed slowly, allowing her heart to return to a normal beat, and smiled as the procession began.

Her cell phone vibrated as the bride and groom joined hands. Slipping outside, Diana pulled the phone free and checked the display. Suddenly she went cold. On the small display was his MatchforLove.com email address. She hadn't answered any of his calls. The message was a text. Diana stared at the small screen, unable to speak. She'd stopped listening to his messages.

The sound of his voice sent her body into overdrive. She wanted to talk to him, but she wouldn't, couldn't. She couldn't trust herself not to forgive him of everything just because that deep voice had whispered in her ear and driven her crazy with desire.

Staring at the phone, she tried to decide if she should answer it. Should she open it and see what he had to say? Her finger was on the delete key. All she had to do was press it and the message would be gone. Her nerves would remain intact and she could return to the wedding. Finally, she opened the email. It said, *Call Emergency Health Flight Services—NOW!* The capital letters jumped off the screen. What happened? Why would she need to call Emergency Health Services? Scott worked there, but she knew no one there, had no dealings with anyone except Scott who even knew of the service.

A phone number accompanied the message, but it didn't specify anyone in particular to ask for. The message was from Scott's email address. Not a personal address, but the one he used for MatchforLove.com. Suddenly Diana panicked. Had anything happened to him? She leaned against the garden wall, her legs suddenly weak, her breath caught in her throat. She'd just seen him. The two of them.

It could be a ruse, but Diana couldn't take the chance. Maybe something had happened to Scott and he needed to reach her. She had to answer. She needed to know. If the message was from him, she could ignore it if she chose.

Immediately, she dialed the number. A woman answered. "This is Diana Greer. I have a message to call this number. Is anything wrong?"

"You need to come here right away," the woman said

"Why? What's wrong?"

"Do you know where we are?"

Diana knew. There was only one airfield in the Princeton area, and Emergency Health Flight Services had their office and planes there.

"Please get here as soon as possible."

"Has something happened to Scott?" Diana's heart was pounding so hard, she could barely hear. Her grip on the small instrument was tight enough to crush it. Her voice grew louder as she tried to get some information.

"I have to go," she said. "We have another emergency."

The woman on the phone would give her no other information, only that it involved Scott. Diana stopped. She slowed her breathing. She had not said that Scott was the emergency. She hadn't said he wasn't, either.

Diana stepped back inside and signaled Teddy. Then she dialed Scott's number. No answer. She called his landline. Again no answer. Diana had to get there. She gave Teddy a shortened version of what occurred and told her she was leaving. Teddy assured her everything was under control.

Diana rushed to the car and sped through the zigzag streets of the township. Route 206 was only a one-lane road, and traffic stopped and started oblivious of her need to open the engine and run every stoplight to get to Scott. Finally she turned into the long driveway and sped down it. She parked in the first available space, not taking into account whether the space was legal or not.

Diana yanked open the door to a cavernous building, then entered and found a long wooden desk with a fiftysomething woman behind it.

"Hello, I'm Diana Greer. I talked to someone on the phone."

"That was me," the woman said. "Catherine Manfred." She offered her hand. Diana shook it.

"Is Scott all right? Has he been hurt?" Diana didn't recognize her own voice. She'd rushed from the wedding and could account for the out-of-breath sound, but the catch in her throat was unexpected.

Instead of answering, Catherine Manfred handed Diana a folder. Diana opened it and found a report showing flight information from Montana to Los Angeles and a medical condition.

"Scott had a heart attack?" Diana could hardly speak. Each word came out separately. Her legs went numb and she gripped the counter, unsure if she could remain standing. "Where is he?"

"Hold on," Catherine said. She rushed around the counter and supported Diana around the waist, leading her to a chair where she sat.

"I'm sorry I frightened you. Scott is not here."

"Where is he?"

"He went to get something to eat, but I saw him go into the hangar a few moments ago."

"But he texted me," Diana said. "Said there was an emergency and I needed to come."

"Sorry, that was me. Scott was headed out. While he checked on something with the plane, I snagged his cell phone and left you the message. I needed to talk to you."

"Why?" Diana asked, looking at the stranger with wide eyes.

"Because you need to talk to him. He's a changed man since you stopped taking his calls. He's irritable and angry and hard to get along with."

"That may not be because of me."

"Believe me," Catherine said, "it's because of you."

Somehow that made Diana feel better. She was glad to hear that he was having at least as much misery as she was.

"If Scott didn't have a heart attack, why did you give me this?" She indicated the folder in her hand.

"It doesn't say anyone had a heart attack. We're not privy to medical details."

Diana looked inside again. She didn't understand what Catherine was trying to say.

"That's why he left you in Montana," she said. Diana looked up. The woman obviously knew more than Diana thought she should, but Diana was still confused.

"If you look closer, you'll see that he piloted a flight where he picked up a child in Waymon Valley, Montana, and flew out to Los Angeles on the day he left you."

Diana checked the dates. She was aware of the exact date and time he'd left her.

"Because of him the lives of hundreds of children have been saved, including the one he brought to New York several days ago. It was all over the news."

Diana remembered the story. "But the call was from Linda."

"And you assumed it was Linda Engles, the vamp who's been calling here for days trying to get Scott to give her some attention."

"I didn't know that."

"Linda Tisdale is a scheduling and dispatch coordinator who works here. *She* called Scott that day. He was in Montana and convenient for getting the child to L.A. on time. Scott let us know he was going to Montana. Of course, he hadn't told us about you at the time and we didn't ask. When we got the call relayed from another emergency service that couldn't respond, he was in a perfect location. As you could tell, he didn't hesitate to answer."

"I feel like such an idiot. I wouldn't talk to him, wouldn't let him explain."

"All is not lost," Catherine said. Her tone was that of a loving mother. "You have a chance to say you're sorry."

"Thank you," Diana said.

"There's just one thing I want you to do."

Diana nodded.

"Don't tell Scott I interfered. He hates that."

Diana laughed.

"You know how men like to think they can handle their own problems," the woman said.

"Women, too."

When Diana misjudged someone, she did it on a grand scale. She left the Emergency Health Flight Services offices, her feet dragging as if she were trying to carry a weight three times her size. How could she have been so wrong? And how could Scott let her believe that he was going to see Linda when all along he was rushing away to save someone's life? She'd told him once he was one of the good guys, yet she didn't let that knowledge keep her from destroying his character when it came to Linda Engles.

Right now Diana needed to talk to Scott. She needed to apologize for her comments, for what she thought of him. She pulled her cell out and dialed his number. She got his voice mail. Disconnecting without leaving a message, she wondered if he was ignoring her calls, since she'd ignored his. She wondered where he was. Where could she find him?

She started into a fast walk, then ran toward the hangar where Scott kept the corporate jet he flew. The wind pulled the curl out of her hair. By the time she reached the edge of the building she was out of breath. The shaded interior temporarily blinded her. It took a moment for her eyes to adjust from the bright sunshine outside.

"Scott," she called. Her voice was weak, and in the cavernous space it could barely be heard. She looked around. The plane sat silently, like a giant white fly on the floor of a big house. "Scott," she said a little louder, taking tentative steps toward the plane.

A man came out from behind the giant bird. "Who are you calling?" he asked. He wore coveralls and had white hair. He was wiping his hands on a shrimp-colored cloth.

"Scott Thomas."

"Up there." He indicated the plane and turned back to whatever he'd been doing before she came in.

Diana looked at where up there was. She walked around the plane and saw the stairs against the fuselage. Scott was inside the plane. Diana took the steps one at a time. She went inside, standing in the middle of the floor and looking first in one direction, then in the other. She'd logged over a million miles in the last five years, been on countless types of aircrafts, DC-10s, crop dusters and 787s, but this plane, except for its scale, could rival Air Force One.

Taking a few steps to her right, she came upon a lounge complete with curved seating, ambience lighting, big-screen television, a desk and chairs. The whole place looked like something out of *Star Trek:* futuristic, functional and designed for comfort. Her breath escaped, and she put a hand to her mouth to keep it from totally leaving her without air. She'd made a huge amount of money from her business enterprise, but she could not afford one engine of this superplane.

She heard a noise behind her and jumped as if she'd been caught doing something wrong. Scott stood there. He wore a pilot's uniform. Diana had never seen him in it. He looked strong and confident, as if he belonged in it.

"Scott," she said, her mouth dry. She wanted to apologize, but didn't know where to begin. She hadn't expected this environment. She expected to be on the ground. This was like being in some futuristic paradise.

"What are you doing here?"

Diana dropped her arms. "I came to apologize."

"For not returning my phone calls?" He came forward.

She wanted to move back, but felt rooted to the floor. "Yes," she said. "But not only that. I need to apologize for doubting you. I know about Linda Tisdale. I know she was the voice on the other end of the phone and not Linda Engles. You left me to go and save a life. I feel so guilty."

Scott came and stood directly in front to her. He slipped his arm around her waist and pulled her against him. Together they gazed into each other's eyes.

"I didn't meet Linda that day," Scott said. "I know you saw us, but what happened didn't really happen."

Diana didn't say anything. She let Scott go on and explain.

"I ran into her at the coffee shop. I was hoping to run

into you." He paused a moment. Diana had intentionally looked for him at the coffee shop when the light turned red. She had not expected to find him kissing Linda.

"It was a friendship kiss," he said as if he could read her thoughts. "We decided that our chance at a relationship had come and gone." He looked at her a long while, his eyes traveling over her as if he needed to take in every detail of her features. "I'm glad you're here," he said.

"Me, too. I've missed you terribly."

"I can't tell you how hard it was for me not to run across this floor and haul you into my arms. It's felt like years since I held you."

"Maybe we could make up for it now," Diana said.

Scott's eyes narrowed. After a moment he moved away from her and went to a wall. Pressing it in a certain place, it opened and a panel came forward. Using a code known to him, Diana heard a motor begin to whir. The sound was muted. Scott looked away from her and she realized he was closing the door of the plane.

"Are we going somewhere?" she asked.

"Oh, yes," he said, his head nodding at the same time. When the door was secured, he closed the panel and returned to her. Taking her hand, he said, "Let me show you around."

They got as far as the bedroom before the tour ended.

A week later Teddy called Diana to take over a wedding. The consultant, Renee, had gone home ill. Teddy had another wedding to do, and everyone else was busy.

"Don't worry about it," she told Teddy. "I'll get right on it."

"What are you getting right on?" Scott asked when she hung up the phone."

"Come on," she told him. "We're going to a wedding."

"Really? Whose?"

"You don't know them."

Within a few moments, Diana was at the bride's house and filling in for the missing consultant. The bride understood, but her mother wasn't sure she wanted the change.

"I assure you, every detail will be promptly accomplished," Diana assured her. "I've done this many times, and Renee is not at her best. You wouldn't want the bride or groom to become ill on their honeymoon."

That got her. She smiled. And the day began. The prewedding photos were done and they proceeded to the church. Diana rushed to complete everything and make sure everyone was ready.

When the bride started her walk down the aisle Diana was relieved. As she had promised, everything went well.

This was the part of the ceremony she liked best. The couple were about to begin a new life. And today was the beginning of it. They had everything going for them. Diana moved to the side. Scott, in the last pew, slid over to give her room. She slipped into the seat beside him. He smiled at her and took her hand.

"Are you done now?" he whispered.

She nodded. For this wedding, her responsibilities ended after the ceremony. The photos and reception were being handled by someone else. Still, Diana liked to stay until the end.

"We're invited to the reception, and I agreed to attend," she whispered.

The minister was at the part where the couple pledged their troths. Diana had looked that up once to understand what it meant. In today's language, they were pledging their lives to each other before these witnesses and the Divine. This part made her eyes misty whenever she had time to sit down and listen to the words.

Holding Scott's hand made the words seem more personal. She wasn't sure why. She hadn't thought of marrying, ever. She had no time for a husband and a family. Both required a lot of time, and she was not interested in a long-term relationship. But the two of them sitting side by side, holding hands and listening to the wedding vows, made Diana think she might like one day to be floating down the aisle on her way to a new life.

"You may kiss the bride," the minister was saying as Diana returned her attention to the front of the church. For some reason she looked at Scott. His attention was on her, and she knew they both were remembering the kiss they had shared at the altar. Although it was at a rehearsal, that made it no less significant in her mind.

The entire congregation stood. The happy couple started up the aisle, wide smiles on their faces. As they approached Diana and Scott, she turned toward them. Scott stepped forward and pushed his arms around her waist, aligning her body with his. Diana forced herself not to gasp or let her weight sag into his body as it wanted to do.

The bridal party came next, followed by the guests. Diana didn't move. She stayed in Scott's arms. Eventually her head fell back on his shoulder and he kissed her neck. A spiral of electricity went through her with a shock as unexpected as her waking up floating on a boat in the middle of the ocean. She was unprepared, ignorant as to how to proceed. She needed help, and it appeared Scott was right behind her, supporting her, providing her with what she needed keep her body upright.

"Shall we go?" he asked. "Or would you like to be kissed in a church for the third time?"

His words pushed her out of his arms, and she stepped into the aisle. Scott caught her hand. They were the last to leave the sanctuary. The bridal party was coming in from the back to begin their photo session.

"Do you like attending all these weddings?" Scott asked.

"I do," she said, suddenly realizing the double entendre of her reply. Covering herself, she went on: "Giving a bride the perfect day makes me feel…" She stopped. They reached her SUV and both climbed in.

"Go on," Scott prompted. "What do you feel?"

"I feel as if I've fulfilled her greatest wish. Sometimes the groom's, too."

"Don't you ever want that for yourself?"

Diana was unprepared for the question. "I never really thought about it." She was driving, but she looked aside, trying to find out where he was going with this.

"I know you aren't looking for a long-term relationship. But since you attend several weddings a year, don't you ever think of it being you in the bridal gown?"

Strange he should bring this up. She'd been thinking that exact thing only minutes ago, as they sat holding hands.

"Once or twice," she admitted.

"Yet you are in a field where the men you meet are on their way to the altar."

"There are the groomsmen," she quipped. "Not all of them are taken."

Scott remained quiet for a moment. In the wedding they had just left, several of the groomsmen were in her age bracket and unattached.

"But you went to MatchforLove.com. Why is that?"

She frowned. Scott leaned forward and looked at her from the passenger seat.

"While there are single men at these weddings, I'm very busy, and most of the ones I meet are either engaged or obnoxious," Diana answered.

"Like me?" he finished for her.

"Like you." Her smile took the sting out of the words. It felt good to be able to laugh at that now.

"I didn't go to MatchforLove.com on my own," she finally said. "Teddy convinced me to go."

"Why?"

Diana sighed. She wasn't sure she wanted to tell Scott the full story, but there was no reason not to. "Getting a business off the ground takes a lot of work," Diana said. Scott nodded. "I've been working night and day for years trying to get the business to support itself. Every ounce of energy I had went into making my wedding planning franchise a success. Consequently, I have no time for singles bars, cafés or blind dates. Coaxed by Teddy, one night I went into MatchforLove. com and filled out the questionnaire. I didn't expect anything to come of it. Even if it did, I was not obligated to respond."

"Why did you respond to me? My profile reads nothing like yours. I didn't leave a photo, so you only had a numeric email address."

"I read what you were looking for in a woman. It was as if you'd read my mind. I thought I'd see if that was true."

"Have you made a decision yet?"

"Let's just say the jury is still out on that."

Diana reached the reception hall and pulled into the crowded parking lot. She parked near the entrance to the parking lot. It was a method of advertising. People driving by would see the SUV and the advertising on the side doors. Since Diana had no responsibilities here, she didn't need to have access to the equipment and materials she took to every wedding. However, if something happened that she could fix, she'd do it.

Ahead of them, a couple got out of their car, along with the two young flower girls.

Diana smiled at them in their perfect little pink-and-white dresses.

"Cute, right?" Scott asked, following her line of vision.

"Jacey and Merry." She told him the girls' names, spelling Merry's.

"She was born during the Christmas holidays?" Scott stated.

Diana nodded. "December twenty-third."

They watched as Merry's dad came up and took both girls' hands.

"I suppose with your business that's not in your future, either."

"What?" Diana asked.

"A husband and kids? They take a lot of time."

"It's a bridge, Scott."

"Bridge?"

"As in one I don't have to cross at this moment. Children change your life."

"Are you saying yours will change? You'll be able to let someone else manage your empire while you play homemaker?"

"Maybe, maybe not. At least while I breast-feed, I suppose I could release the reins." She knew it was the wrong thing to say the moment the words left her lips. Scott's eyes went straight to her breasts.

"Marriage isn't on my mind. As I remember it, you said you weren't interested in a relationship."

"I guess that means we're even."

"Maybe. Maybe not," he quoted her. "Remember that uncertainty principle we learned about in school?"

"What does that have to do with us?"

"You never know when something will happen to change your life. You could fall in love tomorrow. And that could change everything you thought you wanted. The time line you think you own would be cut and pasted down on another road."

"Anybody I know on that road?" Diana wanted to lighten the mood. Somehow they had gotten onto a subject that said more by what was not being said than by the actual words.

"Maybe…maybe not."

Scott had been away overnight. He'd had to fly the corporate jet and several executives to a meeting. They were back. He'd be on the ground in ten minutes. He started his descent into the Princeton area. This height always reminded him of his dad. When he started to come down from the heavens and the earth was no longer somewhere under the clouds. When the trees began to fill in and you could see the green, but not define any roads or houses. It looked like rural Maine, where he learned to fly. Soon he'd see the lights of the city ahead. Usually there was nothing waiting for him except an empty hotel room and a paperback novel. Today Diana would be there. He couldn't wait to get to her. He wanted to run through the airport and scoop her into his arms, rain kisses on her face until she could do nothing but laugh and return them.

But there were formalities first. He shut down the plane's engine, and the attendants opened the doors. There was no ambulance waiting, but there were certain measures required by the FAA. The ground crew took care of them. Scott left his bag, which hadn't been opened during this trip and went into the gate area.

He saw Diana the moment he walked into the small airport. She started toward him. His legs moved, and they were running toward each other as if they hadn't seen each other in years instead of the few hours they'd been apart. He liked seeing her there, liked knowing that she waited for him. He finally understood his friends when they talked about having someone to come home to. He could see himself coming home to her.

Her smile was wide and her arms were out. He closed his around her and swung her around. Then he kissed her in full view of anyone present. Slipping his arm around her waist, he started walking toward the exit.

"Miss me?" he asked.

"Not much." She laughed.

He loved that laugh. He loved everything about her.

"What did you do while I was gone?"

"I sold another franchise."

"That's wonderful. Tell me about it."

"It's in Denver. And that means I'll have to make several trips there over the next few months."

"Aren't you lucky that you know someone with an airplane?"

He only had a flight bag and didn't need to wait for luggage. The business provided him with transportation to and from the airport, but today he preferred to go with her.

"Where shall I drop you?" she asked as they went to her car.

"You didn't come all the way out here to take me home," he told her.

"It's not that far." She flashed him that smile that gave meaning to his day. The top was down and her hair flew about in the sunshine. Scott kept his hands down so he wouldn't run them through it and possibly cause an accident.

"I have news for you."

"Oh, good or bad?"

He frowned. "I'm not sure."

She glanced at him, seeing the confusion on his face.

"My sister is coming to visit. Well, she's coming for a meeting in Philly, but she wants to come up one night and have dinner."

"That's great. It's good to keep in touch with family. Are you two very close?"

"Thick as thieves," he said. "But she's not coming to see me. She wants to have dinner with you."

Diana looked at him as long as the road would allow. "Why?"

"I told her about you."

"What did you say?" Her tone was cautious.

"Only good things."

They reached the turnoff for her house before they got to his. Diana turned right and parked in her driveway.

"When should I expect this visit?" she asked.

"Next week."

As soon as she stopped the car, the July heat made its withering effect felt. Inside the air was cool and comfortable. Scott took Diana in his arms and kissed her soundly.

"I've thought about that for two days," he said.

"Then you should do it again. One for each day."

He did. She smelled of jasmine soap and sweet skin. Scott kissed her deeply. He slipped his arms around her and pulled her slender body into his. He'd missed her more than he wanted to admit. Scott had spent all the time except that of flying the plane thinking about her and what he wanted to do with her. Diana's arms climbed over his shoulders and she joined him in the kiss. It was a long time before they parted.

"I love this dress," Scott told her. He touched the spaghetti straps on her shoulders and pushed them down her arms.

"Why?"

"Because all I need to do is release this zipper." He pulled it from the top to its base. He listened to low crunch of the teeth coming apart. "And it falls off."

"Unlike your clothes," she said, unbuttoning the top button on his shirt. "It takes a lot to get you out of them." With each word she released a button until they were all open. She pulled his tie from his neck and draped it around her own.

Scott bent and kissed her. Her bra was strapless, and

his fingers found and released the catch at the back. Her breasts were caught in his hands. Her skin was soft and warm, and Scott wanted to take her there. Diana's hands, on the belt at his waist, stilled as sensation burst within her. Hooking her fingers in the waistband of his pants, Diana pushed them down. He stepped out of his shoes and the clothes pooled at his feet.

Scott kissed her neck and continued finding naked skin until he reached her breasts. As his tongue lathed her nipples, they tightened and stiffened. Scott had been away only two days, but he couldn't wait any longer for Diana. And from the way she was climbing over him, she couldn't wait, either.

Chapter 11

The main street of Princeton wasn't very long. Except for the students who came and went with the semester changes, it was impossible to live there and not see the same people constantly. So when Diana spied Linda Engles going into the coffee shop, she knew it was time to talk to her.

She'd been angry when she spoke to Linda in the ladies' room, but Diana refused to be vindictive like Linda. And she would not hold a sword over her. Ordering a coffee, she strolled over to Linda's table. She was reading a newspaper and sipping a latte.

"May I sit down?" Diana asked.

Linda looked up and did a double take. She said nothing as Diana took the seat in front of her.

"What do you want?" Linda's voice was fearful and her eyes darted around the coffee shop checking if they were within hearing distance of anyone.

"I'm not here to make a scene," Diana told her. "Or to issue threats."

Linda folded the paper and turned in the seat to fully face Diana. She knew the woman expected some type of altercation, despite Diana's words.

"I'm here to apologize."

Linda's face contorted into a skeptical frown. "I don't understand."

"That night in the ladies' room, I said some pretty terrible things."

Linda nodded. Her face was ghostly white.

"I was very rude. I said some things, issued some threats. I just want to say, you don't have to worry that I would ever use any of that information."

"Wh-why?" she stuttered.

"That's not who I am. I was angry, *very* angry that night. I've been taunted and ridiculed for years and I was no longer able to control how I felt. But I am not a blackmailer. I will keep your secret as long as you want. You need have no fear that anything related to your past will cross my lips."

It took Linda a while to be able to speak. She seemed to be lost for whatever the words were she needed. "I don't understand," she said. "You have a bombshell. You could detonate my life if you wanted. I know I shouldn't ask this, but why are you willing to keep it a secret?"

Diana smiled. "It's not my place to reveal other people's secrets. It reflects badly on me. I operate a business. One that runs on reputation. I don't want my reputation tarnished, just as you don't want yours tarnished. You made a mistake years ago—why should you pay for it the rest of your life?"

"I don't understand you."

. Diana smiled. "That's all right."

"But I treated you so badly. For years I belittled you."

"But if I continue that kind of behavior, it only makes me an offender."

Linda looked at her for a long, long moment. "Thank you," she finally whispered.

Diana could feel the weight that had lifted from Linda's shoulders. Diana got up to leave. Linda called her back. "Can I buy you a cup of coffee?"

"For old time's sake?" Diana smiled.

Linda shook her head. "For all the new times."

It was rare for Scott to wait for a passenger to get off a plane, but he stood waiting for Piper to deplane. She'd called the day before to say she was flying into Princeton and wanted to see him.

Piper was attending a meeting in Philadelphia and would make a small detour to see him. Of course the real person she wanted to see was Diana. Scott had told her a lot about Diana, and it was natural for his sister to want to meet her. When Piper met her husband, Scott arranged to be in a nearby town so he could meet him. After her first marriage failed, he was concerned that she wouldn't make a good choice this time. Not that he would have told her if she hadn't. Scott knew the limits even with family. If she was about to make a mistakes, she had to see it for herself. Scott knew nothing was foretold. There was no way he or anyone could assess the success of a marriage. But when he met Josh Winesap, he liked him immediately. Since then the two men had been the best of friends. And Piper never mentioned him without a smile on her face or a lilt in her voice.

Scott's mouth dropped open when he saw his obviously pregnant sister deplane. She smiled and waved to him. As she came into the terminal and directly into his arms, he hugged her close, feeling her protruding belly.

"When did this happen?" he asked pushing her back and giving her a brotherly once-over.

"Several months ago."

"And with all the emails and phone calls, you didn't think this was important to mention?" Still holding her hands, he raised them and looked at her again.

"We didn't want to tell anyone until the first trimester ended." Putting her hands on her belly, she looked down. "Five months next week."

"You don't have to tell anyone now. They can see." He hugged her again. "Congratulations. You're going to be a wonderful mom."

"And you're going to be a great uncle."

"Have you told Mom and Dad yet?"

She rolled her eyes. "It took an hour to convince them they didn't need to fly up here and take care of me."

Scott laughed, and together they left the terminal.

"So when do I meet her?" Piper said.

Scott didn't pretend not to know who she meant. "I thought you were coming to see me."

"I've seen you. Now when do I get to see Diana?"

"You say that as if you're here to approve of her. We're not even seeing each other."

"Scott, I've heard you discuss jet engines, beating hearts, flying in bad weather, skimming tree tops and a myriad of other subjects. Rarely have you discussed a woman. Yet you've told me more about Diana Greer than any other person in ten years. And even back then you mentioned her a time or two. So yes, I want to meet her. But no, I'm not here to approve. Just hope."

"Hope? What does that mean?"

"It means I hope she's the one for you."

Scott looked at the ceiling even though he was driving. "Not you, too."

"'Me too' what?"

"My buddies."

"Not the ones from the Wall."

"Not them. These are guys I went to college with. They all know Diana and staged, for want of a better word, an intervention."

Piper's head whipped around.

"They didn't kidnap me or anything like that. They just showed up for lunch one day with a lot of questions about me and Diana."

"You and Diana as a couple."

Scott nodded. He didn't trust himself to speak. The idea of a couple had been on his mind, but he'd suppressed thinking about it. Neither he nor Diana was looking for a relationship, especially a long-term one. It was the one question both of them had answered no to on their profiles. Yet he enjoyed being with her. Obviously his sister thought the same thing.

"Are you a couple?" Piper continued.

"We are not."

"Do I hear a *yet* at the end of that sentence?"

"You do not. Both of us were looking for companionship, not a lifemate."

"Things change." She sang the words, an impish smile on her mouth.

The gales of laughter coming from the three women was not what Scott had expected when he walked into the bar. In fact, he didn't expect them to be in the bar. He'd dropped Piper at the restaurant, and she was, at her request, to have dinner with Diana. No one said Teddy would be there, too. Scott started for the table. The three women raised glasses and clinked them together before drinking and again bursting into laughter.

He felt defensive. He didn't know what Piper could be telling them, but he had the paranoid feeling that he was the subject of their regalia.

"What's going on?" Scott asked as he reached the table.

The women answered by bursting into laughter.

"Piper, I hope you haven't been airing the family laundry."

She raised her hand for him to wait until she could stop laughing and get herself under control.

"You can relax," Teddy said. "You're not the subject of discussion."

Scott took the only empty chair at the table. "Who is?"

"I am," Diana said.

"Diana and Teddy have been telling me about some of the things that happened at the weddings they've consulted."

The giggles got to them again, and one by one the three joined into laughter on a joke that he was not privy to. Scott checked the table. There were several wineglasses strewn about and a candle that had burned nearly to its base. "How much have you guys had to drink?" Scott looked directly at his sister's glass.

"Mineral water," she told him.

"I don't remember," Teddy said.

"I'm driving," Diana finished, taking a drink of the dark-colored liquid in her glass.

"So what were some of the wedding stories?"

The question was simple, but again it seemed the three women had lost their ability to speak. Laughter replaced all other forms of communication.

"Diana told us about the troll," Piper finally said.

Diana and Teddy nodded.

"She was a short woman. Pretty and petite, but she'd been to a bridal fashion show and saw a pintucked dress she had to have. It was... Well, let's just say it was something that Scarlett from *Gone with the Wind* could have worn. It was designed for a much taller woman, but she kept adding things to it: a hat, veil, very high heels. And then the umbrella."

"Umbrella?"

"After adding all that stuff, she looked like a troll."

Scott didn't find that funny. "I guess you had to be there," he said.

"I guess so."

After he and Diana stared at each other for a long moment, Piper spoke up. "I hate to cut this short. It's been great." She stood up and pushed her chair in. "I have to sit all day in that meeting tomorrow, so I'd better get to bed."

"We'll do this again," Teddy stated.

"We'll have to," Piper smiled. Each woman stood and hugged Piper. The party broke up and they all headed for the door.

Scott let Teddy lead. She and Piper were in conversation when he took Diana's arm. "What did you really talk about?" he asked.

"We wouldn't lie to you, Scott. We talked about weddings, flying airplanes. You didn't tell me she's a pilot, too. And of course, the most important thing. We talked about you, *Skippy*."

She stood on her toes, planted a kiss on his nose and joined the two women ahead of them. Scott didn't take the kiss as sexual. It was more of an I've-got-a-secret kiss. He wondered what his sister had said. Like Linda, he expected the two women would be like oil and water, or at the least have a standoff. Coming into the restaurant and finding them deep in laughter, looking as if they'd known each other for years, was totally unexpected.

Piper didn't trust easily and apparently neither did Diana, yet the two got on as if they'd played in the same sandbox. And she'd told Diana about Skippy. Scott's dad had told him not to try and understand women. They only changed if you got anywhere near figuring them out.

Today he understood the truth of that statement.

The air was perfect for flying. The wind speed wasn't too strong or too weak. The sky was clear, and Scott was waiting for Diana. He'd invited her to the airfield but had not told her why or where they were going. Emerging from the Porsche, Scott watched her walk to the hangar. Dressed in a pair of pants and a light jacket, she was the picture of sunshine as she strolled across the tarmac. Her hair was pulled back in a ponytail, and she slipped the sunglasses from her crown to cover her eyes.

He stepped out from behind the plane. She smiled when she saw him coming.

"Is this your plane?" Diana asked when she was within speaking distance.

Scott glanced at the plane. He nodded. "My father gave it to me when I graduated from college."

"Most people get interview clothes. I guess this worked as a luggage carrier." She folded her arms and smiled at him. "And you needed some way to get to Montana."

"Naturally," he said.

"Are we going inside?"

He started walking toward the stairs. "I thought we'd go for a ride."

"Where?" Diana asked.

"How about Washington, D.C.? Or Maine?"

She turned on the stairs and looked at him. "Maine?"

"It's not that far. You don't have any wedding planned. You have no franchise appointments. According to Teddy, you're free for a couple of days."

"So Teddy is in on this?"

He nodded. "You should never go anywhere without filing a flight plan."

"And she's mine?"

"She's yours."

After a moment she moved all the way up and stepped through the door. Scott followed, watching her as she looked around the space. The plane seated ten. All the seats were empty. She turned back and looked at him.

"I don't have any clothes."

"I don't think you'll need any." He smiled.

"It might be cold in Maine," she said, a blush painting up from her neck and into her face.

"We have blankets."

"Then I guess I'm out of excuses."

Offering her his hand, she slowly walked toward him and placed her hand in his. Scott led her to the cockpit. He settled her in the copilot's seat and showed her how to put on her headphones.

"Are you sure I should sit here?"

"As long as you don't take the controls, you'll be fine."

He put his headphones on and checked with the tower. After a few routine comments he was cleared. And the two were on their way.

"When did you decide you wanted to be a pilot?" Diana asked several minutes later after they were no longer over the recognizable portions of the state. She had to talk into the microphone for Scott to hear her.

"It wasn't something I decided. It just happened."

"How? Who taught you?"

"My father. He's northern Maine's answer to the bush pilot."

"Really? You're from Maine?"

Scott shook his head. "I grew up in Minnesota. My parents have a house in Maine. We used to go up there every summer. The house is in a remote part of the state. My dad and I would hunt and talk, and he'd take me flying. I think the first time I had the controls in my hands, I was eight years old."

He smiled and Diana could tell he'd lapsed into a happy childhood memory.

"Just holding those controls was like…like nothing I'd ever felt before. I had this big airplane, and with the smallest movement of my hands, it would do what I wanted. The rush I felt was like nothing I could describe. From that moment on, I wanted to fly." He laughed, again at some past memory. "I pestered my dad every minute to let me do it again. I had my pilot's license by the time I was sixteen. I could fly a plane before I could drive a car."

"Did you always fly corporate planes?"

"Other than my dad's planes, I tried a few with the big airlines." His tone told her he hadn't been thrilled.

"Didn't you like it?"

"I didn't like the routine. I had a route. It was like flying all day and going nowhere. I much prefer the corporate jets."

"Nonroutine, I take it?"

"I guess that's part of it. It also allows me a lot of free time. There isn't a flight every day or sometimes twice a day."

"With the world doing email and telecommunicating, is there that much call for a corporate plane, or is it a prestige thing?"

"There's still enough call for in-person meetings, but I'm sure it's prestigious to have your own plane. You can go when you want instead of having to rush things because the last plane out leaves at a specific time."

"Is your dad still alive?"

"Both parents are alive and well and living in Minnesota. My dad is semiretired. He works three days a week, still flies his own plane and operates a ground school for pilots.

"What about you? Did you always want to be a wedding consultant?"

"I'm not a consultant. I run a franchise."

"Excuse me." He winced, as if he'd said something wrong. "Did you always want to own a wedding busi-

ss? There were no courses like that at Princeton, un-
s I missed them."

"How would you know," she smiled shyly. "Your
jor was female anatomy. And that wasn't in the cur-
ulum, either."

"It was not." He pretended to be hurt. "And if I had, I
you were quite knowledgeable to what I was doing."

"You were always in my way, always had a woman
your arm. That is until Linda knocked them all
de."

He dropped his eyes. "Yeah, Linda," he said.

Diana didn't know how to read into that. She de-
led not to pursue it. Linda Engles latched on to Scott
e a leech and the campus gossip had them marrying
en they graduated. Even though Diana hadn't seen
ott since leaving the university, her heart sang that
hadn't tied himself to a woman like Linda.

"Your turn," Scott said. "How did you get into wed-
gs? Your major was either mathematics or computer
ence, wasn't it?"

"Both. I had a double major and double minor,"
ana corrected him. "One of my minors was busi-
ss. I always knew I wanted to own my own business.
idn't know what kind. Then my sister announced her
gagement."

"You have a sister?"

"Joselyn." She nodded. "I also have two brothers.
ins."

Scott gazed at her as if memorizing her features.
ere was so much he didn't know. He'd never taken
e time when they were in college. Now he wanted to
ow everything about her.

"Where do you fit in the mix?"

"I'm in the middle. Brothers are older, sis
younger."

"Anyway, Joselyn announced her engagement a
asked me to be her wedding consultant. I'd never de
it before, and she couldn't afford to hire one. I was go
at organization and details, so I agreed to do it."

"And you found your calling?"

"Sort of. The wedding was rife with changes. T
groom's mother hated everything. Although she's co
to love my sister, she was a force to be reckoned w
during the planning process. The bridesmaids argu
and one left the wedding party. I felt like I was alw
putting down an argument."

"Then what made you go into the business?"

"The day of the wedding, it was like all the pieces
into place. The bride was beautiful; the groom was g
geous and in love. The parents were proud. The chu
was decorated with fragrant flowers. The cake was
livered on time and exactly what the bride requeste
cried during the ceremony."

"You cried," he teased.

"She's my baby sister. And she never looked lo
lier."

Scott saw Diana blink a couple of times, warding
the tears women sometimes shed when they were hap

"When the ceremony was over and all the pho
had been taken," she went on, "when the dancing enc
and the bouquet was thrown and we'd seen the cou
off to their honeymoon and the beginning of their l
together, it all seemed worth it."

She glanced at Scott who was hanging on eve
word, as if she was telling a timeless story that h
been passed from generation to generation for unkno

es. "I know it sounds strange, but I wanted so much
do it again."

"It doesn't sound strange."

"I made up some business cards and went around to
idal and tuxedo shops and left my cards. A few weeks
er I got a call, and that's when it began."

"Was the second wedding as complicated as your
ter's?"

She shook her head. "I suppose if it had been, I might
ve changed my mind about a profession. I like doing
e weddings, making the bride's day the most won-
rful of her life."

Scott smiled at her. The expression on her face had
glow to it. She truly loved what she did, but he won-
red about her choice. He knew her to be an introvert.
was strange to see this outgoing, afraid-of-no-one
oman in front of him.

But as a wedding consultant or even as a business
vner, she'd barred herself from the happiness that
uld be hers. Diana had put herself in a place where
eryone she met was taken or about to be taken. Scott
ondered if she did that on purpose. Was she intention-
ly trying to avoid meeting people?

And how much had his actions played into that de-
sion?

Maine came into view an hour later. Twenty minutes
ter that Scott was setting the plane down on the air-
eld about a hundred yards from the house.

Diana stopped as she came through the cockpit door.
e walked three steps down and stared at the house.
ou said this was a cabin."

Scott was behind her, but she never took her ey
off the distant house.

Scott glanced at the house and back at Diana. "It i

"Look at the size of this place. It's a small hotel."

He looked at the timber-log building with its sol
paneled roof, huge windows and wraparound porch.
suppose it is a little large. Initially it was being built
sales meetings, but after construction began my fatl
decided the location was too remote, so he had it cd
verted to a summer home. Let's go in."

Diana went down the stairs to the ground.

"What's that?"

She looked at the two overnight bags he was carr
ing. He lifted hers. "Your flight plan."

"How'd you get that?"

"Teddy. She packed a bag for you. I don't think y
should spend the weekend completely naked."

They headed for the house.

"How many bedrooms does this place have?"

"I think there are fifteen. I haven't counted the
in years."

"It is a hotel," Diana muttered.

They walked the short distance and went up the sta
to the porch. Scott opened the polished wood door.

"Have you been here recently?" Diana asked, wh
they stepped inside. The smell of furniture polish w
evident.

"I hired a caretaker last week. The place has be
aired and cleaned, and there should be food in t
kitchen."

"I guess going to the corner store could be a pro
lem."

The place was warm. But even in July, the air wou

hill after sundown. Diana walked to the fireplace in the large open room. The fire had been laid, but not lit. On the mantel was a box of long matches. She turned the flue to open, then she lit the paper and the fire began.

"Are you hungry?" he asked. She shook her head. They both headed for the sofa that flanked the fireplace. "Would you like a tour?"

She nodded. Scott reached for her hand. She took it and he pulled her close. They went from room to room on the first level. The place was large enough to hold meetings. Scott had never thought about the size of it, but from Diana's perspective, someone who'd grown up in a semidetached house in Philadelphia, this place was gargantuan.

"Wow!" Diana said when they went into the kitchen. "It's a dream." She turned to Scott. "In my next life I'm going to be a designer. I'll specialize in kitchens."

"Does that mean you can cook?"

"I've been known to boil water without burning the pot." She walked over and opened one of the restaurant-size refrigerators. "How many people did you tell this caretaker to plan for?" The place had everything a person could even think of wanting to eat.

Scott reached over her and grabbed a small bottle of orange juice. Twisting off the cap, he drank half of it.

Diana closed the door. "This place is very remote," she said. "What happens if someone becomes ill or needs assistance?"

Taking her arm, he led her to an outside wall. "This is a satellite phone. It has a solar charger. There are several of them posted around the area. They're in red boxes and attached to trees. There's also a shortwave radio in the den." He looked back toward the other side of the house. "I'll show you how it works later."

"I see your father thought of everything."

"More my mother," he said. "She insisted that we needed to be able to reach help if he was going to have people here."

"Who do we call on these satellite phones?"

"The forest service. Numbers are next to each phone. They know we're here."

"Again, the flight plan?" she asked.

"Safety first," he replied.

They continued the tour, finally leaving the first floor and walking through the many bedrooms and bathrooms on the second level. Scott counted as they went. Other than the master suite, there were fifteen other bedrooms and ten bathrooms.

"Which one of these rooms is yours?"

"The one with the dark red bedspread."

"Maroon," Diana corrected.

"Yeah, that one."

"Which one is mine?"

"Anyone you want," he said. "You have a number to choose from."

"Maroon," she said.

"Good choice."

Chapter 12

While Scott made the fire, Diana found her way round the state-of-the-art kitchen. Her mother taught ll her children to cook, even the twins. Diana smiled, .inking of how she would tell them, "You always have) eat." She didn't require them to learn fancy meals, ıst basic food. Diana had branched out, and during the :an years of getting her business off the ground, she'd ıught herself quite a few recipes.

Tonight she put those lessons to work. She tossed a alad, made glazed carrots, found frozen peas in the reezer and added a thick steak, which she cooked on ıe smokeless broiler. She even baked some fresh bis-uits. The kitchen had a vast amount of spices, and these he used to enhance the steak and the salad. There was wine cooler near the refrigerator. She found a bottle of :d wine, and finding the dining room table formidably ong, she opted to set a small circular table in the den.

"Smells good in here," Scott said, coming throug the door. He looked at the wine bottle sitting on th counter. "Shall I open this?"

She nodded. After a few minutes, the food was o the table and they were sitting down to eat.

"I must say I'm surprised. For a woman who own her own business, I never really expected that you woul know how to cook."

"Reserve your judgment," she teased. "You haven tasted it yet."

Scott took a spoon and dipped it in the carrots. Dian smacked his hand before he could put it in his mouth

"I'll bet your mom used to do that."

"And I'll bet your cook used to do that to you."

"She did."

"The steaks are rare at the moment. How do yo like yours?"

"Medium," he replied. Moments later they wer seated at the table with the food before them. Scott at as if this was the best meal he'd ever had.

"Like it?" Diana asked.

"I didn't realize how long it's been since I had home-cooked meal."

"How long has it been?" she asked, as they move to the kitchen to clean up.

"I guess the last time was when Piper had Thanks giving at her house."

"Thanksgiving was four months ago."

"Not last Thanksgiving, the one before."

Diana frowned. "I suppose I'll have to eat bad foo in the morning, right?"

"Why?" he asked.

"I cooked dinner, breakfast is your job. And I want something worthy of the chefs at the Waldorf Astoria."

"Room service." Scott grinned at her, and Diana knew that smile had more in it than the discussion of food.

Taking their wine, they moved to the sofa in front of the fire he'd built. "It's lovely here," Diana said. She looked up at the high ceiling in the room. "It reminds me of a ski lodge I went to once in Lake Tahoe."

"Do you ski?"

"No." She shook her head. "Do you?"

"Never learned. Never wanted to. You can't ski here, anyway. It's too secluded. Landing a plane here in the winter is dangerous. The runway has too much snow on it, and no one can get here to clear it."

Diana lowered her head to his shoulder. "It must be beautiful here in the winter."

Scott put his arm around her and she cuddled into the crook of it. The fire snapped and crackled.

"Glad you came?" he whispered. She felt his mouth move above her head.

"It's very relaxing. The scenery is good. And the company can be tolerated."

He laughed, his body moving against her. "Who knew Brainiac had a sense of humor?" His hands smoothed her hair. "Do you mind me calling you that? I don't mean it in a sarcastic way."

She shook her head. "I kind of like it, but only when you say it."

Scott turned her head up to look at her. His eyes were dark and filled with need. He set his glass on the sofa table behind them. Then took hers and placed it next to his. She twisted in his arms and watched his movements. When his eyes came back to hers, he ran his hand down the back of her head and pulled her mouth to his. The kiss was soft, tender, loving. Diana went willingly into his arms. She could say the wine led her to it, but that wasn't the truth. She loved this man. She wanted to be here, wanted to be in his arms with him wrapped around her.

The sofa was one of those circular numbers that had been designed to go with the curved well it set in. Scott pushed her back until she was lying under him. He deepened the kiss, and Diana almost lost her breath with the way her body reacted to his. She wanted to devour him, wanted to crawl all over and pull him into her. She wanted the pleasure of lying naked with him and waking with the warmth of his body surrounding her.

She pulled at his clothes, divesting him of his shirt and pants. Her own clothes followed his as Scott touched her. She felt her body tremble beneath his hands. Her breasts were freed and he quickly covered them, first with his hands, then with his mouth. Diana gasped at the wetness of his first touch. Then she reveled in the feel of him, holding his head and arching her back so he could give her more and more of himself.

Her eyes closed as his hands caressed her. He kissed her all over, his mouth touching and tasting every part of her. Diana felt the heat of him. Her hands sought him, roved over his smooth skin. She kissed his shoulders, his pecs, feeling his nipples harden in her mouth. Fire burned in her fingers as they journeyed down his back and over his buttocks. His body was toned, hard from working out. His waist nipped in as she brought her hands around him and took his penis in her palms.

Using both her thumbs, she ran them across the hardness, feeling the hard ridge and throb of his need.

Scott groaned at her touch, but didn't move to stop her. She continued what she knew was an exquisite torture. She watched him. His eyes were closed and his face showed that he enjoyed the feel of her hands. In a lightning-fast movement, he switched positions with her, turning her over on the sofa and beginning the same kind of torture she was inflicting on him. He covered himself with a condom almost at the same time he covered her with his artistic body. Spreading her legs, he entered her. Diana pulled him in, closed around him in a position so tight it said she would keep him there for all time.

But there was no time. Clocks did not exist in this world. They could go on forever, and when they returned not a second would have advanced on any chronometer.

Diana moved beneath Scott. Just the slightest movement causes more pleasure than anyone should be allowed to feel. When Scott pulled back and entered her again, she thought she'd die in the one movement. But he continued. And so sounds came from her. She felt the exertion, felt the pleasure, and she was unable to keep from making a physical sound. Scott's hands pushed into her hair. His mouth took hers in a devastating kiss. His body didn't stop the assault on her senses. Erotic pleasure points emerged from unknown sources.

She melted beneath him. Her hands felt uncontrollable. They raced up and down his back, over the curve of his behind and down powerful legs that were moving up and down as he pushed and pulled inside her. Diana's brain registered no thought. She became only a feeling being. Her body worked with Scott's, as if the two had become a machine that knew the motion of rapture. Passion spiraled between them. Scott held her tighter, his hands on her waist, as he fit his body into hers and out again.

Over and over she accepted his strokes, giving as good as she got. When she felt she could take it no longer, Scott raised the threshold. He pulled her into a sitting position. Her legs straddled him and he pushed into her at a different angle and into a different pleasurable area inside her. Diana sighed, a sound that was not describable. In seconds she was over the edge, trying to force herself not to shout Scott's name and finding it impossible to contain.

Gasping for air, they plunged back to earth. Diana was spent. She clung to Scott, squeezing her legs around him and holding on, as if one or both of them would fall into the open abyss they had created.

Even with ragged breath and a body pounding with the energy of sated sex, Scott's hands roamed Diana's back. He seemed to need to touch her skin, keep her warm with his hands. She loved the feel of him, loved the way he made her feel. She wanted his hands to stay on her for at least the next century. Pushing his fingers up into her hair, he angled her mouth to his and kissed her breathless.

Scott wove his fingers through Diana's hair. She watched his face as he let the strands rain through them, almost as if he was counting them.

Without moving his head or his hand, he turned his eyes to her. Eyes that were soft and hungry. "Promise me you'll never cut your hair."

Diana smiled. "Not even when the style changes to short and chic?"

"You can wear it up, but every night I get to take it down." He bent forward and kissed her forehead, then the tip of her nose and her mouth.

"Not even when I'm old and gray and look like Cousin Itt?"

She meant to get a laugh out him, but his features were soft, but serious.

"Not even then." Again he kissed her. This time deeper, pushing her back into the pillows. "And you're not going to get old and gray."

She pushed him a few inches away. "I'm going to get old and gray."

He shook his head, an impish smile on his mouth. "When we're old we'll dye our hair, you can dye mine and I'll do yours."

"And only our hairdressers will know." They both laughed at the tagline of a commercial they had watched together on television.

"It's a promise," Diana said.

She reached up and pulled Scott's head down. She kissed his forehead, the tip of his nose and his mouth. At his mouth she lingered, feathering kisses inch by inch from one corner to the other. Her body grew as warm as liquid. She stretched under him, positioning herself so he touched her from breast to knee. His body was hard against her softness. Diana loved the feel of him. She touched his hair, smoothing her hand down his neck and across his shoulder.

Scott's leg crossed hers, pinning her down. Diana welcomed his weight. She felt his erection against her leg. The feel of him had her moving her leg up and down against his. She felt the roughness of his skin. Small flames caught from him to her.

The room seemed to change. It was bright morning, and they'd spent the night in each other's arms. Around them she could smell sex, the electric snap of energy that accompanied their coupling. But beneath that was the combined scents they produced. She not only took in the essence of Scott, but reveled in his taste. His mouth devoured hers with a hunger that was deep with need. Diana found it hard to breathe. Yet she was reluctant to let go. She never wanted to be out of Scott's arms. She was as hungry for him now as she'd been only a few hours ago, before the sun rose, before night turned into a new day, before life began.

He pulled the sheet covering her away and lifted his head to looked at her. His eyes roamed over her breasts. He didn't touch them, although his mouth was only a kiss away. His breath on her skin burned it. Her nipples peaked, straining forward, trying to reach his mouth of their own accord. Diana's chest heaved despite her effort to breathe normally. Around Scott there was no normal. Everything with him was fresh and new.

After what seemed like years, his mouth closed over one nipple. Diana groaned at the pleasure that fissured through her. Her body rose off the mattress, pushing her forward toward the pleasure he promised. She wanted more. The need in her ranked up notches. Diana could no longer hold her voice in. Sounds as guttural and primal as the dawn of time came from her. She moved her body, slipped farther under Scott until he covered her totally. She spread her legs, letting his erection settle in the juncture of her thighs. He touched her sweet spot and she nearly toppled them with the writhing that was electrical and shockingly sensational. It was as if he'd found a new erogenous area that had yearned for discovery, but had never been touched. His throbbing body shocked it into being, and she exploded with pent-up pleasure.

Diana didn't want Scott to separate from her, but he took a second to protect them. Then he was back, as hot as a furnace, as needy as she was. His body seemed to hunger for hers with the same intensity that she craved. In a second he entered her. Her pleasure seekers were out and ready. The touch of him opened all doors. She gasped as he began the timeless rhythm. Diana joined in, her hands on his hips, his body pumping into hers. He rose and pushed. She rose and accepted. Together they made love. Her hands roved over him. His body melded with hers. Sensation as tangible as fire soared through her.

She would grow old with Scott, and when they could hardly walk they could still lay together, be together. They could wrap up in each other's arms and remember the fire, remember the long days ahead and the long nights of lovemaking to come. And they would know the secret. They would know that love, however discovered, in either the universe of computer science or campus tomfoolery would find the two people it needed, and nothing could keep them apart.

Diana didn't think she could go burn up any more, but the sudden rush within and the feral nature of Scott's movements told her that he was beyond control. She didn't think about it. She was burning with his love, and she wanted whatever he would give her. He was beyond holding anything. As was she. Like a tigress stalking her mate, she went with everything she had. Her body took on a life of its own, surging up and taking Scott into her, then holding him for a moment before repeating the act. She went on. Her mouth was dry. Her body was burning. She didn't think she could continue, but the passion she felt, the pleasure of holding him inside her, went higher with each stroke. She kept at it. He kept at it. She wasn't sure if they were trying to outdo each other, but the result was too wonderful for them both.

Finally, she felt the scream coming. It started deep in her body, almost as far down as her toes. Gathering sped and burning like a fireball, it grew into a giant wave that crested at their union. Sound filled the room as their climax exploded. Diana didn't know whose voice it was. The two mingled together at their mutual satisfaction.

Scott fell against her. She was slick and sated. She tasted the salt on her mouth as his head brushed her lips. Ragged breaths came from them both. The sound punctuated the air. Under Scott, she still moved. His stationary body still felt good against her own. She didn't know how she had the energy, but he felt too good for her to stop.

The sun rose earlier in this part of the country than what Scott was used to. He opened his eyes. Diana slept next to him, her breathing even and rhythmic. While he'd spent many summers here with his parents and sometimes only with his father, the place took on a different life with Diana next to him. Love swept up inside him and nearly choked him. How had he ever come to this place in life without her? And to think their separate paths only crossed due to the Match For Love program that both had to be talked into using. Thankfully, the universe was on their side.

"How long have you been watching me?" Diana asked.

Scott looked down bringing her into focus. "Since the beginning of time," he whispered.

Diana smiled and raised her arm to encircle him. They were in his bed, the maroon one. After spending so much time downstairs, they finally made to the bed where a repeat of their lovemaking took most of the night.

"Are you hungry?" he asked.

"Yes." She dragged the word out, letting him know her hunger wasn't for any of the stores in the downstairs kitchen.

Immediately his body started to harden. Scott couldn't believe he could want her again so soon, but he knew he did.

Diana pulled herself up. The sheet and comforter fell from her body revealing her breasts. They were nearly his undoing. His hand caressed the perfect mounds before he knew they had moved. Her eyes closed as his thumbs brushed across the sensitive buds. Diana climbed on top of him and took control of their kiss. Her mouth was like a sweet candy to him. He wanted more and more of it, knowing this was a sweetness without end. It wouldn't give him a stomachache, tooth decay or added weight. It could only make him feel good, make him know the passion and rapture of two people who among the billions on the planet had found each other.

In moments they were joined to each other in the most intimate way. Their lovemaking was slower than it had been last night. Mornings seemed to warrant that. Scott wanted it to go on for decades, until a wave of emotion gripped him and the pleasure he felt walled up like a huge typhoon and crashed into him. Without realizing it, his head was banging the headboard as the power unleashed by the two of them writhing together took them on a journey of pleasure that was unbridled.

Scott was out of breath and he'd never lost so much control. He would happily have gone on banging his head if Diana continued her drive to pleasure as she had just done. He had never experienced a woman as he had with Diana.

"We're going to have to get out of here," Scott said, each word took a full breath.

"Why?" Diana asked.

"Because if we don't, you're going to kill me, and then you'll have to call the forest service because you can't fly the plane."

"Who says I can't fly the plane?"

A hundred yards from the house in any direction, the forest grew thick and dark. Scott had given her a heavy jacket to wear. Diana didn't think she would need it until the sun barely made it through the tall trees. The temperature was at least twenty degrees lower inside there. Scott held her hand and led her down a path that had once been there, but now the forest had reclaimed it.

She wore boots that belonged to Scott's mother and were a size too large, forcing her to grip the toes. This made walking hard and tiring.

"How far in do we have to go?" She had no idea where they were going.

"Not much farther," Scott answered.

"That could mean anything from a few yards to several miles." She pushed a branch aside. Most of the trees were evergreens. Their bristle needles scratched at her. Frequently she had to dodge one from hitting her in the face. Grabbing at them with her hands left her with red marks against her skin.

Finally, they emerged into a clearing. A few yards ahead of them was a small stream.

"It's beautiful," Diana said. It was like coming upon an undiscovered oasis. The place was surrounded by trees and mountains. Yet this plaza looked almost land-scaped.

"This is where my dad and I used to come and talk."

The sun was warm here and Diana grew hot wearing the coat. Undoing the buttons, she heaved herself atop a boulder, bringing her knees up and clamping her hands around them. "Tell me about your dad," she said. "You know I know very little about you. Only that your family is wealthy, you come from Minnesota and you have a house in Maine." She looked back at the path they had come from.

"His name is Kevin and he owns a manufacturing business. They make medical instruments."

Instantly Diana had a picture of heart valves and leg braces in her mind. "He started it making tiny instruments for children's surgery," Scott continued. "From there he went into innovative instruments that kept up with medical technology."

"I apologize," Diana said.

Scott turned to stare at her. "For what?" he asked.

"Your roots are humanitarian, not commercial."

"Maybe not totally commercial," Scott said. "We make a lot of money selling those instruments."

"But they help diagnose and cure illnesses, mainly in children."

He nodded. Diana knew that made him a millionaire many times over, but he was providing a valuable resource that was needed to save lives. And Scott had followed in his footsteps even if it appeared tangential.

"Is he still running the company?"

Scott nodded. "They'll have to wheel him out of there."

"Are you planning to join him, become the president of the company?"

Scott shook his head. "I'm not interested in that. He's grooming one of my cousins for that position."

"Are you satisfied being a corporate pilot and dropping everything to fly human organs from place to place?"

"I like the freedom, but the life of a pilot is short."

Diana waited for further explanation.

"It's not something you can do into your sixties and retire from. The plane is an unforgiving mistress. She'll test you at every turn. You have to be on the mark every minute, without fail. Or you will fail."

"What does that mean?"

"It means I'll need to prepare to do something else when flying becomes a younger man's job."

"You say that as if you're an old man."

He laughed. "I know I'm not old, but I also know that I need to plan for my future."

"Got something in mind?"

"I have some investments. And I'm a major stockholder in my father's company. I'm sure I'll find something to do." He smiled and came to stand in front of her.

"What about your mom?" Diana asked. She didn't

want to be distracted by his closeness, but that was a losing gamble. Whether he was across the room or across the country, he distracted her. "Does she work outside the home or is she running the society of Minneapolis?"

"She'd hate to hear you say that. My mom designs jewelry."

Diana frowned. In the back of her mind, she tried to remember something. "Thomas. Amera Thomas?"

"Yes," Scott said

"Amera Thomas is your mother?" Incredulity was evident in Diana's voice.

Scott opened his jacket and looked inside. "I'll check my birth certificate, but I'm pretty sure it has her name on it."

"Designs of Amera jewelry appear in all the bridal magazines. Her creations sell for tens of thousands of dollars. They are as prominent on the red carpet as any Versace, Armani or Vera Wang gown. I am so impressed."

"I'll tell her you said that." He plucked a pinecone from the ground and pulled out extraneous pieces, then presented it to her. "Now it's your turn."

"My family isn't nearly as interesting. And you already know where I grew up," Diana told him.

"But I don't know who your parents are."

Diana sighed. "My mother is an academic book editor. And my father teaches college mathematics."

"I'm sure there's more to them than that."

"My mother specializes in early European history, but she has worked on books from China, Australia, India and Africa. She's a wonderful woman who finds books change the world and she instilled reading in her children. I can probably recite you part of the text of every book I ever read and every one she ever read to me."

"That's impressive. What about your dad?"

Diana smiled thinking about her dad. "He's the typical absentminded professor. If it weren't for my mother, I don't think he'd be able to find his shoes. Although he's a snappy dresser, my mom picks his clothes out. He'll get on a math problem and forget everything else." She stopped to smile again. "We were a noisy bunch of kids. When I come home sometimes I miss that noise. And when I go to check on my parents' house, I remember the antics we did in some of those rooms."

"Sounds like you had a wonderful childhood."

"I did. We didn't have all the opportunities of the world, but in terms of love and laughter, we had the most."

Without them discussing it, Diana slid down from the rock and into Scott's arms. He hugged her close. "I'm glad," he whispered.

"For what?" Diana asked.

"For being normal."

"I didn't say we were normal." She laughed.

"In my field, I see the terrible things that can happen to children. Knowing that those close to me are *normal* is an exception."

Diana understood that Scott wasn't the rich boy she'd imagined. Something he'd seen or been part of had cut deeply into his emotions and he'd pushed it way down. It defined his character, and she was proud of that character.

Chapter 13

Princeton was another planet to Diana Monday morning. Maine was beautiful. Her time there with Scott had been magical. The stream, the trees, the mountains, the house, and most of all Scott. She felt as if their whole world was contained in that small space stripped out of the forest. They talked to each other the way lovers did, the way people in love did. And they were in love. She loved him more than she ever thought she could love anyone.

"How was it?" Teddy asked the moment Diana walked into the office. She looked as if she wanted to tap each foot in a gleeful dance.

Diana went to her and closed the door. "It was wonderful." Diana spun around the room like a sixteen-year-old who'd been asked to the big dance by the cutest boy in school. That was exactly how it felt. She was Brai-

niac, Diana 4.0, the girl hiding behind the long hair and
the best-looking man on campus had just asked her to
the homecoming dance.

"I want you to tell me all about it, but right now, I
have to go put down a crisis."

Diana didn't ask Teddy what the emergency was.
Teddy could handle it. Diana wanted to think about
herself for a moment. She'd done things for others so
long she'd forgotten herself. Now she thought of Scott.
The two parted only a few hours ago, yet she missed
him. She wanted him now…here…today.

But he was unavailable. He had to fly to South Carolina, then to Boston. One of the corporate executives of
the biomedics firm had to get there, and Scott was the
pilot who took him. Even so, she wanted to return to the
house in Maine, with its satellite phone and isolation.

And she wanted Scott to be with her.

Boston was a maze to Scott. With its cobblestone
streets next to major highways and historic districts
around every corner, he couldn't see how horse and
carriage could find the right house, let alone a rented
car. Piper and Josh lived in one of those historic areas.
Their house was a redbrick attached row house with
flower boxes at the windows and a black iron gate that
protected three steps up to the front door. In reality it
was no different from any other house on the street except for the brass numbers above the black lacquered
front door.

Scott opened the gate and ran up the three steps. He
punched the doorbell and waited. Inside he heard the
scurry of feet as someone approached the door. Piper
looked out from one of the side windows. A smile split

her face. Scott found himself smiling, too. Even before she opened the door.

"Well, this is a surprise. What are you doing here?"

He came inside and hugged her. "I had a delivery for Mass General. Thought I'd use it as an excuse to get a home-cooked meal."

"Well, you're right on time. I'm just finishing dinner." She started for the kitchen. Scott dropped his hat and coat on the radiator cover near the door and followed her.

"Where's Josh?" he asked, noticing the absence of his brother-in-law.

"He'll be here in a moment. I sent him to get some bread."

"It smells great in here. What are we having?" Scott glanced at the stove.

"Liver and onions."

"Liver?" he frowned. "When did you start eating liver? If I remember correctly your usual description to the word *liver* is—'ugh.' Must be the hormone thing."

"It's weird, but we don't want to talk about eating habits."

"Don't we?" Scott said. "It's not like I get liver and onions every day."

"You didn't come all the way here for liver and onions. By the way, we also have vegetable soup. And yes, I know this is July."

"So what do we want to talk about?"

"We want to talk about *her*—Diana." She passed some plates and silverware. "Set the table."

Scott took them, glad of something to do. The minute she mentioned Diana he felt himself tense. Piper was on the money. She usually was.

"I liked her. She's smart, funny, can talk about just about anything. I hate it when a person can only talk about themselves and whatever their business is. She knows a lot. Did you know she speaks several languages?"

"Yes, I did." The incident at the church came to mind. Scott forced himself not to relive it.

"Some of the wedding stories she told were hilarious." Piper stopped a moment to laugh. She had to be remembering something Diana had relayed.

Scott walked to the cabinet and retrieved glasses. He set them on the table.

"How do you feel about her?" Piper asked.

He stopped and faced his sister. She'd stopped her activities and was looking at him.

"Oh, my God," she said, her voice low as it dawned on her. "You're in love with her."

Scott took a long moment before responding. Then he nodded once. But once was enough for Piper. She sailed across the room and hugged him. "Have you told her?"

"Not yet."

"I'm thrilled," Piper said. Her smile could rival the Charles River.

"About what?"

Both of them turned as someone spoke from the doorway. Josh stood there holding a long bag with a tube of French bread poking out of it.

"Hi, Scott." He came forward and the men shook hands and gave each other a back-clapping hug. "What brings you to Beantown?" Josh went to Piper and kissed her on the mouth.

"My I-didn't-know-my-sister-was-pregnant discovery. Congratulations, by the way."

"Thanks. Did she tell you about the house?"

Scott glanced at his sister.

"Scott's been a little distracted lately. I haven't gotten around to the house. We can talk about it as we eat. Sit down."

Piper cut the bread and added it to the table with some lemon butter.

"You sit down," Jose told her. "I'll serve."

Piper and Scott took seats and Jose filled their plates. "I hope you like liver," he said, lifting an eyebrow. "I've eaten some strange foods since Piper got pregnant."

"French bread with liver and onions isn't that strange?" Piper defended.

"It is if you don't like liver." They laughed.

"So, Scott, when are you buying the ring?" Josh asked.

Scott nearly choked.

"Does that mean you haven't bought it yet?" Josh didn't wait for an answer. "Take my advice. When you go to pick it out, take her with you. She'll need to choose her own stone and setting."

He looked at his sister. She nodded and put her own hand up. Her ring had a setting around it that had been added after.

"Even if it is an Amera design, let her choose it."

"So," Piper began. "When are you going to ask her?" Her smile, one of those that said she was ready to join in the planning. Scott could almost see her rubbing her hands together, eager to start. He wondered what she and Diana had really talked about that night at dinner.

All Diana had said was a solitary *you*. And then he couldn't get another word out of her.

"Do you think she'll wait until after the baby, so I won't have to wear a maternity dress?"

"I think we should hold off on any plans until the lady accepts."

By Wednesday the construction was driving Diana crazy. There was so much building material and piles of debris she could hardly reach her office. She had to park a few hundred feet way from the building in order to get in. Obstacles were everywhere. Diana held the two cups of coffee she and Teddy shared every day before work began.

"This noise and all these construction materials are hardly conducive to our business." Teddy arrived about the same time. They met in the parking lot.

"It hard to get around them," Diana shouted to Teddy. "And they've practically blocked our entrance. I checked with the fire department, and so far they have not violated any code. But we're not letting him push us away. We leased this place at their insistence, and we're not giving it up."

"I know it's in a convenient location, our lease still has three years to run, we took this property before they built the hospital down the street, and all the trendy establishments weren't springing up, but will our clients cross all this debris to get to our offices?"

"Do you want to move?"

"No, this area is much more convenient for me, too. It's close to both our homes, the area is upscale, and I believe the owners want to rake in more money by throwing us out and charging the next tenant more rent."

Diana nodded. "Also, most of the other services we work with are close by. Moving would cause them an unnecessary inconvenience."

Both women stood looking at the mess the workmen had created.

"Let's see what we can get done before the jackhammers start," Diana said.

She turned, taking the coffee cup she'd set on a pallet of lumber. Teddy screamed. Diana turned back. Teddy was now on the ground.

"Are you all right?"

Teddy didn't answer.

Then Diana saw the blood. Looking back she shouted to the men on the other side of the yard, "Help!" Teddy's leg was bleeding badly. Bending down she pulled some tissues from her purse, along with her cell phone, and began dabbing at the blood. Teddy groaned in pain.

"Hold on, Teddy," Diana soothed. Then she saw the gash on Teddy's leg and knew she needed stitches. "Help!" she shouted again. Teddy had fallen into the pile of lumber and ripped her leg on an exposed nail.

Several men came running. "We need to get her to the hospital," Diana said.

One of them came forward carrying a first-aid kit. He looked at her leg and grabbed something from the kit, which he tied around her leg. Without wasting words, he scooped Teddy into his arms as if she weighed nothing. Teddy cried in pain and turned squeezing the man holding her. Her teeth were clamped on her bottom lip. Diana saw the tears in her eyes and felt her own blur.

"Bring a truck," the one carrying her shouted.

It appeared almost immediately and several of them climbed inside. Teddy whimpered at each bump in the road. With the construction creating an obstacle course, the bumps were plenty. The new hospital was less than a mile from their complex. The staff went into action when they saw Teddy and all the blood. Diana and the men were pushed into a waiting room. After Diana provided all the pertinent information and insurance cards, she returned to the waiting room.

"You're still here?" The three men who'd driven them over stood up.

"How is she?" one of them asked.

"I don't know. I was giving her health information. I want to thank you all." She looked from one to the other. "I couldn't have handled her alone."

"We try not to have accidents, but sometimes they are unavoidable."

"I'm sorry, miss. I put that lumber there. I didn't think…"

"It's all right," Diana said, touching his arm for assurance

"We'll move it right away," the one who'd carried Teddy said. "We best be getting back now. We have a schedule to meet."

"Thank you," Diana said. "I'll let you know how she is as soon as I find out."

He nodded. The three of them headed toward the door.

What are your names?" Diana stopped them. They all turned back to her. "I'm sure Teddy is going to want to know."

"I'm James, miss." James was a massive guy. He was the one who'd carried Teddy. "I'm the foreman. This is Eddie Layton and Kyle Murray." Eddie had driven the truck and Kyle had administered first aid.

"Thank you again."

James, understanding that she was distraught over her friend, touched her on the shoulder. "She'll be all right," he told her.

The other two nodded. "You call us and we'll come take you home." This again from James. He handed her a dirty slip of paper with the construction company logo on it and a phone number. "It's my cell."

"I will."

"Which one?" Scott shouted. He grabbed one of the workers and hauled him close. He probably scared the man, but Scott was past caring. It could have been Diana. "Which one?" he growled at the man. Scott's heart pounded as if someone was beating it with a mallet. Pain like he'd never felt before seized his chest. The men had just told him that one of the women from the wedding company had been hurt.

"I don't know. James and Eddie took her," the man said.

"Took her where?" Scott tried to lower his voice, but he was beyond control.

"The hospital."

He dropped his hold on the man and was back in his car in a flash. With the precision the car was built to perform with, he sprayed gravel and dust behind him as he took off like a horse out of the starting gate. This was his fault. He'd badgered them to move. When Diana dug her heels in, he drew up a different plan, but it used part of the area her offices occupied. They were there every day, going in and out, negotiating the construction materials. It was bound to cause an accident, and now it had.

Scott must have looked like a madman when he burst through the doors of the emergency entrance. Wildly he looked from one place to another, hoping to find Diana. If she had been hurt he couldn't forgive himself.

"Scott."

He whirled around at the sound of his name. Diana was coming toward him. Relief flooded through him like the Niagara River cascading over the falls. He took off at a dead run. He grabbed her, pulled her into his arms and locked his mouth on hers. His arms traveled all over her as he kissed her. It took a moment before he realized she was not responding. He stopped. Lifting his head, he looked at her.

Diana pushed herself back, and he got his first good look at her. If she wasn't hurt, it had to be Teddy. "How is she?" he asked.

"She cut an artery. If we'd been any farther from this hospital, she'd have bled out."

"I'm sorry." He took a step forward. She moved back.

"Go away. I never want to see you again."

"Diana, I didn't mean for this to happen."

"I truly believe that," she said. "But if you hadn't been so hell-fired to get us out of there, your construction people wouldn't have all that dangerous equipment putting us in harm's way." She took a breath. Scott could see she was trying to keep control of herself. "Teddy almost died." She spoke through clenched teeth, but her voice still broke. "And over what? A little bit of land. Well, we'll move, Scott. Our five-year lease is up in three years. At that time, and not a minute before, you can have the office."

"Diana, I—"

"I'm done talking to you. All further dealings between us can be conducted by our lawyers."

Diana turned and walked away. She held her head up and she didn't hurry her steps, but every line of her body was stiff and unapproachable. Scott wanted to kick himself. He didn't dictate the construction plans, but he'd noticed the hazards of the narrow path they had to get to the office doors.

Scott didn't believe the way his heart ached. He'd never felt this bad before. He'd lost her. He could tell by the way she'd felt in his arms. What was he going to do now?

For the past five years Diana had risen each morning with a smile on her face. Going to work made her happy. Even the pitfalls of difficult mothers and bridesmaids hadn't made her want to pull the covers over her head and hide from the world. But for the past week she'd gone through the motions. It was hard to accept the tone of voice of some of the customers, but so far Diana had managed to keep everything going. Teddy was out of the hospital and forbidden to come into the office.

Diana was working with Teddy's assistant, Renee, to make sure everything went well. Renee was a godsend, and Diana considered herself lucky to have her. She filled in the details and kept everything going in the right direction.

As Diana passed the coffee shop, she remembered when she'd seen Scott and Linda sitting inside by the window. They had cuddled so close, they should have gotten a room instead of making a display for the entire township to see. Diana had stopped going to Edward's after that. Now she made coffee in the office or picked up a cup from the construction lunch wagon that came around for breakfast and lunch. It wasn't Edward's fine blend, but it opened her eyes.

"Damn," she cursed and pulled the car into a parking space. She wasn't going to let Scott or Linda alter her routine. She liked Edward's coffee and she'd go to his shop whenever she wanted. She did not have to talk to Scott just because she bought coffee there.

Diana was lucky. Scott was not in the shop. She ordered for herself and Teddy and continued on to the office. She was back in the car before she remembered Teddy was not in the office. Glancing at the two cups sitting on the middle console, she raised a shoulder and decided she could drink them both. Today was a double-cup day, anyway.

Unsure if she was disappointed or elated at not finding Scott waiting for her, she vowed to make this day different. He was out of her life. She was going to be the person she had been before she filled out that stupid profile and got involved with him. She, Diana Greer, was a businesswoman. She had clients to see and weddings to plan. There had been no time in her life for dating to begin with. Her situation now only confirmed what she already knew—that men were a complication. And that Scott Thomas was someone she could not count on.

He'd changed from the boyish college prankster. Now he was a ruthless businessman and he wanted her out of the office. Diana was going to move. She'd resolved last night to talk to Teddy. They couldn't hold meetings or ask clients to risk hurting themselves to get through the construction. They also had other employees, other consultants that couldn't be put at risk. If they had to, they could take office space on Nassau

Street. They could afford it. But they wouldn't totally relinquish possession of the offices until her contract ended. She could still work from these offices. If she had to meet a potential franchise client, she'd arrange for the face-to-face in the new place.

Arriving at the parking lot, Diana found a clear path to the office doors, although she still had to park in the outer fringes of the lot. She gathered her briefcase and the coffee and closed the door.

"Let me help you," James said. He was a couple of steps away from her when she stood up. Diana wondered if Scott had left instructions that anyone going in and out of the building have safe passage to the door. Of course, he was liable for any accidents that were directly due to the construction. Like Teddy's.

"I'm all right, James," she told him.

Still, he took her briefcase and escorted her to the door. Diana wondered: If he hadn't been so dusty, would he have picked her up and carried her to the door? But then that could open up a whole new set of liability issues.

Inside, the assistants had things under control. Diana went to work on finding a new place to relocate. She called a real estate broker she knew in Princeton and made arrangements to see several places with space to rent. It was while she was talking to him that she thought it would make sense to separate the two offices, although she would have liked them to be fairly close to each other. And having a parking lot brought in more revenue than not having one. But she would miss being with Teddy if the two were separated. Walking into her office and having her come in and relax at the

end of the day had become a routine that Diana didn'
want to give up.

Mentally shaking herself, she decided to think abou
that later. When Scott finished all this construction
maybe the place would be better for her and her offices
And maybe he'd be willing to work on a second lease
She was three years from the current lease expiring. By
then the construction would be complete.

"Excuse me, Diana."

Diana looked up from her desk several hours later
She'd been engrossed in a new campaign for the fran
chises. Renee stood in the doorway.

"I'm leaving now. The Garmin wedding is tonigh
and I need to be at the church early."

"No problem. I'll be there to help you out if yo
need anything, even if it's just a second pair of hands.'

Renee smiled, but she didn't immediately turn to go

"Is there something else?"

"Well…" There was hesitation in her voice. "I'm no
supposed to tell you, but if I don't and anything hap
pens…" She trailed off.

"Teddy has asked you to come and get her or some
thing like that."

Renee's eyes opened wide. "How did you know?"

"Teddy and I have been partners a long time. Friend
longer than that." She smiled and relaxed. Renee re
laxed, too. "You go on to the church. I'll pick up Teddy
And I'll bring her."

Teddy couldn't have been more surprised when Di
ana's van arrived instead of Renee. She wore a floor
length gown in a deep wine color. It complemented the
reddish highlights in her hair.

"I knew she couldn't keep this quiet," Teddy said as she admitted Diana into her living room.

"Renee was protecting you," Diana told her.

"I'm fine."

"I know you are. That's why I brought a wheelchair and you're going to sit in it."

Teddy decided not to argue. Both of them knew that argument would get Teddy nowhere. If she wanted to go to this wedding, she'd have to play by Diana's rules. For a moment, Diana wished others would play by her rules.

"Heard from Scott?" Teddy asked, her voice tentative.

"He's no longer a factor in my life. I hate that I ever filled out that profile."

"Tell me the truth. Are you really sorry? Would you feel better if you'd never had any time with him?"

Diana didn't immediately answer. Her heart hurt. She was miserable all the time, and putting on a front that things were normal, that *she* was normal, gave her a perpetual headache. She'd fallen in love with Scott, and there was nothing she could do about it. She'd loved being in his arms. And their lovemaking had been something she wasn't sorry about. He'd made her feel more wonderful, more loved, than anyone ever had.

"Am I sorry?" She hadn't realized she spoken aloud until Teddy said something.

"At least you know now. You don't have to wonder your whole life."

"I know, but that's not a yes or no question."

Diana sat down on the sofa and looked about Teddy's living room.

"What did you like about him?"

Diana smiled. A blanket of warmth settled over her.

"I liked the way I felt when he touched me. He'd whisper in my ear or just sit with his arm touching mine."

"And in bed?" Teddy prompted.

Diana's head whipped around, and she looked at her friend. She was about to push the question aside, then decided the truth was better. "Fantastic," she said.

Teddy smiled. "You should talk to him about it."

"The accident brought it all into focus for me. He still wants us out of the offices and he's doing everything to make that happen. Even making love to me."

Teddy didn't say anything. Diana knew neither of them could definitively say that Scott's actions hadn't been to achieve the goal of getting them to move.

"Well, he's won," Diana said.

"What do you mean?"

She looked at Teddy. "I think we should move. I talked to an agent this morning and I have several places to look at in the next few days."

"I thought we were going to tough it out."

"That was before you got hurt," she told Teddy. "I'm not giving up the offices." Diana went on to explain her plan. "We can't risk having one of our clients hurt, and we certainly can't let it be one of us or the other consultants. Our only option is to move to better surroundings."

"And then what?"

"I don't know. I was thinking of separating the sales offices from the consulting side."

"I would hate that," Teddy said.

"Me, too," Diana admitted. "We can talk about it later."

"Yeah," Teddy said. "Right now, let's go to a wedding."

Chapter 14

Scott was camped on her doorstep when Diana got home from the wedding. She'd stayed longer than usual, telling herself she was enjoying it. But she really didn't want to face an empty house. And then she'd had to take Teddy home. By the time she'd turned into her driveway it was two o'clock in the morning. Scott's car was parked to one side of her two-car garage. She saw him as the van's lights flashed over the porch.

Groaning, she thought, *Not now.* She was not in the mood for a confrontation. She wondered how long he'd been there. Pressing the button to raise the garage door, she drove inside and closed the van's door. Scott opened the door for her the moment she unlocked it.

"I want to talk to you," he said.

"Well, I don't want to talk to you. Now would you leave my garage?"

"Not until I've said what I came to say. You've been avoiding me, not answering or returning my calls. My only alternative was to come here and wait."

"Sorry to inconvenience you."

"Don't be sarcastic. It doesn't fit you."

"Why not?" she countered. "Because the Diana you remember would just keep walking and never reply to the barbs you direct at me? Well, that Diana died. Now you have me to deal with."

Diana was going to have to talk to him sometime. They lived in the same city, so they would inevitably run into each other. She knew she might as well get this over with.

Leaving everything in the van, she got out and went into the house. Her head hurt from all the loud music and dancing she'd done. She hadn't had much to drink, but she'd had a couple of glasses of champagne. The garage door led into the mudroom, which led in turn to the kitchen. A light over the sink provided a small amount of illumination. She hit the switch that threw the kitchen into bright light. The sudden change hurt her eyes. Diana was sure stress had something to do with it, and with Scott on her heels, it was bound to get worse before it got better.

"Would you like something to drink?" she offered, her manners holding from the amount of customer service training she'd had.

"No," he said.

She opened the refrigerator and took out a bottle of water. She opened a nearby cabinet and grabbed a bottle of aspirin. Scott's larger hand took it away from her.

"Hey," she said.

"If this is because you have a headache, fine. If it's because of stress or drinking, they won't help."

Diana twisted the cap on the water bottle and took a long drink. Then she walked into the living room where another low-wattage light burned. She flopped down on the sofa.

Scott came in and took the chair across from her, the same one he'd sat in when she'd woken up with her hangover a couple of weeks ago. It felt like a lifetime ago.

Diana kicked her shoes off and her hair had begun to fall. Reaching up she pulled the pins holding it free. The masses tumbled about her shoulders. She stifled a yawn.

"All right, what do you want to say?"

"I'm in love with you."

Scott didn't know what reaction he would get, but having Diana stare at him as if she'd turned to stone was not one of them.

"Say something," he commanded.

"What would you like me to say?"

"'I love you' would be nice."

"It would," she agreed, but did not return the phrase.

This was going all wrong. Scott had imagined the conversation while he waited on the porch for her to return, but this was not meeting his expectations. He wanted to leave and stood up. Obviously, Diana was in no mood to listen to him or to even consider his declaration. He wouldn't continue to wear his heart out where she could see it and do nothing about it.

"I thought you felt the same way about me," he said. "But I can see I was wrong."

Scott didn't wait for her to say more. He took one

last chance to reach her. He hauled her up from the sofa and into his arms. Squeezing her hard enough to stop her breathing, he found her mouth and captured it in a long, soul-searching kiss.

Diana didn't react in his arms. She didn't resist him, but she didn't participate, either. After a moment he released her and stepped back. Without a word, he left her, closing the door with a soft click. Yet he heard the echo of lost love reverberating behind him.

"You weren't wrong," Diana said very slowly after he was gone. "I love you. I've been in love with you since I fell into your arms that first day I walked onto campus." But there was no one there to hear her.

Teddy returned to full-time work, and Diana had to admit she was glad to have the help. Handling the business totally alone was something she didn't want to do again. The two could be away for vacations or the occasional emergency, but weeks of recovery had laid a heavy burden on her. Diana thought it was time to train some of the assistants to take over when needed.

"You'll never guess who called," Teddy said, coming into Diana's office.

It was late in the day. Time for the two of them to sit and talk for a few minutes before leaving for the night.

Diana turned around to see the Cheshire cat grin on her friend's face. "You're kidding."

Teddy head slowly moved side to side. Diana started to laugh. "How many is this? Three? Four?"

"We are about to meet husband number four."

"Who's the mark this time?" Diana asked.

"Husband-to-be is Giles Marchand," Teddy said.

"Sounds English." Diana's eyebrows rose.

"He is, and he owns a chain of department stores."

"Leave it to Jessica Halston-Wills-Commings-Ol-mstead to find an English lord as her next husband," Diana said, using the last names of Jessica's former husbands.

"I didn't know he was a lord." Teddy took a seat in front of Diana's desk.

"Knowing Jessica, I'm surprised he isn't a king." Diana glanced at the bridal veil lying across the conference table in the corner of her office. "I suppose we're to do our usual extravagant affair," Diana said.

Teddy nodded.

"If she keeps this up, we can count on her to carry payroll and keep us afloat every two or three years."

"This time she wants an English Court wedding," Teddy said. "She's coming in tomorrow to begin the planning process."

"Are we going to England and using Westminster Abbey and all the ensuing grounds?" Diana teased.

Teddy screwed up her face. "Only a little short of that. She wants it at Saint Patrick's Cathedral."

Diana's head came up quickly. "She's not Catholic."

"Tell her that."

Getting out of the SUV, Diana felt a little nonplussed. James didn't immediately come to help her to the door. None of the other workmen came over, either. In fact, the site had only a few men working. She wondered what was going on. Collecting the things she needed to carry in, Diana could have used help today. She was loaded down with books, cases, samples, her briefcase and purse.

Juggling it all, she used her hip to bump the door shut and click the key fob to lock it. Getting inside the door was another circus-style act. Once inside, she dropped her briefcase next to an open office door. Several people looked up at the noise.

James came out. "Can I help you?" He picked up the briefcase and Diana got a look inside the room.

"What is this?" she said, going inside. She put her huge packages on a chair and walked over to a glass-enclosed case. Inside was a mock-up of the complex. Immediately she recognized the building she worked in. If she had any problem identifying it, all she needed to do was read the label. *Weddings by Diana* was printed in block letters on the small roof of a building in the center of the complex.

"This is the design of the area we're building," James said. "It's going to be a medical complex for families of children with catastrophic conditions."

Diana's eyes roamed over the small-scale model that took up the entire surface of a conference table.

"Why is there a playground?"

"Some of the families will live here." He pointed to the housing area. There were semidetached houses and town homes. "Probably the families have other children. This is a place for them to play."

Diana went on to look over the mock-up.

"The major changes have to do with the new hospital." He pointed toward the completed building where they had taken Teddy after her accident. "This area is only a mile from the hospital. Families can visit their children and then have a safe place to come to."

James pointed out a day-care center, a nursery

school, a health center and fitness facilities, even recreational areas for young adults and parents.

Diana glanced over the entire complex. It was obvious her office building was not originally part of the model.

She now realized Scott had bought this entire area to build up for families in need. Why hadn't he explained that to her? Not that she would have listened or believed him at the time. She thought he was just being the same overgrown kid he was in college, and that he wanted her to move for no good reason. He'd never said he was building a medical facility and that his efforts would help families in need—or that her office stood in the way of his plans.

"This has got to have cost a fortune," Diana said. "These families won't be able to afford to live here for extended periods." This property was in Princeton. Land was extremely expensive.

"There will be no charge," James told her.

Diana looked up at the big man. "No charge? How can that be? Especially if this is a viable business."

"I'm not sure of the full details of how that happens, but Mr. Thomas said it was partly family money and partly a perpetual trust that will keep it going."

Part family money, Diana thought. This meant Scott was backing it himself. A wave of love rushed through her. She'd been so wrong about him. He was trying to make the world a better place, and she looked like the ugly capitalist standing in his way.

Well, she wouldn't any longer. She'd talk to Teddy today, and they would figure out how long it would take for them to set up temporary offices in another place. The papers Scott's lawyer had left with her were still upstairs in her office. She'd sign them and send them to him today. There would be some disruption until they were settled, but she was sure they could handle it if they worked together.

"James, what are they putting in this building?" She pointed at the one with her company name on the roof.

"We're leaving that one alone except for the outside. It'll be redone to look like the others, and there will be a private entrance and private parking lot."

"I see." His words made her feel smaller. "What was the original plan for it?"

"Doctor's and dental offices. But Mr. Thomas changed it before construction began."

"Why?" Diana asked unconsciously. She didn't realize she'd said it out loud. She knew why Scott had done it—to placate her.

"Not sure," James said. "But it's providing jobs in this economy, upgrading the hospital to a first-class level and providing a valuable service to kids and parents in need."

"I didn't know," she whispered, but this time only she could hear it.

Diana gathered her belongings. They felt even heavier than they had when she'd gotten them out of the van. "Thank you," she told James and gave him a smile. He was a nice guy, and she could tell that he believed in what Scott was doing.

She turned back. "James, do you have children?"

He smiled. "Three. They are the light of my life and I'm thankful that all of them are healthy, but at any moment any family could need this facility."

Giving his big arm a squeeze, she said nothing, but let him know she understood.

In her office several minutes later, she located the papers and glanced through them. The offer was very fair. She signed them and walked over to Teddy. After explaining what she'd seen downstairs, Teddy signed them, too.

"Where do we go now?"

"We started this in my great room. We could go back there until we find something more suitable. You and I could share that room, and if we remove the furniture in the dining room and the downstairs office, we can put the other consultants in there."

"What about the real estate agent?"

"He had some promising space. None of it was as ideal as we have here, but we may have to give up some amenities for the sake of moving."

"Diana, this is a good thing. Don't look like you've lost your best friend. We'll survive."

Diana smiled at her, but her attitude didn't change. "I know we will. And we'll be better than before."

"That's the spirit," Teddy said. "Why don't we celebrate? Go somewhere after work and forget the troubles of the day."

"What do we have to celebrate?"

"Good citizenship. We're giving up our space for needy children."

Diana felt a little better after Teddy said that. And even if it was later than it should have been, they were doing something good.

"Are we?" Teddy asked after a moment.

"Are we what?"

"Are you concerned about unknown needy children or are you really interested in the man providing for them?"

Diana wasn't one to lie to herself or her friend. "I'm not sure," she said, truthfully.

"You're having problems resolving what your mind tells you and what your heart wants?"

Diana weighed her words for a moment. "He hurt you, Teddy," Diana stated.

"True. And it was serious, but I'm not holding a grudge."

"You think I should forgive and forget?"

"I think you should follow your heart."

"My heart says run to him, but I'm not sure that's the best course of action."

"You could be hurt."

She nodded.

"Are you afraid to take the chance?" Teddy asked.

Diana looked at her. In no way did she appear to have had an accident that could have claimed her life. And she appeared to be giving Diana permission to return to the man who caused her accident. Inadvertedly caused, she amended.

"Diana," Teddy spot softly. Diana looked at her. "Take the chance."

The phone in Scott's hand nearly fell to the floor. "What?" he said. It was past seven o'clock, but he and his lawyer worked late hours. Both were still in their offices. Scott had just returned from a flight and was in the process of filing out the necessary FTA paperwork.

"It came by messenger early this afternoon," the lawyer said. "I was in court and only went through the mail a few minutes ago."

"What were her conditions?"

"She made none. The pages are as pristine as they were when we delivered them. She made no changes."

"And both women signed them?"

"Both signatures are on it."

"Did she give a reason?" Scott asked.

"Nothing. The envelope contained only the contract. Nothing else. Not a letter, not even a sticky note."

"I don't understand," Scott said. He was speaking more to himself than to his lawyer on the other end of the phone.

"Don't question it. You have what you wanted. Now you can go ahead with your original plan for the entire complex."

Scott agreed and rang off. He had what he wanted, but what about Diana? Where was she going? She'd held out on moving for so long, and now without a word of explanation the papers arrived. Something must have happened. Was it Teddy's accident? Diana had refused to speak to him since Teddy had been hurt. He wondered where she was. He hadn't seen her in days. She could do her franchise work from her home. If she needed to take a trip, Teddy or a limousine could take her to the airport without Scott knowing about it.

But he wanted to know where she was. He wanted her close enough to touch, to hold, kiss and make violent love to. He wanted to wake up with her and go to sleep each night with her warm body folded into his. He'd never felt this way about anyone. Until the Match For Love service put them together, he'd have said there was no way she was the one. But he was thinking that not only was she the one, she was the *only* one.

Picking up his cell phone, he dialed her number. He didn't expect her to answer. She hadn't answered any of his other calls. And he was rewarded with the same voice mail message. He'd stopped leaving messages days ago. His number would appear as a missed call, and she would know it was him. She would know he wanted to talk to her. He wanted to explain that he couldn't live without her. He wanted to tell her he loved her, but that was something he couldn't do over a phone. It required an in-person declaration.

Scott was sure she loved him, too. No one could act the way she had when they were making love and be faking it. Being with her was like having fun when they were doing nothing. Her smile, the way she laughed and talked to him. All these intangible things told him that the two of them were in love. But Diana was putting up barriers. He didn't know why. At least not totally. Some of it had to do with his friends and the way not only they, but he also had treated her. And continued to treat her.

Had she had enough? Was she no longer up for the fight with him. Even a fight that put the two of them in the same room. And if he could get her in the room, he could explain.

Scott grabbed his suit jacket and left the office. If she wouldn't answer his call, he'd go to her house. She had to come home sooner or later. And he'd be there waiting for her when that Porsche turned into the driveway.

Five hours later Scott stood up yawning. Raising his arms over his head, he stretched, working the kinks out of muscles that had been stationary too long. Obviously, Diana was better at holding out than he was. It was after one in the morning and there was no sign of her. Giving up, he headed back toward the center of town.

His fingers grasped the steering wheel tight enough

to break it. The woman was driving him crazy, the same way she'd done all those years ago when they were in school together. She hadn't known it then. Now he wasn't so sure.

Chapter 15

Scott looked up at the black-and-white building on Nassau Street. It looked like something one would find in a Swiss village instead of a college town by the Raritan Canal. It had taken him two days to find where Diana had moved her offices. He wouldn't have thought anyone could relocate that fast. And indeed she hadn't. Everything from the walls down was gone from the offices he had asked her to move out of. The desks and credenzas, kitchen equipment, everything that was too heavy for her and her staff to carry remained, but the files, samples, photographs, books and everything that decorated the place and made it a working office was gone.

Scott was unused to Diana giving up. It wasn't like her, wasn't in her nature. But he had the contract she'd signed. And like his lawyer had said, there wasn't a mark on it except for her and Teddy's signatures. They had vacated the premises without a word. Scott asked James if anyone had helped them move. James's answer was negative. No one had even seen them move out. In fact, James was unaware they were gone.

But this was their new location. Scott checked the area. It was the busiest part of the township. While that would be good at times and for some types of businesses, it wasn't for weddings. Diana didn't work on volume, nor did she rely on walk-ins. So why would she accept space here?

Scott went into the building and checked the directory. Weddings by Diana was on the top floor. Taking the elevator, he rode the slow mechanism to the top and got off. The corridor was well lit, and led to legal offices and dental facilities. The Weddings by Diana logo was on the door at the end of the hall. Scott knocked softly and opened the door. He didn't know what to expect. She'd commanded a lot of space in his facility. Here the space was cramped with boxes and books stacked in disorder.

He heard Teddy speaking in a back room. The other consultants seemed to be in each other's way. He didn't see Diana as he looked around. Finally, Teddy came out of the back room and stopped when she saw him. She no longer sat in the wheelchair, but she was clinging to the wall. She had obviously left her crutches behind when she came to the door.

"Scott," she said, her voice low with surprise.

"Where's Diana?" he asked.

"Out of town."

He wasn't sure that was true, but he didn't press the point. "What are you doing here?"

"Unpacking." Her clipped one-word answer stung him.

"Why did you leave?"

"Wasn't that what you wanted? To get your space back so you could complete your facility? Well, you have it."

"Where's Diana?"

"She doesn't want to talk to you," Teddy said.

"So is she really out of town?"

"Yes." Teddy's chin rose half an inch, challenging him for questioning her veracity.

Scott looked around. There were a couple of doors in the office. Both were open and he could see inside them. Diana was not there.

"Would you like to leave a message?" The question was delivered as if he was a tradesman who'd come in with a package that needed a signature.

"I'd like to talk to her."

"Good luck with that," Teddy said and turned back to the room where she'd entered.

He looked at the other women in the room. Two of them only stared back at him. The third one shook her head as if to say she knew nothing.

Scott turned and left the office. He returned to the elevator, pushed the call button and waited. The door opened. At the same time, Scott stepped toward the small space and Diana stepped out of it. They walked into each other.

"Diana!"

"Scott!"

They both spoke at the same time.

"Why did you leave without a word?" he asked.

Diana stepped back as if she needed space. Behind her was the elevator and Scott followed her inside. The door closed and he hit the stop button. He was going to talk to her and if it had to be here, then so be it.

"Wasn't that what you wanted from Day One?"

"Of course, but I didn't expect you to sneak out in the middle of the night and move into space that is obviously too small for your needs."

"The space is adequate for our needs. Teddy and I will adjust and it won't be long before we're either settled in or finding new space.

Diana stared at Scott.

"Why are you looking like you lost your best friend? I thought you'd be happy that we were gone. You have your space and you can build your dental and doctor's offices. The wall around the parking lot doesn't need to be there, and there won't be a blight on the layout you've chosen." She paused a moment.

"Scott, you haven't kicked us out. What you're doing, what you're building for the kids and families is more important than a bridal business's needs. We feel good about giving up our space for the purposes you have in mind." She looked at him. "Our brides will understand why we moved, and they'll be fine with it. Most of our business is done outside the office, anyway."

"Are you sure?"

"I'm sure," she said.

"I don't understand you at all," Scott said.

Diana smiled at that.

"That's exactly what I mean," he said.

"I don't understand," she said.

"I say I don't understand you and you're smiling. Why would that make you smile?"

"I've never been called a mystery woman." She cast a trusting eye at him. "I like it."

* * *

Scott looked perplexed and Diana understood his confusion. She had been one way and then the other. He probably wondered who she was today. The consistent Diana 4.0. In her wake was a new Diana.

"I have a secret to tell you."

He moved closer to her. Diana felt the familiar fear of anticipation. He didn't know how he would react to her words. She'd reacted badly to the same ones when he'd said them.

"What is it?" Scott asked.

"You told me once that you loved me. I never answered you. I didn't return the sentiment."

Diana felt him grow still.

"Well, I am in love with you. I fell in love with you the first day I saw you on campus. From that day to this one, I've never changed my feelings. I love you."

Scott's arms were around her before she could move. He pulled her close, and she felt as if she could no longer breathe without his support.

She reached up and pulled his mouth to hers. Diana felt the hard thudding of his heart against her ear.

"I love you, too," he said. "I don't think I could go another day with coming back and forcing you to say it."

"No force necessary," she told him. "I love you now. I'll love you forever."

"Will you marry me?" he asked.

Diana felt he was holding his breath. She nodded.

At the end of the aisle on her wedding day, Diana paused and looked at the assembled group. Her father held her arm. When she glanced at him, his eyes were glistening. "Don't you start," she told him. "If you cry, I will, too."

He sniffed and they faced the altar. Scott stood smiling at her. A wave of love washed over her. This was her choice. This was the man she wanted to spend her life with. She wanted to have children and watch them playing with their dad on the front lawn. She wanted to make him happy.

Teddy took her place as maid of honor. Her bridesmaids smiled from their positions arrayed across the front, waiting for her to begin her walk down the aisle. Everything was as perfect as Diana could wish it to be. Her ceremony wasn't the showplace event she and Teddy planned for their clients. This was a small service in the open air, on the campus of Princeton University right at the kissing spot. With a few of their most intimate friends and family. The chairs were all filled. Scott's friends watched. After today they would no longer be able to call him the last bachelor.

When the "Wedding March" began, everyone stood. Diana took the first step toward a new life.

* * * * *

We hope you enjoyed reading

Finally a Bride

by *New York Times* bestselling author

SHERRYL WOODS

and

His Love Match

by SHIRLEY HAILSTOCK

Both were originally Harlequin® series stories!

From passionate, suspenseful and dramatic
love stories to inspirational or historical,
Harlequin offers different lines to
satisfy every romance reader.

New books in each line are available every month.

HARLEQUIN

DESIRE

**Luxury, scandal, desire—welcome to the lives of
the American elite.**

Harlequin.com

So, as you can see, my father will stop at nothing to get what he
wants. He doesn't care who he hurts or maligns in the process. I
refuse to let your family become involved."

A frown settled on his face. "That's not your decision to make."

"What do you mean it's not my decision to make?"

"The Steeles can take care of ourselves."

"But you don't know my father."

"Wrong. Your father doesn't know us."

Mercury wondered if anyone had ever told Sloan how cute
she looked when she became angry. How her brows slashed
together over her forehead and how the pupils of her eyes became
turbulent dark gray. Then there was the way her chin lifted and
her lips formed into a decadent pout. Observing her lips made him
remember their taste and how the memory had kept him up most
of the night.

"I don't need you to take care of me."

Her words were snapped out in a vicious tone. He drew in a
deep breath. He didn't need this. Especially from her and definitely
not this morning. He'd forgotten to cancel his date last night with

Raquel and she had called first thing this morning letting him know she hadn't appreciated it. It had put him in a bad mood, but unfortunately, Raquel was the least of his worries.

"You don't?" he asked, trying to maintain a calm voice when more than anything he wanted to snap back. "Was it not my stolen car you were driving?"

"Yes, but—"

"Were you not with me when you discovered you were being evicted?" he quickly asked, determined not to let her get a word in other than the one he wanted to hear.

"Yes, but—"

"Did I not take you to my parents' home? Did you not spend the night there?"

Her frown deepened. "Has anyone ever told you how rude you are? You're cutting me off deliberately, Mercury."

"Just answer, please."

She didn't say anything and then she lifted her chin a little higher, letting him know just how upset she was when she said, "Yes, but that doesn't give you the right to think you can control me."

Control her? Was that what she thought? Was that what her rotten attitude was about? Well, she could certainly wipe that notion from her mind. He bedded women, not controlled them.

"Let me assure you, Sloan Donahue, controlling you is the last thing I want to do to you." There was no need to tell her that what he wouldn't mind doing was kissing some sense into her again.

Don't miss what happens next in
Seduced by a Steele
by Brenda Jackson, part of her Forged of Steele series

Available April 2020 wherever
Harlequin Desire books and ebooks are sold.

Harlequin.com

H HARLEQUIN

DESIRE

Luxury, scandal, desire—welcome to the lives of the American elite.

Save **$1.00**

on the purchase of ANY

Harlequin Desire book.

Available wherever books are sold, including most bookstores, supermarkets, drugstores and discount stores.

Save $1.00

on the purchase of ANY Harlequin Desire book.

Coupon valid until June 31, 2020.
Redeemable at participating outlets in the U.S. and Canada only.
Not redeemable at Barnes & Noble stores. Limit one coupon per customer.

52616671

65373 00076 2   (8100)0 12453

BACCOUP01792

Love Harlequin romance?

DISCOVER.

Be the first to find out about promotions, news and exclusive content!

Facebook.com/HarlequinBooks

Twitter.com/HarlequinBooks

Instagram.com/HarlequinBooks

Pinterest.com/HarlequinBooks

ReaderService.com

EXPLORE.

Sign up for the Harlequin e-newsletter and download a free book from any series at
TryHarlequin.com

CONNECT.

Join our Harlequin community to share your thoughts and connect with other romance readers!
Facebook.com/groups/HarlequinConnection

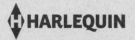

HSOCIAL2020

HARLEQUIN

***Heartfelt or suspenseful,
inspiring or passionate, Harlequin
has your happily-ever-after.***

With new books published
every month, you are sure to find the
satisfying escape you know you deserve.

SIGN UP FOR THE
HARLEQUIN NEWSLETTER

Be the first to hear about great new
reads and exciting offers!

Harlequin.com/newsletters